Dawn of the Broken Sword

Kit Sun Cheah

Ebook ISBN: 978-981-18-4416-4

Print ISBN: 978-981-18-4369-3

Days of Fire

Before the events of *Saga of the Swordbreaker*, Li Ming was a soldier in the Special Military Police. Sign up for my newsletter at https://bit.ly/3xdjuIE and receive a *free* ebook showing his origin story!

Notes on Timekeeping and Calendars

Unlike the rest of the world, which numbers years according to the Common Era, the Zhongxia Republic continues the age-old tradition of era names.

To standardize timekeeping across the breadth of its vast empire, and to placate the peoples it had subdued, the Yue Dynasty created a standard clock and calendar across Xiazhou, based on the norms of its subjects. The power, majesty and influence of the Great Yue guaranteed its adoption across the world, with some minor concessions to foreign powers. Even the Celestial Empire dared not tear down this legacy of its former overlords. With the dawn of the Five States and Ten Corporations, the Yue clock and calendar remained untouched.

1 minute equals 100 seconds.

1 ke equals 10 minutes.

1 hour equals 8 ke.

1 day equals 12 hours.

Each hour is divided into two halves, upper and lower, of 4 ke. The Xia people name each hour according to the animals of the zodiac.

Every week has ten days. Within the Five States, the days are named after the ten heavenly stems.

Every month has three weeks. Reckoned by the phases of the moon, each month has either 29 or 30 days, referred to as a minor or major (or small and large) month respectively.

Every year has 12 months. 7 times every 19 years, the calendar adds a leap month of 30 days.

Chapter One

Five Elements and Twelve Animals

L i Ming stood and breathed.

Left hand extended at chest height, right hand hovering over his belly, head and spine aligned, knees bent, weight aligned over his rear foot, he stood and breathed. And watched.

The world around him awoke. In the pre-dawn darkness, flying insects fled to their shadowed homes. Singing ones fell silent. Trees rustled in a gentle breeze. The scent of earth, rich and fertile, filled Li's lungs. An unseen rooster crowed to the coming sun. In the woods just beyond the edges of his vision, beasts skulked in the shadows.

Amid the motion around him, he was completely still. Still as a pole, rooted as an oak tree, immovable as the distant mountains.

But only on the outside.

His insides pulsed with life and motion. With every passing moment, he made many microscopic adjustments, his attention tuned entirely within. He lifted his extended arm by a hair, keeping the elbow bent. His lower arm floated just above the Girdle Vessel meridian. He curved his fingers, each hand becoming the yawning mouth of a tiger. His rear leg burned pleasantly, propping up seven-tenths of his bodyweight. He shifted his forward foot just a little, bringing it into the perfect position and angle.

All at once, he sank into complete alignment. Tension evaporated. He felt nothing, no muscles, no tendons, no ligaments, no bones. He was a being floating in space yet anchored to the earth, heavy yet free, still yet moving.

This was Sancai Shi. The Three Powers Stance. The foundational fighting stance of wuxingquan. The stance that aligned Heaven, Man and Earth, the stance from which an wuxing man made war. In remaining still, he was practicing zhan zhuang. Standing practice.

The art held many drills and exercises, all of them designed to cultivate different skills and attributes. But the mother of them all was zhan zhuang. Stillness on the outside, movement on the inside, a coiled spring ready to explode in any direction.

In stillness, he breathed.

On the inhale, qi surged through him. It flowed through his nostrils, seeped through his skin, soaked through muscle and bone. It surged down his fingers and feet, gushed through his energy circuits, gathered in his dantian even as fresh air filled his lungs. As he exhaled, softly and silently, a dark cloud of waste qi blew out his nose and dissipated.

Qi was energy. It was the energy of the cosmos, the energy that animated life, the energy that governed the wind and the waters, the energy that set the universe into motion. It was the essence of all things, from the tiniest germ to the largest beast, from the rays of the sun to the gleam of the moon. There were countless kinds of qi, but they were all simply different flavors of the same substance. Qi was subtle, yet its effects manifest in the universe.

Qi was everything.

He relaxed into the breath, sinking further and deeper. Tension in his shoulders and arms melted away. His chest grew light and empty, his back rounded and full. A hot, hard, heavy ball of golden heat gathered in his belly, growing stronger and brighter and larger.

All at once, conscious breathing ended. His belly continued to rise and fall. Energy continued to flow through him, guided by his will, flowing down his fingers and toes, arms and legs, gathering in his dantian. But his breath faded into nothingness, vanishing from his surface mind.

Now he brought his attention to his Huiyin point. The origin point of the conception and governing vessels, the source of yin and yang in the body, it was sited in the dead center of his pelvic floor. He made one last adjustment to his posture, opening his hips.

All at once a shockwave of qi rushed through him. Blasting up his spine, it burned through his energy circuits, a white wildfire burning and purifying every meridian, and exploded out his crown.

He breathed into it. Let the sensations happen. Allowed it to flush out the impurities and blockages within.

A second shockwave. A third.

His muscles trembled. His blood sang. His eyes brightened.

All at once, his qi settled. Now he sensed a tingling at his Huiyin point, a sense of fresh water and golden light rushing into him from the meridian.

He stayed where he was for the space of ten breaths. And, at last, he moved.

Half-stepping with his left foot, he drilled his arms through half-turns, squeezing his shoulders and collapsing his chest, bringing his elbows against his ribs, his knuckles rotating towards the ground. With slow, precise movements, he stepped forward with his right foot, overturning his palms, right arm shooting out out through an arc, left drawing down to his Girdle Vessel. Now he stood in a mirror image of his previous stance, leading with his right side.

Once again, he stood and breathed.

Qi continued to flow through him. Smoother and quieter this time, but it pervaded his being with a soft warmth. His Huiyin settled, now fully open and relaxed. His breath remained smooth, slender, relaxed, unfelt.

There were two ways to practice zhan zhuang. By holding the intention to advance, pressing and pulling the feet together in preparation to pounce like a panther, the practitioner cultivated power. In sinking into the stance, in bringing awareness to the spine and joints, he allowed gravity to draw him into the earth, to make his body heavy and full, strengthening his muscles and bones, tonifying his organs and blood, and exercising his qi.

He did both.

Five minutes for martial power. Another five for good health. Together they made a single *ke* of holistic cultivation.

The classics advised spending at least one *ke* on nothing but zhan zhuang every day. He spent two, one on either side. An extravagant expenditure of time, but here and now, half an hour before dawn, he had nothing *but* time.

One last breath, and he moved again.

He clenched his hands into fists. Compressing into himself, he drew his lead foot back, aiming the second knuckle of his left index finger dead ahead, bringing his other fist back to his hip. He rotated his left fist outwards, cocking his rear foot and hip. He was relaxed yet taut, loose yet solid, a human weapon locked and loaded and ready to fire.

He paused.

Breathed.

Exploded.

Like an arrow shot from a bow, his right fist shot forward at blinding speed, powered by a sharp twist of the waist. In the same motion, he blasted off his right foot, stepping ahead with his left foot. Fist and foot arrived at the same moment. The rear foot shuffled up a half-beat later, the knee pressed up against and behind its opposite partner.

Power surged through him, exploding from his dantian like liquid lightning, blasting down his arm and out his knuckles. An instant after the qi jolt, he angled his fist up slightly, as though trying to strike something with his upper two knuckles. A second wave of qi followed, this time soft and uniform, spreading from his feet to his entire body.

He surged forward, blasting off with his left foot, uncoiling himself anticlockwise, bringing in his right fist and shooting out his left. Another jolt, another twist, another wave.

This was Beng Quan. The Crushing Fist. Expressing the element of wood, it had the form of a straight punch. But to the expert, every motion—the step, the twist, the punch, the retraction—could be weaponized.

Opening training with the wood fist was unorthodox. But, in his experience, it was best suited for *neigong*. For the deep internal work that cultivated health and power, physical and metaphysical.

There was no strength in this technique. No unnecessary tension. Only physics, biomechanics, and metaphysics. In supreme relaxation came supreme power.

He punched again, and again, and again, stillness detonating into motion, motion settling into stillness. His feet followed the direction of his punches, direct and linear, propelling him in a straight line.

Or so it seemed.

Wuxingquan was all circles. Circles that united the practitioner with heaven and earth. Circles that harmonized qi with motion, tapping into the infinite qi of the universe and expressing it in stillness and motion. Circles so small and subtle, the untrained eye saw only direct linear motions.

As he moved, he adapted his feet to the ground. He'd known this hill his entire life. He'd spent countless days training here, in the sun and rain, under clouds and darkness. Every *cun* of the grassy knoll was burned into his brain. He knew the concealed depressions, the gentle rises, the flat patches, every irregularity and every hazard on this little patch of earth. He shifted his steps and angles just so, just enough to maintain his balance and keep from tripping.

Eight punches later, he came to a slope. He stopped and smoothly pivoted around. In a single motion, he kicked high with his right foot and drilled his right fist, extending it out at eye level. He froze in that position for a moment. Then his right foot landed ahead of him, forming a right angle with his body. Turning his palms around, his right hand split the air and drew back to his hip, while his left blew forward and downwards. Left palm outstretched, he continued to sink, left knee spiraling towards his right, bringing himself as low to the ground as he could. Once again, he went completely still, a human spring coiled up and ready to explode, then unwound himself and rose to his full height.

He shuffled his right foot forward, brought his left foot next to his right, and punched.

And continued punching.

He marched up and down the knoll this way, every step a punch, smoothly cycling between motion and stillness, harmonizing breath and motion and qi. He accelerated, ever so slowly, transferring his attention from precision to power, until he was punching as fast as a man could jog, every blow generating a puff of wind.

After fifty punches, he switched sides. Now he led with his right fist and foot, training his left side, and continued punching.

The hundredth punch took him back at the start. He settled into Sancai Shi again. Paused for a breath. Felt the qi roaring through him. And moved.

This time, he shuffled his lead foot forward. As he punched with his right fist, he retracted his left hand, pulled in his body into his foot, and timed the blow to arrive with his rear foot.

Beng Quan had two sides, two variations. Fifty punches for each. Two hundred punches in all.

At the end of the routine, he stopped.

Breathed.

And relaxed.

He stood upright, arms relaxed by his sides, his mind as quiet as his body. His breath remained smooth and silky. Sweat gathered under his shirt, but his muscles brimmed with energy. He was as fresh as he had started out.

And more.

His legs trembled with qi. Within them he felt giant vibrating coils of energy, winding up his calves, his thighs, condensing in his pelvis, rising to his dantian.

He stood where he was, still breathing. Off to the east, the first rays of the sun peeked over the horizon. In that light, in the distance, he saw paddies of rice and taro, fields of tubers and leafy vegetables, Farmers and work animals, so distant they were ant-sized dots, tended to their crops, repeating a cycle that begun in the dim mists of prehistory. The animals of the night retreated to their homes, ceding the land to the beings of the morning.

At the foot of the knoll, the rest of Fuyang Village awoke. The evening watchmen climbed down from the high towers and retreated to the gates. Behind the high walls, children rushed out to play, older adolescents helped their elders with the chores, shop-keepers lifted their shutters and opened for business. The morning watch drew arms and assembled in the central square.

The universe moved in cycles. This cycle, night and day, stillness and motion, yin and yang, had begun long before he was born, would continue long after he was dust. He was but a mote of light drifting through the universe, completely detached from all beings, yet also a part of the grand tapestry of creation. He stood alone, but also in complete union with all things.

He smiled.

One more breath, and he took up the Sancai Shi again.

He flowed through the remaining fists. Pi Quan, the Splitting Fist, rising and falling like an axe chopping wood. Pao Quan, the Cannon Fist, a simultaneous cover and punch, emulating the blast of a cannon as his fists rose and expanded outwards. Zuan Quan, the Drilling Fist, the fist mimicking a geyser as it spiraled forward. Last of all was the most mysterious fist, the fist that gave birth to all other fists: Heng Quan, the Crossing Fist, both hands turning over to mimic the rotation of the planet in simultaneous attack and defense.

This was his morning thousand fist routine. Two hundred repetitions of the five fists, interspaced with zhan zhuang and energy work. The sun was high and bright now, flooding the world in gold and amber. Soft songs, faded to indistinct burbles, rose from the fields. Cows mooed, chickens clucked, dogs barked. The world was awake now.

His body was awake too.

Abruptly he felt the weight of awareness on his right. He pivoted smoothly, facing the line of qi.

Behind him stood a distinguished older man. His hairline was receding, but his bris-tle-like hair remained a vital shade of black. His face carried the lines of his six decades, yet his solid frame packed the muscle of a man twenty years his junior. A neat black beard defined his sharp, strong jaw. He wore the clothes of a common farmer, straw hat and dirty three-quarters tunic and loose pants, but even from the other side of his hill, Li Ming felt his qi, like tidal waves crashing against his body.

"Good morning, Father," Li Ming said.

"Morning," Li Guo An replied, breaking into a smile. "You've been training hard."

And still it wasn't enough.

Li Ming had maintained perfect awareness of the world as he punched his way across the peak of the small hill. The ground, the breeze, the grass, the sounds, the smells, he sensed everything.

Yet somehow, *somehow*, his father had sneaked up on him.

"Today is the last time I'll be training here for a while," Li Ming replied. "Got to make the most of it."

"A fine attitude. I see you've completed the thousand fists. Shall we train together?"

"Have you warmed up?"

Father laughed.

"Of course. I was practicing too, you know."

There was no sign of that. No sweat, no fatigue, nothing but smooth breathing and good humor. But that was the mark of the internal martial artist. The mark of the cultivator.

Father and son met in the middle of the knoll. Keeping two arms' length apart, they assumed the Sancai Shi. For a full minute, they simply stood in silence, readying their bodies, gathering their qi, focusing their will. Their qi merged, becoming a single large field, a pillar of ethereal flame. Finally, Father spoke.

"Five Element linking form."

Beng, Heng, Zuan, Pao, Pi. Wood, Earth, Water, Fire, Metal, the five elemental fists that gave the name to wuxingquan. This form combined all five fists in a smooth unbroken chain, a chain that expressed every step, every principle, every circle that composed the essence of the art. Linear punches, zigzagging blows, covered retreats, cross-stepped crouches, long exaggerated steps into strikes.

These five fists were arranged in the destructive cycle, each element conquering the one that came after it. At the end of the form, they switched to the productive cycle. Metal, Water, Wood, Fire, Earth. A completely different set of movements, yet expressing the same mechanics and energies.

Li Ming moved like a tiger, fast and ferocious, a predator capturing and shredding his prey with every step, the very image of the wuxingquan fighter at the height of his powers. But Li Guo An was something... more. He floated like a fairy, as if completely weightless, seamlessly shifting between energies, every motion an expression of something ineffable and transcendent, something that the ancient sages found no name for but the Dao.

Li Ming felt as if he were chasing his father's shadow. It was like watching a force of nature in motion, irresistible yet invisible, its existence inferred only by its effect on the world. Father was an inexhaustible fountain of energy, discharging great volumes of qi with every move, yet somehow always drawing more from mysterious depths.

Father had dedicated himself to the way of the warrior. In the military he had served in the Special Forces, winning a chestful of medals he rarely displayed. After ten years of service, he entered the jianghu, wandering across Xiazhou as an armed escort. Wherever he went, he maintained his lifelong practice of wuxingquan. Even today, having set aside his sword to embrace the life of a gentleman farmer, he still practiced. He might have washed his hands in the golden basin, but he had never stopped being a warrior.

Next to that, Li Ming's dozen-odd years of training were but the first step in a journey of a thousand *li*.

They paused for a moment to gather their qi. Then they moved on to the Twelve Animals.

Where the five element fists described the essence of the art, the Twelve Animals contained its martial strategy. Each animal embodied a specific quality, a tactical framework to express the five elements. In mimicking the animals, the fighter learned to flank and penetrate, deceive and destroy, advance and retreat.

The average practitioner focused on the animal that suited his physique and temperament best. The Lis practiced them all. The enthusiast reproduced the forms. The Lis used the forms to give shape to qi. The ordinary cultivator moved slowly to grow his qi. The Lis trained for war.

They ran through all twelve animals. Then the Twelve Animal Linking Form, combining the foundations of each form in a single set of movements. Last came the Assorted Form, uniting the Five Elements and Twelve Animals in a winding spiral, the distillation of the art.

The sun continued its inevitable climb. Distant eyes fell on Li Ming, like gentle brushes from an unseen brush. In them he felt only curiosity and approval. He allowed the pressure to pass through him and continued his practice.

Father and son came face to face. Both men were sweating. But again, they showed no sign of fatigue. If anything, Li Ming was overflowing with energy. Hot waves of qi spiraled and crackled through muscles and tendons and bones. He swore he could *hear* it, a background hum just beyond his range of hearing.

"Want to keep practicing?" Father asked.

"Of course."

"Wonderful. Let's work with two man sets."

Every form in the art could be practiced solo. But mastery came through training with a partner. Each form was a catalog of techniques, showing which principles and which step should be used under which circumstances. The roots of the two man sets lay in the linking forms. The attacker began the set with the first fist, the defender with the fist that conquered it.

Father opened with Wood, son answered with Metal. Father blocked and countered with Fire, son extinguished it with flowing Water. Father parried and punched with Earth, son evaded and counterpunched with Wood. Father cut down with metal, son exploded with fire. Father smothered with Water, son crossed and punched with Earth.

They had practiced this set countless times, falling into a dance only they knew, its timing and rhythm and flow unique to the two of them. They moved softly but with maximum intent, aiming every blow at a vital point, meeting every attack as if it were a fatal blow. Every brush of skin on skin crackled like electricity, every clash of bone on bone sparked like steel. Fire and lightning radiated from every point of contact, battering meridians and circuits. In his mind's eye, Li Ming saw flashes of white and green and gold dancing from every impact.

Now it was Li Ming's turn to attack. But it was like grasping at an empty jacket, punching at a phantom, redirecting a raging river. When Li punched, Father disappeared, suddenly reappearing to strike from an unexpected yet calculated angle. When Li deflected, the offending arm lifted off, powering the counter. Every strike came in fast and quick, demanding instant response.

Iron fingers whipped close to Li Ming's face. His eyes watered at the heated wind from their passage. Stone fists rocketed at his torso. He barely slipped out of their path. Steel arms split the air, leaving his bones vibrating long moments after impact. They moved swiftly, trusting in their muscle memory, their qi, in the teachings and in each other.

At last it was over. Father allowed a moment of respite, to gather their breath and straighten out their auras.

"An Shen Pao," Father said.

The Serene Body Cannon. An extended seventy-five step sequence embodying the strategy, the principles and the theory of the art. Every attack had an answer, every counter a recounter, each man taking turns to guide the other. The steps were written in stone, the goal to train smooth, spontaneous response.

They assumed the Three Powers Stance.

Breathed.

Erupted.

There was no time to think. There was only action and reaction, defend and attack, step and strike and step again. Father's qi battered Li Ming, a whitewater river smashing against its banks. Li Ming yielded, and yielded, and yielded again, voiding and redirecting force, issuing force of his own. They grabbed and released, chopped and blocked, punched and parried, their feet carrying them back and forth and side to side across the uneven ground.

Every touch was a thunderclap, every punch a bomb. Qi crackled and exploded and roared in a thousand colors. Even so, they held back only their strength. Everything else—their bodies, their qi, their intent—flashed at the velocity of lethal violence, at the speed of combat.

Father drove a short straight punch into Li Ming's solar plexus. Stepping back, Li Ming warded off the blow and lifted his knee to defend his groin and threaten a kick. Father retreated, bringing his feet together, turning to the west. Li Ming swiveled through an arc, lowered his foot to the ground, and turned to face the dawn. As one, the Lis brought their palms through a circle, bringing them to their chests, clenching them into fists, then back down over their dantian.

They stood.

Breathed.

Said nothing.

Basking in the morning light, Li Ming luxuriated in the qi washing over him. The qi of the sun, the qi of the air, the qi of heaven and earth, the qi of the universe streaming and swelling into and through him. Here, in this moment, he was well and truly alive.

He turned to his left. Father was watching him intently. His gaze was soft and feathery, yet his eyes bright and fiery. Father nodded, Li Ming nodded, and together they turned to face each other.

"Your gongfu is excellent," Father said.

"My fist still can't reach you."

Father laughed.

"In another ten years, maybe. Today, it is enough to earn an entrance into the jianghu."

Li Ming tilted his head in acknowledgment. He'd already known that for months. Known it since the day he'd returned from his two-year term of service in the Special Military Police. Nonetheless, he'd spent every spare moment training, sharpening his skills in preparation for today.

He'd looked forward to this moment for weeks. Yet now when it was upon him, he felt the minutes and hours slipping away, like sand pouring between his fingers. This would be the last time he'd train together with his father for a while. A long while. He wanted to stay a little longer, to learn a little more, to spend just a little more time with Father.

But all things had to end.

"Are you ready to enter the world of rivers and lakes?"

"Only after I'm in it."

"Truer words never spoken. The jianghu is a strange world, a wonderful world, but also a world of sorrow and suffering. Every smile hides a dagger, every promise of gold conceals bloodied blades. Cultivators are the kings of the jianghu, but the weak are meat to the strong. If you believe this is the right path for you, I will not stop you. But you must promise me one thing."

"What is it?"

"Never stray from the way of righteousness. The jianghu elevates the rich and the powerful, but never pursue wealth for the sake of wealth, nor power for the sake of power. Down that road lies destruction. Let the Eight Principles be your guiding star in this world of red dust."

"I promise."

"So be it. Your words and deeds are as one. This is the way of the jianghu, and of the universe. This is the last lesson I have for you."

Li Ming cupped his fist over his heart and bowed.

"Thank you."

Li Guo An returned the salute.

Father and son stood in the silence for a moment more. Li Guo An's eyes softened. His posture rounded out. The years had crept up on him. Among all the men he once and still was, in this moment he was simply a father drawing out one last moment with his son. His heart flared, engulfing Li Ming with warmth and strength.

There was nothing to say. There was nothing more that needed to be said.

"It's time for breakfast," Father said at last. "Mother will be angry if we don't come in soon."

"Let's go," the son said.

Chapter Two

Swordbreaker

Mother had prepared his favorite breakfast.

Steamed buns. Large buns, small buns, buns arranged on a large common plate in the dining room. Every bun sported a small square of parchment paper to prevent sticking. Little colored dots—brown, red, green—identified their fillings. Fresh from the oven, they were hot and moist, but not so moist that the paper shredded in the hand, just the way Li Ming preferred them.

The Lis picked up their buns with chopsticks, transferring them to smaller plates in front of them. Li Ming grabbed a large bun with a brown dot, peeled off the paper, and took a huge bite. Minced pork, vegetables, sauce and crumbled egg filled his mouth. He chewed fast but well, his mouth closed, and immediately wolfed down another bite.

The military had taught him to eat quickly. In training, the instructors allotted just enough time to scarf down a meal before sending the troops back out. In the field, with missions and threats coming at you from any direction and at any time, you had to minimize your downtime. That habit stuck.

Father ate the same way. Like Li Ming, it was one of the habits he'd learned from the military and never corrected.

Mother and Sister, on the other hand, ate with a weird mix of elegant slowness and rural roughness. They ate with their hands, using the chopsticks only to convey food from plate to plate. They savored the meal slowly, smacking their lips and chewing with their mouth open. It was the one thing Li Ming wouldn't miss when he left.

"You've packed your things?" Li Na asked.

"Yes Mother," Li Ming said, trying and failing to keep exasperation from poisoning his voice.

"The jianghu is not going to be like the Army, you know. You must look out for yourself. The law loses all power at the borders of the river and lakes."

"I'm not going rogue."

"You're a cultivator. You're going to be an armed escort. Sooner or later, you'll get caught up in shady business. You must know who you're dealing with and what they want. Always read contracts very carefully. Better yet, befriend a lawyer and ask him to reach contracts for you. Those city people, I tell you, give them a *cun* and they'll demand a *li*."

Li Ming grunted through a mouthful of egg. Once Mother started going, she'd prattle on and on until she ran out of steam. He knew she meant well, but sometimes she just got tiring.

"Do you hear me?"

"Yes Mother."

This time, he managed to avoid rolling his eyes. He congratulated himself by selecting a small bun with a red dot. This one was red bean paste. Light and sweet, the perfect complement to the savory bun. Albeit a bit *too* sweet. Not honest sugar either, rather some kind of artificial sweetener that left a powdery, chemical aftertaste.

"When you become a hero, you must come back and remember us," Li Ying Zhi said.

He chuckled. His younger sister by four years, Ying Zhi still held on to romantic notions of the jianghu. To be fair, Father hadn't gone out of his way to dispel them. When they were children, Father was the local troubleshooter, hunting beasts and bandits whenever they showed themselves, occasionally joining expeditions to the city or the wilds to support the common defense. Father had regaled the family with tales of triumph, and at the dining table he shared the funniest, frustrating, and most surreal stories from the field.

He'd shared with Li Ming a different set of stories. Stories both men would never speak to anyone outside their profession.

"When *you* become a heroine, you must remember us too," Li Ming said.

"*Aiya*, you're the brave one. I'm the smart one."

Li Ming just barely avoided choking.

It was true, though. Li Ming had done all right in school. Nothing spectacular, but then, he was the best martial artist and cultivator in his cohort. Ying Zhi, on the other hand, had consistently earned top scores, and with it a scholarship hand-signed by the President himself. She had her sights set on Taiping University. But first she had to complete secondary school.

Li Ming took his last bun. This one had a green dot, marking lotus seed paste. The skin was thin, leaving a pleasingly large amount of filling. The lotus paste had *just* the right amount of sweetness, just enough to stimulate the tongue without being cloying.

"At least Ah Ming already knows what kind of job he wants," Mother said. "What about you?"

"I just want to keep my options open," Ying Zhi said.

"You've been saying that for years."

She pouted. "I'm only fifteen!"

"Sixteen," Li Ming corrected.

Her pout grew deeper. "Not yet."

"When I was your age, I already knew what I wanted to do," Father said.

"Father, I'm not you."

"You shouldn't be me. You should be yourself. But the sooner you know yourself, the better."

The women cleaned up. Father vanished with the wind, off to tend to some domestic chore or other. Li Ming returned to his room.

It wasn't much. A bed. A wardrobe. A table. A chair. That was all. But it was his. His room, his place, his refuge from the world.

He'd spent two years away from home, from his bed. He knew he could live away from it. And yet, his memories weighed him down. If he didn't move, he'd be stuck here forever.

He grabbed the few things that were left. Keys. Wallet. Flashlights. Knives. Raptor augmented reality smartglasses.

Sleek like a shark, yet built like a brick, the Raptor was designed for the soldier, the cop, the armed professional who needed an edge. Its wide see-through lenses polarized in the sunlight. An abundance of sensors captured visible light, tracked eye movements, imaged qi. Hidden speakers offered clear, rich sound while leaving the ears free to listen to the world.

Li Ming strapped it on and touched the power button. The lenses awoke, displaying power status, clock, quick access apps, signal strength.

The Raptor was a gift to himself, a present for completing his military service and surviving his days of fire. Most city people would be overjoyed at owning such a high-end device, the kind used by the elite warriors of the jianghu.

He saw it as an investment.

The Raptor was a leaden weight strapped to his skull. It was as bulky as a pair of smartglasses could be without graduating to the status of goggles or full-blown headset. He sensed its powerful electromagnetic field, an unpleasant buzzing in his brain, disturbing his qi. Even after sending it back to sleep, the sensation reduced, but didn't go away entirely. Its frame narrowed his field of view. It was all substance and no style, an anti-aesthetic celebrating function but not form, its very presence signaling to the world what kind of man the wearer was.

Most of his life, he'd never needed smartglasses. There was little use for fancy electronics and smartglasses in a country town like Fuyang. As a toy, perhaps, but little else. Phones were good enough, and those could stowed away in radio frequency-blocking pouches that would prevent their electromagnetic fields from degrading a cultivator's qi.

His comrades had laughed at him when he'd fumbled his way through military smartglass training. They'd laughed at him again when they caught him marveling at the myriad glasses and headsets everywhere in the big cities. He, in turn, wondered why people insisted on carrying such heavy weights on their heads and messing up their qi fields everywhere they went.

But, now that he was entering the jianghu, the calculus had changed.

He had to change too.

His rucksack lay next to the main door. Built to military specs, it was colored in a dappled mix of greens and browns and blacks. Webbing lined its outer faces. On the top he had mounted a sustainment pouch, on the back a detachable assault pack. Compression straps and a solid polymer sheet held it upright in a neat, compact package. Inside was the sum of his worldly possessions, mostly clothing and toiletries and other odds and ends.

It wasn't his issue pack. He'd left that one behind in his squad armored vehicle, which a criminal cultivator had flung into a toxic river as easily as swatting at a fly. He'd heard that the vehicle had been recovered, but the Army hadn't returned his kit to him. Typical. The first thing he did when he received his final military allowance check was to buy a replacement.

He opened the triple zips, arranged like a Y, checking his things one last time. Packing cubes with clothing and shoes. First aid kit. Toiletries pouch. Emergency money. Canteens and hydration bladder. Electronics. On and on it went, everything he'd need for an indefinite urban mission.

Mission. Funny he'd use that word. He'd left the military but it hadn't left him.

He checked off everything on his pack list. He had everything. And yet, he had the strange, nagging feeling that he'd forgotten something. It was...

Father materialized next to him.

"Are you busy?"

"Just finished," Li Ming said. "Why?"

"You haven't selected the most important tool for your trip."

"What's that?"

"Weapons."

Behind the Li family's home stood a small structure made of rammed earth. A civilian would have called it a shed. It would have passed for one too, but for the twin latches and the enormous locks on the only door.

Father fished out a ring dripping with keys from his pocket. He sorted them by touch, identifying two separate keys. Same model, same make, but the teeth were just ever so slightly different from each other. These he used on the locks. Then he fished out a *third* key and opened the actual door lock.

A shadowy gloom greeted Li Ming. It was a bright, clear morning outside, but here there was only a perpetual state of twilight. Next to the door, a set of shelves held a collection of odds and ends, including a set of hand lanterns carefully positioned at eye level. Li Ming grabbed one and clicked it on.

Weapons.

Racks of weapons filled the cramped space. A curious smell lingered in the air, the scent of dust and rich loam, of oil and metal, of solvent and paint. Dense qi caressed his skin and hair, brimming with potential, waiting to be expressed in ten thousand forms.

"You cannot enter the jianghu unarmed," Father said. "It's a dangerous world out there. Take any weapon you like."

There were so many of them. Closest to the door were training weapons, staves long and short, training blades with blunted edges and rounded tips, wooden knives that mimicked everything from bayonets to kitchen knives to even more exotic designs. Past those, secured with locks and chains, were cold weapons. Live steel gleamed in the bright light, revealing long spears and short swords and sturdy knives. In the rear, a heavy steel rack held the tools of the modern-day warrior: infinity guns.

"Anything?" Li Ming asked.

"Anything."

Li Ming's first instinct was to reach for the infinity guns. He'd trained with them as a child, along with the other, more conventional, weapons of wuxingquan. In the military he'd further honed his skills and fired guns in anger. Even in a world of supermen and super magic, the gun was a superpower anyone would use.

But.

Li Guo An might have retired from the jianghu, but he was still the leader of the town's unofficial militia. Bandits weren't as much of a threat these days, but Fuyang sat at the edge of the frontier. Past this town was the unclaimed wildlands where beasts roamed free. Most of them preyed on livestock. Too many enjoyed the taste of human flesh.

In an emergency, the town militia would mobilize and draw arms from caches scattered across the town. This was one of them. If Li Ming took an infinity gun, he'd deplete the town's arsenal. Many warriors of the jianghu had gone their entire lives without firing a single shot. But every few weeks, packs of beasts encroached on the borders of the town.

No. No guns. He'd buy a gun with his own money. He wouldn't weaken the collective defense.

Likewise, he wouldn't select any of the training weapons either. They were for *training*, after all. Father used them to teach martial arts classes. Moreover, none of them were designed to kill. An excellent property for a training tool, less than desirable for combat.

Which left him with cold weapons.

Li Ming stood before the blades. There were so many of them, enough to arm a private army. Spears alone they had thirty, spears long and short, spears adorned with tufts of brightly-colored horsehair and spears with naked heads. Swords occupied another rack, straight swords and curved sabers, two-handed swords and paired butterfly blades. A locked cabinet held other weapons, a curious collection of knives, needles, darts, and more exotic armaments.

Before him was a wealth of choices. Any and all of them would serve him well. And yet...

These weapons did not belong to the Li family. They held them in trust for the community, to be used for the common good. They were not intended for private pursuits.

In the age of the infinity gun, there was still a place for cold steel. To city dwellers, they were archaic, to be used for rituals, magic, entertainment, or last-ditch self-defense. But here, in Fuyang, many homes were built of locally-harvested wood. Many mouths depended on the farms and forests. A stray bolt would spark an all-consuming inferno. The militia still had need for steel.

Li Ming sighed. To enter the jianghu unarmed was to seek death. Yet to take a weapon would be to deny it to the community. Sure, Father would be able to afford a replacement for whatever weapon he chose. But it was the principle that mattered, and a man without ironclad principles was no man at all.

And there were no arms stores in Fuyang. Any new weapons had to be shipped in from elsewhere. That took time, time in which anything could happen.

In the end, among the myriad arms laid out before him, there was only one weapon he could choose.

"I'll take this one," Li Ming said.

And, with grave ceremony, drew it from the rack of *training* weapons.

It was too strange to be called a sword. The handle was wrapped in rough beast leather, biting deep into the hand. The hardwood sheath sported a similar wrapping. The round cup guard just barely covered his fingers. Etches on the side might have been words, once, but time had worn them down to illegible scratches. The pommel was shaped like an oversized melon, flaking with rust, counterbalancing its incredible weight. Even so, it was lively in the hand, effortlessly flowing to where Li wanted it to go. The blade itself could not be called a blade. It was a hunk of steel, fashioned like a cross, ending in a sudden tapered point.

It had four edges. None of them could cut.

It had a point. It was always kept sharp.

It was a swordbreaker.

Li Guo An smiled faintly.

"An interesting choice."

"The *only* choice."

Father's smile remained. Li Ming wondered if he had foreseen the calculations that had directed him to this decision. Knowing him, he probably did.

Li Ming drew the weapon from its sheath and held it up to the light. Banded and mottled, the surfaces of the silvery steel resembled a rushing river captured in time. Every edge reminded him of a mountain ridge, steep and sturdy with a rounded peak. The tip was stout and angular, like a four-flanged spear.

The edges concentrated percussive power. With a single blow, it could break a sword or shatter bones. Its tip would defeat even modern body armor. In his own tests, Li Ming had thrust the weapon through plates of scrap metal with ease.

A millennium ago, elite troops wielded swordbreakers in battle, defeating heavy armor with blunt force trauma. In this age, it was an instrument for strength training.

It was *heavy*. At over three *jin* and two *liang*, it was twice as heavy as a saber. Without a cutting edge, it relied on sheer mass and brute force to inflict damage. The Li family used it to cultivate internal and external power, to pack on muscle yet retain precision and fine motor control. The first time Li Ming trained with it, he'd almost dropped it a few times. The following day, he awoke with sore shoulders and forearms. Even Father refrained from using it for anything other than exercise.

Nonetheless, its first and original purpose was for war.

"Do you want it?" Li Guo An asked.

"Yes."

"This swordbreaker has been in our family for four generations. Generalissimo Jiang personally gifted it to our ancestors as a reward for their service in the Summer Revolution. Forged from meteorite steel, it has endured over a hundred years of faithful service on the training field and in the battlefield. It is the most valuable heirloom of the Li family.

"Today I pass it down to you. Use it well, if at all."

Flipping the swordbreaker around, Li Ming snapped it down to chest height, holding it parallel to the floor, forearm resting on the blade. He rested his left hand over the back of his right.

"Thank you, Father. I will."

Li Guo An rifled through the shelves.

"I have one last gift for you."

"What is it?"

Father turned back around, holding up a bracer. It wasn't much to look at, two crude, curved pieces of hardened leather held together by a series of buckles. But mounted on the outer piece was a large egg-shaped crystal, held in place by a cage of bronze.

A reality shaper.

"I can't accept it," Li said.

"It's yours. It's the one you used before you left for the Army."

"It's part of the militia's equipment now, isn't it?"

"I've ordered a replacement. It arrives tomorrow. Don't worry about it."

"Won't the town cultivators need it?"

Father barked a laugh.

"Aren't you a cultivator too?"

"I was planning on buying my own..."

"Shapers are expensive. If you wish to buy one for yourself, you can use this to tide you over until then. Besides, a swordbreaker is a poor match for an infinity gun. You need an equalizer."

Father was right, of course. The military had long ago moved away from cold weapons as primary or even secondary weapons. In a straight-up battle, the gun always outclassed the sword. Or swordbreaker, in this case. But with a reality shaper, with the ability to bend reality to his will, a sword-wielding cultivator was more than the match of a modern infantry squad.

He'd seen it with his own eyes.

Li Ming strapped the shaper over his left forearm. The weight was welcome, familiar, a faded echo of the shaper he had worn there in his military days. The crystal radiated a strange warmth, passing through the aged leather. A pentacle was etched on the crystal's surface, every point of the star ending in a circle. A five element crystal, capable of transforming and expressing stored qi as one of the five classical elements. Among the three major magic systems of Xiazhou, the five element system was the one he knew best.

He touched his mind to the crystal. It was a blazing white sun of infinite potential, ready to become anything he willed it to be. Crystals naturally accumulated qi from the environment over time. Even locked away in a storeroom, the crystal was ready for service.

He detached his consciousness from the egg as quickly and cleanly as a sword stroke. Where intention went, energy followed. If he thought of something too hard, sent his own qi and intention into the crystal, he'd trigger a negligent discharge. *That* was something he would never live down.

"Do you need anything else?" Father asked. "A knife?"

"I have two," Li Ming replied.

"Wonderful. Now listen very carefully.

"When you receive your first paycheck, do not send any money to us. We have enough. Spend it on yourself.

"The first thing you should buy is an infinity gun. The make and model doesn't matter, so long as it is reliable, affordable and accurate enough. Buy a gun, buy a high-quality holster, and train.

"When you have spare cash, upgrade your shaper. A general-purpose crystal like yours won't last long in the jianghu. It's for beginner cultivators, and you're clearly not a beginner anymore. But only buy a shaper and a crystal that you can handle.

"Upgrades and crystals will be your largest equipment expenses in the jianghu. The more powerful you grow, the more you'll upgrade and exchange your kit. Buy equipment that is modular and upgradeable. It's more expensive, but it's a long-term investment. You'll save more money this way than going through a mound of cheaper gear that can't grow along with you.

"Always, always, *always*, save money for the future. Cultivator gear is expensive, and it can be tempting to buy the latest and greatest equipment. Don't fall for that trap. You must always have enough for emergencies. Save not less than one-tenth of your income on long-term savings and spend no more than half your income on living expenses. Including gear."

"It's not the first time you've said this."

"Just reminding you."

Father was being Father again. But he was passing down the lessons he had earned in blood and sweat from his own *youxia* days. Li Ming chose to respond to that, not to the words, and stayed silent.

"The world of warriors is harsh and dangerous, but also beautiful and wondrous. You cannot have one without the other. Keep your weapons close, but don't hold them so tightly you lose sight of the world. Of yourself."

"Understood."

There was the silence again. An easy, comfortable silence. Yet there was a subtle tugging at the edge of Li Ming's consciousness, the awareness that he stood on a threshold. The moment he set one foot past the boundary, he could never turn back again.

There was so much he wanted to say. But they existed only as nebulous concepts, floating like clouds around his mind. When he tried to pin one down, it slipped away like the ticking of a clock. In the end, there was only thing he could say.

"Thank you for everything," Li Ming said.

"You're welcome," Father said.

And it was enough.

Chapter Three

Hour of the Goat

Every day was governed by one of the twelve Day Officers, each representing a type of qi best suited for certain activities—or not at all. Within each day, there were hours of extraordinary auspiciousness, and hours of superlative *in*auspiciousness. Today, for travelers, the astrologers recommended leaving at the hour of the goat.

Thus, for the rest of the morning, Li Ming did everything else he had to do. Final preparations. Prayers to the ancestors and the Fo. Weather and route checks. More checks to see if he had left out anything. At some point he realized it was make-work, but it was a habit he'd picked up in the Special Military Police, a habit he was loath to give up.

With an hour to go, the town militia visited the Li family, carrying with them gifts of food and fruits and rice wine. In the courtyard they held an impromptu feast, a farewell meal for the young master. The women fell into their customary role, serving lunch and tending to household chores, while the men talked of war and business and politics.

"The city sharks will eat you alive. Never, ever do anything without a contract!"

"Your swordbreaker is an unusual weapon. It will attract a lot of attention. Bandits will want to steal it from you. Guard it as if it were your wife."

"You'll find a lot of work in the city. But that's because it's very dangerous. Keep your wits about you."

In between dispensing advice, the militiamen argued the merits of weapons and tactics, magic and martial arts. Somehow Li Ming found himself drawn into a freewheeling debate that encompassed everything from swords versus spears, guns versus magic, yinyang versus five elements versus eight trigrams.

When it was time to go, the militia insisted on escorting Li Ming to the town's sole bus station. This time of day, there were only a half-dozen people in the facility, and half of them were station employees. Everyone stared as the crowd approached. They continued staring as they made their way to the bay of the sole city-bound bus. Their jaws dropped when they saw the swordbreaker mounted to Li Ming's left hip.

Li Ming sat at the rickety bench for the bus to the city. Everyone else formed a crowd around him, chatting and drinking and arguing. It made him totally, utterly, conscious.

He participated in the conversations whenever he could, but still he kept an eye out for the bus.

At last it arrived. Technology was slow to penetrate the countryside, but buses were the exception. Painted a cheerful yellow, the bus gleamed in the afternoon sun, running silent on a cosmic tap. This bus was half-empty. No one got out.

Fuyang was in the middle of nowhere. No one wanted to visit Fuyang. Historic temples and towns down the line overshadowed Fuyang. Once a peaceful farming village, the people of the province, of the nation, remembered it best as a waystation in between Bao An and tourist destinations.

As Li Ming boarded the bus, the militia broke into cheers.

"LI SHAOYE WANSUI!"

May Young Master Li live ten thousand years!

The driver goggled. The passengers stared in disbelief. Abashed, Li Ming waved at the militiamen, paid his fare and scooted to the rearmost seat. The militia continued cheering until he sat.

He hadn't done anything to earn such adulation. He wasn't a celebrity or an idol or anything like that. He was just a young man about to enter the jianghu, like so many thousands of other young men across the land. It was a story as old as Xiazhou itself.

But in paying their respects to him, they were offering respects to his father. And if anyone had earned such honor, it was surely Li Guo An.

In another life, he'd been *Colonel* Li of the Special Forces. He'd climbed the ranks at a rapid pace, protecting the people from the enemies of the Zhongxia Republic. He could have accepted a promotion to Brigadier General, but that would have meant taking a desk job, so he chose to enter the jianghu.

As an armed escort, he traveled the land, once again protecting the people from the enemies of all mankind. After his son was born, he returned to his hometown and invested his wealth back in the village. He bought up large tracts of farmland, and in exchange for a modest rent, he brought in fertilizers and hardy high-yield seeds, ran interference with corporations and governments, and coordinated sales across multiple markets. When he wasn't working, he participated in the collective defense, led the town militia, held martial arts classes, and raised his children.

On occasion, he even helped at the farms.

Li Guo An had left his hometown in rags and returned in silk. He was born in a village of dirt and reshaped it into a town of brick. The people would expect no less from his son.

But how could Li Ming ever step out of his father's shadow?

He didn't know.

His mind churning, he sat in silence, staring at everything and at nothing. When the bus moved off, he barely felt it. He noticed only when the landscape outside the windows blurred into motion. He half-closed his eyes, shutting out the outer world. In his inner world, he tried to chart a course for himself, a path only he could walk. But he saw nothing but darkness.

Finally, as the bus coasted down the highway, he decided to give it a rest. He was only twenty-one, and the world was wide. There'd be opportunities. He just had to find them.

And take them.

It was only a matter of—

The bus screeched to a halt.

Li Ming jolted forward.

He threw his hands up, catching himself before he crashed into the seat ahead of him.

And the bus backed up.

"*Wei!*" a passenger yelled. "What's going on?"

"You're going the wrong way!" someone else shouted.

The bus stopped. Turned. And rolled into motion again.

Li Ming craned his neck. All he saw were forests to his right and smooth asphalt roads. Nothing to—

The bus braked.

And backed up again.

"What's happening?" someone called.

The passengers craned their necks to see.

A bloodcurdling shriek split the air from *outside* the bus.

"Yaoguai! Yaoguai!" a woman cried.

The driver spoke into the intercom.

"Honored guests, we are presently facing difficulties on the road. We apologize for the inconvenience. If there are any military or police personnel aboard, or any martial cultivator, we seek your assistance."

Li Ming's heart thumped in his chest. Electricity crackled in his blood. Now was his time.

Hand on his pommel, he rose to his feet and made his way forward. Through the windshield, a gigantic goat glared at him.

The beast was huge, coming up to the height of a man's shoulder. Its twin horns, black as onyx, curled around in a circle to point at his face. Bony ridges sprouted along its back, defining its spine. Thick brown fur covered its six enormous legs and massive body. Its bare face revealed a flattened skull as hard as steel. Its eyes glittered like fiery rubies.

It was a tietou.

Li sidled up alongside the driver.

"What's the situation?" Li Ming asked.

The driver gulped.

"The beast is blocking the road. When I tried to drive around it, it kept heading me off. What should we do?"

"Is there another route around it?"

"The Military Police closed off the other routes to Bao An. They're hunting beasts in the area. This one must have escaped the cordon. If I take a detour, it will take us... at least two extra hours."

Li Ming grimaced. In his time, he'd conducted many beast hunts and route patrols just like this one. He wouldn't speak of regular troops, but in the *Special* Military Police, manned entirely by cultivators, this wouldn't have happened. Not unless something terrible had happened.

"That's a reality shaper, right?" the driver asked. "Are you a cultivator?"

"Yes."

"Can you destroy the beast? I'll testify to it. You'll get the credit."

It would be an excellent start to his career, *if* he could pull it off. On the other hand, military regulations were clear. Engage beasts from a distance, with firearms. It was too dangerous to willfully close in and engage them with cold weapons. Especially a tietou.

Bitterly he regretted passing up on a gun. But at least he had—

The tietou shrieked again.

Li Ming felt it in his chest, an unpleasant vibration in his bones and organs. The creature bared its teeth, revealing sharp fangs of a tiger and the flat incisors of an ape. Its qi flared, wrapping its body in an ethereal red cloak.

He stared into its eyes. The beast stared back.

"Qi assessment," Li Ming said.

His Raptor responded in an instant, firing up his qi imager. The camera studied the beast's energies, its colors and its intensity, its size and its volume, and returned a result.

Qi score: 898.

The qi scores of most adult tietou hovered around 500 points. This was no ordinary yaoguai. It was a jinhua yaoguai, an Evolved magical beast, one that had learned how to cultivate.

And it was preparing for battle.

"I'm going to draw it away," Li Ming said. "Once I create an opening, drive around and past it."

"Got it. Good luck!"

The door hissed open. Li Ming leapt out, left hand on his pommel. The second his boots touched the asphalt, he wrapped his fingers around the grip and lifted it high, drawing the weapon.

The beast stared, transfixed by the sight of the shimmering silver swordbreaker. Li Ming snapped his left hand to his right hip, passing the handle to his waiting hand, aiming the point at the tietou. He shifted to a two-handed grip, snapped the weapon out in an extended guard, and he advanced.

The beast screamed.

He halted.

It stared at him.

He stared back.

As its name suggested, a tietou had an exceptionally hard skull, harder than steel. Its horns and head were its primary weapons. A headbutt by an ironhead of this size would destroy a car, never mind a man. More than that, the eyes of this beast gleamed with intelligence. An animal intelligence, perhaps, but intelligence nonetheless.

In days of the Yue Dynasty, the state geneticists stopped at nothing to breed the finest military monsters. They had experimented on common goats, warping and twisting them for their own ends. The result was the tietou, an omnivorous goat-ape hybrid, so large and strong the scientists induced it to grow an extra pair of legs to support its mass. As if that wasn't enough, they had meddled with its brains and nerves, seeding them with the dust of ground-up primordial crystals.

Most tietou didn't know they could use magic. The ones that did became walking disasters.

Beast cultivation techniques weren't as refined as humans, but brute strength and raw aggression went a long way. Li couldn't outfight it, even with his shaper.

But he didn't have to.

Li flowed his swordbreaker through wide circles, first going clockwise, then the other way, occasionally cutting across with neat strokes.

"Come on, over here, look at me," Li said.

Slowly, slowly, he crept his feet forward, closing the gap, covering himself with his—

The goat screamed.

And lunged.

But only two steps.

And then it reared back, snarling with bared fangs, kicking at the air with its cloven hoofs.

Out the corner of his eye, the driver silently rolled up to Li's right.

Li breathed.

Gathered his qi in his belly.

And, with an ear-splitting shout, he slashed through the air.

The tietou's eyes flickered, following the point.

And Li extended his left palm.

"HA!" he shouted.

And drew upon the element of fire.

Qi burst from the crystal, flowing down his hands, condensing in his palm, and exploded as a searing bolt of white-hot flame.

Too weak, he realized. The bolt was too weak. The crystal was meant for a child, a novice cultivator, no more. The shaper itself had a low-powered transmission circuit, useful only for low-end utility magic. It wasn't meant for combat. Last-ditch self-defense, maybe, but only against a human. It was too weak to battle a beast as powerful as this.

The bolt struck the beast square in the forehead, right between the eyes. Its qi compressed in an instant, strengthening its steel-hard skull. Smoke blew out from the point of impact, revealing a spot of blackened bone.

It roared, in fury and in pain.

And lowered his head.

Li gulped.

It charged.

Li stood his ground.

It accelerated.

Li twisted his swordbreaker anticlockwise, aiming at its left eye.

It swerved to his left, still bearing down, faster and faster—

He swiveled to the right, throwing his left arm out of the way, and swung the sword-breaker.

Blunted metal struck heavy bone with a heavy crack.

And the beast shot past, missing him by a hair.

Slowing down, it turned back around, readying for another charge.

Li Ming's heart thudded in his chest, in his head. His mouth went dry. That was close. Too close. But he had felt the crack, sensed the force vibrating through its massive body. The tietou was slow, its legs clumsy, trying to support itself. Maybe, with another strike—

The bus horn screamed.

"OVER HERE!" the driver screamed.

Li Ming turned and fled.

Now he sent fire qi into his legs, supercharging them. They pounded like pistons, exploding off the ground with every step. Behind him, the tietou screamed in rage.

He didn't dare look back. He focused his eyes on the bus, on the open door, on the rapidly-shrinking distance between them.

"HURRY! IT'S COMING BACK!"

One two three four five steps and he jumped through the open doorway.

"GO!" Li screamed.

The doors hissed closed. Li seized a grab handle. The driver stomped on the accelerator. The bus rocketed off. Li turned to look through the rear window.

The tietou trotted, slowing to a halt. It fumed at him, its red eyes burning through the glass. Li Ming stared at it, watching it recede in the distance.

"Thank you!" the driver said. "Thank you for your help. You saved everyone aboard the bus."

"It was nothing," Li Ming replied. "Don't mention it."

"*Dajia guli!*" a passenger shouted.

Everyone applaud!

Someone clapped. Another person joined in. And soon the sound of clapping filled the entire bus.

Li Ming blinked. Blinked again. And suddenly he remembered he was still holding on to his weapon. He nodded awkwardly, and hurriedly returned the swordbreaker to its sheath.

"*Li shaoye wansui!*" someone called.

"*LI SHAOYE WANSUI!*" the passengers echoed.

It wasn't right. Li hadn't done anything to earn this. If he were more powerful, or at least had better gear, he'd have burned a hole clean through the tietou's head. If he had a sword, he'd have cleaved the beast in two. If he'd smashed down with a double-handed blow, he might have broken its back. If he were faster, he could have thrust deep into its side. But he'd done none of these.

He'd failed.

The tietou was still out there. It had survived his best efforts to kill it. And it might even remember him.

But that was not what the people saw. All they saw was a cultivator who'd distracted a beast long enough for them to escape. And for them, that was enough.

He couldn't dishonor their feelings.

In the end, he did the only thing he could do.

He brought his fist and palm together over his chest.

"Thank you, everyone."

Chapter Four

The Bright Lights of Bao An

There were several cities in Dongshan Province. But to the inhabitants of Fuyang, only one earned the appellation of 'the city': the provincial capital of Bao An.

Home to a million and a half souls, with twice that number living in the metro area, Bao An was the largest city in the province. For that matter, it was one of the largest cities in the Zhongxia Republic. And yet, somehow, it retained its small town feel.

Life was easy here. Not as slow-paced as Fuyang, but more relaxed than other large cities. The urban core of Bao An, and its satellite commercial and industrial districts, were designed in obedience to *fengshui* principles. Li Ming saw them in the wide, orderly streets, the abundance of parks and trees, the buildings sited and designed in harmony with the heavens, the waters, the earth, and their neighbors.

Bao An Station was right in the middle of the city. As the bus wound through the many streets, he pressed himself up against the window, studying the terrain.

The outskirts of the city retained its traditional roots, defined by its siheyuan. These were courtyard houses, the design ubiquitous across Xiazhou, their origins stretching back for over two thousand years. Multiple siheyuan joined together formed a hutong, a narrow street for foot and light traffic. Several hutong in turned were clumped together into neighborhoods and districts, forming an urban sprawl at once organic and organized.

He'd fought his way through many hutong just like these. But that battle was a lifetime ago. A different time and place, in an urban village abandoned by the rulers. Here, the people honored and cherished their homes. The streets were clean and tidy, the people were well-fed and clothed, the stores were doing a brisk trade, the homes were built with modern materials and to modern codes, yet retained their link to the long-distant past.

Deeper in the city, skyscrapers appeared. But not too many of them. They stood far apart from each other, keeping a respectful distance. In the buffer zones between them lived residential multiplexes, shopping malls, schools, offices. Bao An Tower loomed above them all, the tallest structure in the city, its signature landmark, the edifice that marked its beating heart.

Everything a man wanted in the city he could find around the tower. For commerce he could choose from the half-dozen shopping arcades and office complexes within a three-block radius. If he got hungry, there were a dozen world-class restaurants and a hundred smaller eateries. Short-term travelers could avail themselves of the nearby hotel, while citizens could stay in nearby apartments. Every train, metro, and bus line in the city ran through Bao An Station. From here, a man could go anywhere in the city—and beyond.

A contingent of cops greeted the bus when it pulled into the station. They interviewed everyone aboard, ensuring their safety. The senior officer drew Li Ming aside for a private conversation. Li Ming recounted his encounter with the tietou. The bus driver eagerly backed him up. In the end, the policeman shook his hand, thanked him profusely, and allowed him to leave.

They wouldn't have done this in Fuyang. They wouldn't have bothered with lengthy interviews. They would have mobilized the militia to shoot the tietou. But the city had different rules. And he had to abide by them now.

The station was a study in horizontality and verticality, a fusion of connectivity and commerce. Vast empty space stretched out from the ground floor courtyard to the roof high above, exposing a dozen floors of walkways and shops, gardens and benches, offices and escalators.

Escalators led to the underground rail stations. Escalators headed up to shopping and dining areas. Escalators fed to outdoor atria and indoor fountains. Entire walls of nothing but escalators and steps ran from the ground floor courtyard to the twelfth floor walkways and every floor in between. Escalators and exits pulled him in a dozen directions, sending his mind reeling, unable to tell which way to walk.

Everywhere he looked, he saw a forest of signs, a maze of passageways, rivers of passengers and pedestrians. Most people needed navigation apps just to find their way through the station. The directory showed a staggering array of services and stores, everything from a private clinic to a shopping arcade to a supermarket. He wondered if a man could live his entire life without ever stepping outside the station. Maybe someone had.

First things first. At the tourist information office, he picked up free maps and guidebooks of the station and the city. He had his smartglasses, yes, but a paper map and compass didn't need electricity or fragile circuits.

He followed the signs to the northern exit. Stepped out onto the street. Reoriented himself.

And gaped.

The Bao An Tower loomed over him. The tallest structure in the city, the quarter-*li* edifice was a finger pointed at the heavens, a beacon of blazing blue and bright yellow and stark white light against the coming night. It was the symbol of the city, its proudest and most recognizable accomplishment, having stood since the dawn of the Republic.

He'd seen countless photos and videos of the tower. But there was nothing quite like seeing it for himself.

The Bao An Tower Hotel occupied the fifth to tenth floors. The preferred option of tourists and businessmen on a budget, it charged three hundred and fifty yuan a night. For that kind of money he could eat like a baron for a week.

But that was by Fuyang standards, and he was not in Fuyang anymore.

He booked a room for a week, paying in advance. He dropped his bag in his room and headed back down to the third floor. Here, a goodly selection of restaurants greeted him, offering cuisine from every corner of the globe.

But the prices...

He had no idea how people could afford to spend fifty yuan on a meal, never mind the sixty to eighty to *hundred* yuan these places demanded. The food may look appetizing, the smells were mouth-watering, but the zeroes on the menu turned him off.

In the basement he found a food court. For the stately price of twenty yuan, he enjoyed a large bowl of fish soup with rice. Still a touch more expensive than Fuyang, but everything was expensive in the city.

After dinner, he headed up to the observation deck. Thirty-five yuan for a ticket, a price even *he* found ridiculous, but... a man only lived so long.

And it was worth it.

Shadows swathed the observation deck. Soft lights drew attention to the steps, to paintings, to the wall-length windows, their dim glow enhancing the view of the city. Soft music piped in over from hidden overhead speakers. Couples whispered and giggled by the binoculars. Giggling children hopped and dashed across the soft carpet. A tour guide spoke to his charges through a tinny microphone. Li Ming disengaged from them all and found an empty window.

The bright lights of the city stretched out before him, a dense blanket of amber diamonds, neon reds, ghostly blues, ethereal violets. Gigantic billboards advertised logos, products, blockbusters, so huge he could see them even from here. More ads flashed along the hulls of low-flying blimps, their navigational lights flashing against an empty sky.

In that moment, Li Ming felt like a young god looking down upon an old world, a world ready for the coming of the new, a world that was his to shape to his will.

All his life, he had prepared himself for a career in the military or the police. It was the way of his father and forefathers. But theirs was a more innocent era, where a black was black and white was white and any man could tell the two apart. In his time, the era of the Five States and the Ten Corporations, the world was... complicated.

He would have stayed in the military. He wanted to stay. But the corporations had reached out and touched him, and tens of thousands more. They had used the military as their pawns and made him a hero to draw attention away from their schemes. If this was what it meant to protect and serve the people now, he would have none of that.

But there was no escaping the Ten Corporations. Even here, he could see their logos, burning red like coals, marking the skyscrapers and shopping malls they claimed as homes.

He didn't despise them. He knew the products and services they offered had brought immense benefit to the world. But he had no wish to do their wet work for them.

Yet a man still needed to support himself and his family. More than that, he had to be of use to his family and his nation. For Li Ming, a man of the sword and the gun, there was only one way left.

The way of the youxia.

The only place for such a man was the jianghu. The nature of the jianghu was that sooner or later he'd have to deal with the Ten Corporations. The greater a person's stature, the greater his problems, and the greatest entities of the world would soon encounter the kind of problems only a youxia could handle. Anyone who solved those problems would become a wealthy man indeed.

If he had no choice but to deal with the Ten Corporations at some point, he could at least try to make a lot of money out of it. You couldn't get rich on a government or a private sector salary—not without the right education and connections. And, as a youxia, he could decide whether a job was worth it.

Besides, coming from Fuyang, his only other choices were farmer or merchant, and he knew enough about those professions to know that he would be terrible at them.

Tomorrow, he would enter the jianghu. Tomorrow, he would take the first step to becoming a youxia. He'd have to start at the bottom, but everybody had to start from somewhere. Before you could work for yourself, you had to know how to work for someone else. You had to learn from those who came before you.

Father had written him an introduction for the finest biaoju in the city. In the province. That alone gave him an edge over everyone else. But he knew all that meant was that he'd have to live up to the expectations of two men: his father's and a stranger's.

If he failed, he wouldn't know what else he could do.

Actually, no. He *did* have options. This was just the easiest among them.

No matter what happened, he was ready.

But that was tomorrow. Tonight, *now*, he basked in the bright lights of Bao An.

And allowed himself to dream.

Chapter Five

First and Last Times

Located at the southeast of the city, Luoyang District was one of the oldest neighborhoods in Bao An. Many of the buildings here weren't concrete or brick, but wood or rammed earth. Many hutong were too narrow for cars. People walked or rode bikes; they drove only if they had business elsewhere in the district.

Halfway through the hour of the rooster, the sun burned bright and clear in the cool blue sky. Bells chimed within a walled school compound. Salaried workers hustled into their offices and workplaces. Garbage collectors made their rounds. Expats and tourists emerged from their rented apartments, armed with cameras and smartglasses, ready to take in the sights of the historic district. Housewives, many with toddlers in tow, made their daily grocery runs.

Li Ming stared out the window of the robot taxi, taking it all in. The first time he'd visited this district, this was the first time he'd overnighted in the city in years. Back then, he was just a teenager, and robot taxis were only beginning to populate the roads.

The taxi was a bright white pod on wheels, neat and compact, seating only two. Three of the pods could fit in the space of two regular vehicles, perfect for the tight streets of the outlying districts. The ride was smooth, quiet, clean. No annoying radio, no unwanted conversation, just blissful silence.

At last, the taxi deposited him at the mouth of a hutong. The computer demanded a hundred and fifty yuan. Exorbitant. But this was the big city. And if this were a taxi with a human driver, the fee would be easily double that.

The display produced a brightly-colored three-dimensional matrix code. He aimed his Raptor's cameras at the code. A window popped up, taking him to Aitan. It was an all-in-one social media platform, incorporating instant messaging, social feeds, and digital payment.

The app requested authorization to make payment. He looked at the approve button and blinked thrice, slow and deliberately. A green checkmark appeared. The computer beeped and the door swung open.

It wasn't his first time using a robot taxi or making mobile payments, but his last time was over a year ago. The novelty still hadn't worn off.

Standing at the entrance of the hutong, Li Ming paused to study his surroundings. This place was once the domain of the upper crust of some distant dynasty. Even today, he saw the traces of their heritage. Ancient stone walls, tall and imposing, demarcated the borders of the neighborhood, preventing passers-by from looking in. The street was paved not with cheap asphalt but with smooth blocks of quarried stone. Painted in dazzling shades of red and blue and green, the gate towered over Li, as though daring him to enter.

He inhaled deeply. Let it out.

He was here now. He was committed.

He stepped through.

The narrow street flowed through a gentle curve, following the lay of the land. Two- and three-story buildings lined the road, the signboards announcing tea houses, a bakery, snacks, accessories, souvenirs. The ground floor was for commerce, the upper floors for habitation. Knots of people ambled up and down the street, checking out the wares on offer. Bikes lined the road, leaning against walls and utility poles.

As he passed, a dozen ditties assaulted his ears. Pop music clashing with traditional instruments. Advertising jingles and radio broadcasts. A hundred screens blaring everything from the news to the latest blockbuster to gamestreams.

Delicious scents wafted through the air. Vendors sold grilled meat skewers, freshly-baked biscuits and buns, roasted sweet potatoes, and more. The tea houses offered an astonishing range of teas, many of which he'd never seen in Fuyang. Green tea, black tea, ground tea, fermented tea; pearl milk tea, plain or served with everything from honey to milk to fruits; tea from faraway mountains and exotic locales.

Deep in the hutong, commercial activity ceased. Here now were siheyuan. Most of them had been converted into multi-family units, marked by the abundance of doors and windows. A few, however, had retained the original design. These he recognized by their solitary gates.

And now, at last, he stopped in front of the largest among them.

Heavy steel doors, painted a deep crimson, protected the entrance. Next to it was a small intercom. A portico extended out into the street, two stone pillars supporting a sharply-arched roof. A pair of guardian lions, carved from stone, flanked the gate. One was a male with a paw perched on a ball, the other a female holding down a lively cub. Gold characters splashed across the black signboard.

Dayong Biaoju.

Li gulped. Breathed. Stepped up to the intercom.

And knuckled the doorbell button.

He waited.

Breathed.

Waited some more.

As he waited, he sensed a slight pressure falling over his body. Someone was peering at him through the camera unit mounted on the panel.

A loud click issued from the speaker.

"Wei? Qingwen nin shi nawei?"

Hello? May I ask who is this?

The speaker was an older man, his voice deep and smooth and confident. He'd used the word *'nin'*, the polite way to say 'you', even though Li Ming was much younger than him.

"Li Ming, from Fuyang. I have an introduction letter from Li Guo An."

"Ah, Mr. Li. Please wait a moment. We will come to you shortly."

He stood. He waited. He watched the street.

Gravel crunched. Heavy bolts snapped. The double doors swung inwards.

A woman stood before him.

Slender as a reed, tall as a willow, skin clear as jade, she came up to Li's nose. An augmented reality headset encircled her temples, the dark visor swiveled up to reveal eyes like limpid autumn water. Her red qipao, tailored to flatter her figure, revealed broad shoulders, muscular arms, a sturdy neck. She'd done up her hair in an elaborate black bun, held in place with chopsticks. Delicate gold earrings dangled from her earlobes. On her right forearm, she wore a reality shaper, an ornate construct of gleaming leather and brass, holding a blazing white sphere.

This close to her, he could sense her qi field, a palpable force electrifying the air, a pair of green wings folded protectively over her body. Her shaper crystal brimmed with qi, ready for immediate response. She was no mere mortal.

She was a cultivator.

A powerful one, too, at least as powerful as him. Maybe even more.

Their eyes met. A golden spark leapt across the space between them. Electricity crackled down his spine. In that moment, deep, complex emotions swirled up within him. A sense of recognition, of familiarity, of deep intimate knowledge, of *joy*.

But how? This was the first time they'd met.

Her eyes widened. Her lips parted, ever so slightly.

His breath caught in his chest. His heart paused.

And just like that, the moment was over.

Her face flushed with color. She blinked and looked away, an awkward smile creeping across her face.

Li Ming breathed.

And cupped his fist over his chest.

"Nin hao. Woshi Li Ming."

Hello. I am Li Ming.

She breathed sharply. And, as she exhaled, she blossomed.

Every muscle relaxed and loosened. Her spine lengthened and straightened. Her head lifted into perfect alignment with her body. Her arms flowed into a perfect mirror of his salute.

"Nin hao. I am Cai Yan, daughter of Cai Mengyang. Thank you for coming. Please, come in."

She stepped aside, spreading her arm to welcome him inside. Passing through the gate, he found himself in a small walled garden.

Flowering shrubs and potted plants stood on a field of gravel. A waterfall burbled away in a corner. A winding path of flagstones led to the inner gate. The scent of jasmine and honeysuckle flavored the air.

As they stepped away from the entrance, the double doors swung shut on unseen hinges and locked themselves. Suddenly he felt like he had entered a private sanctuary, a world made only for the two of them.

"Let me show you to my father," Cai Yan said.

"Thank you."

She was nervous. Her voice caught in her throat. But so was he. He didn't trust himself to say anything more complex than basic greetings.

"You must have come a long way," Cai Yan said.

"Two hours by bus," he replied.

"Two *hours*? I heard Fuyang was on the frontier, but I never really knew what that meant."

He mulled over a range of responses for a while. There were so many things he could say, so many things that he could *not* say. In the end, he simply breathed and spoke from his heart.

"It can be hard to reach."

She chuckled.

The inner gate was almost as grand as the main entrance. But its portico was guarded not by stone lions, but by trees. They were *penjing*, tiny trees carefully cultivated to mirror the size and scale of full-grown trees in the wild.

Cai Yan pressed her thumb to the fingerprint reader by the gate. As before, the double doors unlocked and opened for them.

"This way," she said.

The inner courtyard was a weather-worn square of bare concrete. It reminded Li Ming of a parade square in a military base. But instead of the armored vehicles and markings he was used to, a tree stood in a patch of grass at every corner.

Side halls flanked the square. Long and low, their gray tiled roofs arched in dramatic sweeps. While inspired by traditional designs, they were built from modern concrete and reinforced glass, and the doors were guarded by security panels.

The main hall stood at the far side. Taller and wider than the outlying buildings, it was the center of the compound. The facade was clean, neat, elegant, but Li Ming sensed the weight of countless centuries emanating from its heart. Here was the headquarters of Dayong, the biaoju that had clawed its way to the pinnacle of the Bao An jianghu. So many promising biaohang had served with the company, winning wealth, glory and immortality. There was only one way for him to join their ranks.

He had to prove himself worthy.

Verandas ran along the inner perimeter of the wall, joining the halls together. The pillars were crafted from real wood, fire-hardened and painted a deep red. *Dougang,* interlocking wooden brackets, joined the pillars to the roof. He wondered if they were genuine structural reinforcements, or mere decoration.

He sneaked a look at her. With eyeblinks, he activated his qi assessment app.

Qi score: 16384.

Over three thousand points higher than him. But she didn't look older than him, at least, not much older than him. She couldn't have trained that much longer than him. Maybe the Cai family had its own secret cultivation techniques. Or, more likely, their wealth purchased the potions and pills and elixirs needed to supercharge qi development.

Cai Yan took him around the square, under the shelter of the walkways. The hustle and bustle of the street faded into a distant murmur. Here there was only a blessed quiet.

"It's peaceful here," Li Ming murmured.

"Thank you. Father enjoys a tranquil environment. Our guests and clients do, too," she replied.

"Where's everyone?"

"The household staff is indoors. Our biaohang are all out. The rest of the family is around the back."

"It's just you and me here?"

"And Father."

Of course.

Two steps later, the words 'household staff' jumped out at him.

The Cai family had servants.

Of course they did. A home as opulent as this needed servants. Maids, butlers, cooks, gardeners, housekeepers, whatever they were called, people who cared for the house and its family. This was the first time he'd met anyone so rich they could afford servants.

But what else did he expect? Dayong was one of the leading armed escort agencies in the province. How could they *not* have servants?

Cai Yan showed him into the main hall. Cold air washed over him, so cold it raised goosebumps over his flesh. Dark leather sofas and glass tables clustered in the corners, leaving wide aisles to walk through. Vases of fresh plants adorned every table and corner. Paintings hung from the walls, a mix of calligraphy and landscape shots. In the warm yellow lights, the parquet floor gleamed.

The western side of the hall was a single large room. Bookshelves stretched across the left-hand wall, groaning under the weight of books and trophies and decorations. By the door, cream-colored sofas surrounded a wooden table. Potted plants stood by the curtained windows. Framed certificates and news clippings covered the walls.

At the far corner, silhouetted in the morning light, a man stood behind a worktable.

He was a cultivator, no doubt about it. His energy flooded the room. It was steel wrapped in fire-hardened leather, a sword waiting to be drawn. For an instant he seemed like a giant, looming tall over Li Ming, ready to unleash overwhelming violence at the slightest provocation.

He was no giant. But he came close. As tall as Li Ming, maybe even taller, he was built like a bomb. Sleek and clean-limbed, he was lean muscle and rock-hard bone and nothing more. His darkened skin spoke of many hours under the sun. His spine was erect, his hair thick and dark and full. He appeared to be in the prime of his life. But behind his Raptor smartglasses, his hard eyes carried the weight of many decades.

"Father, this is Li Ming," Cai Yan said.

Li Ming snapped to attention, fist and palm meeting over his heart.

"Cai shishu, jiuyang daming, xinghui xinghui!"

Greetings, Martial Uncle Cai! Your great name precedes you!

Cai Mengyang smirked, waving his hand in casual dismissal.

"Ni hao. There's no need to be *that* formal. We don't stand on ceremony here. Come, sit."

Cai Mengyang wore a dark jacket and matching trousers. Clean, simple, elegant, its deliberate understatedness was itself a powerful statement. As Li Ming approached, he noted the fit of the cloth, the way it shone under the light, the crisp lines that defined his figure. The suit seemed to make his body disappear, yet highlighted his face and posture. Handmade, Li Ming guessed, probably silk or a synthetic substitute.

Li Ming sat on a leather chair in front of the worktable. The surface of the desk was a single slab of solid black wood. A bank of sensors and holographic projectors stared at both men. As Cai Mengyang reclined against his own chair, Li activated his qi assessment app.

22872 points. The highest score Li had seen yet in Bao An. Only one in ten cultivators ever broke the twenty-thousand point barrier. Those who did walked as gods among men.

"Would you like anything to drink? Coffee, tea?"

"Boiled water, please."

"Very well. Xiao Yan?"

Cai Yan nodded, and withdrew from the room.

Cai Mengyang turned his attentions to Li Ming. His gaze was like twin lasers boring into his soul. Li Ming matched the intensity of his stare, open and unafraid, neither defiant nor submissive, simply signaling a readiness to meet anything he sent out.

Cai Mengyang smiled.

"I understand you have a letter for me."

"Yes. One moment."

Li Ming dug into his backpack and retrieved his document organizer. The first slot held a pair of envelopes, one white and one yellow. He removed the white envelope and handed it over with both hands.

A red wax seal secured the flap. Cai Mengyang inspected the seal, holding it up to the light. Nodding, he broke the seal, extracted a sheath and papers, and began to read.

The civilian world, with its love of electricity and efficiency, had long ago adopted telephones and electronic mail as the medium of business communication. The jianghu, however, held fast to tradition. Cai Mengyang would appreciate the personal touch. Father had sent him a heads-up last week, but this letter served to verify Li Ming's identity.

"You're Li Guo An's son," Cai Mengyang said.

"Yes."

"This is the first time we've met. How is your old man doing?"

"Hale and hearty, as always."

"Good, good. I heard he retired a wealthy man."

"We've comfortable. He spread the wealth around the village, especially to the farmers. He liked to say that society would starve without the farmer."

"Sounds like something *he* would say. I presume your family knows of your intention to join the jianghu?"

"Yes."

"How do they feel about it?"

When Li Ming first announced his intentions, it had sent his family into a state of shock. Mother nagged and nagged for weeks and months, hoping to dissuade him. Sister vacillated between encouraging him and wanting him to find a safer career. Father had kept his peace for the most part, but behind the scenes he smoothed things over with the women.

"Waiting for your father made me an old woman," Mother had said. "Waiting for you could kill me."

Only much later, on the bus to Bao An, did he finally realize what she actually meant. She had spent weeks, months, years, worrying about her husband, about whether she would open the door one day to find a priest and a dour messenger in dress blues. When he was away, she did her best to raise the children.

For his part, Father didn't wander too far from home. But before the birth of his children, his jobs had taken him all over Xiazhou, all over the world. He stayed at home for half a year, then spent the other half fighting bandits and training protectors. The separation had taken its toll on Mother.

But she was tough. And he had made his choice.

"They accept my decision," Li Ming said at last. "It took a lot of talking, but they finally came around."

"I see. The jianghu is no ordinary industry. It is a whole new world, both a part of and apart from the outside world. It has its own rules, logic, traditions. Every year, countless people find many reasons to enter the jianghu. What's yours?"

He had spent weeks, months, preparing for this very question. The response came automatically to his tongue.

"I want to protect people."

The older man's eyes twinkled behind his lenses.

"Really? You think you're some kind of hero?"

"No, not at all. In the Army, I served in the Special Military Police. The idea of serving and protecting the people resonated with me. I decided to make it my career. No better way to do that than in the jianghu."

"You could have signed on as a professional soldier."

"Soldiers have to do what the government tells them to do. The government must do what the voters and the Ten Corporations want them to do. What the Ten Corporations want may not always be the right thing to do. Soldiers cannot say no—or, if they do, they must resign. In the jianghu, you can always refuse."

"An idealist, *en?*"

"A world without virtue is a world without light."

"Pretty words. But what do you think are these virtues?"

"*Qian. Zun. Zheng. Xin. Zhong. Yi. Ren. Yi. Heng. Yong.*"

Modesty. Respect. Righteousness. Trustworthiness. Loyalty. Determination. Endurance. Willpower. Perseverance. Courage.

Cai Mengyang laughed.

"Fine words. But these martial values are for those who wish to study martial arts. Not necessarily the real world."

"We are martial cultivators. We hold in our hands the power of life and death. The power to cripple, kill and destroy. We must hold ourselves to higher standards."

"Why?"

"Without virtue, we are but beasts."

"Guo An's letter said you were a fine man. He didn't say you were a deep thinker."

Li Ming shrugged uncomfortable.

"I do not know what my father said about me. I am here only to present myself."

At that moment, Cai Yan returned, carrying a serving tray. She placed a cup of water before Li Ming, and another cup of tea in front of her father. She moved with effortless grace, every motion clean and efficient. Li Ming couldn't help but study the play of her muscles and fingers. Then he realized her father was watching him stare.

A tiny smile played across her father's face.

Li Ming gulped.

"Thank you, Ms. Cai," he said.

"You're welcome," she replied.

And retreated.

"Do you have any previous work experience?" Cai Mengyang asked.

"Just my service in the military. I've prepared a resume for you, as well as the results of my latest medical screening. Would you like to see it?"

"Please."

Li handed over the other envelope. Cai Mengyang removed a sheath of documents and slowly flipped through the pages. As Cai Mengyang read, Li sipped at his water. It was hot, hot enough to blunt the bite of the chilly air without burning his tongue.

"You said you served in the Special Military Police," Cai Mengyang said.

"Yes."

"You were part of the Capital Battalion. Taiping is far away from here. How did you end up serving over there?"

"I heard that at the time I graduated from the Special Military Police Academy, the Capital Battalion had suffered heavy losses. They sent me there to make up the numbers."

"Are you familiar with Taiping?"

"Not at that time. Until I'd joined the military, I'd never been to Taiping."

"It must be challenging. New environment, new culture, new duties."

"I adapted. It worked out well."

"Indeed, Staff Sergeant Li. It says here you won a combat meritorious promotion *and* the Medal of Valor."

Li Ming kept a poker face. He hadn't asked for any of that.

"I simply did my duty."

"And what was your duty, exactly? What were the circumstances leading up to it?"

Li Ming steadied himself with a deep breath.

"In my final week of service, the Capital Battalion was dispatched to clear the urban village of Shanxia. The Hong Shun Tang had seized control of the area. Our job was to disrupt their activities, capture or kill their leaders and facilitators, and restore law and order to the area."

He described the operation as he'd experienced it. Two days of fire and smoke, two days that had left permanent scars in his psyche. Cai Mengyang interrupted often with questions, teasing out every detail. Li Ming answered what he could. As he spoke, he reminded himself to breathe fully and deeply, to be in the moment and release any emotions that arose.

Finally, he finished his story. The men sat in silence for a moment, sipping at their beverages.

"It sounded like you've been through a lot," Cai Mengyang said. "I'm glad you made it home safely."

"Thank you."

"With an achievement like this, I'm surprised the military didn't try to retain you."

"I told them I was done. They respected my decision."

"And why were you done?"

"I..."

"Too many bad memories?"

"Not exactly. It's... As I said earlier, a soldier can't say no."

"But a youxia can?"

"Perhaps. But I'm not applying for the position of a wandering hero."

"You completed a ten-day training program at Nine Star Security Consultancy. One of the most prestigious programs in the country. You want to become an armed escort?"

"Yes."

"With a man of your record, many doors in the jianghu will open to you. Why here? Why sign up for an armed escort agency?"

"I have to start from somewhere. Might as well start here, with my *shishu*."

"Funny you should call me *shishu* when we've never met."

"That may be so, but you've trained alongside my father. That makes you my *shishu*."

"Guo An says he taught you martial arts. Which arts were those?"

"My foundation is in An Family wuxingquan and yizhang. In the military, I've also picked up other techniques from other styles, including the Army's combatives program."

"How many years have you practiced? Ten?"

"Twelve."

"A good number of years. In that case, I'm sure you know the name of our fortieth generation grandmaster."

Li Ming smiled.

"*Shishu*, I was not aware that our lineage had so long a history. I only know that the current grandmaster is merely the fourteenth generation lineage holder."

Cai Mengyang smiled even wider.

"I misspoke. What is the name of the current grandmaster?"

"An Long."

"How do you trace your lineage to him?"

"My father first studied the art from his father. Later, when he was stationed in Bao An, he trained under Gong Jun. That was when he met you. Together, you two traveled to visit Shigong An, where you learned directly from him. My father passed down the art to me."

"I see. What is the origin of the name of wuxingquan?"

For a moment Li Ming wondered if Cai Mengyang had misspoken. He'd pronounced 'wu' with the rising tone, not the dipping tone.

"Each of the five fists represents the five elements. By understanding the five elements, you understand the universe."

"A textbook answer."

A flicker passed across the older man's face. Li Ming wondered if he'd failed a secret test.

"Please show me your Sancai Shi," Cai Mengyang said.

Li Ming stood and paced a safe distance from the desk. He relaxed into the stance, letting muscle and bone flow into the stance long ingrained into his memory. As he lifted his arms into place, he sank his weight into the floor.

Cai Mengyang watched him like a hawk, studying every angle, every motion. Unconsciously, Li Ming altered his posture, spreading his fingers a little more, redistributing his weight just a bit, shifting his lead foot a touch more to the right.

"Very good. Show me the Five Element Linking Form, both the productive and the conquering cycles," Cai Mengyang said.

"Armed or empty hand?"

"Whichever you are most comfortable with."

Li carefully withdrew his scabbarded swordbreaker and placed it by his backpack. He knew the armed forms, but the empty hand form was burned into his blood. He returned to the center of the room and assumed the Sancai Shi.

Exhaled.

And exploded into motion.

He turned off his conscious mind, allowing his *yi* to guide his *qi*, and his *qi* to guide his body. Intention was everything, but intention did not have to be conscious. He let the movements happen naturally, his awareness grounded in his body and expanding to encompass the world around him.

This was a performance, yes, but it was also moving meditation. His body was in constant motion, his mind was totally still. Together they expressed the five fundamental energies of this ever-changing universe, five basic movements in complete alignment with the laws of Heaven and Earth.

"Well done," Cai Mengyang said. "Show me the sixth fist."

"*En*? The sixth fist? What do you mean?"

There was no such thing. There were only five fists. It was right there in the name of the art.

Cai Mengyang's face hardened. His eyes dimmed. His lips tightened.

"Never mind. Please demonstrate the Assorted Form."

Li Ming wondered if he had failed another test. As quickly as the thought emerged, he breathed it out, then focused his intentions and energies on the form.

He flowed up and down the length of the office, shortening his steps to compensate. Twisting and torquing, he exploded into motion, settled into stillness, flowing from one state to the other. He lunged and pecked and punched in violent bursts, flowed through smooth arcs and circles. He hopped and pounced and advanced, then he squatted and spun and retreated.

Something prickled at the edges of his conscious. An idea. Yin and yang, shape and form, stillness and motion. But the more he grasped at it, the more it slipped away from him. He let it go, focusing on his form.

And suddenly the set was over.

"Excellent work," Cai Mengyang said. "What about the Golden Butterfly and the Silver Bee?"

Li blinked. Was that another test?

"I haven't heard of that."

A shadow fell over Cai Mengyang's face.

"Ah."

"Is something wrong?"

"No, nothing. Don't worry about it. Show me the yizhang that you've studied."

Yizhang was the art of the changing palm. Based on the eight trigrams, it was the microcosm of a universe always in motion, always changing from one form to the next. The art was nominally defined by its twisting, spiraling, circular movements, the opposite of wuxingquan's direct attacks, but the An family taught yizhang and wuxingquan as complementary arts. Teachers usually encouraged practitioners to master one art or the other, but to gain full understanding of the system, of the principles of movement and cultivation, students had to learn both.

Li Ming only had six years of training in yizhang. Just enough to recognize that there were deeper principles beyond what he little he knew. He saw their shadows, grasped at their silhouettes, yet they always slipped away from him, hiding just behind the next palm, the next step, the next spin, disappearing when he arrived.

Even so, he tried.

He began with the single and double palm changes. The foundational moves, expressing the essence of change itself. Then came the Heaven Palm, seamlessly flowing into the Earth Palm. Pure yang and pure yin, they were the from which all other palms flowed. The remaining forms followed in quick succession: Fire, Water, Wind, Thunder, Marsh, Mountain.

These were the eight mother palms. In them lay the entirety of the art. Some schools melded the palms together, forming sixty-four palms. The An Family focused on the eight mother palms, for mastery of the eight allowed the practitioner to freely execute infinite palms.

"Not bad," Cai Mengyang said. "But I see it's not your primary art."

"I spent most of my time on wuxingquan."

"It shows. Your movements are very linear. Very direct. There's more wuxing in your palms than yizhang. Remember that yizhang is the art of flowing around the enemy. It is not the art of blasting through him."

"Understood. Thank you."

"Now there is one last form I wish to see."

"Which is that?"

Cai Mengyang walked around his desk and folded up his sleeves.

"An Shen Pao."

Li Ming drew himself to attention, and saluted.

"Shishu, qing."

Cai Mengyang returned the gesture.

"Qing."

The men assumed the Sancai Shi. Straight away, Li Ming saw the subtle differences between their stances. Cai Mengyang was taller and heavier, his center of balance higher off the floor. His legs were like coiled springs, ready to burst into motion. His hands were slightly higher than what Li Ming was used to, yet remained within orthodox practice.

His subconscious mind whispered how he should adjust his moves. His conscious mind went blank. He breathed.

They began.

In the first moment of contact, their fists brushing past each other to explode into empty space, it felt like touching a live wire. Electricity radiated from the point of contact, penetrating to the bone.

The opening steps signaled the speed of the set. Cai Mengyang went full bore, holding nothing back, and Li Ming accelerated to match. They stepped back. Reset their stances. Paused for a heartbeat.

Li Ming launched a Beng Quan.

Cai Mengyang parried.

And it was on. A complicated dance of feet and fists, hands and hips, offense and defense and counteroffense. Clothes slapped against skin with audible claps. The ground trembled with every footfall. Qi erupted from every moment of contact, burning hands and arms and legs. Still they continued, punching and probing, clearing and striking, fully intent on landing a killing blow, fully confident that conformance to the choreography would protect them.

One last punch. One last parry. Then the men stepped back. Turned. Brought their fists over their *dantian*. And looked at each other.

Cai Mengyang smiled.

"Excellent. I see your father taught you well."

"Thank you. He is a great teacher."

"No doubt about that."

They returned to the desk. The workout had done Li Ming good. Now he was warm. Not so much that he was sweating, just enough that he was now comfortable in the chilly air.

"For someone as young as yourself, you have a stellar resume," Cai Mengyang said. "Good grades in school, superb service record, solid martial skills. Any biaoju would be eager to hire you. The jianghu will certainly welcome you with open arms."

Li Ming's heart leaped into his chest. Did he pass?

"Thank you for coming all this way to Bao An. You must be tired after such a long test and such a vigorous workout. Do you have a place to stay?" Cai Mengyang asked.

"Yes."

"Good. Do you have any questions?"

Li Ming realized he hadn't asked *any* questions up to this point. He didn't know if it were a good or bad thing, only that he was here now and he had plenty of questions.

But, really, there was only one question that mattered most.

"What's it like being a biaohang?"

Cai Mengyang's eyes hardened into twin spears illuminated in moonlight. They pierced into Li Ming, through him, breaching his face to penetrate his soul.

"Challenging."

"Could you elaborate?"

"The nature of our work means that you won't have a fixed schedule. You must be prepared to answer the call any time of day, any day of the week. No exceptions. Your house might have burned down, a family member might have passed away, but if you are on duty, you answer the call.

"Life in the jianghu is not about you. It is never about you. Beasts and bandits will not wait for a time when it's convenient for you to beat them up. Likewise, when we are protecting a client, we will be working on the client's schedule, not ours. When the call comes, someone out there needs out help, and they need it right now.

"If you don't have an assignment, you're free to go anywhere and do anything you want. But when we call you, you must report here within a half hour. Day or night, if the call comes, you answer.

"Once you're on the clock, you don't knock off until the job is done. Expect to skip meals, sleep, family time, weekends, holidays. In busy months you'll have to work assignments back to back without downtime. You'll be suitably compensated, but make no mistake: you'll have to earn every yuan. Are you *sure* you want this?"

"Sounds like the military. With the bonus of not working on quiet days."

Cai Mengyang laughed.

"*If* we hire you, and I'm not saying that we will, our standard contract runs for six months. If, after those six months, you still enjoy being a biaohang, we'll discuss options for extension."

"Understood."

"We don't expect you to work all the time, of course. You're entitled to five days of vacation leave, ten days of medical leave, and five days compassionate leave. We require at least two weeks' notice before you apply for vacation leave.

"However, this *is* the jianghu. Don't expect to use all your vacation time. Or *any* of it, for that matter. Unused vacation days will be converted to paid work days at the end of your contract. Before you ask, no, we *don't* offer overtime."

"I see."

Li Ming had wanted to ask about salary. He'd done his research, of course, and Father had confirmed it, but there was nothing like asking the source. But before he could open his mouth, Cai Mengyang cut him off.

"I think I've taken up enough of your time. I enjoyed speaking with you and seeing some of your gongfu. I'm going to make a few calls, talk to some friends. I'll let you know my decision by the end of the week."

"Thank you, *shishu*."

"You don't have to call me that. We're not in a training hall. Call me Mr. Cai if you wish. Or *laoban*, if you prefer."

"Understood, Mr. Cai."

"Come, let me…"

His voice trailed away. A grin dawned over his face.

"Mr. Cai?"

"I just remembered I had some work to do. My daughter will see you out."

They stood and shook hands. Mr. Cai led him to the door. Ms. Cai sat at one of the sofas, headset visor lowered, hands swiping through various gestures. No mere entertainment device, the headset was a spatial computer, designed for the intersection of business and war.

"Xiao Yan, please see Mr. Li to the door."

"Okay."

She blossomed, unfolding to her full height, lifting the visor from her eyes. Li gawked for a moment, until he remembered where he was. She caught his eye and offered a mischievous dimpled smile.

"This way, Mr. Li," she said.

They walked to the secondary gate in silence. Li Ming didn't trust himself to say anything intelligent. Despite her confidence, he sensed a skein of nervousness under the surface. It resonated with him, threatening to infect him.

This was another test, he decided. That had to be why she was dressed like this and acting this way. She would report everything he said and did to her father. Which meant he had to be on his best behavior.

"What do you think of Bao An?" she asked.

He bought a moment with a breath.

"It's been years since I last came here. A lot has changed. But a lot remained the same too."

"Ah? How so?"

"The city core is always changing. New shops, new displays, new products. But the historic districts at the outskirts remained the same."

"The outskirts change too. Business is hard these days. The shops down the road barely last a year or two."

"But your biaoju remained?"

"Yes. We've been in business for one hundred and fifty years."

"One hundred and fifty? Your company dates to the Celestial Empire?"

"Oh yes. My great-great-grandfather founded it. It's been in the Cai Family hands since then."

"Incredible."

"It's a dangerous world. There'll always be a need for security."

"Always a need for youxia."

She laughed. It was like the tinkling of a windchime.

"Biaohang, yes. But youxia? The only youxia these days are in the movies."

"Maybe it's a good thing."

Standing by the main gate, the sun painted her in a golden sheen, as if a master sculptor had chiseled her out of a sunbeam. Her eyes were twin whirlpools, soft and dark and deep, so deep a man could lose himself in them forever. He drank her in, burning the sight into his memory.

And, he sensed, she was doing the same.

He cupped his fist over his heart.

"Thank you."

She smiled and returned the salute.

"Hope to see you soon."

Chapter Six

Terrain

L i Ming had nothing on his schedule. It didn't mean he had nothing to do.

The day after the interview, he awoke at his accustomed time, a half hour before dawn. The hotel room was cold and dark and lifeless. The only illumination came from the city lights shining through the curtained window, distant and distorted. He groped around the headboard until he found the room control panel. One eye closed, he clicked on the lights.

Above his head, a bright yellow light clicked on. He squinted against the sudden illumination. Slowly, as his vision adjusted, he opened his other eye and rolled off the bed.

In the tiny bathroom, he shaved and brushed his teeth. He marveled at the disposable toothbrush and toothpaste, the one-use tubes of shower gel and conditioner, the dedicated shaver power socket, wondering how such things even existed. In the countryside, and in the military, he'd learned to make the most of everything he had. One-use-only items seemed so... *wasteful*.

Barefoot, he padded to the sole window. The room was patterned off a Celestial-style fangzhang, a small square with just enough living space for a sole man, plus a tiny hallway to accommodate the closet and the bathroom. He had to squeeze between the bed and the opposite wall, careful to avoid brushing against the television.

A writing desk and chair looked out the window, offering a grand view of Bao An station and the main street. The streetlights were still shining bright, but already the city was waking up. Cars and buses flowed down the roads in iron rivers, building up to the morning rush hour. People pulsed in and out of the station at regular intervals, blood cells propelled by an unseen heart.

Between the bed and the desk, Li Ming had a small strip of bare floor. Five steps across, one step wide. It had to be enough. Back to the wall, he assumed the Sancai Shi.

Zhan zhuang. The Five Element Fists. That was all he had space for. As he moved, he shortened his steps, minimizing his motions. His legs brushed up against the bed and the desk, and he punched into empty space. Every fifth step he shortened his strikes, turning them into palms, stopping them just shy of the wall.

Briefly he thought about brushing up on his yizhang. It'd been a while since he'd deliberately drilled it. He knew he was getting rusty. He'd felt it back at the escort agency. But here... here was not the place. There just wasn't enough space.

And there was more to life than just wuxingquan.

A thousand fists later, he grabbed his keycard, Raptor and a towel and headed out.

The hotel gym, sited on the fifth floor, was small but complete. It had treadmills, weights, fitness machines, even a punching bag in the corner.

Which was currently in use.

A stout young man whaled away at the bag, alternating between whipping strikes from unorthodox angles to traditional kicks and full power punches. He exhaled sharply with every punch, moving around and into the bag, chasing it as it swung around. With every blow, qi pulsed from his body, filling the room.

He was a martial cultivator. Not a novice either. His strikes were clean, his footwork nimble, his breath perfectly synchronized with his movements. But he was careless.

Never let strangers see you train, Father had warned. Only your fellow disciples. Never let anyone else see your true strength, lest they steal your techniques and devise a stratagem to defeat you.

The Raptor claimed this cultivator had a score of 15324 points. Not anyone worth crossing, that was for sure. Li Ming shied away from the bag, heading instead to the weights corner. With every breath he drew his qi into himself, suppressing his aura. Nobody needed to know there was another cultivator in the room. He didn't want to be drawn into unnecessary fights, especially with a job application in the works.

For the next half hour he worked the dumbbells, full-body supersets that worked the arms, chest, legs. There was just no substitute for raw muscle power. Their qi scores being equal, a strong man almost always beats a weak man. He finished the session with a short run on the treadmill, three *li* in ten minutes.

It was an excellent time, for a regular human. For a military cultivator, it was the gold standard. Elite cultivator athletes, those who participated in marathons and sporting events, those who used specialized cultivation methods to become lighter, faster, stronger, would have left him in the dust. He appreciated the discipline and the talent needed for such competitions, but they weren't for him. His focus was on the martial way.

As he left the gym, the other cultivator remained, still slamming the bag at full power. He barely noticed Li, and Li returned the favor.

Back in his room, he enjoyed a cold shower. He made a mental note to figure out how to deal with the dirty clothing. Back home he'd have done it himself. For a fee, the hotel offered same-day laundry services. He could afford it *now*, but was it something he needed?

He'd scrimped and saved over the past two years, squirreling away as much of his meager military allowance as he could. Even so, with the prices he'd seen in Bao An, he didn't think it would last long. Two months, maybe three at most. Every last yuan counted.

He could figure out his own laundry, he decided. Along with all his other expenses.

He enjoyed breakfast in the hotel restaurant. His room fee covered it, and he might as well make the most of it. From the modest breakfast buffet, he assembled a mix of buns and egg pancakes. There was other international cuisine too, but today he craved familiar tastes.

He spent the rest of the day walking the streets of Bao An. In the military he'd learned the importance of learning the terrain. If Bao An were to be his new area of operations, he had to know the lay of the land.

He began with the city's downtown core, circling through a widening clockwise spiral. He strolled through shopping malls, marveled at skyscrapers, walked down wide boulevards. He goggled at the huge variety of goods on sale, many of which he'd never see in Fuyang. The prices, too, left him awestruck. By his rough calculations, everything was about twice as expensive as Fuyang.

It could have been worse. In Taiping, everything *began* at two and a half times dearer than Fuyang.

Everywhere he looked, the world of the jianghu interpenetrated the world of men. Digital billboards announced an upcoming bout between two fighters. The faces of famous cultivators graced ads for clothing, tech, skin whitening products, supplements. Low-level cultivators thronged pharmaceutical halls, snapping up pills and elixirs and manuals promising good health, smooth cultivation, greater power.

There was so much to take in, *too* much. But the jianghu was *everywhere*. At a movie theater he saw a poster for this year's version of the legend of the eight immortals, this time starring a cast composed entirely of immortal cultivators. A private hospital published endorsements by celebrity immortals, all of them testifying to the efficacies of their rejuvenation and longevity treatments. A cultivator gear shop stocked nothing but brands and products used by military, police and movie immortals.

The xian were so beautiful, so perfect. Every last one of them was the image of youth. Sparkling eyes, full heads of styled black hair, clear skin, toned muscle. The men were uniformly tall and solid, either packed with muscle or glamorously androgynous. The women were visions of idealized femininity, with hourglass proportions and flawless skin, soft curves and delicate limbs, as regal as warrior-queens or as ethereal as lotus blossoms shrouded in mist.

The ads said they were forty, fifty, sixty, even eighty years old, but they were all preserved in time. The oldest was an eighty-eight-year-old man who appeared a distinguished forty. Most of the rest were frozen in time, locked between the ages of sixteen and twenty. All of them had their faces and bodies sculpted by the hands of master artists to reach heights of beauty unattainable by mere biology.

Li Ming had read once that in some distant, bygone era, the only way to achieve immortality was constant, disciplined cultivation. Only a rare few exceeded the age of eighty, and never a hundred and twenty-five. The Celestial Empire had changed that. Having unlocked the secrets to life extension, rejuvenation and negligible senescence, they opened the doors to eternal life. But only for the rare few who had earned the absolute trust of the Emperor.

Even in the era of the Zhongxia Republic, things hadn't changed much. Anyone could purchase a rejuvenation and beautification package on the open market. But a single treatment cost as much as what a white-collar worker would earn in a year. Maybe two. For most people, the best they could hope for was graceful aging, of spending their twilight years in perfect health. Only the richest and most famous members of society could afford a treatment schedule that kept them in perpetual youth.

And most of them were cultivators.

For some reason, his distant ancestors had foregone the gift of immortality. But maybe, in his time, he would break that tradition.

He wondered how life would change after that.

Learning the human terrain was just as important as the physical terrain. Li Ming studied how people walked and talked, how they dressed and acted, the slang and gait and brands unique to Bao An.

Clothing in Fuyang was rough and dull, chosen for durability, practicality, and cheapness. Here, clothing was bright and vivid, announcing something about the wearer, be it his profession or aesthetics or simple rebellion against the modern world.

He'd left his old clothes behind in Fuyang. They were the garments of a farmer, but he was not one. He'd packed instead the clothes he'd bought in Taiping in his military days, the clothes of a city dweller. In his jacket, jeans and boots he blended right into the crowd.

But only if he kept his mouth shut.

His accent marked him as an outsider. Everyone in Fuyang spoke with broad, slow accent, elongating or slurring vowels. Here in Bao An, everyone spoke quickly, a beat and a half faster than he was used to. After his time in the capital, he had picked up the terminal rhotic 'er' and exaggerated tones that marked the Taiping dialect. In Fuyang he'd suppressed these habits, but this city brought them out again. When he spoke, he blended the accents of the farms and the capital in a strange mix. It stood out so much, listening to him was like a needle to the ear. The Cais hadn't commented, but surely strangers would.

That was all right. With enough exposure to Bao An, he'd pick up the accent soon enough.

In the north, he visited the city's oldest extent temple, founded in the Yue Dynasty, and paid his respects to the Fo and the Pusa. Then he crossed the road to honor the city god in his shrine. To the west, in a shopping district, he enjoyed a quick lunch of rice noodles with pork dumplings and a generous helping of vegetables, the *only* thing he could afford here. At the east he caught a movie in a shopping mall, the first time he'd watched a show since he'd left the military. In the evening, he wandered the Bamboo Street Night Market, nibbling on barbecued meats and buns.

Martial cultivators were everywhere. Everywhere he went, one in a hundred people marked themselves as more than men. Their qi melted into the background, undetectable until they were up close, but they dressed and carried themselves differently from the crowd.

Many wore weapons openly. Swords, knives, shapes, batons, other weird and exotic weapons from every corner of Xiazhou. They dressed to draw the eye: flashy coats, old-fashioned clothing from previous dynasties, stylized re-interpretations of police and military gear. Swaggering through the streets, every motion, every gesture, every word, was a declaration of their exalted status.

When a sole cultivator walked a street, shopkeepers called out for his attention, seeking his patronage. Civilians flocked to teams of cultivators traveling together, taking photos, seeking autographs, offering promotions. But when cultivators from rival associations shared the same street, everyone went quiet and slunk away.

Li Ming followed the wisdom of the crowd. But now and then, he caught people staring at his swordbreaker, his reality shaper, his smartglasses. Many of them were cultivators with smartglasses of their own, assessing his qi, determining if he were friend or foe, predator or prey.

He was too visible, he realized. In this sea of swords and sticks, his swordbreaker stood apart. Those who noticed his weapon were wondering what he was armed with, and what it said about the kind of man he was.

He needed new kit. But he couldn't afford it, yet.

Police cultivators patrolled the streets alongside their mundane counterparts. These he identified by their shapers. Combat cultivators carried two, one on either forearm. An extravagant expense, but it made the most of their abilities. Whenever cultivators gathered in groups, the police were always waiting nearby, ready to jump in. They kept the peace the best they could, but it was a tense peace.

On the train back to Bao An Station, he filed his observations away in his mind, letting them sink into his brain, becoming a part of his being. In his room, he spent three ke in deep meditation, circulating qi within him, winding down for the night, before going off to bed.

The next two days passed in similar fashion. Gongfu in the morning, breakfast at the hotel, a day-long walk around the city, meditation, bed.

The universe operated in cycles. The city had its own cycles, its rhythms, its patterns of activity. The initial interview at Dayong was on Ding-day, the third day of the week. The day after was Wu-day, the mid-week break. It seemed like the entire city was out and about. But the next two days, Ji and Geng, were workdays.

In daylight the streets were quiet*er*. Everyone was busy working or studying. When lunch hour came, they flooded the eateries and malls, then vanished just as quickly. In the evening, after work, they surged out again, this time lingering in the night streets and markets. Li Ming tracked it all, noting traffic patterns, bus and train timings, popular stores and vendors, the things you can only learn through direct observation.

In the afternoon of Geng-day, just as he was about to tuck into a bowl of egg noodle soup, his phone rang. Unknown number. But Li Ming already knew who was on the line.

"Li Ming, it's Cai Mengyang, Dayong Biaoju. Are you busy?"

"No, not at all," Li Ming replied.

"Wonderful. Your references check out. We would like to invite you to our selection test."

"When is it?"

"Tomorrow, sixth hour. Meet us at the Police Academy."

"Understood. Do I need anything?"

A pause.

"Exercise clothing."

Chapter Seven

Softness and Weakness

The Bao An Police Academy was like every other military base he'd been to. High forbidding walls topped with barbed wire and cameras. Gates manned by heavily-armed guards. Instructors barking a quick cadence, the recruiters shouting along in a ragged chorus. Flags fluttered high and proud in the breeze. The men wore deep blues instead of camouflage greens, the signs displayed the crest of the Bao An Civil Police instead of formation insignia, but otherwise there was little obvious difference from an army camp.

Li Ming arrived two ke before the appointed hour. He'd dressed for the occasion, black jacket paired with plain white shirt, blue sweatpants and running shoes. In his backpack he carried two changes of clothes, one to dress down, another for the journey back. The guards had mistaken him for a recruit when he'd showed his face, a sure sign he'd done something right.

He'd thought he was early. Instead, there was a man waiting for him.

The stranger wore humble clothes, a white tunic over black pants and moccasins. But he carried himself with the bearing of a prince. His skin was the color of deep bronze, burned from a lifetime under the sun. Armies of fine lines marched across his long, almond-shaped face, the face of a man too young to command such creases. His cheekbones were huge, twin boulders flanking an arrowhead of a nose. Thick platinum hair flowed like a mane down to his jaw. His mustache and beard were equally thick, framing a pair of pale lips twisted into a frown. His bushy eyebrows threatened to meet in the middle, capping a set of sleek smartglasses, themselves protecting eyes colored a startling shade of amber.

He was a Yue.

An actual full-blooded Yue. Li Ming had never seen one before, not in person. The closest was on the big screen or in the news. After the fall of the Yue Dynasty, the Yue mainly kept to their homelands in the west. After decades of suppression by the Celestial Empire, they were only beginning to make their way east again, to exchange deserts and steppes for asphalt and concrete.

He was a cultivator too. His qi field was an all-consuming fire, burning everything that came close. Even from this far away, Li Ming felt the heat and the pressure emanating from him. In his mind's eye, he saw a solid wall of red and orange. He was not someone Li Ming cared to trifle with.

The Yue stared at Li Ming through his smartglasses, his face locking into a scowl. Then, just as abruptly, he looked away and left Li Ming alone.

Li Ming returned the favor. Behind his back, he checked the Yue's qi score.

17482. On the cusp of breaking into the upper ranks of the jianghu, Li Ming recalled. An incredible achievement for anyone. Especially for someone who looked so... young.

Was he a prodigy? Or simply far older than he looked?

This was the jianghu. It had to be both.

As the minutes passed, cars pulled into the parking lot outside the base. More men stepped out, dressed in loose exercise clothing. They retrieved bags of gear and gathered around the Yue. The Yue was coldly indifferent to them, nodding and exchanging greetings, and said little else. Yet he listened to every word they said, while keeping a watchful eye on the world. And Li Ming.

The newcomers glanced at Li Ming, long enough to check his qi score. He did the same. They floated between the high sixteen hundreds to low nineteen hundreds, and did nothing to hide their qi fields. It was a palpable force pressing up against his own, sensing every bit of him, probing for softness and weakness.

They were watching him. Judging him. But also ignoring him, seeing how he would respond to their presence. Li Ming didn't know if he should walk over and introduce himself or stay put and wait for the Cais. All he knew was that he didn't know who they were, and they made no attempt to reach out to him.

The Cais' arrival settled that question. They pulled up in a black sports utility vehicle, parking right in front of Li Ming. It looked like an ordinary car, but it rode low to the ground on rugged run-flat tires. A fresh wave of qi washed over Li Ming, like water waiting to condense and transmute into hardened steel, the kind of qi he associated with a shield generator.

Out came the Cais. Dark shirts, dark pants, dark shoes, plenty of pockets. Cai Mengyang accessorized with a worn, heavy jacket. Cai Yan smiled and waved at Li Ming.

"Good morning," she said.

"Morning," Li Ming replied.

"You're here early," Cai Mengyang said. "Well done."

"Thank you. Are the others with us?"

"Of course."

Cai Mengyang gestured them over. The biaohang swaggered over, their eyes boring into Li Ming. Li Ming straightened as he approached.

"Gents, this is Li Ming. He'll be running through the selection test with us," Cai Mengyang said.

Li Ming punched his palm over his heart.

"*Qianbei, xing hui!*"

The biaohang laughed.

Li Ming blinked.

"We're not your seniors. Not unless you pass," the Yue said.

His accent was a little off, flowing like a relentless river, smothering the tones that differentiated words. But it suited his voice perfectly, smooth and deep and rich like liquid chocolate.

"Ah. Sorry about that," Li Ming said.

"Nothing you need to be sorry for," the Yue replied.

"Our work demands a high level of fitness and skill," Cai Mengyang said. "Every three months, or whenever we sign up a new candidate, we run through our combat qualification tests. The police academy kindly lends us the use of their facilities for this purpose.

"For you, this test is part of your selection process. If you fail, you will not be allowed to join us. You must pass—and pass *well*. Just scraping by is not enough. If you cannot meet our standards, the work is too difficult for you."

"Understood. What are the requirements?" Li Ming asked.

"Our test is based on those used by military cultivators. I trust you remember them?"

"Yes."

"Excellent. Unlike the Army, we do not adjust standards for age and sex. We also do not have separate tiers for special forces, combatants, and service personnel. The only passing standard is the gold standard. Think you can handle it?"

"Yes."

"Confident. Good. But I must add: you will perform the combat and physical fitness tests back to back. All in the same day. Are you *sure* you can handle it? You can always back out and reschedule if you're not ready."

Cold fear nibbled at Li Ming's heart. At Fuyang he'd maintained a strict physical fitness regimen. He was confident in his martial skills. But it had been a while since he'd trained with a gun, trained *seriously* for combat, not just beast hunting. It was the one flaw in his daily workout regimen, the one weakness that could undo him.

But he was here now.

"Let's do this."

The cultivators had brought their own gear. Helmets, armor, load carriage gear, most of all, their weapons. Their kit was as individual as the operator, personalized for their unique body shapes and types, each a statement of their strengths and intended use cases.

Li Ming had loaners from the Police Academy stores.

His helmet was old and musky, stinking of stale sweat and dandruff. The armor carrier was a touch too big, the trauma plates thick and awkward. But that paled to the weapons.

The armorer had granted him a Type 82 Infantry Weapon. The standard-issue infinity gun of the military, it had been adopted by many police departments all over the nation. Sleek and solid, it was the weapon he had trained on. But it wasn't *his* weapon.

This gun was stock. After leaving the factory, it had been left untouched save for firmware updates and armorer-level maintenance. It was so old and banged-up, its paint had peeled off in long scratches to reveal dull metal underneath. He'd used custom guns for so long, he had to remind himself of the original weapon's capabilities and limitations.

To supplement the infinity gun, they'd given him two reality shapers and a Type 38 handgun, also government issue, also factory stock. He knew he could run a Type 82, run it well, and a shaper was a shaper no matter what make or model they were, but pistols... the Army gave him just enough training to competently handle one and left it at that.

He was committed. It was too late to back out.

At least they had given him time to refamiliarize himself with his borrowed arms. Running against a clock, he field stripped and reassembled the Type 82 in just over half a minute. He performed the same feat with the handgun.

It wasn't impressive. They were energy weapons. They only had a handful of working parts, all of them easily accessible and manipulated. He remembered a time when he could perform this feat in forty, even thirty-five, seconds. He was slowing down.

But Cai Yan looked impressed. And he'd beat the military standards. That was what mattered.

At the known distance range, they allowed him to zero the weapon. The others blazed through the process, reconfirming their own zeroes. Li Ming went slow and steady, following the textbook.

He lay prone on the hard-packed earth, legs splayed wide apart, toes pointing outward, arms and elbows forming triangles of solid bone. The others had brought bipod-ready weapons. He made do with a sandbag.

Downrange, fifty *chi* away, the target filled his sights. A man-shaped silhouette of thick steel, blasted and pitted and pockmarked. White painted circles drew the eye to its center. There, a circle of red paper filled its holed-out heart.

The manufacturer claimed that the Type 82, zeroed at the factory, never needed recalibration. Li knew it was a lie. Factory zero was good enough for most work, but at the level of performance he was expected to live up to, every little bit of precision counted.

Plus, who knew what the previous handler had done with this weapon.

"Shooter, stand by," the range officer called.

Li Ming settled into the position, sinking deep into the earth.

"Shooter, fire when ready."

The scarlet reticle, big and bold, stared at Li Ming through the scope. A huge hollow circle with a precision dot in the middle. Not his preferred set-up, but he'd make it work.

Utilizing a sophisticated swinging mirror array, the sight showed him the view from the muzzle. All he had to do was move the red dot over the target and fire.

Move the red dot over... a red dot.

He shifted this way, then that way, jiggling up and down, trying to distinguish between his sight and the target. At last the dot settled on what he reasonably believed was dead center of the silhouette.

He thumbed off the safety, setting it to single shot. His ring finger tapped the fire mode wheel, ensuring it was set to half-power.

He breathed.

Exhaled.

Fired.

There was no recoil. No physical sensation of firing. Just a click and peal of thunder and a flash of searing light.

Li Ming released the trigger. Smoke wafted from the target, obscuring his vision. He reapplied the safety and waited for judgment.

"Shooter, on target!"

This weapon might be old, but its users had honored it. That much he could grant to the cops and cadets.

He performed the same feat with his pistol. The shot had singed the edge of the hole, but the range officer had decreed it a fair hit. Now he was ready to take on the course of fire.

In the military, there'd be classroom lectures, marksmanship simulations, dry runs, rehearsals. Not today. Today the biaohang would run the course cold.

He would run the course cold.

As his assistants set up the targets, the range officer delivered the briefing. Nothing Li Ming hadn't heard before, but he paid attention all the same. When the range was ready, they took to their lanes.

Li Ming surveyed the field before him. White tape marked the limits of the lane. A sandbag rested nearby. In the distance, a bright white berm, scorched and blackened in many areas, served as the backstop.

He'd been in many ranges just like this one. All he had to do was repeat his performance there, and he'd be fine.

"Shooters, ready your weapons!"

Li Ming took up his infinity gun and set it to standard power. At this range, a half-power shot would fizzle out long before impact.

"Advance to contact!"

Li Ming advanced.

Sweeping left and right, finger off the trigger, hands tightly gripping his weapon, he walked down the lane, coming closer, closer, closer to the sandbag.

His heart thudded in his chest. Sweat gathered over his neck and in his armpits. He inhaled softly, exhaled smoothly, waiting for—

"CONTACT!"

Li Ming threw himself to the prone, landing right by the sandbag. Hurriedly he set himself up, supporting his weapon on the bag, and threw the magnification lever to 4X.

"TARGETS!"

Downrange, five hundred *chi* away, a single target popped up. The red dot was only slightly smaller than the target. Li Ming aimed, pressed the trigger, saw it go down in a puff of smoke, heard the clang of the strike.

A half-beat later, two targets appeared. He burned them down in eyeblinks.

Three targets popped up. But the one on the left was painted blue. No-shoot.

He blasted the other two.

Now came a *moving* target, a man running left to right. Li Ming led the target, saw red against black, fired.

It went down, and four targets popped up. Li Ming got the first one, turned to the second, squeezed—

Missed!

Fired again and the target went down.

He serviced the last two. Then two more targets rose—

One target. The right-hand one was a no-shoot. He shot the other one and—

Yellow light crackled around the target.

Shielded target. This one needed multiple shots. He rested the red dot on the target and fired one two three four *five* times and the shield collapsed and it dropped.

The next target was another running man. The first shot splashed against a shield. The next missed. The next hit. The fourth blew through it and took it down.

Now came a triple set. All of them shielded.

Every hit on each target added a half-second to the exposure. A beginner would be tempted to burn down the targets one by one. But if he tried that, the other two would get away. The smart move, the only move, was to service the targets with a single shot each, sweeping back and forth, pounding the shields with rapid fire.

He got the first. The second. The third—

The gun beeped angrily.

Li Ming snarled. The Type 87 had overheated.

An infinity gun had infinite ammo. Its cosmic tap drew qi from the world and transformed it to power. It did *not*, however, have infinite heat capacity.

The stock Type 87 had a mere thirty-shot capacity, and a cooldown of one second per shot. He'd burned through it all, and now he had to wait until it cooled off before he could shoot again.

Untouched, the third target went down.

Li Ming sighed.

"Shooters, advance!"

Li Ming picked himself up and jogged down the lane.

It wasn't enough to shoot fast or shoot well. He had to shoot fast *and* well *and* manage his weapon's heat capacity. He had to time his shots and exposures to give his gun a chance to cool. It had been *too* long since he'd done this.

At the four hundred *chi* lane, he went down to the prone again. No sandbag this time. At least the weapon had cooled off completely.

Once again, fifteen targets. A mix of singles, groups, runners, no-shoots and shields. The last five were shielded too. No misses this time, but he was little slower, and the last target got away.

That was okay. He didn't have to be perfect. He just had to be good enough.

Two hundred *chi*. He knelt by the line and waited. Another fifteen targets. *Two* misses this time. He was tense, *too* tense. He breathed out, reminded himself to relax.

One hundred *chi*. Standing offhand. He leaned into the gun, keeping it in the compressed low ready, watching for—

Threat.

Fire.

Repeat.

Conscious thought melted away. He moved, he assessed, he fired if needed, he moved on.

Fifteen targets.

All fifteen down.

"Move to shaper line!"

Li Ming slung his weapon and ran again. The moment he reached the seventy-five *chi* mark, two targets popped up.

He raised both hands and touched the crystals within his borrowed shapers.

They were yinyang crystals. Government issue. There were no five element crystals available in storage. But he knew how to use them.

A bolt of lightning leapt from either crystal. In a flash they crossed the length of the range and struck the targets. Both went down with resounding booms.

All around him, the other biaohang used other magics. He sensed the roar of fireballs, the shattering of ice crystals, flashes of light, snatches of sound. He ignored them all and breathed in, feeding the depleted crystals the qi of the world, preparing them for—

Two more targets.

Once more he raised his arms, once more he fired. The government-issue crystals were only half-charged, but they had to do. This time he poured out their power as twin jets of focused flame. Fire had always come easy to him, and they just had to remain coherent enough to cross the distance and strike the targets.

The right target went down.

The left stayed up.

Not enough qi to be registered as a decisive hit. If he had his military-grade shapers, this wouldn't have happened. But he'd rushed this shot, hadn't given the shapers enough time to recharge.

He charged his qi. Aimed.

The target went down.

Li Ming sighed.

"Shooters, move up!"

He jogged again. At the twenty-five *chi* mark, he rested his hand on the butt of his pistol. And waited.

"Prone fire!"

Li Ming drew his pistol and hit the deck. Weapon extended straight out, finger off the trigger, he waited.

This was the slow fire range. And by slow, they meant you had an extra second to aim. It wasn't much. It had to do.

Two targets. One shoot, one no-shoot. The moment he tagged the former, two more came up. Both shoot targets. Then a runner. And four targets.

Four *shielded* targets.

He took his time, working a slow, steady cadence, letting the handgun breathe between bolts. The Type 38 had a mere fifteen-shot capacity. He had no margin for error.

And all four went down.

"Kneeling fire!"

He rose to a knee. Waited an eyeblink.

Another eight targets. A single, a triple, a shielded runner, a shielded triple. He burned six down. On the seventh, the gun billowed hot steam and shut down.

He swore and saw the remaining two targets disappear.

"Shooters, move up!"

Li Ming holstered his weapon and ran to the fifteen *chi* mark. Hand on the grip, he waited.

"Shots from holster!"

A target popped up. He drew, fired, saw a shield spark. Three more shots and it went down. He scanned and holstered.

Next was a runner. Li fired five times, missed two, and it went down.

Now came three targets, two shielded targets with one no-shoot in the middle. He fired in singles, left and right, right and left, working back and forth, taking care not to flag the no-shoot as he moved, and took down the two targets.

"Shooters, proceed to the five-*chi* line!"

Now this was the part he hated the most. He steeled himself with a breath, and readied.

The first phase was easy enough. A shielded quadruple to be taken with rapid fire. Then a short pause, to allow the pistol to cool off. And then:

"Strong side, fire!"

A single target came up.

Li Ming pressed his left hand against his chest. Drew with his right. Fired. Reholstered.

Runner. Shielded. He fired four shots, missed with one.

Shielded triple. He took his time, going for center of mass hits, and burned them all down.

"Weak side, controlled pairs!"

This was the part that killed him. As the target came up, he twisted around with his left hand, freed the handgun from the holster, aimed, fired.

Hit.

A good start. And he maintained it. Somehow, *somehow*, he'd killed all five threats without a miss.

Not bad.

"Cease fire! Cease fire!"

And it was over.

The biaohang gathered at the start line. Emotions bubbled up within Li Ming. He let them all out, refusing to allow them to take form and substance. The test was over. Whatever happened next would happen.

One by one, the range officer tabulated the scores and passed them out. Half of the biaohang had obtained a perfect score. The other half threw only three or four shots at most.

And there was him.

"Infinity gun stage: sixty targets, fifty-six destroyed. Reality shaper stage: four targets, three destroyed. Infinity handgun stage: thirty-five targets, thirty-three destroyed.

"Infinity gun shots fired: one hundred and forty-two. Infinity gun hits: one hundred and thirty-eight. Reality shaper shots: four. Reality shaper hits: four. Handgun stage shots: ninety-five. Handgun hits: ninety-two.

"Target destruction rate: Ninety-two point nine percent. Long gun accuracy rate: ninety-seven point one-eight percent. Reality shaper accuracy rate: one hundred percent. Handgun accuracy rate: ninety-six percent."

The biaohang sniggered. Li Ming ignored them.

"How did I do?" he asked.

Cai Mengyang frowned.

"You're the worst performer in the group."

"Yes."

"On the other hand... you had to use borrowed equipment. Equipment you hadn't trained on and hadn't optimized for yourself."

"Yes."

"That's no excuse. We have to use whatever kit we have available, not just the kit we can bring to the job."

"Yes."

"Is there anything more you can say that 'yes'?"

"Of course."

Cai Mengyang snorted.

"Our standard is no less than ninety-five percent accuracy, ninety percent target destruction, and *no* no-shoot targets. You *barely* made it. But you passed."

Li Ming exhaled.

"Thank you."

"Don't thank me yet. You still have more tests to go."

"Let's get to it."

Chapter Eight

Good Enough

The biaohang changed into exercise equipment and convened in the stadium. Equipment filled the football field at its heart. Barbells fitted with heavy plates. Medicine balls. Stone locks. Tires strapped to a sled. Brightly-colored cones and tape.

The sight took Li Ming way back, back to a year ago, back to his time in the Capital Battalion of the Special Military Police. He'd participated in countless physical fitness tests just like this one. He knew he'd survive.

The question was whether he was good enough.

A pair of physical training instructors led the team through warm-ups. Twisting lunges, high kicks, leg tucks, push-ups, circles and swings and stretches and turns, revving up the body for action. They finished with a five-minute jog.

As they recovered, the instructors briefed the biaohang. This was a standard physical fitness test, going by military requirements. No surprises here. But there was only one standard. The gold standard.

And that Li Ming wasn't sure if he could hit.

But he was here. He just had to do it.

Finally, the men paired off. Li Ming found himself assigned to the Yue.

"Good luck," Li Ming said.

The Yue grunted.

The first test item was the deadlift. Three reps, slow and controlled. The higher the weight, the higher the score. The barbell was loaded with plates weighing one hundred *jin*, the minimum allowable weight. A pile of plates rested nearby.

Li considered the barbell for a moment. And added more weight.

And more.

And more.

And more.

At last, he had mounted every plate on the barbell. He stretched. Rubbed his hands. Looked at the instructor. And the Yue.

"Begin when ready," the instructor said.

Li Ming positioned himself by the bar. Adjusted his feet. Checked his posture. Squatted. Gripped the bar.

Breathed in.

Held.

And exploded upright.

"One!" the Yue called.

Li Ming lowered.

Paused.

Breathed.

Lifted.

"Two!"

Down.

Breathe.

Up.

"Three! Down!"

He set the barbell down. Stepped back. And sucked down more air.

"Three reps of three hundred *jin*," the instructor said. "Full points."

The Yue took to the barbell. Without hesitation, he cranked out three deadlifts, full power and full speed, wearing a bored expression on his face.

They jogged over to the medicine balls. Li Ming stood at the very edge of the field, holding the ball against his chest, and turned around. The Yue checked his position, laid down measuring tape, and nodded.

Li Ming held out his arms. Squatting, he brought the ball down to his ankles. He stood back up, bringing it to chest height. He repeated the gesture, once, twice, and on the third rep he exhaled sharply and tossed the ball high and over his head.

"Six and a half *chi*," the Yue called.

A passing grade. But Li Ming wasn't satisfied with it.

"You get another throw. Want to try again?" the instructor asked.

"Yes."

He breathed. Concentrated. Brought his qi to his belly and arms. And threw.

"Eight and a half *chi!*"

Better. It wasn't a perfect score, but it would still place him in the top physical fitness band.

When it was the Yue's turn, he didn't even wind up. He just squatted, grabbed the ball, and threw.

Twelve and a half *chi*. Perfect score.

Next up, hand release push-ups. As many as he could crank out in a minute. There was no art to it, no secret trick, just good form and brute strength.

Li Ming assumed the position. The Yue squatted next to him, stopwatch in hand.

"On my mark. Three. Two. One. Go!"

Li Ming dropped to the concrete. Lifted his palms off the floor for a moment. Pushed himself back up. Over and over and over again, pumping as fast as he could. Next to him, the Yue counted off his score.

"Three!" the instructor called. "Two! One! Time!"

Li Ming relaxed, sprawling over the ground. His chest burned. His arms ached. Still...

"Forty-four push-ups," the Yue reported.

He'd done better. But that was in his military days.

The Yue cranked out fifty, another perfect score, without even breathing hard.

On to the next station. This was the part that washed out the greatest number of troops. He breathed deep, flooding his lungs with air, bracing himself for what was to come.

"Combat maneuver test!" the instructor said. "Prepare to sprint to the red line!"

Li Ming lowered himself to a running position.

"Go!"

He sprinted. Arms swinging, legs pumping, he dashed from one end to the field to the other, charging for a line of red tape.

"Low crawl! Crawl to the yellow line!"

Li Ming dropped to the floor and wriggled his way across the grass. In the military there'd be men shouting encouragements and timing and advice. Here there was nothing, nothing but silence. That was all right. He pushed on, syncing his breathing with his movements.

The moment he touched the finish line, the instructor shouted again.

"High crawl! Move to the green line!"

Now with his forearms and lower legs, he propelled himself back across the grass. The dry field resisted him, pushing back against his elbows and knees, forcing him to adjust. His breath shortened, his muscles ached, but still he continued.

"Stone lock sprint!"

He scrambled to his feet and grabbed a pair of stone locks. Thirty *jin* each, they represented a typical one-handed load on the field. He sucked down a breath and ran, this time weaving between two lines of cones. The Yue ran alongside him, watching his feet, keeping him honest.

The weights dragged down his arms. His hands threatened to fly open. He added qi to his grip, gritted his teeth, kept on running, turning, running again, and at last he reached the finish line.

"Tire drag!"

Three tires sat on a sled next to the instructor, strapped down into place. A pair of tough nylon drag handles extended from the working end of the sled. Li Ming grabbed the handles and hauled the load, once again weaving through the obstacle course.

Blood rushed to his face. His breath came in short puffs. Li Ming took shorter, quicker steps, moving through exaggerated arcs to maneuver the sled.

Gasping, panting, he dragged the load past the end point.

"Sprint! Sprint to me!"

Li Ming dropped the load. Turned. Sprinted.

He poured every bit of energy he had left into the run, charging his lungs, legs, arms. The world faded to gray, narrowing down into a tube. He ran, faster and faster, aiming for the end line—

"Time!"

—blasted through.

And slowed to a halt.

He bent over, wheezing and huffing, drinking air in great gulps. The instructor marked down his scores, then it was the Yue's turn.

As before, he effortlessly ran through the course. At the end of it, he was only beginning to sweat, breathing smoothly but audibly.

The head instructor walked about the group, updating their scores. At last, he spoke to Li.

"Forty-seven points so far. Not bad. But to pass this test, you must complete the run in twelve and a half minutes or less."

This was *harder* than military standards. Right on the edge of special operations standards. But he'd done it before.

Once.

"I can do it," Li said.

"Good. Everyone, take a five minute break. We'll begin on my mark."

Li breathed.

He did nothing but breathe. In the breath, he expelled waste and inhaled qi. He recharged and supercharged himself, directing qi to restore his strength, rebuild his muscle, erase his fatigue. Gradually, his breath recovered, his pains faded, and—

"Time for the run."

The biaohang took their places at the running track. A large gateway marked the starting point. Li's breath was still heavy, his limbs felt rubbery, but he would manage.

They pinned tags to their chest. Embedded with microchips, every time they ran through the gate, the system would track their laps on a nearby display board.

"You will run six laps around the track," the instructor said. "Keep to the first two lanes. The system will call time as you pass by. If the system doesn't track you, raise your hand, but keep running. On your last lap, enter the gate through the fourth lane. Ready?"

"Ready!" the biaohang called.

"Go!"

They began with a slow jog. One by one, they passed through the gate, using the innermost lane. Li slowly accelerated, reaching full speed just as he reached the gate.

The machine beeped.

It was on.

Consistency was key. He had to strike the fine balance between speed and stamina. Too fast and he'd burn out before the end, too slow and he'd fail. He aimed for a two-minute pace, the standard he aimed for the last time he passed the test. As he approached the end of the lap, he accelerated past Cai Yan. She ignored him, he ignored her. It was every runner for himself.

"One minute, ninety-five seconds," the gate announced.

Too fast. He ordered himself to slow down, to conserve his strength.

"Two minutes!"

Perfect.

For the next two laps he maintained the pace. But fatigue set in again. His feet slowed, his lungs burned, his chest tightened.

Three more laps. Just three more laps.

At the fifth lap he clocked in at 2:02. Off the standard, but acceptable. On the sixth lap he came in at 2:08. *Not* acceptable. He sped up, or tried, but his chest grew heavy and his lungs tightened and his heart squeezed. He slowed down, just a mite, drinking in more oxygen, forcing himself past—

"Two minutes, five seconds. Last lap."

How much time did he have left? He didn't know. His brain refused to compute. All he knew was that he had one more lap. Just one more lap.

He breathed. Forced down more energy into his limbs and lungs. Shortened his steps. Leaned in. He pulled out every trick he knew to speed up, reduce energy expenditure, but it wasn't enough. He was still slow, slower than the first lap.

He turned the last corner. And sprinted.

It was an all-out burst of energy. Every last molecule of oxygen, every last bit of qi, everything he had went into this last dash.

The gate loomed into the distance. He broke off, moving to the fourth lane. His chest heaved, his nose and mouth worked like a bellows, his limbs swung through shorter and tighter arcs, closing the distance to—

"Stop!"

He staggered. Slowed. Stopped.

Everything hurt. His arms and legs, his chest and lungs. He was done. Completely, totally, done. He brought his attention to his breath, to his qi, jumpstarting the recovery process.

The biaohang ahead of him huddled together, whispering among themselves. The ones behind him burned through their last lap. Li ignored them, slowing his pants down to long, slow, breaths.

A few minutes later, the instructors gathered them together, and read out the scores. Once again, they left Li Ming to the last.

"Twelve minutes, forty-two seconds. You've passed the physical test. Congratulations."

Li Ming grinned.

"Thanks!"

He was done. He was in. He was—

Cai Mengyang held up a hand.

"Wait. Don't be so happy."

"What do you mean?"

"You have one last test."

Li Ming clenched his fists. And sighed. Of course there would be one last test. They weren't military. They were cultivators.

"What's the test," Li Ming said, too exhausted to turn his words into a question.

"We are a biaoju. In the gravest extreme, we must be able to defend our clients with physical force. Unlike athletes, we do not have the luxury of tapping out. We must *win* our fights, or at least hold off the threat long enough to evacuate the client. Even when exhausted, we must still be able to defend ourselves, and our clients. Thus, the final test: sparring."

"With who?" Li Ming asked.

The Yue stepped up.

"Me."

Chapter Nine

Brotherhood of the Fist

"What are the rules?" Li Ming asked.

"One round of three minutes," Cai Mengyang replied. "Empty hands only. No lethal or crippling blows. Full speed, but control your power. Your strength *and* your qi. No one is going to the hospital today. Or the morgue. Any questions?"

"Any safety gear?" Li Ming asked.

The Yue smiled unpleasantly.

"Do you need any?" the Yue asked.

"Your house, your rules," Li Ming said.

Cai Mengyang smiled.

"We don't normally train with safety gear. Not for a sparring session like this. I trust you'll be able to control yourself."

Li Ming nodded. "When do we start?"

"So eager?" the Yue asked.

"Take a break, a short one," Cai Mengyang said. "We're not gods or devils. How long do you need to catch your breath?"

In it, Li Ming sensed another test. Too long and the veteran biaohang might look down on him. Too short and Li Ming would gas out long before the round was over. He had to choose carefully.

"Five minutes," Li Ming decided.

Cai Mengyang maintained a neutral expression.

"Alright. Five minutes."

The Yue walked away, stretching and twisting. Li Ming breathed, resetting his brain and body, watching him at work.

The Yue was light on his feet, but every step was filled with power. It was as if he were driving himself forward, ever forward, on a string of exploding firecrackers.

In the middle of the running track, he hopped and bounced around, punching and kicking at shadows and imaginary enemies. He was readying mind and body for battle, and yet he was giving away nothing about his style, nothing beyond blows common to all striking arts. Or maybe his was a generic style, something like sanda, a free-form style encompassing punching and kicking and wrestling.

Whoever the Yue was, he was formidable.

Li Ming walked and stretched and breathed, keeping his muscles warm and loose. Life returned to his lungs and limbs. His chest eased. His heart slowed.

When he was ready, he assumed the *wuji* position. Feet shoulder length apart, weight perfectly balanced, he stood with his arms hanging loosely by the sides, palms facing the rear. He elongated his spine, held his skull upright, hollowed his chest, touched his palate with his tongue.

And breathed.

Now he charged himself with qi, reinforcing his muscles and bones, nerves and sinews. Qi trickled through his meridians, barely detectable, but it was smooth and steady and warming. He would need all the extra qi he could get.

The Yue saw him. Paused.

Stood as still as a post.

And drew qi into himself.

You just had *to perform qigong in front of him,* Li Ming thought.

And now that the Yue was gathering and exercising his qi, Li Ming had to do it too. If the Yue started throwing qi-augmented blows, Li Ming needed defensive qi to shield himself. And if the Yue believed Li Ming would enhance his own strikes with qi, he'd draw in even more qi. It was an arms race, a microcosmic reflection of the jianghu.

"This isn't a competition," Cai Mengyang said. "It's not about winning or losing. We want to see your stamina, your techniques under pressure, and most of all, your spirit. To pass, you just have to show me what you've got."

"Does the Yue know that?"

Cai Mengyang paused.

"I'll remind him."

Cai Mengyang ambled over to the Yue. Li Ming continued breathing. The Yue continued condensing qi. Cai Mengyang whispered something to the Yue. The Yue grunted a single word. Cai Mengyang departed.

The Yue continued cultivating.

So Li Ming had to.

The men squared off, not quite locking eyes, but still aware of each other, still studying the other's technique. Cai Mengyang paced the track, occasionally checking his watch, glancing between the two of them, talking to the other biaohang.

Li Ming needed an edge. But whatever he did with his body, the Yue would see it. So he changed his breath.

On the inhale, he expanded his diaphragm downward, towards his toenails. On the exhale, his diaphragm contracted. His chest and abdomen remained still.

It was internal breathing. The deepest, most subtle kind of breathing, filling the lungs and oxygenating the blood more efficiently than other breathing methods.

As he breathed, new sensations came over him. A feeling of coolness wrapping over his skin. He soaked it in, still breathing, still filling his lungs. Presently he felt qi flowing down his legs and into his feet. As he exhaled, it flowed back up, returning to his dantian.

His fatigue melted away. Strength returned to his limbs. His chest and lungs grew light.

He was ready.

"Are you ready?" Cai Mengyang asked.

"Yes!" Li Ming called.

The Yue nodded mutely.

"Take your places!" Cai Mengyang ordered.

The men squared off on the third lane, in front of the cultivators and the instructors. The Yue glared venomously at Li Ming, a tiger eying his prey. Rooted to the rubber, his qi erupted like a volcano, shooting up his legs, up his spine, out his crown, circling around to rain lava down on the earth. The qi wave rushed over Li Ming, threatening to wash away his own.

Li Ming raised his own qi. Or tried. He was tired, depleted, and even after the intense breathing exercise he was barely at eighty percent of his strength. Even so, he drew qi from the heavens and the earth, reinforcing his center, standing fast against the storm.

They stood there for a moment, sizing each other up, their spirits locked in battle, a typhoon battering a rock. The Yue stood tall and strong, a fist taller than Li Ming, his body completely relaxed. Under his clothing, the Yue's muscles were iron cords and coiled springs. Even after the marksmanship and fitness test, he seemed fresh and ready for a fight.

Li Ming sensed he had to get close. It was the only way to survive.

Fortunately, he was a born infighter, and it was the fight strategy of wuxingquan.

With a soft smile, Li Ming cupped his fist over his chest, the slap of flesh on bone audible across the square.

The Yue smirked.

And returned the salute.

"Guard up!" Cai Mengyang called.

Li Ming unfolded into the Sancai Shi. It was a slow, deliberate, conscious effort, perfectly aligning joints and tendons, sending his weight into the earth. In that moment, the last of his lingering fatigue floated away, the tension in his muscles dissolved.

He was ready.

The Yue assumed his guard. Deceptively loose and sloppy, he bladed off towards Li Ming, right side forward, fists at chest height. But his legs were firmly planted, feet ready for instant action.

"Touch fists!"

Li Ming extended his left fist. The Yue bumped his right knuckles against Li Ming's. In that moment of contact, like the closing of a circuit, a powerful surge of electricity rushed down Li Ming's arms and jolted his heart.

An invisible fist punched Li Ming in the chest, cold and burning. Li Ming winced, his hand jerking away. And suddenly the sensation faded.

What the devil was that?

The Yue offered no answers. He merely glared at Li Ming, a beast in human skin, an apex predator armed with the most powerful weapon on the planet: the marriage of brain, body, and qi.

"Begin!" Cai Mengyang cried.

The Yue exploded.

Right hand cupping his ear, elbow aimed at Li Ming, he flung his arm behind him and rocketed off the ground like a human spear. Li Ming's brain blanked for a fatal moment, unable to comprehend what he was seeing.

The point of the elbow smashed into Li Ming's right breast. Years of training took over, and Li Ming relaxed into the blow. He spun with it, shedding the energy, pivoting clockwise and bringing his left palm chopping down.

Li Ming's forearm nailed the Yue's shoulder. And suddenly the Yue was past, blazing off into clear space.

Li Ming staggered aside. The blow *hurt*. If he hadn't rolled with it, if the Yue had aimed just a little lower and to the side, it would have shattered his ribs. Was *this* how Dayong trained?

Very well. If this was how the Yue wanted to play, he'd play too.

The spectators yelled cheers and encouragement. Their voices faded into a blur. Here and now, there was only Li Ming and the Yue, crossing the rubberized lanes to re-engage.

Li Ming swiveled, orienting himself towards the Yue, arms assuming the Sancai Shi. But the Yue was slightly ahead of the curve, now advancing on Li Ming. The Yue threw a blistering series of straight-armed punches, too far away to connect, covering his approach.

Li Ming waited.

Now the Yue was a step away from contact. He threw a left jab. Li Ming parried it down and fired a right cross.

The fist ploughed solidly into the Yue's abdomen. The Yue jerked forward, wrapping his body around the blow. Li Ming twisted around, going for an uppercut—

The Yue leaned away, slipping the blow. And retreated three more steps.

The gut shot was a solid hit, but the Yue showed no sign of damage. Li Ming advanced, now throwing a straight punch at—

Shielding his face with his elbow, the Yue crashed in, swinging his other elbow around.

Aborting the punch, Li swung his lead hand down, already knowing he was too—

The elbow speared into his sternum. It rocked him backwards, sending him staggering away. It was a good shot, and at the last moment he had sensed the Yue pulling back. If he had landed with full power, it would have broken bone.

The Yue was an infighter too. So much for the primary plan. Now for the backup.

Li Ming hopped away, making distance, breathing through the pain. The Yue pursued, crouched over, elbows shielding his head. When he was just outside arm's reach, the Yue shot up and threw covering punches again. Li Ming parried the shots as they came, circling around as they went. Most men would tire themselves out quickly, but the Yue seemed to have infinite stamina, and Li Ming's own was quickly fading.

That was all right. He just needed an accurate measure of the man's reach.

The Yue closed again. Li Ming greeted him with a mid-level roundhouse kick. The Yue crouched, intercepting his shin with rock-hard forearms. Li Ming bounced off and swiveled around into another roundhouse kick. The Yue shifted, this time trying to catch the leg.

Li Ming hopped, torqued and snapped his leg down at the Yue's face.

The Yue blocked, his arms forming a cage of bone. He took the shot on his forearms, turning ever so slightly, shedding the energy of the kick. But the blow unbalanced him, sending him back a step. Li Ming brought his foot down and—

And the Yue exploded into motion, right palm describing a huge arc, swiping down at Li Ming.

Li Ming flinched. Iron fingers rocked his forehead and slashed down his face, missing his eyes by a hair's breadth.

And the Yue kept coming, windmilling his arms in lethal overhead blows. His stamina was endless, his attacks relentless. Li Ming jumped back, back, and back again. Somehow the Yue had *extended* his reach, stretching his chest and back, bringing his arms to maximum extension. Li Ming took another shot, an iron palm blowing through his outstretched hand and hooking it away. The Yue closed again, arm coming down to split the air—

Li Ming crashed in with Pao Quan, left forearm rising to deflect the blow, right fist blasting into the Yue's sternum.

The Yue exhaled sharply and staggered back.

Li Ming stepped in with body shots, close-range shovel hooks, one and two and three, every punch landing with power and authority, and on the fourth shot the Yue jumped away and out of range.

Li Ming panted. He was gassing out. But the Yue was as fresh as ever. Li Ming didn't know how much time was left, only that it wasn't time *now*. The Yue was *good*. Scary good. He could dish out *and* take punishment. He was proficient in long *and* short range attacks. Even if Li Ming were in top form, he didn't think he could win this fight.

Wait.

He didn't *have* to win, did he?

That's right. This was not a contest or a life-or-death fight. This was simply a sparring match. A test of fighting spirit. What did it matter if he won or lost, so long as he remained standing at the end of it?

Li Ming smiled.

The Yue hesitated. His qi faltered. And, just as quickly, it reconsolidated into an impenetrable palisade.

The Yue grew more cautious. He circled around Li Ming, testing and probing his defenses. Li Ming moved with him, his arms flowing up and down, side by side, adjusting and readjusting. Now and then their hands made contact. The Yue tried to clear them the away, but Li Ming flowed through tight circles and quickly readjusted.

The Yue was getting frustrated. His movements became faster, tighter, tenser, easier to see. He was used to taking the offensive, to overwhelming his opponent with sheer brute force. But now he'd sensed something had changed in Li Ming, and his former strategy wouldn't work. Even so, he kept testing and tapping, seeking a point of weakness.

So Li Ming gave one to him.

Li Ming extended and dropped his left arm just so, leaving his head open. The Yue hooked the arm away and crashed in, his slashing forearm a bone blade aimed at Li's temple.

Li spun in a tight circle, stepping his left foot behind him, rotating his left forearm up to guard his head. The arms collided. Li continued his turn, his right palm turning outwards and extending, and smacked the Yue's temple.

It wasn't a hard hit. But it had come out of the blue, taking him by surprise. The Yue stumbled. Li completed the circle and pounced, firing a straight fist at the Yue's head.

The Yue covered up. Knuckles thudded into a meaty forearm. Li readied his other fist, feeling the Yue's defenses. The Yue shifted left and right, guarding against the blow. Li went high, the Yue covered, and Li snapped back and drilled his fist into his belly.

The Yue dropped, crashing his forearm into Li's, robbing the fist of his strength.

The counter *hurt*. He felt it all the way in his marrow. Li disengaged, once again taking up the Sancai Shi.

The Yue had excellent offense and defense. But his defense *during* his offense was lacking. There was the way to victory.

But Li Ming wasn't much of a counterpuncher.

And he didn't have to win this fight.

More testing. More probing. More circling. The clocking was ticking down. Time was on Li Ming's side, not the Yue's, and both men knew it. The Yue strained like a dog on a leash, caught between the desire to finish things and the desire to not be hit.

They continued jockeying for position, seeking positional advantage. Points of dull pain throbbed through Li Ming. Everywhere he'd been hit ached. He ignored them all, filling his lungs with *qi*, giving himself the strength to carry on.

"Twenty seconds!"

The words injected new life into the Yue. With a shout, he rushed in, windmilling his arms once again, slashing through unpredictable angles. Li Ming backed up, feeling his timing, his rhythm, his intent. The Yue lashed out again, and now Li Ming stepped off to the side, deflecting the arm with his own, and corkscrewed his fist into the Yue's liver.

It should have been a clean hit. He felt the ribs compress under his knuckles. The Yue simply exhaled. His muscles stiffened, forming a living shield of tight, impenetrable tissue. And then he whipped around with an elbow.

Li got his hands up. The elbow crashed through his defenses, blowing him off his feet. Li landed on his butt. The rubber track absorbed and cushioned the force, but it still *hurt*. Sucking down a breath, he forced himself back up.

Now the Yue showed a reaction. Bending over, he pressed his right hand to his injured liver, holding his left arm out in a long guard.

"You okay?" Li Ming asked.

The Yue glared at him.

"You could always end it if it hurts too much."

The Yue crouched deeply, forming a horse stance. He brought his left fist to his jaw, aiming his elbow at Li. His right hand rested on his injury.

He scratched his thumb across his nose.

"Come on," the Yue said.

Li Ming approached.

Paused.

And sank into the Sancai Shi.

"After you," Li Ming said.

"Ten seconds!" Cai called.

The Yue shrugged.

"Okay."

And exploded.

He launched himself off the ground, fist outstretched, aimed at Li Ming's face. Li Ming swiveled aside, his right hand splitting down to—

Missed.

The Yue swooped down low, vanishing from sight. Li Ming's stomach sank. Firm arms wrapped around Li Ming's left. Li Ming twisted, wedging his arm against the Yue's. The Yue sprang up, levering Li Ming up and out.

Li Ming wrapped his leg around the Yue's and shoved the Yue's face away with his free hand. Swiftly he encircled the Yue's arm with his other arm, wedged his head against the Yue's, grabbed his elbow, and pulled.

The grip broke.

Li Ming stepped back. Then punched at the Yue's head—

The Yue shot out his forearm, blocking the blow. Closing in, his other hand snaked around, grabbing and snapping Li Ming's left shoulder into him. The Yue snaked around the forearm, wrapped his other arm around Li Ming's neck, stepped in and swept his legs out.

For a heart-stopping moment, Li Ming fell through space. The Yue pulled up at the last second, softly dropping Li Ming on the rubber. The Yue knelt on Li Ming's belly, twisting Li Ming's right arm aside. He chambered his fists by his hips, sucked in a breath—

Li Ming twisted, left arm rising, right hand sliding through the gap behind his legs—

The Yue punched—

The fist careened off Li Ming's left forearm and Li Ming's hand shot up to grab—

"TIME!"

They froze.

Exhaled.

Relaxed.

Li Ming dropped his arms to the ground. The Yue stood up. Li Ming scooted a safe distance away, paused a moment to catch his breath, and picked himself back up.

"Salute!" Cai called.

Li Ming punched his palm over his chest.

The Yue did the same.

"That's all. Well done, everyone!"

Everyone clapped. Even the instructors joined in. Their voices came rushing back into Li Ming's consciousness. And now he remembered that he had an audience, one that had gathered to judge the fight. Judge him.

Li Ming extended his hand. "Thank you. You fight well."

The Yue shook.

"You're a fierce fighter. I see you studied An Family wuxingquan and yizhang."

"You recognize the specific family style?"

"I've trained with the boss often enough."

"Ah. You studied shifangquan, yes?"

The Fist of the Ten Directions. The art of bodyguards and warriors. Renowned for its aggression, it had a single strategy: attack, attack, attack. There was no retreat, no sophisticated evasions, just simple, direct and powerful blows, designed to end the fight instantly.

It was also the most famous martial art of the Yue people.

The Yue nodded.

"Correct."

"Must be very useful for a biaohang," Li Ming said.

The Yue's chest puffed up.

"I have used it many times. Every time, I won."

"He's one of the finest martial artists in our agency," Cai Mengyang added.

And of course, Cai Mengyang hadn't mentioned him at all. But maybe that was the point, to see if Li Ming could handle surprises like this one.

"What's your name?" Li Ming asked.

"Ghazan."

The Yue people customarily used only a single name.

"I am Li Ming. Pleasure to meet you. I hope we can work together soon."

Ghazan nodded. "Me too."

"I believe Mr. Li has passed the test. Ga San, what do you think?" Cai Mengyang asked.

Ghazan had pronounced his name as a single word. Cai Mengyang had split it into two, speaking each word with the first tone, high and flat. The Yue's eyebrows twitched.

Li Ming made a note to learn how to properly speak his name.

"He passed," Ghazan said.

Cai Mengyang turned to the crowd.

"And what about the rest of you? Has Mr. Li passed?"

"Yes!" Cai Yan exclaimed.

"*YES!*" the men echoed.

And clapped.

And cheered.

Their applause and voices filled the stadium. Li Ming saluted them, adding a little bow.

Everyone fought everybody else. Even Cai Yan got in the act, using the intricate circles of yizhang against a biaohang taller and stronger than her. As he pressed her with relentless forward charges, she circled out of the way to deliver strikes and takedowns from unorthodox angles. Through three minutes of nonstop movement, she managed to hold her own, a sign of excellent gongfu. After the fights, the biaohang cooled down and headed off in the direction of the locker room. When the Yue was out of earshot, Cai Mengyang spoke.

"I see you made a new friend."

Li struggled to find breath and brains to answer the question. His mouth spoke the only words that came to mind.

"I hope so."

Cai Mengyang laughed.

"The jianghu is the brotherhood of the fist. After trading blows, everyone becomes brothers."

"Sounds romantic."

A moment later, his brain reminded him that those words didn't match what he'd seen on the streets.

"We all have to live in this world," Cai Mengyang said. "The world of men and the world of the rivers and lakes."

"I see."

"And with this in mind... I saw your counter to Ga San's final attack."

"My body just acted on its own."

He'd come *this* close to delivering a quick, vicious groin strike. An excellent reflex—for combat. Not for sparring.

"Lucky the clock ran out when it did."

Something in Cai Mengyang's tone suggested it might not have been a coincidence.

"*Xie tian xie di,*" Li Ming said.

Thank the heavens and the earth.

"Hard training is good training, but we share the same sky. We have rules for a reason."

"I'm sorry. But I didn't know any other counter to that move. And he was so... so *intense*. It was like fighting for real."

"That's a bad habit of his. I'll speak with him about it later."

"Thank you. But I have a question."

"Yes?"

"Groundfighting is not part of wuxingquan or yizhang. How would you counter that technique?"

A long pause.

"In a life or death confrontation, in a serious fight... I would have done the same thing you did."

Chapter Ten

Welcome to the Jianghu

The biaohang's attitudes changed as dramatically as night becoming day.

The Dayong team enjoyed breakfast in the academy canteen. Clustered in a group, the biaohang bombarded Li Ming with questions. Where he came from, his experience, his military service. After much probing, he finally relented and discussed the events of Shanxia.

But left out what happened after.

The biaohang seemed impressed. They showered him with advice, information, opinions. It was like being part of the town militia again, only this time he was surrounded by a higher class of warrior. In between bites of steamed buns and sips of tea, he listened carefully to his seniors, filing away fact away in his mind. It was like drinking from a fire hose.

Cai Mengyang drove Li Ming back to the Dayong compound. As his daughter worked on her headset, he made small talk with Li Ming, asking after his family, his town, how he found life in Bao An. Li Ming relaxed, as best as he could.

But the scent of Cai Yan's deodorant, subtle lavender and sweet citrus, was distracting.

Back inside the main hall, inside his office, Cai Mengyang got down to business. At last, he finally discussed the one thing Li Ming had on his mind, the one thing that the jianghu despised with one breath and craved with the other, the one thing that made the world go round.

Money.

"Our basic day rate for a new biaohang is three hundred and fifty yuan. This covers training, investigations, audits, assessments, and days when there's nothing to do. This *also* includes weekends and holidays. For a protection or escort job, it'll be bumped up to five hundred and fifty. For high threat assignments, you'll receive one thousand yuan a day. If a violent incident occurs while you're working a detail and you successfully resolve it, you'll receive high threat payment for that day.

"Beast hunts use a different compensation scheme. The client will pay us a bounty for every confirmed kill. As a junior biaohang, you will receive one share of the bounty, as well as one share of any bonuses we may be awarded.

"Finally, in the future, you may have clients who request your services by name. For a personal contract like this, you may set your own rates with the client, especially if they request for services we don't normally offer. We will help with negotiations and provide support, in exchange for thirty percent of the fee."

Li Ming ran the numbers through his head. If they paid three hundred and fifty yuan per day, and there were thirty days in a month, then...

His eyes boggled. The basic monthly pay was twenty percent *more* than what a farmer would earn in Fuyang. And since Cai Mengyang had previously hinted that there would be a lot of work...

"How much is the average salary per month?"

"It depends. Our income is as unpredictable as the weather. Most months, it's around twenty-five thousand yuan. In busy months, it can be twice that. Even more."

Li Ming had read of such income figures. But to hear someone say that to him was something else. More than that, it was the casual way he had said it, as though the numbers were just trifling figures to him.

Now Li Ming understood the appeal of the jianghu. Excitement, adventure, glory, power, and most of all, wealth.

"Do you have insurance?" Cai Mengyang asked.

Li Ming blinked.

"Well, I'm still covered under the military's insurance policy."

Cai Mengyang shook his head.

theIt's extremely basic. It won't cover what we do. We have a partnership with an insurance company, one that caters to the jianghu. We could sign you up for their insurance coverage, as a supplement to or replacement of the military policy. But the cost will come out of your salary."

"How much?"

"Seven hundred and fifty yuan a month. You can find alternatives on your own, but this is the preferential rate for Dayong."

"What other costs are there?"

"Not much. The insurance plan covers medical and dental care. We'll provide all the equipment you need for the job. If you want to use your own gear, you may, subject to approval, but you'll have to pay for them out of pocket.

"We'll cover your phone bills, up to five hundred yuan a month, and transportation costs of up to seven hundred yuan. For on-the-job meals, you'll receive an allowance of two hundred yuan a day, unless the client covers them. You'll also receive a one-off clothing and equipment allowance of up to ten thousand yuan. It sounds a lot, but trust me, costs will add up.

"The major cost for you is lodging. Do you have a place to stay?"

"The Bao An Tower Hotel."

Cai Mengyang frowned. "It's overpriced for a budget hotel and doesn't have the amenities for a high-end one. It's not worth it."

"I was hoping to find cheaper accommodations. Haven't found anything yet."

"You could stay here."

Li Ming blinked.

"Here? What do you mean?"

"We have a guest house for our biaohang. You can use one of the unoccupied rooms. Electricity, water and Net access is free. There are bathrooms, a kitchen, lockers, everything you need for long-term stay. You can cook, too. For this, we charge rent of three thousand five hundred yuan a month."

Li Ming smiled. "Rent, huh."

"You can get cheaper in the city, but with fewer amenities and services. You'll also need to get your own lockers. Plus, you'll save time and money on transport. For the price, it can't be beat."

"Seems like you have to pay for everything in the big city."

"That's city life for you. But if you're worried about money, if you work with us, you'll never go hungry."

"I'll take a room at the guest house."

"Excellent. Do you have any other questions?"

"I heard some biaoju issue pills and elixirs to their staff. Does yours?"

"We don't. Every person is unique. Without a medical prescription and long-term monitoring, the haphazard use of pills and elixirs could disrupt your qi and cause long-term harm. Instead, you'll receive discounts for these supplements if you purchase them through our partners."

"Sounds fair."

Cai Mengyang placed two sets of paper on the table, and a pen.

"Here are the terms we discussed earlier. Please read and sign every page."

Fuyang ran on verbal promises and handshakes. Cities demand contracts. Growing up, Li Ming had heard many horror stories of unscrupulous lawyers and unfair contracts. He read every page, every line, every word, with extra care. He read both agreements front to back, twice, then signed them.

And just like that, he was part of Dayong.

"Thank you," Boss Cai said. "We're glad to bring you aboard."

"I look forward to working with you," Li said. "When do we get started?"

"How soon can you start?"

"Immediately."

"Good, good. Report to work next Jia-day, lower half of the fifth hour. Bring all your things with you. The first day is for admin, orientation, logistics, and all that stuff. The day after that, the real work begins."

"Understood."

The men stood. Boss Cai shook Li Ming's hand.

"Welcome to the jianghu."

Three days later, at the gates of Dayong, Li Ming found himself face-to-face with a young man in a blue suit who was *almost* the splitting image of Cai Mengyang. And Cai Yan.

"Cai Yong," he said, shaking Li Ming's hand. "Yes, I'm the boss' son."

"Is anyone else in the family who *isn't* involved in the business?" Li Ming asked.

"Our grandparents have retired, and Mother doesn't work. It's just me, Father, and Yanyan."

"What do you do here?"

"I manage field operations. Father handles the business and strategy. When we deploy a team, I'm usually in charge. But sometimes Father likes to get hands-on too."

"What about Cai Yan?"

"She's a magic specialist and field medic. She also escorts clients who require a female protector."

"Who's the elder sibling?"

"I am. By forty minutes."

"Twins? You two certainly look a lot alike."

"We get that a lot."

Passing through the outer gate, Li Ming asked, "How many biaohang do you have?"

"Including you and me, twelve. In two months, three of them will complete their current contract. We're also expecting another four or five of our regulars to return in the next six weeks."

"Regulars? Return? How does that work?"

"Many biaohang prefer to float around the escort circuit. They work for one company for a year or two, take a break, go somewhere else and work for another company, and so on. The ones who keep returning to work for us are our regulars."

"Ah. They sound just like youxia."

Cai Yong laughed.

"We're just doing a job. A job that requires a lot of travel, a job that happens to be dangerous and difficult at times, but also a job that pays well."

As he opened the inner gate, Cai Yong glanced at Li Ming's hip.

"That's a strange weapon you've got there."

"It's a swordbreaker."

"A what?"

"Swordbreaker."

"Not a sword? I don't think I've met a martial cultivator who uses one."

"Me neither."

"Why did you pick it anyway?"

"Family heirloom."

"Ah. Sentimental value?"

Li Ming shrugged. "We don't exactly have very many weapons to spare."

"You came from Fuyang, yes? That farming town about two hours away?"

"Yes."

"Ah."

There was something in that word that grated against him. A sense of superiority, perhaps. Li Ming had heard it all the time from city dwellers who thought themselves above farmers. He'd learned long ago not to let how he felt show.

In the main courtyard, Cai Yong gestured expansively around him.

"The side halls are for visitors and employees. The eastern hall is reserved for our biaohang. The western hall is for our housekeeping staff. They're busy now, but if you're staying here, you'll see them soon.

"The main hall is the heart of Dayong. This is where we entertain clients, discuss business, plan operations, and carry out our daily work. Every workday morning on the fifth hour, everyone gathers here for briefings and assignments.

"The west wing of the main hall contains the offices. You've been there before. If… *when* you need to file paperwork, we've got computers set up for you.

"The east wing is the armory and storeroom. The storeroom is open to everyone, but only the Cai family has the keys to the armory. If you want to store something here, just let us know.

"Past the main hall is the inner courtyard and the Cai family residence. That's off-limits. If you're not invited, please stay out. The doors to the inner residence are all locked with keycards, so you shouldn't accidentally wander inside.

"All weapons and shapers must be secured. You are free to go around armed while on company property, but whatever you're not carrying must be locked up. You can use your room locker or the armory. Personally, I'd recommend the locker. You'll want ready access to your gear, without relying on someone else.

"Common sense rules apply. If you choose to carry a gun, keep the safety on and the weapon pointed in a safe direction. If you have cold weapons, they stay in their sheaths. If you wear a shaper, do not discharge them on company property without a good reason. But if you must use your weapons, judicious aim will be greatly appreciated.

"When you're not working, you're free to use the training equipment whenever you please. You'll find them inside the general storage shed next to the biaohang house. Just return them when you're done. Of course, if you have your own kit, feel free to use them too.

"You'll find that our policies are very relaxed compared to other companies. We're all professionals here. We're all part of the jianghu. We trust that you know how to follow instructions and handle weapons properly. But just so you know, if you cause a negligent or accidental discharge, if you willfully injure or otherwise harm a fellow biaohang, if you cause significant damage to the property, you are gone. No appeals. And you will be referred to the Civil Police. If you're still alive."

Maybe Cai Yong meant it as a joke. But the words pricked at Li Ming's heart again.

Approaching the biaohang house, Li Ming studied the security measures. The windows were made not of glass but toughened transparent ceramic. An electronic lock with an analog backup secured the only door. A camera dome peered down from the eaves.

Past the door, Li Ming found a small but comfortable living and dining room. The furniture here was cheap and functional, wood and faux leather, not as high class as the ones in the main hall but comfortable enough. The air conditioner kept the house at a pleasantly cool temperature. Sniffing, Li Ming picked up a whiff of sweet air freshener.

The kitchen was tiny but well-supplied. The fridge was filled with frozen meats, but few fresh items. The cooking utensils looked practically brand-new. Full bottles of cooking oil and condiments rested on the counter. Li Ming wondered if anyone actually used this room.

Past the kitchen was the laundry room and bathroom. The shower was still wet, but the washer and dryer were silent. At the fair end, a door led out to an empty courtyard.

It was a tiny patch of concrete. Ten paces across, five paces wide. There was nothing here, just four walls and a floor and the open sky. The floor was cracked in many places, as though a giant had stomped his way back and forth across the ground.

"This is one of our secret courtyards," Cai Yong said. "The other side hall has one too. You can use this place to meditate, practice martial arts, or otherwise do something you don't want guests seeing."

"Including the laundry?"

"Sure. But if I were you, I'd hire someone else to do it. You just won't have the time or energy."

"Who can we hire? The housekeeping staff?"

Cai Yong's eyes twinkled.

"If you pay them. Our contract with them doesn't cover laundry for biaohang, so you'll have to negotiate with them directly. There's also a laundry service two streets down. If you're in a rush, use the laundry. They offer same-day dry cleaning service. Our housekeepers can't do that."

The other half of the house was dedicated to habitation. Four bedrooms, plus a closet and a second bathroom.

"The room closest to the door is Ga San's. The others are empty," Cai Yong said.

"No one else lives here?" Li Ming asked.

"For now. Only singles and junior biaohang live here. Those with families live in the city."

Li fished out his phone and turned on his compass.

"What are you doing?" Cai Yong asked, mystified.

"Checking for my lucky direction."

"Fengshui? Really?"

"Why not? This entire compound is built according to fengshui principles."

The biaohang house was sited on the east of the compound, and the main door faced west. The bedrooms were sited on the northwest and west sides of the interior. It was no coincidence. The original builders had constructed the compound in conformance with ancient principles, and though successive generations of renovations had erased most traces of the past, the orientation of the house had remained.

Li Ming clucked his tongue.

"What's wrong?" Cai Yong asked.

"All the rooms sit in unlucky directions."

Northwest was the Five Ghosts sector. West was Life Threatening. Both were terrible.

"Are you seriously telling me that the location of your bedroom will decide your fate?" Cai Yong exclaimed.

"When I was young, I was weak and sickly. I had colds and fevers and other illnesses all the time. The doctors couldn't help much. In the end, a fengshui master advised my parents to shift me to another room, which was in my Heavenly Doctor sector. Since then, I've never had major health problems."

Cai Yong sighed.

"Well, if you're so concerned about fengshui, you could always find lodging elsewhere."

The ancients believed that Five Ghosts and Life Threatening were terrible, but only because of the context of their times. Five Ghosts carried the qi of emptiness. It led to betrayals, gossip, backstabbing. But in emptiness, too, lay an understanding of deeper and higher truths. Priests and magicians used this sector to exorcise their inner demons and gain deep insight into the nature of mind, consciousness and reality.

Life Threatening was the sector that invited calamity into your life. It attracted illness, accidents, and disasters. But, used properly, it opened the door to sudden windfalls and explosive growth. And the business of a biaohang was to bring order to chaos—and get paid well for doing it.

In truth they weren't terrible. If anything, they were ideal for a martial cultivator seeking the fast track to growth. *If* he knew how to make the most of them.

"Do you really have to think so hard?" Cai Yong asked.

No. He didn't. He just needed the room that would best fit his needs, and what he needed was...

Li Ming walked to the room at the end of the hall.

"This one," Li Ming said.

Cai Yong unlocked the door. The air was stale, the qi stagnant. But otherwise the room was well-maintained. There were two single beds, separated by a nightstand. No sheets and pillowcases, only aged mattresses and stained pillows. A long desk and two chairs sat next to the window. Two double-door lockers stood where a closet would go. Each locker had a dedicated slot for a long gun, lockable drawers for handguns, and racks mounted on the inner doors.

"Each room sleeps two people, but normally we only have three or four biaohang staying with us at any one time," Cai Yong said. "If we have more tenants, we'll let you know first before moving someone in."

"Are we supposed to get our own linens?"

"We've got some in the storeroom. We'll draw them later. And, yes, you'll need to take care of the linen too. Either work out a deal with housekeeping or use the laundry service."

"And locks?"

"We'll provide them too." Cai Yong squinted at Li Ming's pack. "Is that all the stuff you're carrying?"

"Yes."

Cai Yong shook his head. "That isn't nearly enough for a biaohang."

"I'm new to the job."

"You can use our kit. But if you work for other companies in the future, understand that not everyone is as generous or as well-stocked as ours. You should get your own kit." He paused. "Also, you need to upgrade your shaper. That shaper is for kids. You're way too powerful for it."

"It's on my wish list."

Li Ming dropped his backpack in the locker and followed Cai Yong out.

"What do you think of this place so far?" Cai Yong asked.

"It's *huge*. And you said there's another residence behind this compound. I've never seen a home as large as this before."

"Is that so, Li *shaoye*?"

Li Ming winced. How the devil had the Cais learned about that?

"That was a joke. My family home isn't even as large as the biaohang house. This is the first time I've visited such a grand estate. You can feel the history in the air."

"Yes, we've had it since the time of my ancestors."

"The Celestial Era, if I recall."

"Yes. Back then, our fifth-time great grandfather was the governor of the city."

"Really! That explains a lot. Your family goes back a long way, doesn't it?"

"We can trace our lineage all the way to the Yue Dynasty, and beyond."

"Fascinating... But..."

"But?"

"If you'll pardon my directness, how did this property remain in the family hands after the Revolution? Didn't the new government confiscate the lands of the officials of the Celestial Empire?"

"My ancestors were dedicated to serving the people of the province. They were also fortunate to have come from wealth. They used their resources to help the citizens whenever they could. They even opposed their fellow bureaucrats and civil servants when they felt the system had wronged the people.

"They saw firsthand the inefficiency, corruption and decadence of the Late Celestial Empire. When civil war broke out, they defected. They welcomed the revolutionaries with open arms, raised their own private army, and fought at the front lines. For their service, they were allowed to keep their property and holdings, though they had to give up their government positions.

"That, by the way, was how and why Dayong was founded. My ancestors needed a new job, and there were plenty of beasts, bandits and warlords to go around."

"It worked out well for them, didn't it?"

"Indeed. *Shanyou shanbao, e you e bao.*"

Kindness is repaid with kindness, evil is repaid with evil.

Inside the main hall, the men parted ways.

"I need to prepare for an upcoming job, and you need to sort out the rest of the admin stuff. Go see Yanyan. She'll help you take care of the rest."

"Understood. Thank you for your guidance."

"No problem. I'll see you in the field soon."

He felt her before he saw her.

Her qi field was warm, soft, fluid. It was like immersing himself in a pool filled with water heated to just the right temperature. She was the opposite of every male cultivator he had met in Bao An. Just as powerful, maybe even more so, but the quality and the type of qi was markedly different.

Cai Yan was the queen of the small bullpen Dayong used for an office in the east end of the hall. Or, rather, she was the only person in the office at present. Seated at the large corner table at the opposite end of the room, she smiled as he entered.

"*Zao an!*" she sang.

Good morning!

"*Zao,*" Li Ming replied. "Your elder brother sent me."

"He *really* told you he's the elder brother?"

"He's not?"

"He thinks forty minutes somehow makes a difference." She sniffed. "Our birth charts are almost identical."

"Birth charts?"

"You know, bazi birth chart?"

"Ah."

Bazi was an ancient form of astrology, so old its origins were lost in the mists of time. With the date and time of birth, a bazi master could learn everything important about a person: personality, career, relationships, health, critical life events.

"Have you ever done a birth chart before?" she asked.

"My parents preferred fengshui. They're not into bazi."

"It's a shame. Bazi, fengshui, they are all part of Zhongxia metaphysics. They complement each other in different ways."

"You sound like you know a lot about metaphysics."

Her eyes sparked.

"It's part of my job."

The second he sat at the desk, her energy shifted. Now she was completely in work mode, her attention totally focused on her screen.

"I'll need your identification card," she said.

He fished it out of his wallet. It was a palm-sized piece of plastic, blue with pink tints. His twelve-year-old face frowned at him. A stranger's face, long vanished into the mists of time.

She held the card to a scanner by her keyboard. Her computer beeped. Holding up the card, she compared the reverse and the obverse to the screen, her eyes flicking back and forth, going line by line.

"Interesting," she said.

"What is?"

"Your name. It sounds similar to the characters for 'dawn'."

"A fengshui master chose the name."

"Ah..." She cocked her head. "*En?*"

"What's wrong?"

"You came from Fuyang. That's a country town, isn't it? But your accent... You sound like you come from Taiping. Maybe not the city, but the surrounding towns."

"I served in the Capital Battalion of the Military Police. Everyone's accents rubbed off on me."

"Ah."

She returned the card.

"I'm going to submit this information to the Ministry of Cultivation. By law, when a cultivator takes up a job in the uniformed services, or in the jianghu, the Ministry must be informed. If you change jobs, the Ministry must also be informed. They want to track the activities and movements of all cultivators. But, really, this is just a formality."

"What about the background checks?"

"You've already cleared them. You wouldn't be here otherwise."

That explained the waiting period between the initial interview and the test.

"By tomorrow, you'll officially be registered in the Jianghu Association. Have you heard of it?" she asked.

He grinned and spoke with this thickest provincial accent.

"I'm just a dirt bun from a poor farming town. I don't know anything about how the world works."

She laughed.

"*Zhen shi de!* You're a real joker, aren't you?"

"I do my best."

He couldn't help it. There was just something about her that brought out that side of him.

Still chuckling, she shook her head.

"The Jianghu Association is the official martial cultivator association of Xiazhou. It coordinates clients and cultivators, provides resources and legal aid, and represents the interests of the jianghu to governments and corporations.

"Members are ranked according to their experience, qi score, and accomplishments. There are five ranks: iron, bronze, silver, gold, platinum. Iron is for newbies like yourself. Platinum-ranked cultivators are the most powerful in the world, the ones who respond to national crises.

"Governments all over Xiazhou have wildly different regulatory and licensing schemes for cultivators. The Association has representatives in every nation to smoothen the process. The ranking system serves as a universal permit. The most important thing you need to know is that the type of jobs you can accept, and the equipment you are allowed to purchase, is limited by your rank.

"Iron-ranked cultivators can only accept basic jobs like bodyguard work and beast hunts. They are also restricted to buying civilian-grade equipment. *However*, Father is ranked gold. As such, his authorized employees—including yourself—will be allowed to carry gold-ranked equipment in the field. But that equipment is company property. You can *not* carry it in your personal time.

"You may also participate in missions rated higher than your rank, but only as part of a team led by a senior cultivator of the appropriate rank. This is for your own safety.

"Finally, if you care about such things, the Association maintains a leaderboard of its members. You can see how you rank in relation to every other member. The system tracks successful missions, commendations, qi scores, and other such factors, and gives you a number to represent your score. As a newcomer, you'll be ranked dead last. But don't worry. That will only last for a few days, maybe a week at most, before someone new joins the jianghu. Or if someone leaves it."

"It sounds complicated," Li Ming said.

"It's this or negotiate with local, provincial and national governments, with clients, with police, with all the other stakeholders the Association liaises with for us."

"That's fair."

"Government regulations also require us to update your qi score at least once a quarter. Company policy is to update once a month."

"Just like the military."

"Father said that too. The Association's ranking system uses qi score as one of its major criteria. The sooner you rank up, the more lucrative jobs you can accept—and the more powerful gear you can buy. For the six months you're with us, making ranking up your top priority."

"Understood."

She lowered her Eight Eyes visor into place.

"Smile!"

He smiled.

A heartbeat. Two. Three.

She raised the visor, wonder on her face.

"Interesting... You have a qi score of thirteen thousand six hundred and eighteen points. After Ghazan, you have the highest qi score among newcomers to the jianghu I've seen so far."

"What was his?"

"Sorry, can't tell you that. Etiquette, you know. You'll have to ask him yourself."

The jianghu had strange rules. In the Special Military Police, troopers would answer that question without hesitation. On the other hand, in the military, everybody knew they were on the same side.

"Anyway, with a score as high as yours, you've already cleared one of the major hurdles to obtaining a bronze rank," Cai Yan continued. "Now you just need at least six months of work experience, a recommendation, and a thousand job points."

"Job points?"

"The Association ranks jobs by their complexity and danger. The bigger and more dangerous the job, the more points a martial cultivator will receive when he completes it."

"How long will it take to earn a thousand points?"

"If you're working with us? If you're lucky, three months."

"If you're *not* lucky?"

"Three weeks."

The next half-hour trudged along in a lengthy briefing. House rules, corporate policies, procedures, occupational health and safety, on and on and on. Li Ming was no stranger to such matters. He'd endured more than enough of them in the military. Nonetheless, he sat through it all, and for his reward he received the official Dayong biaohang guidebook.

And an identification card.

"This is your biaohang card," Cai Yan said. "This card identifies you as part of our biaoju. It is a supplement to your own national identification card, but it does not replace it. When you're acting in your official capacity as a biaohang, you can use it. But it does not store your national identification number or registered address. This card is also your personal keycard. You'll need it to access the controlled areas in the compound. Keep it on you at all times."

Li stored it in his wallet.

"You shouldn't do that," Cai Yan interrupted. "Keep your biaohang card in a separate card holder."

"Why?"

"If you're off-duty, you might not want people identifying you as a biaohang. You don't want to be a target."

"Some martial cultivators are so famous, people recognize them on sight."

"Yes, but you're not them. You don't have a reputation, and you're not as powerful as them either. That makes you a target for bandits and other criminals. You'll want the option to remain incognito."

"Fair enough. But I don't have a card holder."

"Put it on your to-buy list."

With the admin matters out of the way, Cai Yan brought him on a mini tour of the main hall. The reception area, the office, the conference room, the side halls.

The armory.

She held her keycard to the reader. The machine beeped once. Red lights flashed. She stooped over, bringing her face in front of the camera. The lights turned green. A bolt retracted with a heavy snap. She swung the security grille open, fished out a set of keys and unlocked the door proper.

"High security," Li Ming remarked.

"Government regulations."

"It's tighter than a military armory. We don't need facial recognition for that."

"We're private sector. We aim to exceed the standards."

The armory was a cramped room, not much larger than his own. Li Ming had expected the scent of oils and lubricants, metals and dirt. All he got was dust. He'd anticipated racks of weapons, gun safes, high-security tough boxes, shelves of supplies.

He saw a machine.

Tall as the room, wide as an elephant, it was a hunk of dark metal, so dark it swallowed the light. A blue bar illuminated a small control panel mounted at eye level on the right. It vaguely reminded him of a vending machine.

In a sense, it was.

"Is that an interspatial storage machine?" he asked.

She smiled. "Never seen one before?"

Interspatial storage was the final miracle of the Yue Dynasty. By strange magics or stranger sciences, they found a way to create pocket dimensions that could hold vast quantities of goods. When the Great Yue fell, the science was lost. Only recently had the scientists of the Zhongxia Republic figured out how to reproduce it, and only imperfectly.

"I have," he said defensively. "I just never had a chance to use one."

"Never? But weren't you in the military? Don't they use interspatial storage?"

"Only in logistics units, or in units that need to haul around bulk goods and materials. The Special Military Police didn't need that capability."

"I see. Need an explanation on how this works?"

"Please."

She cleared her throat for effect.

"This is a Model 9000 Interspatial Storage Machine from Zhenbao Dynamics. With a storage capacity the size of a five-bedroom apartment, it is an ideal long-term storage solution for businesses with large inventories, such as Dayong.

"This machine holds all our weapons and accessories. Like the armory itself, access to the machine is restricted to the Cai family. It uses a combination of keycard and fingerprint access. However, I can authorize you to draw specific items from it. You'll still need a Cai family member to let you in, but this way you can quickly access your gear once you're inside."

"Interspatial storage machines need a lot of electricity, don't they? What happens if the power is cut?"

"We have our own cosmic tap."

"Dayong has its own cosmic tap?"

"This machine has its own cosmic tap. Dayong has a separate tap. The Cai home has another one too."

Li's eyes boggled.

"You have *three* cosmic taps?"

"Four, actually. The last is for the storeroom."

Numbers swam through his head. For the price of a small-scale cosmic tap, he could buy a house in Fuyang. The cost of *four* taps was...

"You look shocked," she said.

"With the tap you need to keep an interspatial machine going, you could power all of Fuyang."

"It consumes a *lot* of electricity, doesn't it?" She paused and smiled. "Or you don't use much electricity at home?"

"No. Not until ten years ago."

Now it was her turn to be shocked.

"Ten years ago?! How long has Fuyang been around?"

"Since the Mid-Celestial Empire."

"What? I... How... How is it even possible?!"

"Beasts roam the wildlands. They chew on power lines, destroy utility towers, attack generators. It's an ongoing problem, even today. Even if they leave the infrastructure alone, it's too dangerous for technicians to perform maintenance and servicing works without an armed escort. Fuyang experienced blackouts and brownouts all the time."

"You didn't have electricity for centuries?!"

"We have solar panels, water condensers and hydrogen crackers. But they're ancient, or just reserved for essentials. For the most part, we just learned to make do."

"That's... I want to say it's unbelievable, but..."

"Yes, well, we got by. Father got fed up with the situation, so he pooled together some money with the rest of the village, and we bought our own cosmic tap. Now Fuyang has all the electricity we need."

"I didn't know countryside life was so... so..."

"Backwards?"

"I thought so too, but I didn't want to insult you."

"It's not an insult if I agree with it." He sighed. "Going to Taiping was a shock. There was so much I had to learn in such a short time."

"Which do you prefer? The city or the farm?"

"The city is crowded, noisy and expensive. But the standard of living is also much higher. On the other hand, Fuyang has a significant advantage over Bao An. And Taiping, for that matter."

"What's that?"

"The ability to practice gongfu in the great outdoors anytime you want."

She sighed. "You're really a martial arts *zhainan.*"

"In this line of work, it's an asset."

Shaking her head, she walked to the control panel. She held up her keycard to the scanner, pressed her thumb against the reader, and punched in a command in the control panel.

The outer surface of the machine flashed to life. It was a gigantic screen, now split into large and small boxes demarcated by bright blue borders. Arrows and windows hovered at the sides of each box. But each box was empty.

No, not empty. It was a darkness so deep that nothing escaped.

"The machine has a wide range of configurations," Cai Yan said. "This is the tactical loadout configuration. It lets the user draw many items at ones. The window above each frame tells you what it's for: infinity guns, load carriers, accessories, and so on. Use the arrows to navigate between items. If you press the icon at the lower right corner, you'll call up a list of all items tagged to that frame."

"The machine tags items automatically?"

"It's not that smart. We must key it ourselves. But that's the Cai family's business. As for you, pick the loadout you want and I'll register it for you."

"What can I pick?"

"Anything that isn't already registered to someone else. I've already filtered those out. You can pick the gear you want."

There were so many choices. So. Many.

Sights. Slings. Goggles. Crystals. Cosmic taps. Fire control units. Upper and lower receivers. Blades. Breaching tools. Grenades. Shapers.

And guns.

Lots. And lots. And lots. Of guns.

"I can draw anything?" Li said, a grin growing across his face.

"Anything."

His grin illuminated the room.

"What's that grin for?" she asked.

He didn't answer. He was too busy.

He scrolled through the catalog, going back and forth, jumping from one frame to another at rapid speed, dancing between the guns and the gear at random. He called up his Net browser on his smartglasses, compared different equipment and took furious notes. He swiped left, swiped right, swiped again, bouncing between various options.

"Can you filter out stuff that isn't my size?" he asked.

"Sure," she said.

"Can you also filter out items by brand?"

"Which?"

He told her. It was a short list.

"How many items can I draw?" he asked.

"How much stuff do you need?"

"Just asking."

"You can draw whatever fits into the frames."

His face fell for a second. Then he went right back at it, scrolling through the selections, glancing at his screen, doing even more research. In a minute, he settled on his choice of gear. But the guns...

There was a wealth of handguns. Full-sized duty pistols for military and police. Backup guns for concealed carry. Snub-nosed guns for ultra-deep concealment. Target guns for precision and competition. Oversized hunting guns for dangerous predators, both two- and many-legged.

There were enough long guns to equip a platoon of troops. General purpose infinity guns. Precision weapons for hunting and sniping. Personal defense weapons. Single-shot ultra-powered guns. Heavy-duty repeaters. The one species of long gun they didn't have were infinity cannons, but the repeaters came close.

And the brands... He recognized all of them. In the military they were objects of desire. In the jianghu they set the standards for the industry of arms, for the forest of warriors. Every last one of them was top quality, forged from lessons earned in blood, proven in a hundred battles and a thousand streets.

Any one of them would a superb choice. But which was best?

"Is it really that hard to choose?" she asked. "Most other biaohang would be done by now."

"You said I could choose anything, right?"

"Yes..."

"But I can only draw what fits in the frames, yes?"

"Yes... And so..."

"So I need to pick the best choice."

She sighed.

"Don't worry about getting the best choice. If you change your mind, or if you want to use another piece of gear, we can arrange that for you. Just pick what you think you need. And if you need specialist gear for a specific job, you can come back here."

His grin redoubled in intensity.

"Why are you so happy?"

Still ignoring her, he touched the screen a few more times. Flipped back and forth a couple of times. Nodded to himself. Stepped back.

"Done!" he pronounced.

"*Finally,*" she muttered.

"I want to inspect the gear."

And see how the machine works, though he'd never admit it to her.

She sighed.

"Suit yourself."

She hit a button.

The machine hummed. Blue light spilled from the gap between the frame and the screen, defining a door. The humming grew louder, deeper, a sound that oscillated in the depths of Li's being.

The machine chimed politely.

The door swung open, revealing a shelf that neatly corresponded to the grid he'd seen on the display, a shelf stocked with the gear he'd chosen.

"Just like that?" he said.

"Just like that," she said.

With great reverence, he set everything on the floor. Spare parts. Accessories. Cleaning kits. A sling. Shaper. Handgun. Infinity gun.

"You look like a kid unwrapping his birthday presents," Cai Yan said.

Li took the long gun in his hands. "Do you know what this is?"

"It's an infinity gun."

He sighed.

"This is a Sima Clan Arsenal Avenger. Patterned on the military's Type 82, it was designed to participate in the Special Forces General Purpose Battle Weapon competition, and won.

"It is overengineered in critical areas for maximum reliability, shaved down in nonessential places to reduce weight, and its point of balance was shifted just slightly forward for better ergonomics. It will operate in any terrain, anywhere in the world, and will stand up to torture that will break a lesser gun. The handguard uses the Empty Lock negative space mounting system. This minimizes forward weight without sacrificing structural strength. The whole weapon can be field-stripped without tools."

He pivoted, smoothly bringing up the weapon, finger off the trigger, muzzle pointed at the wall.

"It's incredibly well-designed. It points exactly at where I want it to go. The Type 82 is a bit front-heavy and there's some noticeable drag. The pistol grip is positioned at just the right angle and position for maximum comfort, and I can swap out the grip module so it fits my hand perfectly. The stock has an integrated adjustable cheekpiece. With it you can obtain a strong cheek weld and optimal eye-to-optic focus.

"The optic was designed in partnership with Steiner-Muller. Highly rugged, rock-solid housing, crystal-clear lenses. It's zeroed right from the factory. You won't have to touch it once you've confirmed the zero, even if you've banged it around. It'll shoot to point of aim out to a *li*."

He canted the weapon and checked the cosmic taps mounted on the butt and forward of the trigger guard.

"Voight Energy Dynamics. The finest name in the business. This is as high end as it gets. It draws and converts qi from a small field forward of the tap, small enough that it won't suck in the firer's qi, yet large enough that it can sustain continuous fire for as long as the heat sinks hold out. Other manufacturers draw from a larger field, but VED uses a highly efficient design and prioritizes user safety."

"You seem really into this," Cai Yan said.

"You live and die by your weapons. Is this gun stock?"

"We've never touched it."

"The output crystal comes from the Sima Clan's ateliers. Guaranteed ninety-nine point nine hundred and ninety-nine percent shot-to-shot precision and repeatability. It's shaped to focus energy forwards, minimizing waste heat and energy. To suit Special Forces requirements, it is one-third more powerful than standard military-issue crystals and replenishes twenty percent faster.

"It is also tightly integrated with the fire control unit, ensuring maximum precision, performance and repeatability. It maintains one-tenth minute of angle accuracy out to half a *li*. Type 82s only manages one-half minute of angle out to the same distance.

"The Avenger has a thirty-five shot heat capacity, maximum rate of fire of eight hundred shots per minute, and an overheat cooldown time of twenty-eight seconds. If you stick to single shot, one shot per second, at standard power, you can practically fire it forever."

His thumb clicked through the fire selector. His eyes widened. His finger rotated through the fire mode wheel. His jaw dropped.

"This uses the safe-1-continuous fire selector and the half-standard-double-breach fire mode wheel. How on earth did you get your hands on a military-grade fire control unit?"

Now Cai Yan smiled.

"Father is a gold-ranked cultivator, remember? He can buy equipment normally restricted to military and law enforcement."

Li shook his head in awe. "This is the official weapon of the Special Forces. It's *beyond* regular military and law enforcement. This is the kind of gear we dream about using while in the Army."

"Why didn't you?"

"Because it's expensive. For the price of one of these you could buy three Type 82s, or even a full-sized infinity cannon. It's also heavier by about a *jin*. It doesn't matter to Special Forces soldiers with their powered armor or exoskeletons, but it *will* matter to line infantry who aren't issued such kit."

"You are such a *boy*."

"And what does *that* mean?"

"You love your guns."

"You have to know what your weapons are capable of."

"I'm sure you'll get along swimmingly with Elder Brother."

"He likes guns too?"

"He could talk for *days* about them. Every weapon you see here, he bought."

"Excellent taste."

"Next you're going to tell me all about the handgun you picked."

"The Golden Legion is Sima Clan's interpretation of the Type 38 pistol. While retaining the controls, manual of arms and modularity of the original design, the Golden Legion was optimized for high-speed combat shooting under stress. This includes a high-power high-precision crystal, a large VED pistol cosmic tap, modular grips—"

"All right, all right, I get it!"

"I thought a biaohang like you would be interested in weapons."

"Only as much as I need to carry out my job. I'm more of a backline supporter. Magic is my forte, not guns."

"I could talk about shapers all day if you want."

She rubbed her temples, as though soothing a headache.

"Please. Enough. My head hurts enough as it is."

"Fine... But I have to say, it seems the company favors reality shapers from Chang An. While I prefer Five Mountains, Chang An is also an excellent choice."

"Why do you prefer Five Mountains?"

"Their shapers are optimized for the five element system. You *can* use eight trigrams or yinyang if you want, but it's less efficient."

"Interesting. I use the eight trigrams myself, and the Chang An line is best suited for sustained magic."

"I'm not a dedicated shaper, but I've worked a lot of magic in my time. Could I have two reality shapers?"

Cai Yan shook her head.

"I can only give you one. Company policy. We don't have that many to go around, and most cultivators—those without your kind of training and experience—won't be able to handle two. We won't stop you from using two, but you need to buy the other one with your own money."

"You've got plenty of shapers, don't you?"

"For now. A few more cultivators will be joining us, and they need shapers too."

He sighed. "Well. At least this one is a step up from the one I have now."

She looked at his shaper. Then at the company shaper. And back at his.

"You *sure* you can use the Chang An?"

"What do you mean?"

"Your shaper is a generic model. It doesn't even have a brand name. You sure you're powerful enough to use the Chang An?"

"Of course I am. If I weren't, I wouldn't even..."

She chuckled. "Wouldn't even what?"

He shut his mouth. Shook his head.

"You're making fun of me."

"Now we're even. Is this everything you need, or do you want to ogle your kit some more?"

"I need to customize it to my requirements."

"You're going to take all day, aren't you?"

"Only as long as I need."

"I don't have all day. After I'm done with you, I need to get back to work. And we still need to register you for the storeroom. Put your kit away. We'll come back here once we're done with all the other logistics stuff."

"Alright, alright," he grumbled. "Let's go."

Chapter Eleven

Form of the Swordbreaker

The rest of the day passed in relative peace. The moment he'd set up and arranged his room, he transferred all his issue gear to this room, and began the laborious task of fitting them to his body. He cinched down straps, fastened buckles, wiped down his kit, inspected crystals, mounted pouches on his plate carrier, tended to the ten thousand things a soldier needed to do to prepare his equipment for war.

He didn't mind. It was a rhythm he was long used to. He lost himself in the process, immersing himself in every moment, scrutinizing and readying his gear. He studied everything as though he were a child seeing it for the first time, seeing every item with unclouded eyes and a mind free from conceptions, learning how to identify every item by shape, color, touch. More than just preparation, it was a ritual, familiar and vital, an anchor and a compass in these ever-shifting times.

He left his room just once for the afternoon meal. The second he was done, he retreated to his room and continued his preparations. Everything had to be perfect. Every loose strap had to be secured, every spare thread burned off, every buckle locked in the sweet spot between comfort and security. When he was finally done, he returned his kit to the armory.

He wanted to keep them in his room. Cai Yan vetoed the idea immediately. Government regulations. This was silver and gold-ranked gear; as a mere iron-ranker, he couldn't own them, only use them under the direction of a senior cultivator. Once he no longer needed them, he had to return the kit to its original owner. The only kit he could keep in his locker was the gear he was allowed to own.

Which, for all intents and purposes, was his swordbreaker and his utility shaper.

He spent the evening wandering the streets and alleys around Dayong. He studied the geography, the layout of the stores and homes, how the alleys transitioned between planned grids to organic sprawl and back again. He watched the flows of traffic, human and vehicle. He noted the danger zones, the places where a predator might lurk, and developed countermeasures. Most importantly, he identified the eateries, the laundry service, public transportation options, the essential services and locations in the area.

He returned to the biaohang house at the twelfth hour, the last hour of the day. There was no one in sight, but he sensed a powerful qi presence deep in Ghazan's room.

After a quick shower, he returned to his room. He spent the rest of the night reading through the employee guidebook, catching up on the news, scrolling through various feeds and websites. At the close of the hour, he tucked himself into bed, and fell into a deep sleep.

He awoke to a curious sound. A string of rhythmic banging, like the sound of drum, but distant, muffled, distorted by the glass window and wooden door. Eight bangs, a pause, another eight bangs, and the cycle repeated.

He scanned the world, fists ready. But there was no intruder. The sound had come from further off. And it was too regular, too repeated, for it to be the sounds of someone breaking in or otherwise causing harm. Not at this hour.

It was one *ke* before the fourth hour. One *ke* before his alarm was scheduled to ring. He didn't think he'd be able to go back to sleep. He disabled the alarm, swung out of bed, and trudged out of his room.

The banging grew louder, fiercer, more insistent. Now he recognized the sound as shoes stomping concrete. A sound he had heard countless times in the military. For a moment it propelled him two years into the past, into the parade square of the Capital Battalion, into the military rituals prior to morning physical training.

He snapped himself back to the present and investigated the source of the sound. Past the kitchen, past the laundry, past the door to the secret courtyard, he saw it.

A man stood two paces from the door. He was completely still, completely focused on his inner world. He turned his head to his left, his arms flowing up to guard his chest. Abruptly he exploded into violent motion, arms swinging through wide arcs, feet stomping the ground with every blow. In the pre-dawn dark he was a hurricane of violence contained in a tiny space.

Ghazan.

The routine carried him to the other end of the courtyard. He relaxed. Straightened. Breathed.

And turned to Li Ming.

Ghazan's eyes seared into Li Ming. Li Ming met his gaze with equal intensity.

For a moment, the men stood and stared.

"Shifangquan?" Li Ming asked, finally.

"Yes," Ghazan said.

"I was wondering what that sound was. Were you training?"

Ghazan grunted.

"I'll leave you to it," Li Ming said.

Ghazan continued staring until Li Ming closed the door.

As much he'd like to watch, to study the explosive forms and movements of the art, Li Ming had his own training to tend to.

He armed himself with his swordbreaker and washed up in the bathroom. Shaved off the beginnings of a beard and mustache. Trimmed the small hairs of his nostrils and between his eyebrows. Splashed more water on his face. He felt almost human, but fatigue clung to him like a leaden weight.

Fortunately, he knew the answer to that.

In the middle courtyard, he stood in the exact center of a square. Dayong was quiet. The world was still. But for the non-stop stomping, he allowed himself to believe that he was the only man awake in the world.

Then a woman in a black uniform emerged from the servants' home, broom in hand, and disappeared in the direction of the outer garden. Just like that, the spell was broken.

He followed his military morning routine. Zhan zhuang. The Five Elements and Twelve Animals. The major forms. The entire routine was timed to last for three *ke*.

As he trained, he saw more servants emerge from the house, going about their duties. The stomping continued unabated, Ghazan training with him, together yet separate. The sky lightened slowly, gradually, but the first rays of the sun had yet to show.

One last punch, and he flowed through the closing form. He stood upright, feet together, arms loose by his side. He breathed, slowly and smoothly, letting the qi flow through him. Liquid lightning surged through him, spiraling up his legs, coursing down his arms, shooting through his spine. As he breathed, he relaxed, releasing the tension in his muscles, allowing the qi to move even more smoothly.

One last breath, and he moved on to weapons.

Cai Yan had granted him access to the general stores. He made use of that now, piling a cart with training weapons. Every weapon covered in the An Family Wuxingquan syllabus.

A double-edged straight sword. A saber. A two-handed longsword. A long staff. A short staff. And of course, the foundational weapon of the art, the weapon upon which every movement was derived from, a spear.

Back in the courtyard, he began with the spear. Sliding thrusts, subtle deflections, circular smashes, horizontal swings, every movement was an expression of the five elements, an ancestor of the five fists the world knew today. Wuxingquan was born on the blood-soaked battlefield of antiquity, a method to rapidly prepare levied troops for war. The wuxingquan of today was merely the spear expressed in two fists.

Now warmed up, he moved on to the other weapons. Every weapon form was different, taking advantage of its unique properties, yet they all boiled down to the five elements. After completing a set, he switched to his swordbreaker, attempting to replicate it, to adapt it, to find a way to use it.

Or, rather, he tried.

As he worked through the straight sword form, he spotted Ghazan at the edge of the square. Wielding an enormous spear, almost twice his height, the Yue flowed through the forms of his art.

Like wuxingquan, shifangquan was also built upon the spear. But where the An Family trained in a variety of weapons, all lineages of shifangquan viewed the spear as the beginning and the end of the art. The true shifangquan practitioner was a spear specialist, and Ghazan was a master.

In every step, Li Ming saw the power, the ferocity, the aggression that defined the art. But it was a controlled aggression, laser-focused on the singular purpose of efficiently destroying the enemy, every movement quick and clean and explosive. Man and spear moved as one, the artist becoming the art, the weapon an extension of the body, the body an instrument of qi, the qi an expression of intent.

Shifangquan was vastly different from wuxingquan. The tactics, the mechanics, the footwork, they were so different. But the relentlessness, the power, the focus, these Li Ming appreciated, even if he saw only the outward manifestations and not the subtleties that made them work.

Li Ming sensed Ghazan would very much have preferred to train alone, in secret. But the hidden courtyard was too cramped for such a huge weapon. He had no choice but to train here. And he was watching Li as intently as Li was watching him.

Li Ming was used to being watched. In the Special Military Police, when he trained on base in his off-time, inevitably he would attract an audience. But they were his fellow troopers, eager to learn new and better ways to carry out their duty. He taught them some of his art, and they in turn shared what they knew. They were united in common cause; they were all part of the same world.

But here… here was different. Li Ming and Ghazan were supposed to be part of the jianghu, part of the same world, yet Li Ming sensed an unbridgeable gulf between them, a great wall that would never fall.

Not today, anyway.

Li Ming continued training. Saber and swordbreaker, staff and swordbreaker, drawing inspiration from the short weapon forms to express the five elements in his swordbreaker. But they were different, *too* different, for a clean translation. He had to adapt.

Orange rays streaked across the sky. Shadows melted in the growing light. The servants continued their chores. In the square, the men continued. Li Ming stepped and pounced, advanced and retreated, his feet light and quiet. Ghazan attacked, and attacked, and attacked, every step exploding like thunder, stopping only when he had reached the other end of the square, retreating only enough to make space, and attacked some more, every step powerful and audible.

At last Li Ming completed his final set. And still… there was something not *quite* right. Something off. Something he was missing…

A shadow loomed over Li Ming. Li Ming automatically swiveled towards it to find Ghazan standing a respectful distance away, the butt of the spear grounded firmly against the floor.

"You seem deep in thought," Ghazan said. "Something wrong?"

Perhaps it was his accent, a muddy river that elongated the vowels and added stops and soft vocalizations in strange places. But it sounded like a strange mix of concern concealing arrogance. Li Ming chose to respond to the former.

"I'm trying to figure out how to use a weapon," Li Ming replied.

"Which?"

"My *jian*," Li Ming said, pronouncing the word with the dipping tone.

"Your *jian*?" Ghazan asked, speaking it with the falling tone.

"No, no, *jian.*"

Li Ming articulated the last word carefully, enunciating the descending pitch and the slight rise at the end.

"What's the difference between the two?"

Li Ming held up the double-edged straight sword.

"This is the *jian* you're thinking of."

Li Ming drew his swordbreaker.

"This is the *jian* I'm referring to."

Ghazan drew closer, scrutinizing the swordbreaker.

"Your *jian* has four edges?"

"The edges aren't sharp. It's just a bar of steel with a rectangular cross-section. But the tip will puncture sheet metal."

"I've never seen a weapon like it before. How is it used?"

"I don't know."

"You don't know? Why are you using it, then?"

"I'm trying to figure it out. The swordbreaker is not part of the formal wuxingquan curriculum, but I'm hoping to adapt it to the principles of the art."

"Why didn't you choose a cold weapon you were familiar with?"

"This was the only weapon available."

"Better to fight with your bare fists than with a blade you don't know."

"I know this weapon. Back home we used it as a training tool. We ran through weapons forms with the swordbreaker to develop muscle and whole-body power. We used it loads of times. But I want to use the swordbreaker the way it was meant to be used, as a weapon, not as a weight."

"Why not use your sword forms?"

"That's what I thought too. But they don't translate well. The thrusts work. But not the slashes. With a slash you draw the edge over the target material. But the swordbreaker doesn't *have* an edge. The body mechanics aren't *quite* right."

"Your swordbreaker is a short weapon," Ghazan said, carefully enunciating the dipping tone. "Why did you take the long weapons?"

"The spear was for warm-up, to practice the body mechanics. As for the miaodao... Well, the swordbreaker may have a short 'blade', but the handle is long enough to fit two hands. I thought there was something in the miaodao form I could use."

"Your miaodao has a curved blade. Your swordbreaker is straight. Different body mechanics."

"Yes..." Li Ming shook his head. "Tricky, isn't it?"

"How is the swordbreaker supposed to be used?"

"It's an impact weapon, designed to shatter bones through armor."

"Why not use your short staff form, then?"

"I could. But the form doesn't quite translate either. Here, I'll show you."

He picked up the short staff, holding it in both hands, and executed the opening steps.

"The first few movements work well. They are single and double-handed swings and smashes. Simple enough, right? But we come to *this* move."

He pivoted through a tight arc, snapping the staff horizontally in front of him.

"This looks like a block against an overhead attack. But its hidden application is a hooking thrust, either to strike the temple or to maneuver around the opponent's guard so you can finish him with a horizontal blow. To do this, you need to grab both ends of the staff. Now if I try this with the swordbreaker..."

He dropped the staff and executed the same movement.

"As you can see, I'll have to grab the blade with my bare hands," Li Ming said.

"The edges aren't sharp. What's the problem?"

Li Ming blinked.

Blinked again.

That was true. The grip was uncomfortable, but it wasn't impossible. He would never do this with a sword. But this was a *swordbreaker*, a sword with no edge. And with the hand gripping the blade, he could convert the hooking thrust into a precise jab to the throat.

"Ah," Li Ming said.

Quickly he flowed through the rest of the form. Through the turns and the steps, the swings and the recycles, the evasions and the counters. Everything he did was a perfect mirror of the short staff form, only with a weapon with the appearance of a strange sword.

"It works," Li Ming said. "Thanks!"

Ghazan chuckled.

"You're welcome."

In that moment, the gulf between them closed. The distance was still there, his guard was still up, but now Ghazan seemed to acknowledge that Li Ming, too, was part of the same world.

"Good morning!" Cai Yan called.

She stood at the edge of the square. Behind her, her father and brother strolled to the main hall.

"Morning!" Li Ming replied.

"You've been training hard," she said, approaching the men.

"A spear left alone gathers rust," Ghazan said.

"Did you train too?" Li Ming asked.

"Yes," she said. "We train in the back courtyard in the mornings."

"I see. I would have liked to train with you."

A small smile crept across her face.

"*Wo?* Why is that?"

"It's been too long since I practiced yizhang. My spear is rusting. You practice yizhang, don't you?"

"Only a little bit."

"I saw you sparring during the test. Your 'little bit' went a long way. And you can't train a two-man set alone."

"I'm sure some of our biaohang study yizhang."

"The only one I know *now* is in front of me."

"Are you actually asking me to train with you?"

"We have to keep our skills sharp, yes?"

She smiled, her face flushing.

"We open for business soon."

"Plenty of time, right?"

She looked over her shoulder. Cai Mengyang was nowhere in sight, but the lights flicked on in the main hall. Cai Yong crossed his arms and grinned at his twin.

"I guess I could spare a few minutes," she said.

Li Ming slapped his palm over his fist.

"Thank you for the lesson, Cai *shijie.*"

She laughed. "You! You're impossible!"

Ghazan looked away, his shoulders quaking, covering his mouth with his hand.

Li Ming and Cai Yan faced each other in the middle of the square. As one, they flowed into their guard. Standing obliquely to each other, they crossed their arms over their torsos, right arm over the dantian, left over the chest, palms loose and open, knees bent just so, bodies turned to face each other.

"What shall we do?" Cai Yan asked.

"The first two-man set. You ready?"

"Let's go."

They circled around each other, planets orbiting an unseen star, first going clockwise, then smoothly pivoting around and walking anticlockwise. This was circle walking, the foundational exercise of the art. Within circle walking were many of its key principles. In this form, it had a hidden application, of stealthily closing the gap.

Closer and closer they approached, their feet cutting through subtle angles, the circle becoming an ever-narrowing spiral. Their fingertips brushed against each other. Their wrists touched. Their forearms clung to each other.

And they flowed.

Forearms and palms, kicks and knees, snatches and deflections, grabs and releases, they were in constant motion, always changing, always moving. Circle steps became linear drives became sideways shuffles. Attack became defense became counterattack.

Li Ming had practiced this form many times. But this was different. When crossing hands with other martial cultivators, every contact was an eruption of qi. An explosion of energies that demanded a response, one that defended against the attack that could be seen and the one that could only be felt.

Here, with Cai Yan, there was none of that. She was steel wrapped in silk, transforming to cloud and rain at the slightest touch. She came with total commitment, but when they touched, she melted away, leaving only the faintest impression behind. He chased her shadow, but she was gone when he arrived. She snatched at him, and when he hooked her away she borrowed his energy to dissolve into the air. When he responded, her arms met his, and for a moment he felt something strange, something like a sword sheathed in a swirling stream, and she was gone and he was somewhere else.

Too soon, far too soon, the set ended, and once again they found themselves facing each other, now having swapped their starting points.

"Next set?" Li Ming asked.

"Sure."

Where the first set was broad and expansive, this one was tight and close. So close he could smell her, sweetness laced with sweat, so close their breaths intermingled. No more circle stepping. In its place were sudden shifts in vectors and directions, the true application of combative footwork. They went high and low, striking and grabbing, melting into each other's energies.

As they moved, Li Ming caught movement in his peripheral vision. Faces known and unfamiliar at the edge of the square. Eyes trained on them. His ears picked up soft whispers.

But she was completely, totally, focused on him. Her eyes were wide open, bright like bonfires, looking past him to the side, keeping him in his peripheral vision. Even so, her body reacted to his, meeting the forces he sent out, directing force at the openings he exposed.

The set ended. But they didn't stop. They simply moved on to the next set, and the next, flowing with the energies. Qi flowed into their bodies, gathering in their bellies, shooting out their fingers and feet. The air grew thick and heavy, their movements drawing in the qi of the heavens and the earth, the qi that fueled their next step, and the next, and the next.

She was soft, he was hard. She erupted from stillness, he settled into movement. She twisted around, he went straight in. She stepped in, he slipped away. There was no offense, no defense, for every movement combined both. They were in a constant state of flux, smoothly changing from posture to posture, technique to technique, vector to vector, making a thousand different alterations every moment to meet the other's physique and temperament and tempo, changing and changing and changing again, melding and merging into a unified whole.

They danced.

In that dance Li Ming felt himself slipping away. There was no him, no here, only the movements and the steps, following a choreography charted by masters long gone, a continuation of their centuries-long legacy, an expression of the higher and deeper and subtle and profound principles those unknown sages had captured in motion, a manifestation of yin and yang and the infinite and the supreme.

And just like that, they spiraled away from each other, now back at their starting points, back in their original postures.

For a long moment, they looked at each, breathing and saying nothing. He had ten thousand things to say to her. None of them could be spoken. They had already been expressed in the sets. All he could do was stand and breathe, and drink in the sight of her, palms outstretched, body twisted, hair loose, as serene as a Pusa.

"You two done flirting yet?"

And just like that, the magic was gone.

"We've got a job," Cai Yong continued. "Be in the main hall in two *ke*."

The words yanked Li Ming back into the real world. Now in his peripheral vision, he saw men streaming into the main hall. His fellow escorts, all of them strangers to him. Ghazan slipped in among them. Cai Yong waited nearby, an amused expression on his face.

Li Ming swiveled around, bringing his feet together, cupping his fist over his heart.

"Thank you for training with me."

Cai Yan smiled, and flowed into a mirror of his salute.

"Thank you."

"We should do this more often."

Her eyebrow raised.

"Was that an invitation?"

His lips twitched into a crooked smirk.

"Do you want it to be?"

She laughed.

"I might just take you up on it."

Chapter Twelve

Borrowed Glory

In the team room, six biaohang sat around the table. Li Ming, Ghazan, four more. The veterans studied Li Ming with the eyes of tigers, scrutinizing every *cun* of his appearance. Li Ming acknowledged their gaze with a brief nod, firm and respectful, confident but non-challenging.

They looked like civilians. One man wore a loose jacket and casual jeans. A second matched a dark long-sleeved shirt with work pants. The other two had off-the-rack officewear. They wore their hair long and styled, either clean-shaven or with neatly groomed beards, the hairstyles of civilians the world over. They matched their clothes with watches, phones, bags, smartglasses, every accessory the white-collar warrior needed.

But for their auras, they could have passed for civilians.

Their qi flooded the room. It was like sitting in a hot spring, in a river, in a furnace, all at the same time. The energies swirled and crackled about, jockeying for space and supremacy, before settling into an uneasy peace.

Underneath their clothes, Li Ming made out their muscles. Thick necks, broad shoulders, massive biceps and forearms, huge calves and thighs. Their clothes emphasized their lines while hiding the swell of their muscles. But there was no concealing the way they moved and lounged with ease.

They were all watching him. Judging him. Holding him to their standards. He might have won their approval during testing, but that was the past. Respect had to be earned every day. In the face of such pressure, there was only one thing he could do.

Exceed the standards.

"This job is a close protection detail," Boss Cai said. "Low risk, no known threats, but the client is a celebrity, and you know how fame attracts weird people."

"Who's the client?" Ghazan asked.

"You might recognize the name. Dong Hai."

A ripple passed through the room. The veterans exchanged a knowing glance. Ghazan's face tightened.

Li Ming blinked.

"Who is he?" Li Ming asked.

"You don't *know* him?"

That was Jiang Long, the man in the jacket, the oldest-looking cultivator in the room.

"Never heard of him," Li Ming said.

"Unbelievable..."

"Go easy on the new guy," the biaohang next to him said. "This is his second day in the jianghu."

Song Huizhong was the most relaxed among the veterans, sprawled all over his chair. He had gone for an outdoors look, the look of a construction worker, a contractor, a man who worked heavily with his hands—though his hands were strangely smooth and delicate.

"Who is Dong Hai?" Li Ming asked.

"Professional fighter signed with the Supreme Martial Immortal Championship," Boss Cai said. "This week, he is coming to Bao An to make his shot at the world super heavyweight championship."

"I think I saw an ad for that," Li Ming said.

Jiang Long laughed.

"You think? Dong Hai is one of the biggest names in the Supreme Martial Immortal Championship. He has a perfect record of fifteen-zero, winning twelve fights by knock-out, six of those in the first round. He's widely tipped to be the next champion."

"Our job is to make sure he can fight in peace," Boss Cai continued. "Mr. Dong and his retinue will fly into Bao An on the afternoon of Geng-Day. We will meet them at the airport and escort them to the Bao An Theater House for the pre-fight conference. After that, we will take them back to the hotel.

"On Xin-Day, Mr. Dong will hold a meet-and-greet with his fans in the afternoon and have dinner with his closest supporters and sponsors. The following day, he will make final preparations for the fight. Fight night is on Gui-Day. After the fight, Mr. Dong will take a day to rest and recover. He will fly back home on the morning of Yi-Day.

"This is a ten-day contract, starting today. Standard rates. We'll have four days to prepare for his arrival. Any questions so far?"

"He's a fighter, right?" Li Ming said. "What happens if he's hospitalized?"

"That's never happened before," Jiang Long said.

"If it does, we'll renegotiate with his agent," Boss Cai said. "The last time we escorted a fighter who was hospitalized after a fight, we signed a contract to protect him while he was recuperating. Six weeks of easy money."

"I remember that one," Song Huizhong said. "Easy but boring. We just stood outside his room all day and kept an eye on the doctors."

"Is his itinerary confirmed?" Ghazan asked.

"That's the itinerary the agent gave us. But expect it to be fluid. On his rest and recovery day, he might go on a tour of the city."

A sour note crept into Ghazan's voice. "Do we have to play tour guides?"

"We could hire one and focus on protecting him," Boss Cai said. "But be prepared to show the client around the city if we can't get a guide."

"We should charge extra for such services."

"What the client wants, the client gets," Jiang Long said.

"Team assignments," Boss Cai said. "Jiang Long, you are the detail leader. Among all of us, you know the most about the professional fight circuit. We're counting on you to liaise with the client and his party."

Jiang Long swelled up. His eyes sparkled.

"No problem, boss."

"Huizhong, you're the second in command."

"Roger that," Song Huizhong said.

"Kang Brothers, you're in charge of the vehicles, as usual," Cai said.

"Understood," the older of the two suited men said.

"Ga San, you're the advance party."

Ghazan nodded mutely.

"Li Ming, you're the body man."

Song Huizhong grinned.

"Little Brother, you've got the best role."

Li Ming didn't think so. The most traditional of bodyguard positions, the body man's role was to shadow the client everywhere he went. If something went wrong, the body man's sole task was to get the client to safety.

And, if necessary, shield him with his own body.

"I'll do my best," Li Ming said.

"Come on, show some excitement, why don't you? People spend their entire lives wishing for a chance to get close to a fighter like Dong Hai. You get *paid* to do it," Song Huizhong said.

"I'm just not into combat sports."

Everyone in the room slunk away from Li Ming, frowns creeping across their faces. Even Ghazan looked away.

"*En?*" Li Ming muttered.

Song Huizhong clapped his arm around Li Ming's shoulder.

"Little Brother, you don't know what you're missing out. Combat athletes like Dong Hai are the pride of the jianghu. They are the face of the profession. *Everybody* looks up to them. Everybody wants to be them."

Li Ming glitched. His heart demanded he say something in response. His brain agreed. But somewhere between the realm of ideas and the realm of words, his answer was lost in translation.

"If you're done with the horseplay," Boss Cai said, "you've got a job to plan."

"Okay..." Song Huizhong said, suddenly sobering up. "Little Brother, before we get into the thick of things, there's something you need to know about Dong Hai."

"What is it?" Li Ming asked.

"Dong Hai is... intense. Don't let it get to you. It's an image he cultivates for his fans. No matter what happens, stay cool. Focus on solving problems, not on proving whose ego is bigger. You'll have enough to take care of as it is."

"Roger," Li Ming said. "Thanks."

The elder Kang smirked.

"Little Brother knows his manners! We'll make a biaohang out of him yet!"

Li Ming expected it. The old birds always picked on the new guy. They were testing him, probing him, seeing how he would respond to stress and provocations. Losing his temper would only cause them to lose their faith in him. There was only one right response here.

"Let's get to work," he said.

The next four days passed in a blur.

There was so much to do, so much to prepare for, so many unexpected hassles to deal with, before the client came. Route reconnaissance, security sweeps, liaisons with stakeholders. Jiang Long rotated Li Ming through various duties, letting him taste different aspects of the job.

He rode with the Kang brothers through the streets of Bao An, preparing and plotting routes. He trailed Jiang Long as he coordinated with the Civil Police. He partnered with Song Huizhong to study Dong Hai's hotel, identify vulnerabilities and exits, and smooth things over with the management. He helped Ghazan prepare the ground at Bao An Coliseum.

They started work early and ended late at night. They sorted out permits and paperwork. They rehearsed actions on site, everything from escorting the client to the room to driving him around to evacuating him under fire. Through relentless pressure testing, they identified and corrected flaws in their plans. Li Ming barely had time to eat, much less rest or train or cultivate.

And just because they weren't busy enough, new problems cropped up.

Dong Hai's entourage expanded, doubling, then tripling in size. Public relations adviser, image consultant, private doctor, local fixer, friends, friends of friends, the list went on. The biaohang scrambled to persuade the hotel to make room for them all. Alternating between flattery and browbeating, Jiang Long convinced the management to shift around some guests and clear out an entire floor.

With the group came new reasons for the police to harass the biaohang. With the increased group size, the paperwork the team had submitted no longer applied. Li Ming spent hours on end filling in forms alongside Ghazan while Song Huizhong liaised with the licensing authorities.

The Kang brothers sourced for more vehicles to accommodate the enlarged group. Suddenly Li Ming found himself sharing a rented car with Ghazan. Li Ming had a driver's license, but the last time he drove was months ago, at the Nine Star training program. He had no experience driving in the streets of Bao An, and no time to prepare. The client was due the following day and they still had other business to tend to.

"I'll drive," Ghazan said. "You take care of the client."

That worked for him.

The one thing they did not have to worry about was gear. The escorts brought their own. Deep concealment rigs, specialized pistols, hidden weapons, shapers, all of them as individual as their owner.

Li Ming went with his issue kit.

The Golden Legion was a compact pistol, but not compact enough to conceal inside his waistband. At least, not without pointing the weapon uncomfortably close to a sensitive part of his anatomy. His clothes fit his frame too well for inside the waistband carry, and he didn't have oversized clothing. He resorted to mounting his holster on his right hip and hiding it under his jacket.

The gun was for emergencies. He stowed a folding knife in each of his front pants pocket and a flashlight in his waistband, and mounted his shaper on his left forearm. It wasn't the setup he liked, but it was the one he could work with.

At least until he could afford his own gear.

On Geng-Day, at the hour of the goat, the team set up at Bao An International Airport. It was a full hour before Dong Hai's arrival. Even so, a huge crowd congregated in the arrivals hall. Hundreds of people, a small army of fans, armed with signs and T-shirts splashed with Dong Hai's face and name. Clustered among them, journalists held up cameras and microphones and press passes. There were so many of them, the Airport Police set up a cordon to hold them back.

"Didn't we warn the agent not to announce the client's arrival?" Li Ming asked.

"He said he received our message," Jiang Long said. "He didn't actually agree to it."

"We need to contact the client, tell him to leave through an alternate exit."

"No point," Ghazan said. "He wants to make a grand entrance."

"We have to try."

Jiang Long punched a number into his phone. Waited. Frowned.

"Agent's phone is off. Going to try the alternates."

As Jiang Long worked the phone, Song A full hour before Dong Hai's arrival addressed Li and Ghazan.

"We've planned for this. Just stick to the plan. Stay here and monitor the crowd. I'll speak with airport security."

They had plans for every possible scenario. A mob of fans was one of them. Ghazan, his skin and hair marking him as an outsider, sat by a pillar, pretending to be a businessman waiting to meet a client flying in from overseas. Li Ming infiltrated the crowd, making his way to the front.

It was slow going. The fans were packed close to each other, leaving little room to breathe. There was an unusually large number of young women among them, many holding small children close to them. Li Ming had expected a predominantly male crowd, but he figured most of them would be working at this hour.

He slipped through gaps in the crowd, zigzagging through them, twice doubling back to pick another route. He was a ghost, his presence unseen, unfelt, unnoticed. The crowd's qi field trembled with anticipation, growing larger and denser with every passing ke. People whispered among themselves, escaped into their screens, yammered into phones. Li Ming drew his qi into himself, condensing into an impenetrable outer layer, sealing off his essence from the outside world. He was a moving void, a part of yet apart from the crowd, noticeable only by his absence of presence.

The crowd was thickest at the front. A veritable wall of living flesh, pressed tightly together, converging on the exit. A line of eight Airport Police officers stood fast before them, keeping them back by sheer presence. Behind the cops, travelers streamed out the arrivals hall, wide-eyed and gaping at the gathering mob.

Li Ming couldn't break through them. Not without going hands on. Instead, he hovered just behind the front lines, locking eyes with the Airport Police one by one. Equipped with smartglasses, their facial recognition cameras would pick his face out of this crowd and identify him as one of Dong Hai's bodyguards.

If the paperwork had been processed correctly.

If the bureaucrats had deigned to inform the field officers.

If the cameras worked as advertised.

So many ifs.

Jiang Long's voice filtered into Li Ming's earpiece.

"The crowd is growing larger behind you. Huizhong and I are going in. Ghazan, maintain situational awareness."

Li Ming touched his wrist to his leg, felt the hard plastic of his push-to-talk switch, and clicked it twice.

The chatter grew louder. Individual conversations blurred into background babble. The fans shifted about, surging their way forward and to the sides. The Airport Police spread out, and summoned backup to help manage the crowd. Through it all, Li Ming kept one eye on the crowd, another on the exit.

"Client has disembarked the plane and is now going through Immigration," Jiang Long said.

"Any way we can convince him to leave through an alternative exit?" Song Huizhong asked.

"He insisted on meeting his fans. And he'll meet us with them too."

"He wants to do the linkup in front of the world? Is he joking?"

"Dead serious." Jiang Long sighed. "We'll have to roll with it."

Li Ming sensed a disturbance in the crowd. Glancing to his right, he saw Jiang Long make his way forward, positioning himself next to Li Ming.

"You nervous?" Jiang Long asked.

"I don't like it when things don't go according to plan."

"Me neither. Just follow my lead and we'll be fine."

Civilians scurried out the hall. The cops shifted from side to side. Their supervisor whispered into his radio. The crowd stirred. A large group of men, and a few women, approached the door. At their head was—

"Dong Gong! It's Dong Gong!"

Dong 'the Duke' Hai swaggered through the entrance.

"DONG GONG! DONG GONG! DONG GONG!"

The screams drowned out all thought. Li Ming's earpiece blocked out the noise, saving half his hearing. He crammed his finger into his other ear, wincing at the pain.

Note to self: buy earplugs.

Dong Hai had *presence*. He was huge, towering over everyone around him. His suit strained at the seams, barely containing his enormous muscles. He'd left his collar undone, showing off a gargantuan neck. His bald pate gleamed into afternoon light. With furious blinks and eye gestures, Li Ming activated his qi assessment app.

Qi score: 23134.

A stupendously high qi score. A score possible only through decades of focused training and a strict regimen of supplements. A score worthy of a champion.

Smiling, Dong Hai punched his palm in front of his swollen chest. His qi roared like a typhoon, washing over Li Ming, demanding attention and recognition.

"Dong Gong has arrived!" he boomed.

The crowd erupted in cheers.

"Let's go," Jiang Long said.

Jiang Long waved with his right hand. With his left, he discreetly lifted his biaohang card from his breast pocket. The police supervisor nodded and gestured at his subordinates. A small gap opened in the police line, allowing Jiang Long and Li Ming through.

"Mr. Dong!" Jiang Long shouted, extending his arm. "Long from the agency!"

Dong Hai keyed on Jiang Long. On Li Ming. Smiled. And shook Jiang Long's hand.

"Pleasure to meet you! Who's your friend?"

Li Ming held out his hand.

"Lin! I'm your close escort!"

Once on the job, the men used operational aliases. It was too easy for an enemy, or a potential threat, to track down a biaohang who worked under his real name.

Dong Hai gripped.

And squeezed.

Li Ming's fingers buckled. His nerves screamed. His muscles folded. Li Ming surged qi through his body, reinforcing his hand, squeezing back with every last bit of strength he could muster.

It wasn't enough.

Bombs exploded in his knuckles. His palm threatened to give out. Blood pulsed through constricted veins.

Li Ming held firm, still squeezing, and pumped his captured hand once. With the other, he gently tapped Dong Hai's hand.

Dong Hai grinned.

And released.

"Looking forward to working with you," Dong Hai said.

"Me too," Li Ming said.

His hand throbbed. Pain crackled through his bones. Li Ming held his hands in front of him, left over right, and poured qi into his hand. The energy reinvigorated abused tissue and sinews, soothed aching nerves, kickstarted the healing process.

It still hurt. Just less.

Dong Hai worked the crowd, grinning and waving, issuing greetings and thanks. His entourage walked in his wake, basking in borrowed glory. The journalists swarmed all around, angling for better shots. The Airport Police interposed themselves between Dong Hai and the crowd, moving along with him.

Jiang Long softly tapped Dong's hand, subtly guiding him to the elevators. Li Ming kept his face away from the cameras as best as he could. Song Huizhong floated among the sea of faces, keeping pace with the group.

Ghazan reappeared at the elevators. Two more cops stood beside him. Together they formed a security screen, blocking off access. As Jiang Long called the lift, Dong Hai waved one last time to the crowd.

"Thank you all for coming!" he shouted. "See you on fight night!"

The crowd cheered. A few fans pressed forward. The Airport Police held firm, pushing them back.

"That's enough!"

"Don't cross this line!"

"Let Mr. Dong through!"

The elevator doors opened. Ghazan entered. Dong Hai and half his entourage flowed in. Li Ming, the last man in, closed the door.

And a blissful silence fell on the world.

Li Ming heaved a quiet sigh of relief.

"Drivers, we're coming down," Li Ming whispered.

"Roger," the younger Kang said.

The elevator left them out at the basement parking lot. The younger Kang was waiting for them. A short walk away, the elder Kang watched over the cars.

The protectors hustled their charges inside the vehicles. Ghazan, Li Ming and Dong Hai had a car all to themselves. Dong Hai sprawled all over the back seat. Li Ming squashed himself in next to his bulk.

"Looking forward to the fight?" Dong Hai asked.

"Yes," Ghazan said.

Li Ming blinked.

"You a fan of combat sports?" Dong Hai asked.

"I enjoy everything to do with martial arts and cultivation."

Dong Hai laughed.

"A healthy attitude. You're a Yue, aren't you?"

"Yes."

"You've learned the Yue *wushu* too?"

"Shifangquan."

"A powerful style. People say it's the art that subdued Xiazhou. I fought a few fighters who used it. Beat them all."

Ghazan bristled. His qi became a field of spikes.

"That's why everyone says you'll be the next world champion," Li Ming said.

"I *am* the champion. The world just doesn't know it yet," Dong Hai said.

Irritation gnawed at Li Ming's heart. With a breath, he let it go.

"Lin, you practice *wushu* too?"

"A little bit," Li Ming replied.

"Yes? What style?"

"Wuxingquan, mostly."

"Ah, wuxingquan. You know, my first pro fight was against a wuxingquan player. On the opening bell, he threw a straight punch, you call it the Beng Quan. I slipped it and uppercut him in the chin. Perfect counter. He went down right there and then. Fastest knockout in my career. Didn't even need magic."

"Impressive."

"I've fought... seven wuxingquan fighters in my career. None of the fights lasted longer than a round. Four of them didn't even last a minute." He sniffed. "How old are you?"

"Twenty-one."

"A good age. If I were you, I'd switch to another style. Plenty of time to learn something useful."

How many people have you killed with your *style?*

Raw fury rushed through Li Ming. His fists clenched. Then he reminded himself that he was on the job. This job was not about him. It was *never* about him.

Dong Hai didn't notice. He turned to Ghazan.

"What's your name?"

"Gengji."

"Interesting name. How many years did you study shifangquan?"

"Twenty years."

"And you're how old?"

"Twenty-eight."

"*Wa...* That takes a lot of dedication. Don't go rising up to conquer Xiazhou again, you hear?"

Red rage blasted through Ghazan's aura, a pillar of flame so hot and intense Li Ming saw a flash of scarlet before his eyes.

Dong Hai didn't notice. He was busy looking out the window.

"The rest of the guys are here. Finally."

Six days, Li Ming reminded himself. *Just six days of this and I'll never see him again.*

Chapter Thirteen

Beast Without Shame

In the world of the jianghu, in the combat sport circuit that defined the rivers and lakes for the people in the world of mortals, the Supreme Martial Immortal Championship was its undisputed ruler. The most famous entertainment company to emerge from the forest of warriors, anything it wanted, it got.

Cities and nations competed to secure hosting rights. Megacorporations climbed all over each other to land sponsorships and advertising slots. With a single word, the company could commandeer any location anywhere in Xiazhou to promote its events.

Today, for the Bao An Brawl, it chose one of the city's most iconic landmarks: the Bao An Theater House.

The oldest theater in the city, it hosted weekly performances, specializing in classical operas. Several times a year, it hosted full *xiqu* performances, lasting for two, three, even four evenings. Music, song and dance, acrobatics, martial arts and drama were the key ingredients of *xiqu*. Today, it was being rigged up for a performance of a vastly different—yet uncannily similar—kind.

Technicians bustled about, arranging lights and audio systems, cameras and furniture. On the main stage, they set up a huge screen. Li saw dozens of logos, the logos of the sponsors that made this fight possible, caught in between the faces of the main fighters. Long tables stood in front of the screen. Place cards marked out the seats of every fighter, shouting their names and social media handles. Next to every card was a bottle of mineral water and a can of energy drink, their logos turned out to face the cameras.

The technicians set down a podium in between and ahead of the tables, emblazoned with the names and faces of the main fighters, the words 'Bao An Brawl', and the date of the fight. And a reminder that it was on pay-per-view.

A sea of chairs faced the screen, rapidly filling up. Journalists occupied the front ranks, wearing their press passes prominently around their necks. Fans piled into the rear seats, dividing themselves into tribes.

The lights went out. Music played, a high-energy track with booming drums and electronic beats. A video played on the screen. Two fighters standing in a ring, the referee between them, the camera zooming in on one man.

"Declaring the winner by submission, Iron Body Qiong!"

On the screen, the current champion pumped his fist into the air.

The rest of the video was a highlight reel, showing off the accomplishments of the men on the main card. Punishing combos, spectacular strikes, victory after victory. The segment closed with a short statement from either fighter.

"Two men enter the ring, one man leaves on his feet," Dong Hai said. "I'm going to be that man. I'm going to bury him."

"He wants a shot at the championship, he's welcome to try," Qiong Wu Xiu Er said. "But everyone knows that my iron body is unbreakable."

The video ended. Lights flashed back on. From stage left, the President of the Supreme Martial Immortal Championship, Bai Zhihao, strode to the podium. He was once a boxer, and he still carried himself like one, a solid mass of muscle gliding through space.

"Good afternoon everybody!" Bai Zhihao called. "Thank you for waiting. Taiwuxian 381, the Bao An Brawl, takes place in four days. How excited are you for the fight?"

The fans cheered, whistling and yelling and clapping.

"That's not excitement. You can do better than that!"

As one, the crowd roared, filling the house with vocal thunder.

"All right! I hear you! The world hears you! In four days, at Bao An Coliseum, we will see the most exciting match-up of this season. Dong Hai versus Qiong Wu Xiu Er!"

The fans shouted in glee.

"Ladies and gentlemen, Duke Dong!"

The challenger strutted up on the stage. Men and women screamed his name. Waving and smiling at his fans, Dong Hai took his place at his table.

"Iron Body Qiong!"

The reigning champion took to the stage, hoisting his three championship belts high. Though he was a foreigner, the home crowd showered him in adoration. The applause, the cheers, the heat and the noise, everything doubled and redoubled, drowning out Dong Hai's fans. A murderous glare flashed across Dong Hai's face, quickly settling into a scowl.

"*TAIWUXIAN! TAIWUXIAN! TAIWUXIAN!*" the fans chanted.

Iron Body Qiong saluted his fans and took his seat. When the crowd finally went silent, Bai Zhihao introduced the other fighters on the undercard. Three pairs of men of lesser renown. This time the applause was restrained, polite, just enough for courtesy.

"We're ready to take questions," Bai Zhihao announced. "Who wants to go first?"

A journalist shot to his feet.

"How do you expect the fight to play out?"

Dong Hao snatched up the mic.

"People say Qiong-mou has an iron body, but I know he's got a glass chin. I've watched his fight vids, I've seen him stagger many, many times. His chin is as poor as his name. One good punch and he'll be down for the count, I guarantee it."

Iron Body Qiong smirked.

"You see that?" Dong Hai continued. "He thinks he can beat me. He thinks he can take my shots on his iron body. Not so fast, poor man. I'm going to blow you away. I can even tell the whole world how I'm going to do it, and you won't be able to do anything about it."

Iron Body Qiong leaned into his mic.

"Duke Dong sure likes to punch a lot. I worry about the state of his hands when I'm done with him."

"You can just stand there and eat my punches if you like," Dong Hai retorted.

The fans laughed. Even Iron Body Qiong smiled.

"Dong Hai can't go the distance. He doesn't have the heart. He'll wear himself down, he'll leave himself exposed, he'll give me everything I need to take him down."

"Oh yes? You say I don't have the heart?"

Dong Hai lifted his can of energy drink from the table, dramatically popped it, and slugged down a long pull.

"I've got the best team in the world in my corner. I've been training for years for this. With my team, and with Yellow Dragon, I can fight this war to the finish. You want to go the distance with me? Bring it!"

Dong Hai slammed the can back down, showing the logo, a golden grinning dragon, to the cameras.

Off in his corner, Li Ming laughed into a sleeve. Ghazan shook, his face contorting, trying to hold himself back.

"I heard of product placement in tournaments, but this is ridiculous!" Li Ming exclaimed.

"It's all show business," Jiang Long said.

The questions followed a similar cycle. Someone asked a question. Duke Dong said something inflammatory. Iron Body Qiong smiled and responded neutrally. Duke Dong launched a fiery retort. They were psyching each other out, putting up a show for the fans, hyping up the rivalry and the pending battle.

Li Ming wondered how much heat there was in Dong Hai's words. He was aggressive and boorish, no doubt about it. But the headline fighters would earn a cut from the fight's total earnings, above and beyond their purse. The greater the drama, the more eyeballs they could pull, the more money they would make.

The undercard fighters, in contrast, were calm, composed, even laughing at the headliners' antics. Their payouts came from the fight purse, plus a victory bonus to the winners. They weren't paid for pulling in viewers. They could relax and field questions without worrying about their image.

The questions came fast and furious. Impressions about the other fighters. Comments on their training regimens. Contracts and earnings. Sponsorship deals. Every time Duke Dong found a way to needle Iron Body Qiong, bolster his own image or promote a product, often two or three at the same time.

Four ke later, Bai Zhihao brought the conference to a close. Scantily-clad ring girls took to the stage, escorting the fighters to the podium. Both men faced each other, Duke Dong sneering down his nose at Iron Body Qiong, fists clenched. Bai Zhihao interposed himself between both men, arms on their shoulders. The journalists rushed in, cameras at the ready.

"Get ready," Jiang Long said. "This might get wild."

The air crackled. Red-hot qi rolled off Duke Dong, smothering Iron Body Qiong. Iron Body Qiong's own qi wrapped protectively around himself like a shell, shedding the enormous energy wave. Caught in the backwash, Li Ming felt like he had a front row seat to a volcanic eruption.

"You're a midget," Duke Dong said. "You're too short for this fight. You can't even reach me."

"This close, I'm tall enough to reach your face," Iron Body Qiong replied.

Quick as a snake, Iron Body Qiong's hand darted out, lightly tapping Duke Dong's enormous nose.

"You dare?! YOU DARE?!" Duke Dong blustered.

And seized Iron Body Qiong's collar.

"Go!" Jiang Long called.

Li leapt on the stage and sprinted over. Iron Body Qiong peeled off the hand and rammed a forearm against Duke Dong's chest. Duke Dong snapped his head forward, just barely missing Iron Body Qiong's skull. Iron Body Qiong's own bodyguards jumped in. Duke Dong grabbed for Iron Body Qiong's head. Bai Zhihao wedged himself between the men. Li Ming moved to Duke Dong's side, wrapped his arm around his massive trunk, and pulled.

He might as well try to move a mountain.

"That's enough!" Bai Zhihao shouted.

Duke Dong growled, lashing out. Ghazan grabbed Duke Dong's shoulders, pulling him aside.

"Stop it! Save it for the ring!" Bai Zhihao yelled.

Li Ming torqued, twisted, stepped, trying to find an angle of attack, a point of weakness, something he could use. But Duke Dong was good. He was rooted deep, shifting and twisting his body, standing firm against Li Ming and Ghazan.

The undercard fighters joined in, pinning the fighters' arms, keeping them from touching each other. They huffed and strained too, but Duke Dong was as unshakable as ever.

"Break it up!" Bai Zhihao ordered.

At last Li Ming felt an opening, a sudden void in Duke Dong's stance. Li Ming pushed into it. Duke Dong shuffled back, ever so slightly.

And relented.

The fighters stepped away from each other. Dong Hai and Qiong Wu Xiu Er now stood side by side, the undercard fighters forming a line beside them. As one, they struck up fighting stances.

"*Taiwuxian! Taiwuxian! Taiwuxian!*" the crowd chanted.

Cameras flashed. Fans cheered. The bodyguards retreated.

The fighters stood there for half a minute. Long enough for everyone to take their photos. Then they saluted the crowd and left the stage.

"What a farce," Li Ming muttered.

"They are showmen," Ghazan said. "We are biaohang."

Dong Hai was disciplined. Li Ming could give him that much.

He stuck to the plan religiously. Once he arrived at the Jing An Hotel, he locked himself down in the Presidential suite. The largest suite available, it boasted two bedrooms, a grand dining room, a spacious living room. The second he settled down, he changed into exercise gear and went to work.

He warmed up by practicing his moves and combos under the watchful eye of his coach. He went smooth but slow, working on perfecting his body mechanics. When they were satisfied, the coach broke out striking pads. Dong Hai went hard, striking the pads with full force, throwing punches and palms, forearms and elbows, knees and kicks. Every impact was a bomb blast, rocking the coach back.

They went for a full hour, taking short breaks to sip water. If anything the coach needed more rest time than Dong, kneading his battered arms and legs. At the end of the session, Dong Hai seemed full of vigor, as fresh as he had started.

After a shower, he sat down for a room service dinner. Pork chops with baked potatoes and a healthy dose of vegetables. He ate like a wolf, barely pausing to chew.

He passed the evening hours studying fight footage of his rival and discussing fight strategy with his coach. Li Ming stood in a corner, listening to it all, taking copious notes. It was a masterclass in high-level martial arts. Timing, angles, footwork, magic, body mechanics, opportunities for counters, identifying tells, a ruthless frame-by-frame dissection of the current champion, putting them all together to construct a master plan to take him out.

Before bed, Dong Hai enjoyed a light snack. A banana, a serving of nuts, and a bottle of beast essence.

In cultivator circles, beast essence was an essential elixir. Composed of beasts processed under high pressure and mixed with herbs, regular consumption boosted energy levels, improved focus, and strengthened the body. Top-tier martial cultivators considered it as important as food and water. Companies spent decades and billions researching and developing the optimal mix of beasts, herbs and manufacturing methods to generate specific effects.

The Special Military Police issued a daily ration of one bottle a day. From the lowest bidder, of course. It was so generic it didn't even have a brand name. Dong Hai had chosen

Cinnabar Mountain, one of the oldest and most prestigious brands in the field—with a price to match. In his time, Li Ming savored every sip of beast essence. Here, Dong Hai gulped down the black broth like water, downing the small bottle in one go.

The following morning, Dong Hai awoke at the fourth hour. For the first half-hour, he did nothing but qigong, flowing through a staggering array of postures and movements. Slow and deliberate, he resembled a glacier in motion, titanic and unstoppable, effortless and inevitable. His qi field pulsed a solid red, washing out the living room. For the second half, he ran thousands of laps around the suite at a rapid pace, clocking up ten *li*. At the end of it, he was coated in sweat, but the only sign of fatigue was some heavy breathing.

"Why don't you train in the hotel gym?" Li Ming asked.

"No outsiders get to see me train," Dong Hai said. "Too many spies in the circuit. You're lucky you get a chance to watch."

After catching his breath, he sat down for his first meal. A bowl of oatmeal and chopped bananas, soaked in milk, flavored with honey and cinnamon. He ate slowly, savoring every bite. He relaxed for a while, watching the television, chatting with his friends, reading on an old-fashioned smartphone.

At the sixth hour, he exploded into motion. Bodyweight exercises, hundreds, *thousands*, of reps. He began with familiar exercises, push-ups and squats and tuck jumps, then proceeded to complex movements so exotic Li Ming had no names for them. In between sets, he rested for a mere minute; in between exercises, he paused just long enough to gulp down water.

When the hour of the horse arrived, he retired for a long, long bath. He returned just in time for a room service lunch. Chicken breasts, roasted yams, sprinkled nuts, another banana.

After the meal he gulped down a dozen supplement pills, washing them down with a bottle of beast essence. The potent cocktail would strengthen his qi, accelerate recovery times, enhance cognition, repair muscle and cartilage and bone.

Li marveled at the sight. That was a thousand yuan gone, just like that. An unobtainable commodity for a nobody like him. An essential for a high-level fighter like Dong Hai.

Dong Hai rested some more, sipping on pomegranate juice. His friends trooped in, all of them carrying duffel bags. Lounging about the living room, they chatted about current affairs, the weather, financial instruments, movies, a dizzying range of subjects covering everything but the coming fight.

The hour of the goat approached. The coach clapped his hands. All chatter ceased. Dong Hai stripped down to a pair of boxers. He had the body of a fighter, not a showman, a stout torso shielded by heavy muscles and fat. His pecs were granite, his lats were like bat wings, but his abs were smooth.

He warmed up in a corner, stretching and hopping and bouncing, throwing punches and kicks. His friends changed, donning helmets and mouth guards, groin guards and body protectors. They warmed up by themselves and cleared the furniture, leaving Dong Hai to shadowbox in a corner.

At last Dong Hai donned his own protective gear and gave his coach a thumbs-up. On cue, the friends backed off into a corner. One of them stepped up, clenching and unclenching his fists. Dong Hai met him in the middle of the living room.

The coach held out a fist.

"*Li!*"

The fighters saluted, right fist punching into their left palms.

The coach extended his arms.

"Begin!"

Dong Hai stepped in with a long jab. His partner covered up, taking the shot on a meaty forearm. Dong Hai crashed in, punching and punching and punching, his partner danced away, shedding the blows as he went. Dong Hai relaxed for a second to catch his breath, and the other fighter snapped a kick at his groin. Dong Hai blocked it just in time and crashed in with renewed strength.

It was sparring. But it was a few degrees shy of full-on fighting. Iron Body Qiong was renowned for his defensive skills and endurance, his footwork and his kicks, and Dong Hai's partner mimicked his fighting style. Dong Hai in turn worked his fight strategy, hiding feints among his storm of blows, striking whenever his partner fell for a fake.

Out came the magic. Glowing white gauntlets appeared around Dong's fists, reinforcing his blows. His partner's armor turned gray, reinforced with metal qi. Blasts of sound and white light thundered around the fighters. Both men sucked down qi, accelerating their moves, strengthening muscles and sinews, hardening their bones and armor.

The Supreme Martial Cultivator Championship prided itself on its minimalistic rules. No lethal or crippling attacks. No tearing up the environment. No weapons. Everything else was fair game. The fighters used special shapers calibrated for combat sports. They allowed the wearers to draw qi into their bodies with full power, but project only a small amount out into the world.

Even so, a fighter's fists were deadly weapons.

After three minutes, the coach ended the first round. Dong Hai retreated to a corner to drink and rest. The next friend stepped up, psyching up for the round, checking the straps on his gear. After a minute of rest, the fight began anew.

Sparring continued in this fashion. Dong Hai fought a new challenger every round. His friends changed their tactics, simulating different plans the champion might use while sticking to his strengths. Dong Hai's partners were good, but he was the best. They fought when they were fresh, Dong Hai rested on a little between rounds, but still he dominated them all.

They went the distance. Ten rounds. A full title match from start to finish. Dong Hai started strong, he finished even stronger. No matter what Iron Body Qiong could throw at him, Dong Hai was ready.

Li Ming was amazed. He had no idea a human could withstand such punishment. True, Dong Hai was a martial cultivator, but even cultivators had limits. Or so Li Ming had thought. Dong Hai was drenched in sweat, his breathing was ragged, but he held himself like a warrior-king fresh from the battlefield. He showed no sign of pain, if he indeed felt pain at all.

Dong Hai went off to take another shower. His friends returned to their rooms. When he stepped out, room service had another meal waiting. A bowl of fish and egg porridge.

The moment he finished his meal, they departed for another hotel. The Bamboo House, the newest and trendiest five-star hotel in the city. Designed by one of the world's most famous architects, it was a fifty-story column, boasting outdoor gardens every ten floors, its lines clean and organic. A hotel fit for a champion.

"Someday, I'm going to live in a place just like this," Dong Hai vowed.

Li Ming didn't see the point. Next to the Bamboo House, the Jing An Hotel was just a boring concrete cube. Even so, the suite was luxurious beyond Li Ming's comprehension. That room alone was larger than his home. How much more luxury can a man enjoy before he got sick of it?

Dong Hai had originally planned to stay in this hotel. The protectors had vetoed it. With a public event scheduled here, if a troublemaker wanted to find Dong Hai, he'd have a known nexus to work with. After a heated argument with the agent, Dayong laid down an ultimatum: cancel the meet and greet or find somewhere else to stay.

Dong Hai had chosen the latter. But the way he looked at hotel, it was if he were a barbarian planning his next conquest.

The hotel staff had prepared the third floor ballroom for the occasion. A single table. A chair. Two security guards. And many, many, *many* lengths of velvet rope.

The entourage showed up with half an hour to go. Even so, there was already a light crowd mingling outside the ballroom, taking advantage of the free drinks. Song Huizhong was already on site, coordinating operations with the staff.

The more observant among the crowd noticed Duke Dong's arrival. Duke Dong smiled and waved at them. At least this time they had the courtesy not to shout. Too loudly.

Li Ming and Ghazan quickly hustled Duke Dong inside the ballroom. Duke Dong sat upon his chair as though it were a throne, planting his feet squarely on the ground. He laid out a series of pens before him and plastered on a huge smile.

"I'm ready. Let's do this," Duke Dong said.

"We're still half an hour from the official start time," the agent said.

Duke Dong waved his hand. "Is there anything else to take care of?"

Everyone conferred briefly.

"Nothing else," the agent said.

"Then we shouldn't keep the fans waiting. Let them inside."

They swarmed in, winding their way through a maze of velvet rope. Duke Dong rose to his full height, letting his qi expand to fill the room, greeting them all with powerful waves and a brilliant smile. Li Ming and Ghazan stepped aside, disappearing into the celebrity's shadow.

Duke Dong worked his magic. He signed his name on books, shirts, gloves, shapers. He took photos and videos. He flexed his muscles and posed beside a never-ending stream of gorgeous women. He rolled up his sleeves, showing off his custom-made shapers, and pulled off a series of tricks. Bright flashes, thunderclaps, fireballs, electric bolts, all the parlor tricks he had tried in sparring.

"Show us the Whirling Storm!" someone shouted.

Duke Dong obliged.

He stood a distance from the table, gesturing everyone to keep aside. Gathered his qi into his body. Clenched his fists.

"*HAH!*" he shouted.

And exploded into motion.

Swinging his arms in wide circles, he took a series of long steps, then jumped off the ground and launched into a spinning kick. And again, and again, and again. Twisting and turning, he whirled across the length of the hall, kicking and kicking and kicking again, punctuating each movement with ferocious forearm and palm strikes. A loud whoosh accompanied each strike, the air itself compressing and fleeing before him.

Ghazan snorted and looked away. Li Ming forced himself to focus on the crowd, to watch for knives and guns amidst the forest of phones and cameras. It was a captivating performance, but it was only a performance.

Li Ming had heard that the most famous cultivators of the jianghu had signature techniques and forms. This was Duke Dong's, a complex routine of tornado kicks and long-range punches, making full use of his monstrous reach. Li Ming wondered why fighters like that showed off their best moves. They were giving away their tricks for free. Or maybe Duke Dong was signaling that was so confident in his prowess, he could afford to reveal his secrets.

Or maybe showmanship was just part of the game.

He repeated the form six more times, in between more signings and photos and videos. Duke Dong was indefatigable. He'd spent a full day training, and yet here he was, training even more. He ruffled his suit a little, but otherwise he showed no sign of weariness.

At last, at the hour of the dog, the agent closed the event.

"That's all for today! Thank you for coming!" the agent shouted.

The crowd began to chant.

"Dong Gong! Dong Gong! Dong Gong!"

Duke Dong raised his fist in the air.

"Thank you for your support! Stay tuned for fight night! I will be your next champion!"

The crowd went wild.

Li Ming and Ghazan hustled him through the cheering mob. People wanted to stop him, to shake his hand, to pose for more photos. Jiang Long and Song Huizhong ran interference, keeping the fans from getting too close.

The protectors brought Dong Hai up to the eighth floor. In the elevator, Dong Hai adjusted his clothing, checking himself in the mirror.

"Do I look alright?" Dong Hai asked.

"You look disheveled," the image consultant said. "Here, I'll fix your clothes."

"Come on, I'm a fighter. I should look like one."

She smoothed out his sleeves and patted down his jacket.

"You should look like a champion, not just a fighter. You need to look handsome, powerful, elegant. You're a lion in man's clothing."

She undid his collar, showing off the swell of his neck.

"There you go. Now you look like a hero."

Dong Hai puffed up his chest and lifted his chin.

The hotel restaurant treated Dong Hai with the courtesy due a duke. The head waitress personally welcomed him and led him to a private room in the back.

There was a single round table with twelve seats. Dong Hai sat down, defining the head of the table. His agent sat across him. The consultant departed, her job done. Li Ming and the bodyguards stood around and pretended to be furniture.

"One day," Dong Hai said, "I'll host my private parties in a grand setting. There'll be so many guests, so many from the elite of society, we'll have to book an entire ballroom. I'll be the world champion, and everyone will know it."

"One day, Duke Dong," the agent said. "One day."

One by one, Duke Dong's private guests trickled in. They all bore gifts, baskets of expensive elixirs and pills, everything the self-respecting martial cultivator needed to gain an edge over the competition. Li Ming recognized none of them. But they were all immortals.

The men were handsome beyond compare, the women beautiful beyond dreams. Their hand-tailored clothes fitted them perfectly, silk and wool and other designer fabrics, communicating their status without mentioning a brand. Every movement was fluid and elegant, their speech refined and courteous. Everything about them was, quite simply, perfect.

"Ladies and gentlemen," the agent said. "On behalf of Duke Dong, thank you for coming here to meet us. It has been a long and arduous journey. With your patronage, we have taken Duke Dong to the finals. We are deeply appreciative of your support.

"One more fight. One more fight, and Duke Dong will be the next Supreme Martial Cultivator. He is the most powerful and accomplished fighter of the fight season. He is an undefeated fighter with fifteen victories to his name. He has dominated the super heavyweight class for years. All this was thanks to you.

"As a token of appreciation, we invite you here to share a modest meal with us. It might not be much, but we hope you enjoy the food and drink we have selected just for you. We look forward to your continuing support.

"Now, please give a round of applause for the man of the hour, Duke Dong!"

They clapped. They cheered. They shouted praises and encouragement. Duke Dong basked in it all, standing to salute them.

The waitstaff took that as their cue to begin the dinner service. A procession of waiters and waitresses marched into the room, serving hot tea, delivering napkins, placing bottles of sauce and condiments on the central glass turntable, and at last, appetizers. A large plate stocked with spring rolls, peanuts, cold vegetables, slices of century egg.

The guests chatted as they ate, keeping their conversation focused on politics, the economy, investment opportunities. Duke Dong listened intently, chiming in on occasion, but ate only two slices of century egg.

When the last of the appetizers were gone, the waitstaff swooped in. They removed the used plates, set fresh ones, served a bowl of rice for everyone, topped off the tea.

The rest of the meal arrived in swift succession. Shark's fin soup. Spinach. Chicken. The immortals ate heartily, spinning the turntable round and round, using serving spoons to scoop generous portions. Dong, however, maintained a disciplined diet, no more than two or three mouthfuls per dish.

As dinner progressed, conversation turned to business. Sponsorship deals. Advertising. Merchandise. Endorsements. The immortals represented as astonishing array of interests: pharmaceuticals, sports equipment, reality shapers, apparel. They fawned over Duke Dong, promising opportunities to show his face, to wear their brands, to use their gear. They spoke the language Duke Dong understood best, not yuan and fen, but performance enhancement and audience growth. The agent injected himself into the conversation at key intervals, booking slots for follow-on meetings.

For dessert, the waitstaff served plates of honeydew. Now Duke Dong indulged himself, munching down an entire slice. He wrapped up his conversations and rose to his feet.

"Thank you all for coming," Duke Dong said. "I hope you've enjoyed dinner. In two days, I will put up a fight the world has never seen before. Until then, take care and stay safe. Goodnight!"

One by one, the immortals left. Duke Dong shook their hands one by one, whispering promises in their ear. The agent hung back, flitting between the guests, taking down last minute notes.

At last it was just Dong Hai and the protectors. Dong Hai inspected his gifts, studying them one by one, nodding his approval.

"Excellent," he pronounced. "Lin, carry them for me."

"Excuse me?" Li Ming said.

Dong Hai frowned.

"You heard me. Carry the baskets for me."

Li Ming shook his head.

"I can't do that."

"What do you mean, 'I can't do that'?"

"I am your biaohang. If I am to protect you, must keep my hands free at all times."

Dong Hai glared at Li Ming. His qi washed over Li Ming, filled with man-killing rage.

"Who do you think you are? I pay you! I am your boss! You will do what I say!"

Li Ming met the glare with a look of his own, neither defiant nor submissive, just a steady calmness. His heart trembled under the pressure, his blood raged, his hands readied for war.

He breathed out.

"Mr. Dong, we are your protectors, not your porters. We cannot do our jobs—"

"You dare talk to me like that? Go die! You're just a biaohang. I'm the next champion! Go to your—"

Jiang Long cut in.

"Excuse me."

A wave of water qi washed over the men. Cool and soothing, it doused Dong Hai's fire. Dong Hai blinked and turned to Jiang Long.

"What seems to be the problem?" Jiang Long asked.

Dong Hai's eyebrows furrowed.

"I asked your man to carry the gift baskets for me. He refused. Deal with him immediately."

"Mr. Dong, we happen to be in a hotel. I'm sure the bellhops will be pleased to help you carry your gifts. That should solve the problem, right?"

Dong Hai pointed a thick finger at Li Ming.

"That's not the point! I hired him to help me. He refuses to take my instructions."

"To do our jobs, we must keep our hands free at all times," Li Ming repeated.

"He is correct," Jiang Long said. "The bellhops can take care of the gifts for you."

"Correct? What do you mean 'correct'? I hired you, didn't I?"

Now Jiang Long drew himself straight, staring into and *past* Dong's gaze.

"You hired us to be your biaohang. Not your valets."

"You too?! You are all—"

The agent hurried over.

"Dong Gong, it's been a long day, hasn't it? We should go back to the hotel and rest."

Dong Hai frowned. The agent rubbed his arm and back soothingly, subtly turning him away.

"Come on, you're tired. You've trained hard all day. It's almost time for bed. This is a small matter. Just let the bellhops take care of it. No need to get worked up, right?"

"Fine," Dong Hai spat. "But you, Lin, don't think I won't forget this."

Dong Hai spun on his heel and stormed off.

"What a piece of work," Li Ming muttered.

"Don't let it get to you," Jiang Long said. "It comes with the territory."

"*Wo yiting ta kaikuo shuohua jiu zhidao ta shige buyao lian de chusheng,*" Ghazan growled.

The moment I heard him speak, I knew he is a beast without shame.

It was the most Li had heard Ghazan speak in a single breath.

"We're stuck with the client. But at least you did the right thing," Jiang Long said. "Come on, the day isn't over yet."

Three days, Li told himself. *Three more days and this will be over.*

Chapter Fourteen

The Fight Game

L i Ming might have done the right thing, but every action carried a consequence.

Dong Hai spent all of Ren-Day pent up in his suite. Jiang Long switched the team's duties around, placing Ghazan indoors, condemning Li Ming to guard the corridor outside. The schedule said today was a rest day. Nothing more strenuous than daily cultivation. His friends visited him for a marathon chitchat session, and room service prepared epic quantities of food and drink.

Li Ming would have liked to see how a high-level martial cultivator trained, the training tips and secrets he shared with his fellows, what a professional athlete did in his downtime. On the other hand, he was glad he didn't have to interact with Dong Hai now.

Gui-Day passed in similar fashion. Li Ming stood watch in the corridor, rotating shifts with Song Huizhong and the Kang brothers. Ghazan reported that Duke Dong was readying preparing the fight, and had locked himself inside his bedroom, forbidding everyone, even his protectors, from entering.

Two hours before the fight, they set off.

The Coliseum was the largest sports stadium in Bao An, one of the largest in the nation. Twenty thousand people could comfortably fit under its domed roof. Already mountains and seas of people formed up at the doors, waiting to be let in. Enterprising hawkers worked the crowd, selling tissues and T-shirts, snacks and swag.

The staff let Dong Hai in through a side entrance. They guided the party through the winding internal corridors, reciting a brief history of the building. The agent seemed impressed. Li Ming listened with half an ear, his mind focused entirely on the world around.

Dong Hai barricaded himself in the locker room. The rest of the team stood guard and swept the building, working alongside the Coliseum's security staff. Along the way, they encountered Iron Body Qiong's security team, performing a sweep of their own.

The detail leaders shook hands, exchanged credentials, and conferred briefly. Their principals might be rivals, but they were fellow professionals, brothers of the jianghu. The biaohang were here to do their job and do it well. Coordinating with each other, they inspected the seats, hallways, entrances, every point of interest, and pronounced them all clear.

The headliners remained in the locker rooms. The undercard fighters warmed up and psyched up. Fans streamed into the stadium. As the seats filled up, Jiang Long sent Li Ming and Ghazan to handle the most critical job.

Watching the cars.

Li Ming understood its importance. The last thing anyone needed was for some crazed stalker to set an ambush near the vehicles, or to sabotage them. After his altercation with Dong Hai, Jiang Long wouldn't want to do anything that might upset the client's focus. Banishing Li Ming to the basement and setting him on guard was the only rational thing to do.

But Li Ming would miss the fight.

He didn't mind too much, though. He couldn't stand crowds. The thought of watching a stadium packed with tens of thousands of screaming fans sent shudders down his spine.

At least Ghazan wasn't much of a talker. He was a rock. Plant him in position and he would never leave. He stood by the cars, vigilantly scanning all passing people and vehicles. The stadium had reserved a corner of the lot just for them, but Li Ming knew that signs alone never stopped anyone.

"The undercard fights have started," Jiang Long radioed. "Anything to report?"

"All quiet down here," Li Ming replied.

"Roger. Keep us posted."

Two hours. Two long hours of standing around with nothing to do. He'd pulled longer shifts in the military, but two hours was still two hours.

"Do you need a break?" Ghazan asked.

"No. Why?"

"I'm going to practice gongfu."

Li Ming grinned. "Dedicated, aren't you?"

"In the jianghu, gongfu is life."

It was the way of the rivers and lakes. If you do not train regularly, you will be defeated by someone far more dedicated than you—and it will be your fault.

Ghazan pressed his back against a wall, standing ramrod straight. He took two steps forward, consciously maintaining his posture. He stayed that way for the space of three breaths. Then he spread his feet apart and squatted, sinking into a deep horse stance.

He breathed.

Li Ming felt the qi rushing in and out of Ghazan, streams of fresh qi pouring into him, waves of stale qi billowing out. He drew from a wide area, sucking in all energy around him as if he were a cosmic tap. Li Ming felt Ghazan pulling on its his own aura.

"You're stealing my qi," Li Ming said.

"Sorry."

Ghazan dialed down, controlling his draw, contracting his presence. The pulling sensation ceased.

"Better?" Ghazan asked.

"Better."

Ghazan stayed motionless for a full ke. Two ke. Three.

"You've got powerful legs," Li Ming remarked.

Ghazan grunted.

"You want to practice too? I'll stand watch," Ghazan said.

"Sure. Thanks."

The men exchanged spots. Bringing his left side forward, Li flowed into the Sancai Shi. Went still. And breathed.

External stillness, internal movement. The essence of zhan zhuang. He breathed deep, moving qi through him, making hundreds of microadjustments to his posture, his feet, his hands, his fingers. The air was stale, filled with rubber and concrete dust, but beneath that was an undercurrent of purity. He sank his weight and opened his perineum, letting energy rise from the ground, up his spine, and out his crown. Warm waves of electricity washed through him, calming and comfortable. In them he sensed tension, blockages, restrictions, and adjusted his body some more.

And suddenly there was nothing. Nothing but the sensation of his feet anchored to the earth, his breath effortlessly filling and departing his lungs, his energies circulating through in, breathing in and out with the rhythms of the universe.

An urge rose within him, his qi directing his body. He melted into it, allowed it to move, and his body moved with it. His body settled once again into the Sancai Shi, now right side forward.

His qi came to rest. His body followed. And at last, his mind.

Time passed.

Presently his internal clock hit zero. He breathed, relaxed, and returned to a neutral stance.

"Is that the Santi Shi?" Ghazan asked.

The Three Bodies Stance. It was what other branches of wuxingquan named the foundational posture.

"My lineage calls it the Sancai Shi," Li Ming replied.

"Which lineage is that?"

"An Family."

"Never heard of it."

"It's an obscure branch. We don't even know who the actual originator is. All we know is the first head of the lineage received his teachings from a General Gong. He was purged from the military during the late Yue Dynasty. The general never revealed who had trained him."

"I see. Do you do a lot of standing practice?" Ghazan asked.

"Yes. It's the single most important practice."

"More important than learning to fight?"

"It teaches structure, relaxation and internal power. But you have to do it right."

"Standing practice doesn't teach you how to express power in a fight."

"That's why we have the forms."

"I'd like to see one."

Li Ming raised an eyebrow. Ghazan, the man who trained in secret, isolating himself from everyone else, was asking to see his form? Was he trying to steal Li Ming's techniques?

Even if he were, what did it matter? Wuxingquan's power lay in its small circles and internal mechanics, so subtle to be practically invisible. Even Li had difficulty analyzing a form done right, and *he* knew what was in it.

Stepping in front of the car, he looked all around. No vehicles, no passers-by. This late into the fight, everybody who wanted to be here had arrived. With a breath, he assumed the Sancai Shi. Breathed again. And ran through the Five Element Linking Form.

He moved swiftly but smoothly, imbuing every step and every strike with power. Hard, visible power, the kind of power Ghazan was looking for, the kind of power that concealed the hidden power of the art. He emphasized the punches, the steps, the turns, and in them hid the circles, the spirals, the torques.

He returned to his starting point, back in Sancai Shi.

"Not bad," Ghazan said. "Not bad at all."

"Thank you."

"Was that the Five Element Linking Form?"

"Yes."

"I've never seen one like that before."

"Different branches have their own versions of the form. For that matter, they have their own versions of *everything* in the art: Five Elements, Twelve Animals, even Sancai Shi."

"Interesting. The branches I've seen use linear footwork. Their forms just march forwards and backwards, sometimes turning around. Yours is more... circular. More circular movements, more sidesteps. It's unlike any other wuxingquan forms I've seen."

"The An Family teaches wuxingquan and yizhang as complementary arts. You can see the influences from each other."

"My lineage teaches complementary arts too."

"Really? How?"

"Shifangquan is famous for the spear and the elbow. Fuguazhang is renowned for its explosive long-range palm techniques. The Wu Family teaches both arts as a single integrated art, the way it was originally taught by the first grandmaster of the lineage."

"So that's where the splitting palms came from."

Ghazan smiled. "It caught you off guard, didn't it?"

"Yes. I was expecting you to crash in, not try to strike from long range. Got me a couple of times."

"I didn't expect you to slide out of the way too. From what I'm told, wuxingquan practitioners like to meet a threat head on."

"Our arts are full of surprises. Speaking of which... it's your turn."

"My turn?"

"Yes. Show me one of your forms."

He blinked. "*En...*"

"You don't have to show me a secret form. But I'd like to see how you move."

"All right, all right."

Ghazan stepped in front of the car. Breathed.

And exploded.

He opened with a stylized salute, bent his knees, and stepped into his stance. He paused for a moment. And exploded into a series of punches and splitting palms. Every step produced a strange sound, a stomp combined with rushing air and scraping soles, reverberating in the parking lot. His qi erupted from him, exploding outwards like a geyser.

The lights above his head brightened. Dimmed. Brightened again. He was emitting so much qi the circuits were surging. Even from a distance, Li Ming felt his energy washing over him, hard and cutting, electric and fiery.

Every step was sharp and linear, every strike explosive and abrupt. But where Li Ming expected short, direct attacks, he saw circles. Circles small and large, circles that granted power both immense and subtle, flowing seamlessly between the two expressions.

This wasn't the shifangquan Li Ming thought he knew. This was the shifangquan practiced by the ancient grandmasters, who had seen the need to fight at every range, up close and at a distance, to synergize the line and the circle to express ultimate power in every extremity. The shifangquan that traced its lineage to the Xia troops of the Red Banner Army in the service of the Yue emperors.

And if Ghazan knew the principle of the circle, then wouldn't he have seen the small circles of wuxingquan too?

Just as well that Li Ming hadn't shown any of the higher-level applications of the art.

Finally, Ghazan closed the form, and relaxed.

"Wonderful!" Li Ming said. "What form was that?"

"The Small Frame. It is the essence of the art. Every principle and stance is contained within it."

"I can see why it's so deadly."

"Shifangquan is designed to end the fight immediately. Among all the facets of the art, that appeals to me the most."

Ghazan's voice went flat. His eyes hardened. Now Li Ming was standing before a human predator, likely someone who had used his art in war, and prevailed.

Someone just like him.

"The main event has started," Jiang Long reported over the radio.

"Finally," Li Ming said.

"Who do you think will win?" Ghazan asked.

"Iron Body Qiong."

"Why him?"

"He's the champion. He's got the record and the experience to match."

"I say Dong Hai will win. He's younger, faster, stronger. If anyone can pound Iron Body Qiong into submission, it's him."

"Strength isn't everything."

"*Power* is everything. And Dong Hai has the higher qi score. He'll knock Iron Body Qiong down, either with his fists or his magic."

"Qi scores aren't everything either."

"You're joking. In our world, only two things matter. Power and qi. It's even part of our ranking criteria."

Irritation flashed through Li Ming. Before his brain could stop him, his mouth opened.

"In the military, I killed martial cultivators more powerful than me. Three of them with my bare hands. They had hundreds, even thousands, more qi points than me. But I won."

Ghazan's eyes glowed with a strange light.

"How did you do it?"

"I..."

Sense-memories flooded his mind. Bone cracking under his boots. Blood spilling over his hands. Terrible winds. Thunderous explosions. Steel sinking into flesh. As suddenly as it had come, annoyance faded into a dull heartache.

Li Ming shook his head.

"Not today."

"Excuse me?"

"Not today. I don't want to talk about it today. The point is, I've defeated men much more powerful than me. You can't say Dong Hai is the better fighter on qi points alone."

"He's got strength, stamina, strategy, high-quality gear. And he has the edge in qi. He's going to win. I can feel it."

"We'll have to see how the match plays out."

"Not going to bet on it?"

"I'm not the gambling type."

"Really? I heard you Xia people enjoy betting on everything."

Li Ming raised an eyebrow. Ghazan smirked.

Li Ming chuckled.

"Gambling is part of our culture. But I don't have any gambling luck. I stay far, far away from it."

"A wise choice."

The men continued alternating between training and standing watch. Ghazan revealed no more forms or techniques, and neither did Li Ming. They simply repeated the forms they had demonstrated, over and over again, breaking up the monotony with zhan zhuang. Every moment was an opportunity for cultivation, and this was no exception.

Five ke later, Jiang Long radioed again.

"The match is over. We're moving on to the post-fight press conference."

"Roger that," Li Ming said.

"Who won?" Ghazan asked.

A pause.

"Our client. Victory by knockout in the last round. He finished Iron Body Qiong with a tornado kick to the head."

Ghazan pumped his fist into the air. "I knew it!"

Li Ming frowned. He should be glad that his client had won. And yet...

"Why are you so happy?" Li Ming asked.

"I was right."

"That's it?"

"Nothing deeper to it than that."

Li Ming grunted. "I don't like the fact that he won."

"Why?"

"As you said, the client is a beast without shame."

"It's how the fight game is played."

"I don't want any part of that game."

"We're in the jianghu. We can't avoid it."

"We can always choose not to play the game."

"The jianghu is a small world. You might not want to play the game, but sooner or later you'll brush shoulders against the players."

"I'd rather focus on applying martial arts in the real world."

"Me too."

"We should train together more often."

"Maybe."

"Just 'maybe'?"

"I like training alone."

"So do I. But we won't get better if we don't practice with someone else. That's why two man sets exist."

Ghazan pondered in silence.

"I'm not going to force you to train with me, but I think we can get better if we do," Li Ming said.

More silence.

"Sure," Ghazan said, at last.

"Thanks. I'd like to see some of your shifangquan."

"Only if you show me your wuxingquan."

"Deal."

Chapter Fifteen

Cross Spears

The rest of the contract proceeded without a hitch.

Dong Hai spent Jia-Day recovering from the fight. He slept, he ate, he practiced qigong, he ate some more. His opponent had worked him over, breaking his nose, cutting up his face, dislocating a rib. But, as Dong Hai liked to remind the world, he'd broken Iron Body Qiong.

First thing in the morning, Dong Hai visited a chiropractor to reset the rib. The healer carefully loosened his pecs and hammered the bone back into place. Dong Hai groaned and breathed through it all. It was the only sign of pain he showed.

The second he returned to the hotel, Dong Hai and his agent started talking about future deals. Sponsorships, advertising, product placements, social media campaigns, renegotiating his contract now that he was the super heavyweight champion of the world. The agent did most of the talking, with Dong Hai listening intently. The facial wounds suggested many heavy blows to the head, yet Dong Hai seemed cognizant and intelligent.

In the evening, Dong Hai brought all his friends for a celebratory feast at a five-star restaurant. This time Dong Hai cut loose. Meat, vegetables, seafood, desserts, copious amounts of tea and rice. They demolished enough food to feed a platoon of soldiers, and Dong Hai signed the check without even looking at it.

Dong Hai and his entourage left at dawn the following day. The escorts saw them to the departure hall. Dong Hai insisted on shaking everyone's hands.

"Thanks for keeping us safe," Dong Hai said.

"You're welcome," Li Ming said.

Whatever lingering animosity there might have been between them had evaporated in the flush of victory.

When the client left, so did the biaohang. They parted ways at the airport, going in separate directions. The job was over, and now they could finally relax.

Li Ming had nothing to do and nowhere to go. But the contract had taken its toll. Irregular meals, inadequate sleep, dealing with the client. He needed a break too.

He hopped on a succession of buses and trains, making his way back to Luoyang District. He wasn't in any hurry, not right now. He spent his trip staring out the windows, watching the city and the people around him. He was dressed like them, but he was not of them. They were all mortals, but he was a martial cultivator and they were not. They were blissfully ignorant of the of the rivers and lakes, and barring unusual circumstances, would never need to know the deep undercurrents swirling through them.

An indescribably complex emotion arose within him. Loneliness? Jealousy? Pride? All of the above? He couldn't put a finger on it. All he knew was that he had chosen this path, a path open only to those who possessed the talent and the dedication to pursue it, and all he could do was walk this path to the end.

But what was this path? It involved martial arts, cultivation, and magic, but what was the purpose? What was the end goal? What did he hope to accomplish?

He had no answers. Only an endless string of questions.

He thought again of the promise he'd made to himself on the streets of Bao An, staring up at the posters of the immortals. Was it worth joining their ranks if it meant becoming someone like Dong Hai?

No.

He'd win a way to immortality, one that didn't involve giving up everything that made a person a decent human being. There was no point in becoming more than human if it meant discarding everything that made you one.

The moment he exit the Luoyang metro station, his phone rang.

"Ready to take another job?" Boss Cai asked.

Li Ming was exhausted. He wanted to collapse into his bed and sleep all day, or at least do nothing until tomorrow. But he remembered what the senior biaohang had said during the entry interview.

If the call comes, you answer.

And here was the call.

"Yes," Li Ming said.

Days of never-ending duty flowed into nights of nonstop vigil. Jobs came one after another. Protecting a client from a stalker. Performing a security assessment of a home and business. Escorting a minor celebrity on a weekend getaway in Bao An. Li Ming barely had time to breathe.

Finally, a week after Dong Hai's departure, his schedule cleared up. Now he had time for extensive training in the morning. Not enough to train everything he wanted. Only everything he needed.

He awoke a ke earlier than usual and rushed through his morning ablutions. Ghazan was already up and training, stomping back and forth in the secret courtyard. The men might have agreed to exchange martial skill, but personal training always came first.

In the inner courtyard he blazed through a shortened version of his morning routine. Cultivation. Zhan zhuang. One hundred fists. A quick run-through of the varied linking forms and animal forms. It was the routine he practiced when he was on duty in the military, when he had a schedule to keep—or when he had other elements to train.

As he trained, he saw each form with fresh eyes. The punches were obvious. But the footwork, the kicks, the grapples, the counters, they were all hidden in the movements. They were out there, in the open, disguised as extravagant swings, exaggerated retractions, small turns and rotations. But he had to find them.

The practice of wuxingquan was eighty percent solo, twenty percent with others. Before he could practice with others, he had to excavate the depths of the art.

Slowly, he began to see the techniques. Father had told him what to look out for, what each move was supposed to do. But the forms simply practiced the internal dynamics needed to carry them out, making them big and expansive so the practitioner could consciously train them. In combat, the movements were small, quick, subtle, invisible until impact. As he performed the large movements, he thought about how to shrink them, how to make them compact, how to adapt his body to the principles and the techniques to his body.

As the first rays of the sun crept over the city skies, Li worked with his swordbreaker. The short stick form was brief and direct. Strike, strike, strike again; block and counter, evade and counter; an interplay of attack and defense where both became one and the same.

As he worked the form, he looked for options. He had heard of how sticks could be used for grappling. He'd learned a few basic baton grappling methods in the Special Military Police. Were there other applications, other branches, other tricks hidden in the form?

The only way to find out was to practice.

He worked his way across the square, the swordbreaker swooshing through the air with every swing. Now that he had the form, he departed from it, finding and exploring follow-ups and finishers, alternative targets, responses to attacks.

There was so much potential. So much to explore. So little time to do it all.

In the end, though, a swordbreaker was a swordbreaker. Its shape dictated its purpose, the same way the shape of the five fists dictated how they would be used. It was a smashing weapon, a crushing weapon, and occasionally a thrusting weapon. It could be used to augment a lock or a grapple, but that wasn't what it was designed for.

But the edges... the blunt edges were wickedly designed. A stick or baton would spread the pressure of a lock against a curved surface. The swordbreaker would concentrate it along a thin ridge. If he weren't careful—or if he really needed to—breaking arms and hands would come easily.

One last rep, and he returned to his origin point. He sheathed his swordbreaker and pulled out his other training weapon for the morning.

A fan.

A traditional folding fan, made of bamboo and fabric. With a flick of the wrist and an audible crackle, he opened it into a red half-circle. Another flick and the fan folded closed.

He had no illusions about using the swordbreaker on duty. It was a long weapon, too long and too eye-catching for many of the jobs a biaohang would be asked to complete. Most of the time he would only be able to use short weapons. Or weapons that didn't look like weapons.

Hence the fan.

Most wuxingquan schools didn't have a fan form. An Family Gongfu was unique. It had *two* forms, one for both branches of the lineage.

Li stood in silence. He regulated his breath, gathered his qi, steadied his heart.

And begun.

He lunged and stabbed, grabbed and kicked, spun and parried. A quick snap and the fan unfurled. More thrusts, more swings, more steps, working his way back and forth down a narrow line, every gesture a graceful flower hiding a martial root, every circle concealed in linear motion.

He folded his fan. Went still. And allowed the qi to circulate through him.

Warm and pleasant, liquid and electric, it surged through his body, following his meridians. As he breathed, he guided it through him, tracing a circle that began with his nose, sank to his dantian, curved around his perineum, ascended his spine, curled around his skull, and ended with a soft exhale.

Five breaths later, he flowed into the yizhang fan form.

Now the circles were obvious. Circle steps and spins, swings and slashes, and yet every circle abruptly changed into a sudden thrust, a flash step forward, before swirling through a circle once more. This set had larger, wider movements than the wuxing set, more visible to the observer, yet it took him through different interpretations of many of the same principles, and ended where he began.

He stood again in zhan zhuang, breathing, cultivating the qi rushing through him. But two breaths later, he felt eyes boring into the back of his head.

"Was that a fan?"

Li Ming swiveled neatly around. Ghazan stood at the edge of the courtyard, his arms crossed, wearing an amused expression.

"Yes," Li Ming said.

"Why do you train with a fan? Nobody carries fans around anymore."

"Body mechanics and footwork."

Ghazan shook his head.

"There's more to it than that. You wouldn't train in something you don't think is useful."

"How did you know that?"

"Why else do you spend so much time on empty hands, but so little on classic weapons beyond your swordbreaker and short stick?"

"The fan develops many useful attributes."

"But it's not useful in the modern world."

A hot twinge ran through Li Ming.

"You sure about that?" Li Ming said quietly.

"Who else carries a fan these days?"

"It's not about the fan. It's about what the fan represents."

"Which is? Preservation of history?"

Li Ming pulled his folding knife from his pocket and thumbed it open.

"Watch."

He flowed through the forms once more, this time with minor adaptations. With each thrust, he shifted the knife subtly in his hand, supporting the butt against his palm. Every swing became a slash, a hook, a shear, a hooking thrust. Flicks became back cuts, swift and sudden. He went low, blade tracing an arc to fend off a low thrust, then popped high to thrust at—

The memory of flesh and blood seared through his brain.

Skin, firm and springy, parting under the point. Blood gushing over the blade and his hand. The smothered terror of dueling an immortal.

He ripped out the point from an imaginary neck, breathing out as he went, and the moment faded.

He continued the steps, every motion elegant and stylized, yet hiding an application. Twice more the phantom sensations returned. Twice more he breathed through them and carried out.

He'd heard that the body stored emotional trauma, and that intense neigong brought them back to the surface. This was the first time he'd experienced it for himself.

If Ghazan noticed, he didn't speak. He just watched Li Ming, studying every step, every thrust, every slash.

Finally Li Ming ended. He closed his knife and put it aside.

"Your fan form is a knife form?" Ghazan asked.

"Yes. But it's not common knowledge."

"The forms are very stylized."

"They teach attributes and principles, as I said. In real life the movements would be close and tight."

"I don't see how that's possible."

"I made it work."

"You killed someone with it?"

A jumble of memories roared through him. Fire and lightning screaming in a tiny room. Steel whirling and flashing about. Shields detonating in actinic flashes. Blood, blood, more blood. A man curled up in a pool of blood, whispering—

"Yes."

Ghazan raised an eyebrow.

"When?"

"Recently enough that my knife hasn't gone rusty."

Ghazan nodded slowly.

"I see. You've done well to survive the encounter."

"Thank you."

"In shifangquan, our forms aren't so... so big. There's still some exaggeration, but not so much as yours. Even our weapon forms are similar to the application."

"I'd like to see that."

Mirth danced in Ghazan's eyes.

"I hear your art is based on the spear. I'd like to see your spear work too."

"Sure. Let's get spears."

"And armor."

Maybe it was his accent. But it sounded like a statement, not a question.

"You want to cross spears with me?" Li asked.

"I've never seen the An Family wuxingquan spear in person before."

"Let's do it."

The Cais' humongous training spears were more properly long staffs. The spearhead was little more than foam secured with tape and sprinkled with chalk dust, but at the high speeds a spear could travel, it could still cause damage.

Both men grabbed helmets. A dense mesh protected the wearer's eyes and face, thick cloth protected the rest of the head, and a flap of reinforced padding defended the throat from accidental strikes.

"You're going to keep your smartglasses on?" Ghazan asked.

"We need to keep track of time."

"Sure you won't cheat with that?"

"How?"

"There are apps that read body language, including a fighter's movements. They draw attention to threats and suggest responses in real time."

He'd heard of apps like that. But he'd never gone hunting for them. He trusted his eyes and mind more than a machine.

"I don't have an app like that."

"No smartglasses. Just to keep things fair."

"What about timekeeping? My Raptors don't have an external speaker."

"I'll get my scroll."

Ghazan hustled to his room. As he waited, Li strapped on a padded jacket and slipped on a pair of thick sparring gloves.

Ghazan returned, a scroll in his right hand. Resembling a pair of thick tubes joined together, the portable computer was heavy and ruggedized, the kind the military and police favored.

"I'm ready when you are," Ghazan said.

"You don't want any more armor?" Li asked.

"Armor like yours just gets in the way."

"How so?"

"You'll find out." Ghazan cracked his neck. "Shall we cross spears?"

"How long do you want to go for?"

"How long do *you* want?"

"Three minutes."

"Fine by me."

Ghazan pulled the tubes apart, unrolling a thin, flexible screen. He spoke something in his native tongue. The device chimed and replied in the same language.

"We start in one minute," Ghazan said.

The men set their devices down under the shade of the tree, took up their weapons, and squared off in the center of the courtyard.

The men faced each other, their spearheads touching. Ghazan glared at Li through his mask, his qi fierce and powerful. Hot, fiery energy washed over Li, a flood threatening to wash him away. Li stood fast, a rock against the storm, watching Ghazan's hands, shoulders, hips, feet.

The scroll beeped.

Ghazan thrust.

His right hand shot the spear forward, left hand held fast to guide the weapon. It was a sliding thrust, bringing both hands together, extending the weapon to maximum length while maintaining balance.

The same thrust wuxingquan used.

Li Ming twisted his weapon through a circle, knocking it aside, answering with a counter-thrust to the face. But he was a little too slow, a little too late. Ghazan leaned back, expertly dodging the blow, twisting just enough to bring to spear off-line, and launched a riposte. Li Ming turned aside, but not enough. The spearhead struck him squarely on the breastbone.

Li Ming tapped his chest.

"Good hit."

Now Li Ming understood why Ghazan had forgone armor. Ungloved and unencumbered, Ghazan wielded the weapon as though it were a fifth limb, a natural outgrowth of his body. Li Ming's heavy gloves were clumsy and awkward, robbing his hands of the feel and dexterity needed for high level spear work.

Too late to do anything about it now. He just had to work with what he had.

Ghazan dominated the match. Li Ming had trained in many weapons, but Ghazan was a master of the spear. His movements were quick, explosive, brutal, constantly attacking, constantly pressuring forward. Even in the retreat he lashed out with a thrust or a tight swing. No wasted movements, only probes, fakes, a sudden stroke like a thunderbolt.

Li Ming did his best to keep up. But Ghazan was in his element, and it had been too long since Li Ming had trained with the spear. Li Ming parried, smashed, pushed Ghazan's spear aside, but somehow the weapon always flowed back around, back in line with Li Ming's body.

Ghazan's timing was uncanny. Whenever Li Ming thrust, Ghazan allowed the spear to enter his airspace, to reach past his arms, to reach the point of maximum commitment, before swiftly knocking it aside and retaliating. At that fatal moment, off-balance and off-line, Li Ming had no way to defend save for backing up and hoping for the best. Which didn't usually work.

Ghazan was superb, but not perfect. Twice Li Ming touched him, once to the chest, once to the face. But both times provoked a storm of counters, sliding thrusts launched at long range, forcing Li Ming back, occasionally taking him in the head and body.

Li Ming couldn't fight like Ghazan. He couldn't hope to beat a shifangquan fighter at his own game. He had to use his own fight tactics, his own art.

He targeted Ghazan's head, keeping his thrusts short and sharp. Enough to threaten him, not enough to provoke a parry. Ghazan kept his guard up, protecting his upper body. Li Ming slipped offline, linear movements hiding small circles, slid the spear down—

And swung.

The spearhead rapped Ghazan's unprotected knuckles. But lightly, light enough to register a hit.

"Hit," Ghazan acknowledged.

And attacked.

Li Ming guarded high and low, one parry flowing into the next. Ghazan kept up the pressure, giving him no room to breathe. Li Ming caught a shot to the forehead, the sound of the impact echoing against the blow. Li Ming called it, and Ghazan thrust again and again. Li Ming backed up—

And his rear shoe touched a root of a tree.

Another thrust.

Li parried. Stepped. Swung.

Slashed Ghazan's arm.

"Hit."

Ghazan backed up. Li Ming slipped into the gap, circling around Ghazan. Ghazan moved warily, presenting his spear forward.

Ghazan favored linear movements. He could throw thrusts at blinding speed. He had the stamina to keep this pace forever. But circular footwork... now *that* was something he had difficulty with.

Ghazan attacked. Li Ming ate another body shot. Ghazan thrust again. Li Ming circled right, subtly widening his footwork, increasing the distance. A third thrust. Li Ming circled out with a vertical parry, then ran his spear down the length of Ghazan's shaft, going for the hands.

Ghazan twisted, bringing his spear high by his temple, voiding the blow. Abruptly he thrust, going for Li Ming's head. Li Ming side-stepped, Ghazan's spear whooshing past his ear, and tagged Ghazan's thigh.

Ghazan acknowledged the hit. Then took the next point. And the next. And the one after that.

Circular movements, Li Ming reminded himself.

Ghazan thrust. Li Ming parried across his body. Ghazan swung suddenly, flowing with the energy, stepping in with a rising butt strike. Li Ming jolted back, surprised, the wood scraping against his padded glove.

"Hit," Li Ming said.

Not a solid hit. But it *had* caught him off-guard.

The clock ran down. The men continued exchanging blows. Li Ming focused on circling, on parrying, on countering when he could. Ghazan aimed to cut him off, to close off his movements with powerful thrusts, to knock away his spear and land a well-aimed thrust. Ghazan was far more successful than Li.

Li Ming's blood threatened to boil. He breathed it out. Unchecked emotion was the enemy, and it would give Ghazan another advantage. Li Ming breathed out his emotions and focused on meeting Ghazan with the entirety of his being.

Ghazan thrust. Li Ming turned, and the spearhead brushed against his face mesh. Ghazan returned to the guard, exposing his head. Li Ming snapped his spear through a small circle, just enough to bump Ghazan's weapon aside, and thrust. Ghazan leaned back—

Not far enough.

The spear struck Ghazan full in the face. Li Ming retracted the weapon just as quickly, taking up a full guard. Ghazan thrust, Li Ming parried, and—

The scroll beeped loudly.

The men backed up a step. As one, they lowered their spears. Li Ming cupped his fist over his heart. A moment later, Ghazan did the same.

The men peeled off their helmets and armor and checked their points.

Ghazan counted six chalk marks on his body. Li Ming found twenty-one.

Heat raced through Li Ming's heart. Twenty-one strikes. Twenty-one times he could have died on the field. Unacceptable.

But that was merely a reflection of his own lack of skill.

"Your spear work was amazing," Li Ming said. "Your thrusts were incredible."

"Thank you. That last strike at the end was beautiful. I didn't see it at all," Ghazan said.

Ghazan smiled. A genuine, open smile, a smile of respect and recognition.

And that was enough.

There will always be someone better than you, Father had said. *Always strive to be better than the man you were yesterday.*

As they doffed their safety gear, Li Ming saw the Cai family pass through one of the side gates leading to the inner residence. The men headed to the main hall. Cai Yan strolled to the courtyard.

"Busy training?" she asked.

"We're just finishing up," Li Ming said.

"Ah? I recall someone asking if he wanted to train with me. It seems I have a bit of time now, but..."

Li Ming chuckled. Straightened. Saluted.

"Li *shidi* humbly requests to train with Cai *shijie*."

She laughed. Full-throated and unreserved, a laugh from the belly.

"*Zhenshi de!* I already said you don't have to be so formal!"

"Even so, under certain circumstances, decorum must be observed."

She shook her head, catching her breath, her hair fanning out like a black wing.

And saluted.

"Very well. I accept. And next time, don't stand on ceremony. I don't like it when people do it."

"Understood."

"We only have two ke before I have to get to work. Is there anything you'd like to cover?"

"*En...* I think..."

Sirens howled in the morning light. Dozens, hundreds of them, joined in an infernal chorus, a strident screaming growing louder, higher, climbing to a crescendo, reverberating in every street in every direction.

Cai Yan's eyes widened.

Li Ming's blood chilled.

They were civil defense sirens.

Bao An was under attack.

Chapter Sixteen

Get Your Guns

"**G**et your guns!" Li Ming yelled.

Everyone ran to the armory. The Cai men rushed over to join them. Talking into his smartglasses, the eldest Cai unlocked the door. Li Ming rushed for the interspatial storage machine. He raised his keycard to the reader, jammed his thumb against the fingerprint scanner, hit the button for his preconfigured loadout.

The machine hummed. Blue light spilled from the edges of the access door. Li Ming reminded himself to breathe, to remain calm. The sirens were still screaming, alternating between high and low tones every six seconds.

Raid warning. Attack was imminent—whatever that attack may be.

At last the machine chimed its readiness. Li Ming yanked the door open. His gear floated in mid-air, suspended in their frames, ready for immediate deployment.

"What gear do we need?" Li Ming asked. "What's the situation?"

"Beast attack!" Cai Yan replied. "Take everything!"

Li Ming snatched his war gear from the frames. Infinity gun, handgun, battle belt, plate carrier, reality shapers, helmet, gloves. Cradling his kit in both hands, he bumped his back against the door, slamming it shut, and raced to a corner of the room.

His hands flew, his body followed, his heart settled into a clear lake. He'd kitted up countless times in the past two years, so many times every movement was burned into his muscle memory. He snapped on his armor, the straps already adjusted for a snug fit. He buckled on his belt and patted down his pouches. Everything was where he'd placed them. He fastened his issue shaper—the good one, the one from Chang An—on his right forearm. He slipped on his radio headset and strapped his helmet over it. He donned his gloves. Stowed his handgun in his holster. Slung the infinity gun over his shoulder.

Secured his swordbreaker to his belt.

In half a minute, he was ready for war. Looking up, he saw Ghazan hustle over, equipment in hand. The Cais, all three of them, were now lining up in front of the machine.

"You're taking your swordbreaker with you?" Ghazan asked.

"It's a family heirloom. I couldn't just leave it in the courtyard."

Ghazan's set up was remarkedly different from Li Ming's. His plate carrier was stripped-down, the trauma plate just large enough to cover his vital organs, while leaving a generous shoulder pocket to shoulder a weapon. His sidearm was enormous, a massive hunting handgun designed for the most dangerous beasts on the planet. He had strapped on a shaper on each arm, doing double duty as armored bracers. Ghazan's infinity gun was an Avenger like Li Ming's, but it had an extended handguard and mounted only a single accessory.

"Is that a bayonet?" Li Ming marveled.

Ghazan pointed his weapon at the ceiling and hit a catch. A matte black blade sprang out from the handle, huge and wicked.

"Yes."

As the Cais kitted up, the patriarch delivered a running update.

"A horde of beasts have breached the city's southern defenses. The police is mobilizing to contain them. Civilians are advised to stay indoors and out of sight. Our mission is to protect the hutong. This appears to be a simple horde. No reports of coordinated attacks elsewhere in the city. I'll keep you advised on the situation."

"What kind of beasts are they?" Li Ming asked.

"Yaoshu."

Everybody cursed.

The origins of yaoshu were lost to the mists of time. Historians still argued over whether the Yue Dynasty had deliberately created them, bred them from existing species, or simply found them in the wild. But everyone agreed on one thing.

They were living weapons.

"I've recalled all our biaohang," Boss Cai said. "They'll be here in a half hour. Until then, we hold in place. The Civil Police will contain the beasts."

"Yaoshu are monstrous," Li Ming argued. "We have to deploy *now*."

"Terrorists have been known to use yaoshu. If you go out now, in that get-up, you might get shot by accident. Besides, we don't know where they are. We don't want to go on a wild goose chase. Let the cops find and fix them. We'll finish them."

"The cops aren't cultivators."

"They're volunteers. They know the risks."

"Is there a Special Military Police garrison around here?"

"They're stationed outside the city proper. They can't deploy in Bao An without permission from the city government. The police is the first line of response."

"And the jianghu?"

"We're the closest."

Now kitted up, they rushed outside. The housekeeping staff retreated into their abode. Training weapons and armor lay scattered across the courtyard. There was no time to put them away.

Three people stood by the main hall. A tall, regal woman in a long white dress. Behind her, a short man and an even shorter woman in semiformal tunics. Li Ming hadn't met them yet, but their resemblance to the Cais was startling.

They were all armed with infinity guns.

"Mengyang, the beasts are coming," the man said. "Get ready."

"Understood."

Boss Cai spun on a heel, addressing the group.

"Li Ming, I don't think you haven't met them yet. My wife, Liyue, and my parents."

Li Ming nodded at them.

"Pleasure to meet you," Li Ming said.

"The Cai elders will stay here to guard the house. I will set up a command post in the outer garden. The rest of you, guard the street. If anyone seeks shelter, let them inside. If you see a beast, shoot on sight. If you see an armed man, challenge him and verify his identity. If he's one of us, link up and continue the mission. Do not let armed strangers enter, but do not accidentally shoot a fellow member of the jianghu."

They raced to the gate. Boss Cai continued talking into his smartglass, setting up a conference call. Ghazan took point, Li Ming behind him.

"Li Ming, you ever hunted yaoshu before?" Ghazan asked.

"Twice."

"Then you should know what to expect."

Death. Danger. Terror. Li Ming felt his insides quake. But the biaohang around him were calm, their expressions neutral. He breathed out, slow and deep, allowing his mind to settle. He could not, would not, *must not*, infect them with his fear.

"We're going to split into two teams," Cai Yong said. "Ghazan, you're with me. We're going left. Li Ming, go with Yanyan. Go right. Limit of advance is the end of the hutong. Shut and barricade the gates."

The gate swung open. Li Ming and Ghazan stepped out, swiveling to cover their respective arcs. The Cais dashed across the narrow street, taking up position in doorways.

"Let's go!" Cai Yong said.

"Cai Yan, follow me!" Li said.

"Roger!" she said.

The sirens continued to scream. Beneath the wail, Li Ming picked up a faint, indistinct sound. He fiddled with his ear protection settings, blunting loud noises and amplifying soft ones.

Hissing.

Deep and sibilant, flowing from the deepest insides of a thing that hated all life. It was a warning, an alarm, a signal to attack.

And the gate to the hutong stood wide open.

Li Ming brought his weapon to the compressed ready. He clicked the fire wheel to half power. In such close quarters, a full-power shot would easily burn through a target and strike something or someone behind it.

Approaching a lamp post, he scanned up and down, left and right, his ears pricked, ready to respond to the first sign of—

A black blur rushed through the mouth of the hutong.

"CONTACT FRONT!" Li Ming screamed.

Its name meant 'demon rat'. Li saw little trace of the rat, but plenty of demon. It was a male, as large as a motorbike. Its rough, jet-black fur drank in the light, hiding spines running down its back. Vicious claws clacked against asphalt. Saliva dropped from bared fangs, as sharp and curved as sabers. A pair of golden globular eyes glared out at the world. It waved its tail back and forth in the air, its sharp bony point darting about at random. Li Ming scanned it with his qi assessment app.

287 points.

Middling as monsters went, but dangerous all the same. As the thought flashed through his head, it opened its mouth and hissed.

Li Ming shot it in the face.

Its head vanished in a burst of red. The beast threshed, issuing a horrible liquid gurgle. Its spine darted back and forth, shattering a window. A girl screamed.

Li Ming fired again, and it went still.

And three more yaoshu charged through the entrance.

Li Ming snapped his sights to the closest. Red dot and circle floated over a snarling monstrous face. He fired. Snapped to the next threat. Touched his finger to the trigger and its torso erupted in blood. Turned to the last one—

It pounced.

Supercharged with qi, this one soared through the air, teeth bared, claws out, tail arched to expose its stinger—

Li Ming fired. Cai Yan fired. The twin shots caught it in its chest, blowing out plumes of vaporized meat and blood. The dying beast spun around in mid-air, claws swiping at Li Ming's head, jaws yawning wide.

Instinctively Li Ming lunged in, thrusting his weapon high, ducking his head low. The muzzle smashed into the yaoshu's chin, slamming its mouth shut. Claws scraped against his helmet. The monster fell to the road, writhing and bleeding, limbs cycling through the air. Li Ming jumped back and fired, again and again, until what was left of it went still.

"Li Ming! Are you okay?" Cai Yan called.

Right hand on his weapon, Li Ming patted himself down with his left hand.

"I'm okay!"

Li Ming stepped clear of the gory mess, continuing his advance. Police and ambulance sirens howled, joining the choir of sirens. Infinity guns shouted in every direction. The scent of death, iron-rich blood and stinking waste, filled his nose.

More yaoshu screeched in the distance. Shots echoed down the street. He peeked over his shoulder, long enough to confirm that there were no beasts behind them, and trained his attention on the mouth of the hutong. The scent of blood and death attracted yaoshu, and...

And there was an open window.

Jogging over, Li Ming yelled at the top of his voice.

"Close and lock your windows and doors!"

No response.

"You! Inside the house! Close and lock your window!"

A young girl popped up at the second-story window.

"Close—"

A pack of yaoshu charged through the open gate.

"DOWN! DOWN! DOWN!" Li Ming screamed.

Li Ming thumbed the fire selector down to continuous fire and raked the mass of writhing muscle. Actinic blue flashes whited out his visor. The bolts shattered concrete, vaporized flesh, ignited hides. Demonic screeches tore at his ears.

He fired at flesh, fired at motion, fired at everything that might be a target. But there were so many, so many—

Cai Yan shouted.

A tongue of white flame roared from her outstretched shapers. It washed over the street, stripping off hides, broiling and liquefying flesh in an instant. The scent of sweet pork and burning grease choked Li Ming's nostrils.

And the flames cut out.

What remained of the pack lay heaped across the narrow street. Greasy bones gleamed amidst shredded tissue. Meat melted and burned. Rats writhed in their death throes. Small flames danced among the remains, throwing out thick clouds of foul, greasy smoke.

"Did we get them all?" she asked.

Something stirred. Something shifted. Bone crackled.

Quick as a snake, a yaoshu erupted from the mound of the dead. It scrabbled up the wall with its hooked claws and contorted its body bonelessly, passing its head through the window—

Li Ming swiveled and fired.

Its tail fell off, twitching and trembling. The demon rat shrieked and squirmed into the house.

The girl screamed.

Li Ming ran. With every step he filled his muscles with fire qi. His legs grew hot, his arms crackled, his body enkindled in an inner flame.

He jumped.

Rocketing through the air, he released his weapon and caught the windowsill. The girl screamed again. Li Ming hauled himself up and over and through the window.

The demon rat crouched in the middle of the room, turning to the new threat. Venom-laced saliva dribbled from its mouth. Blood dripped from its stump. The girl backed herself up in a corner, still screaming, arms flailing.

The yaoshu turned to Li Ming.

And pounced.

He seized the handle of his swordbreaker with his left hand, exploded off-line and drew his weapon across his torso. The yaoshu crashed headfirst into the blade's steel ridge. It fell to the floor, twisting and writhing, trying to get back up. Li grabbed the swordbreaker in both hands and drove the tip into its skull. The hardened point punched deep, penetrating the brain.

One last twitch, and it went limp.

Its qi dispersed, melting into the world. It was well and truly dead now. Li Ming yanked the swordbreaker free.

The girl lay in the corner, staring at Li Ming in mute horror.

"It's all right now," Li Ming said.

She said nothing.

And an old woman appeared at the door, a walking stick in her hand.

"Who are you?" she rasped.

"I'm a biaohang," Li Ming said, slowly backing up. "I work for Dayong. I stopped the monster."

She looked at the beast. At Li Ming. At the child.

And smiled.

"Thank you! You saved my granddaughter! Thank you *zhang guan*!"

"Just doing my job," Li Ming said. "I'll be taking my leave. Close and lock the window after me."

Li Ming wiped the blade off on his sleeve and pants, careful to soak up every drop, cursing at himself. He'd brought a blade to war, but not something to clean it off with. If he sheathed the weapon without cleaning it, the blood would dry and jam the swordbreaker in its sheath. From now on, he had to incorporate rags into his go-to-war load.

He filled his shapers with earth qi. Braced himself. And hopped out the window.

As he fell, he sent the qi shooting downwards at his feet, twin upside-down fountains of pale yellow light, slowing his descent. He landed as lightly as a cat. Snatched up his infinity gun. Scanned.

Cai Yan was right beside him, an expression of concern on her face.

"Are you alright?" she asked.

"Yaoshu eliminated. Everyone inside the house is safe."

She sighed softly. And nodded.

"Understood. I'll extinguish the flames. Cover me."

She aimed her shaper at the bodies. A stream of cold water gushed out. Working her arm back and forth, gulping down all the qi she could grab from the smoky air, she doused the flames and hosing down the bodies.

Li Ming covered her, ready to respond to a third wave.

The last of the fires died. Wending their way through the charred corpses, they made their way to the mouth of the hutong. Li Ming kicked away the corpse at the narrow entrance. Cai Yan grabbed the double doors of the narrow gate and swung them shut.

"What are you doing?" Li Ming asked.

"Securing the hutong."

She slid a heavy bolt into place. A second. A third.

"What about the other hutong?" Li Ming asked.

"They have their own emergency response plans. Their own gates."

Madness. In Fuyang, if anyone spotted a beast, the entire village mobilized. Only children and noncombatants locked themselves down like this.

"We should stand guard outside the gates, burn them down as they come, keep the gates open until—"

Her eyes hardened. Her voice turned to steel.

"They are yaoshu. If we leave the gates open, if they overwhelm us, the entire neighborhood is finished. If humans want to come in, they can knock."

He couldn't find any fault in her logic. But Dayong was the most well-armed and well-trained armed organization in the district. Didn't they have a responsibility to protect everyone?

A shrill voice cut through his thoughts.

"JIUMING AH!"

HELP!

Chapter Seventeen

Hero

"I'm going to help," Li Ming said.

"Our orders are—"

"Our *mission* is to protect the weak."

Li Ming filled himself with fire qi. His muscles brimmed with renewed vitality. His heartbeat kicked up a notch, supercharging his organs with fresh blood. Heat swirled around and into him.

"We need to lock down the hutong," she insisted. "Don't be a hero!"

"Stay here if you want. I'm going."

Li Ming leapt.

In a single bound, he cleared the gate of the hutong. As he vaulted over the high wall, he flashed his fire to earth. Just enough to cushion the shock of his fall. He readied his weapon and scanned.

The sirens reverberated endlessly in the empty streets. Cars sat abandoned in the middle of the road. Yaoshu chittered nearby, their voices loud and urgent.

"*JIUMING!*" the same voice screamed again.

Li Ming ran.

A half-dozen yaoshu lay strewn across the road, their faces and bodies peppered with small-bore wounds. They'd been blasted to oblivion, their qi dispersed into the universe. The bodies formed a trail pointing to an alley.

Li Ming hopped over the blood and bodies, rounded the corner, saw—

An open gate.

Past the doors, two policemen lay face-down in a lake of blood, their entrails spilling out of their bodies, clutching infinity handguns in their hands. They were both dead, their qi completely dispersed.

Li Ming shook his head. They'd done their best, but it wasn't enough.

"*YAOGUAI!*" a woman screamed. "*YAOGUAI OVER HERE! HELP!*"

A baby shrieked at the top of its lungs.

Weapon at the ready, he passed through the gate. His heart screamed at him to rush in now. The warrior within reminded himself that he was alone. If the yaoshu ambushed and killed him, no one would come to save her.

Past the gate, the hutong was a long straight road. This was a residential area, the street lined with single-story houses, but many residents had turned their front doors into roadside stalls. Li Ming saw boxes of fresh fruit and vegetables, baskets of buns and biscuits, flimsy tables groaning under the weight of assorted sundries. Faces peeked nervously from curtained windows, tracking his passage. The baby continued to wail. The yaoshu's cries grew louder.

"BIAOHANG!" Li Ming yelled. "I'm here to help! Where are you?!"

"OVER HERE!"

Li Ming ran.

Narrow alleys in between the homes led deeper into the neighborhood. Li Ming approached the nearest. He pied the corner as he approached, side-stepping through a semicircle to clear the unknown space.

The alley was tight. Barely wide enough for a man to squeeze through. Claw marks scored the walls. Li Ming steeled himself with a breath and—

Wood shattered.

"*JIU—AAAAAAH!*"

He ran.

Rushing down the alley, scraping against the walls, holding his Avenger at the low ready, he stepped out into the space beyond—

Yaoshu.

A pack, a swarm, a *horde* of yaoshu. They scurried across a small courtyard, scrambling all over each other.

This place was once a siheyuan, converted into a multi-family complex, now a feeding ground for demon rats. Yaoshu feasted on bodies in the middle of the courtyard. A dog, an old man with a blood-soaked broadsword, a girl, three yaoshu sliced in half. Yaoshu assaulted the surrounding houses, crawling through windows, flowing through doorways. Yaoshu faced from point to point, squeaking and screeching at each other, seeking opportunities to feed and to kill.

Li Ming was only one man.

He shouldn't be here. He should back up, call in artillery, call in air support, call in a martial immortal with an ocean of qi at his disposal. He should turn around and run away before they noticed. Everyone here was lost. There was no use staying. There was only death here, waiting for him, greeting him with a forest of fangs and countless claws. He had to—

The baby wailed.

Li Ming's breath caught in his chest.

He released it.

Stepped out into the siheyuan and swung up his weapon and fired.

The bolt caught the nearest yaoshu in the head, obliterating everything above the neck. Instantly he swung and fired, swung and fired, as if he were back on the range, blowing away triples and quads. When a yaoshu filled his sights, he pressed the trigger and moved on to the next, the next, the next.

The beasts rallied. They flowed into a single swarm, massive and vicious, and charged into the teeth of his guns.

He welcomed them with fire. There were so many, *so many*, he couldn't take them all. He switched to continuous fire and sprayed them down, left to right, near to far, burning them down—

Smoke burst from the muzzle of the infinity gun. The sights screamed an alarm.

He ran.

Sprinting down the alley, long gun banging against his hip and back, Li Ming drew his Golden Legion. The rats screamed in rage and triumph, chasing him. There were so many, so close, he heard their claws scraping against concrete, their stingers grinding against brick, their voices joining in a cacophonous chorus of war.

He blasted out into the street.

Turned.

Aimed.

Yaoshu flooded down the alley. They scrambled all over each other, they clambered up the smooth concrete walls, they jostled against each other, they were a wall of demon rats shrieking for blood and meat.

He couldn't kill them all. The pistol didn't have the heat capacity for that. His Avenger wouldn't cool down in time. He had to break, to run, to get out before—

He fired.

He fired and fired and fired, working the trigger as fast as he could, filling the alley with sun-hot plasma. They were packed so close, so tight, there was no need to aim. They were so fast, so furious, there was no *time* to aim. He pointed and fired and pointed and fired again and kept on going.

The demon rats exploded in droves. And they still kept coming, and coming, and *coming*, and the handgun spewed a cloud of white smoke and cut out.

He stood firm, holstered his pistol, raised his left hand, the hand with the utility shaper. His animal mind screamed that he had to run, that he was going to die here, that this was madness.

The rest of him released the thought and flashed qi to fire.

Wonder of wonders, the small orange bolt caught a yaoshu in the head and killed it.

Li Ming raised his other shaper. Fired a second fire bolt.

This one was long and large and bright, bright and hot as the sun. It slashed through the alley, incinerating all it touched. The survivors hung back for a moment. Then charged again.

No space to draw the swordbreaker. No time to deploy the knife. Only one thing left to do.

He flowed into the Three Powers Stance.

"BRING IT!" he screamed.

The air crackled. Metal sang. His hair stood on end.

Li Ming leapt aside.

Lightning crashed down from the heavens. Thunder rocked his world. His visor blacked out, his ear protection kicked in, and for a precious moment he was blind and deaf. Shock waves buffeted him, driving the air out of his lungs.

"Li Ming! Are you alive?!"

Cai Yan.

His sight cleared. His vision returned. Li Ming shook his head. The world shook with him, dragging his brain with it. He grimaced, squeezed his eyes shut, and pressed his middle finger to his philtrum.

In between his nose and upper lip, here was the Governing Vessel 26 meridian point. The only acupuncture spot he could access that treated dizziness. Inside him, an energetic circuit closed, and qi surged.

"Yes," he replied.

The dizziness grew stronger. Nausea built within him. He breathed into it, letting his body process and release it.

"Why are you here?" Li Ming asked.

"The Kang brothers took over. I followed the sound of the guns."

The nausea faded. The world returned to its axis. His head settled. Li Ming opened his eyes again to see Cai Yan in her martial splendor, her face frozen in a frown.

"Thanks," Li Ming said.

"No problem. Did you really have to—"

The baby shrieked.

Cai raised her shapers. An invisible shock wave blasted forth, blowing the piled corpses away.

"Come on!" she called.

Li Ming led the way, stomping over mounds of packed flesh, holding his breath until he was clear of the abattoir.

There, in a house to his left, the baby continued screaming. Li Ming steeled himself with a breath, crossed the blood-soaked concrete, and entered.

A man lay by the main door. His right hand held a handgun in a death grip. Two dead yaoshu lay by his feet. The rest of him was ripped up beyond recognition.

Past him was a woman, covering a cot with her body. Dozens of puncture wounds ran down her back. Her legs were shredded to the bone. Blood pooled on the floor. But the cot remained immaculate.

Beneath its mother, the baby screamed.

Gently, he pulled the woman off the corpse, laying her on the floor. Cai Yan rushed past him and reached into the cot.

"Shh, it's okay, everything will be okay."

She scooped the baby up to her bosom, rocking back and forth. The infant continued to wail at the top of its lungs.

"I'm here. Don't look. Just breathe. You're safe now. Everything will be fine."

The baby stopped. Sucked down a breath. And cried again. This close to it, Li Ming's ear protection kicked in.

Cai Yan continued cooing and rocking, soothing the child. Li Ming took up his Avenger and checked the sights. It was ready for action.

"I'm going to check for survivors," Li Ming said.

"Go. I'll stay here."

Li Ming walked the courtyard, his qi senses tuned to the max. He peeked through windows. He hunted under beds. He looked inside cabinets and cupboards. He checked every nook and cranny.

He found plenty of bodies, human and yaoshu, clawed and chewed and stabbed and sliced and shot and shredded.

There were no survivors.

He returned to the house. Cai Yan hummed a lullaby. The baby had finally gone quiet, clinging tightly to her.

She looked up and raised an eyebrow.

He shook his head.

Her face fell. And hugged the child closer.

Heat bloomed deep within his chest. Here and now, Li felt like there was just him and her and the child in the entire universe. And if anyone, anything, tried to threaten them, he would pour out the full measure of his wrath on them, destroy them so thoroughly there would be nothing left of them.

Then Cai Mengyang got on the radio.

"All Dayong call signs, fall back to the command post. We are mounting our counter-attack."

Chapter Eighteen

Friction

"WHAT THE DEVIL DID YOU DO?!"

Li Ming had never seen Cai Mengyang angry before. Now he had assumed the form and face of the King of the Underworld, his eyes flaming and furious, lips locked in a furious scowl, hands clenched into fire-forged fists.

"You were ordered to secure the hutong! Why did you leave?!"

"I heard a civilian call for help," Li Ming said.

"You abandoned your post!"

"The gate was locked and secured. There were no other yaoshu in sight. I judged it was—"

"The city is under attack! There's a swarm of yaoguai rampaging across Bao An! You went off all by yourself! Did you think you were a hero? Were you in a hurry to be reincarnated? What the devil were you thinking? Why did you do it?!"

Li Ming had no answer to that.

Ever since the first Li stepped out the mists of unrecorded history to settle in a tiny farming village in the middle of nowhere, the bloodline was fated for death and violence. His line had the gift of aggression, one they had used to leave their mark in history.

Soldiers, policemen, biaohang, the men of the line had always turned to the profession of arms. In times of peace, they beat their spears into plowshares and eked out a living from the dirt, or else assumed a civilian career and melted into the masses. But when beasts prowled and raiders roamed, when the nation called, when the innocent cried out for justice, out stepped the Lis, ready to destroy the enemies of the people with sword and gun and bare hand.

Duty was an all-demanding goddess, her altar soaked in the blood of the vicious and valorous. Before the ancestors, before the gods of the celestial realm, before even the Fo and the Pusa, the Li men worshiped her first and foremost. Wherever she beckoned, they followed. They fought, they bled, they killed, they died, but always that cold deity was never far from their minds.

It was how he was raised. It was what his ancestors would have demanded of him. It was the destiny of his lineage. Who was he, a mortal man, to turn away from the footsteps of his forefathers?

He had no words to explain all this. Why did he do it? Might as well ask, how could he *not* do it?

Instead, Li Ming said, "People needed help."

"You disobeyed—"

A shrill voice wailed.

Just like that, the tension in the air vanished. Cai Mengyang blinked, his expression melting. Li Ming glanced to his side.

"*Ba*, you're scaring the baby," Cai Yan chided.

Mrs. Cai cradled the child to her chest, singing softly.

"Take the baby inside," Cai Mengyang said. "This is no place for children."

The outer garden bustled with furious activity. Civilians huddled in a corner, whispering among themselves, anxiously working their phones and glasses. Housekeeping staff tended to them, bringing snacks and beverages. The biaohang of Dayong waited at the gates, weapons ready. Everyone studied Li Ming and his boss.

Mrs. Cai, still singing, headed inside. Mr. Cai sighed. In that one breath, a torrent of fiery qi exploded from his lips and sank deep into the earth. He turned to his men.

"We don't have time to waste. It's time to get to work."

Just like that, the anger was gone. Li Ming understood now that it was just an act. He had to dress down Li Ming in front of the others, had to demonstrate that his orders were absolute, that discipline was paramount and recklessness was suicide. At the same time, there was no way he could fault Li Ming for saving the baby. Not if he were still human.

Boss Cai set a slate on a stone table. The flat black pad, embedded with phased array optics, generated a volumetric projection, a three-dimensional map of the street. Twenty biaohang gathered around him, dressed in an odd mix of casual and outdoor wear, yet armed to the teeth. He accounted for everyone and began his briefing.

"The situation has stabilized. The Civil Police has locked down the district. Everywhere north of Avenue 81 is cordoned off. The yaoshu will not be able to break through into the city proper. One ke ago, the city government has hired us to mop up the remaining yaoshu.

"The government has traced the incursion to a breach in the southern City Barrier. As long as the breach remains, beasts of all kinds can infiltrate Bao An. We don't know yet if the breach was caused by an accident, beast damage, or human activity. That's not our concern right now. We do know that there aren't any other major incidents going on around Bao An, so we can reasonably assume this event is nothing more than a beast horde. But don't get complacent.

"We will deploy from our compound and sweep south through the district. We will split into three squads. Cai Yong will lead Squad One. Mr. Song will take charge of Squad Two. I will lead Squad Three.

"Squads One and Two will comb through the district and make their way towards the breach. Squad Three will remain on standby here to protect the civilians, coordinate police activities, and act as our reserve.

"This is a joint operation. As you clear critical avenues and streets, the Civil Police will flow in behind you to tighten the cordon. The Police Tactical Unit will secure and hold key locations and rescue civilians.

"The military is also involved. The Air Force has deployed drones to Bao An. The Special Military Police has sealed off the highways and are sweeping the wildlands. They are also escorting a detachment of engineers to the breach.

"There's a lot of moving parts here. A lot of potential for friction. I want all of you to wear your biaohang cards. If your kit doesn't have Dayong or biaohang patches, slap them on now. We do not want any misunderstandings with the police or military.

"Our area of operations is Luoyang District, and *only* Luoyang District. If an incident occurs deeper within the city, let the police or other biaoju take care of it. If you spot a beast past the breach but you can't shoot it down, do not under any circumstances pursue it. Leave it to the Special Military Police. Am I clear?"

Boss Cai glared at Li Ming as he said the last words.

"Clear," Li Ming said.

"I want you to be extra careful out there," Boss Cai continued. "Medical support is limited. Ambulances will *not* come in without heavy police escort. If you're injured, you'll have to rescue yourself.

"Stock up on antivenin. No less than two doses per shooter. If you're feeling especially paranoid, break out your auxiliary armor. Rescue what civilians you can. But remember: the priority is to kill the beasts. The faster we get this done, the safer everyone will be.

"We will conduct a tactical patrol to the breach, neutralizing all beasts we encounter. If the Special Military Police are there when we arrive, great. If not, we will hold the breach until they do. Once they arrive, they will take control of the breach. We will back clear the streets back to Dayong. The hunt will officially conclude once we return.

"This is a hunting contract. You'll be paid for every credited kill. Record your kills. This bounty will come from the city government. It supersedes your salary for today.

"You want to kit up, go to the bathroom, do it now. We deploy in one ke. Team leaders, on me. We'll plot our routes."

Li Ming was woefully underdressed for this job. Just a T-shirt and exercise shorts. By some minor miracle he hadn't been scratched yet. But he wasn't going to bet on it.

Back in his room, he changed into his urban tactical uniform. Colored in dazzling shades of gray, the thick flame-resistant fabric was reinforced with shear thickening fluid, offering protection from shrapnel, heat and claws.

He swapped his shapers, moving the Chang An to his left forearm, then filled up his canteens and hydration bladder. He thought about getting more auxiliary armor pieces from the armory but... no. No time. Besides, armor was for bad luck, not bad tactics. Against melee-type beasts like yaoshu, the tried and true method was to blast them from afar.

Ghazan had a different philosophy. He emerged from his room decked out in full armor. Helmet reinforced with face guard. Plate carrier bulked out with hard plates and soft armor inserts. Curved plates protecting his deltoids, biceps, quadriceps, calves. Over it all he wore a powered exoskeleton, allowing him to move effortlessly despite the weight.

"Feeling paranoid?" Li Ming asked.

"We will be fighting in extreme close quarters. Every piece of armor helps."

"In my time in the Special Military Police, we found that mobility was far more important than armor. Especially when dealing with beasts."

"In the military, did you have medics, aircraft, and reinforcements at your disposal?"

"Yes."

"We're biaohang. We don't. Every little advantage helps."

"I can't afford a loadout like yours."

Ghazan smirked behind his visor.

"After this job, you will."

The biaohang regrouped in the courtyard. The elder Cai rattled off team assignments. Li Ming, Ghazan, Cai Yan, and the Kang brothers would serve under Song Huizhong.

"We're going to cover the eastern half of Luoyang," Song Huizhong said. "We'll zigzag our way through the hutong and the streets and make our way south. Our area of operations will be defined by the police cordon to the north, the outermost streets to the east, Taodong Boulevard to our west, and the breach to the south.

"We will split into three two-man teams. Li Ming and Ghazan on one team, Kang brothers on the second, myself and Ms. Cai on the third. The first two teams will patrol the roads at ground level. Ms. Cai and I will dominate the rooftops. We will spot targets, snipe them, and drive them towards the ground teams with magic."

"How many yaoshu should we expect?" Li Ming asked.

"Sensors estimated some two hundred yaoshu made it through the breach."

Kang the Elder whistled. "A huge horde. Haven't seen one of those for a while."

"I thought the Special Military Police was supposed to break them up in the wild," Kang the Younger said.

"That means more money for us," Song Huizhong said. "But more work too."

"Standard rules of engagement?" Ghazan asked.

"Yes."

"Standard payment scale too?"

"Correct."

"Excellent."

Ghazan turned to Li Ming, a murderous gleam in his eye, his bayonet fixed.

"I will take point. Cover me. If any beasts make it past me, engage it."

Li Ming blinked. Blinked again.

"Are you seriously telling me you're going to hunt yaoshu with your bayonet?"

"Why not? My people hunt beasts with long spears. I heard you do the same too, out in the country."

"We use spears only because we don't want to set our houses and farms on fire. Even then, we fight in spear walls of at least five men. If we can use magic or an infinity gun, we'll use those instead. It's much safer that way."

"Bounties are assessed by the weight and quality of the harvested beasts. An infinity gun will blow away a sizable portion of the beast, and with it, your reward. A single well-placed thrust will kill a beast with minimum tissue damage."

"Are you serious? You'd risk your life for money?"

"We are biaohang. It's what we do."

"Forget it, Li Ming," Song Huizhong said. "When Ga San first joined us, he insisted on hunting with a long spear. It took ages to convince him to switch to a long gun—and only because he bought a bayonet to use with it."

"*Yao qian buyao ming*," Li Ming said.

You desire money, but you don't value your life.

Ghazan hefted his weapon.

"It is perfectly safe. With the bayonet, I have two *qiang* in one. I can keep the beasts at a distance."

Trust a martial cultivator to treat a gun as if it were a spear. On the other hand, not too long ago, Li had done the same. Albeit without a bayonet.

"And if the yaoshu gets too close? I won't be able to shoot them off you," Li Ming said.

"My hands are enough."

From any lesser man it would been an idle boast. Ghazan had said it as if it were a fact.

"Overconfidence kills quickly."

"Fear freezes your spear."

The men beheld each other for a long moment. Ghazan held himself with complete self-assurance, a man who knew he was a master of the spear and fist, a man who had hunted dangerous beasts with a spear and would do so again. All Li Ming knew was that his martial knowledge was inadequate, but the gun deployed at the right range made up for that.

Nonetheless, he knew that if Ghazan got into trouble, he'd be there to save him.

And Ghazan would do the same.

"The Civil Police are here!" Boss Cai called. "Let's move!"

Li Ming gestured at the gate.

"Point man up."

Ghazan smiled.

"Follow me."

Chapter Nineteen

Food Chain

Li Ming was no stranger to urban hunts. Dayong's tactics was a variation of the ones the Special Military Police used. But where the latter had manpower, firepower, magic power, Squad Two only had six martial cultivators.

They'd have to make it work.

Winding through the streets of Luoyang District, Li Ming maintained total vigilance. In every moment the universe spoke to him in all its myriad ways. He just had to perceive it.

The air was clean, though thicker and dirtier than Fuyang. In the distance, beasts screeched and guns answered. Civilians pressed their faces up against windows and doors, though none dared to leave their homes.

A bubble of tense silence surrounded the team. Plasma fire and beast cries scraped at its fragile walls. But still, there was nothing. No beasts, nor signs of beasts. Just abandoned cars, empty streets, locked doors.

But contact was imminent. Li Ming could feel it in his bones.

His body threatened to drown out his consciousness. His belly grumbled. His skin chafed. His mouth dried out. The last he addressed with a small hit of water. The rest he ignored. He hadn't had breakfast. Already he felt his muscles flagging.

But that was a trick of the mind. A momentary weakness, no more. He just had to push through it.

He relaxed. Not a dropping of the guard, but a calculated release of unnecessary tension. His shoulders softened, his neck loosened, his legs limbered. With every step he breathed in the qi of the cosmos, charging his dantian, reinvigorating his muscles, processing every data point the universe offered to him.

A soft sound scratched at the edges of his hearing.

"Freeze!" Li Ming ordered.

Across the narrow alley, Ghazan froze.

"What's wrong?" Ghazan whispered.

"Anybody heard that?"

"I do," Cai Yan said.

Cai Yan and Song Huizhong navigated the rooftops to Li Ming's left. The homes here had arched roofs of curved ceramic tiles, yet they moved as gracefully as cats, keeping upright and balanced.

"Where's it coming from?" Song Huizhong asked.

A tin can bounced off an alley.

"Pig hour," Li Ming replied.

Li Ming quarter-turned to his left, bringing his weapon to the low ready. Halfway down the road, a tiny alley wended between a pair of houses.

Ghazan crept forward, his infinity gun held low by his hip, as though it were a spear. Li Ming followed, taking small, stealthy steps. He swept his head back and forth, eyes wide open, watching the world in his peripheral vision.

A black shape darted out the alley.

Li Ming turned—

A black cat.

The cat darted across the road and hid under a low table.

Li Ming exhaled.

And remained on guard.

Something had scared the cat.

He extended his qi senses, sending his consciousness to the alley, and past the alley. Living souls registered at the edges of his awareness, radiating fear and boredom.

But past the alley, he felt... hunger.

"Something's in the alley," Li Ming said.

"I feel it too," Ghazan said. "Moving up."

"Wait!"

Ghazan didn't wait. He forged on ahead, bayonet thrust out at the world. Li Ming hustled, trying to keep up.

At the mouth of the alley, Ghazan pied around the corner. And went still.

A yaoshu screeched.

"Ghazan!" Li Ming shouted.

Ghazan rooted himself to the earth, his qi concentrating in his body, flowing down his hands.

And thrust.

Swifter than a snake, he punched the bayonet into the unseen alley. A yaoshu screamed. He tugged. The blade held fast. His qi flared, and with a powerful yank he freed the bayonet and leapt away.

Claws swiped futilely through empty space. A tail lashed back and forth. Li Ming and Ghazan stayed clear, watching the beast die. Ghazan stared at the yaoshu, readying himself for a second blow. Li Ming scanned and—

"Contact!"

A pair of yaoshu climbed up on the roofs, hissing and screeching, coiling up for a fatal pounce. Ghazan, still focused on the threat before him, didn't see the one above him.

Li Ming snapped his weapon up to the nearest beast and fired. The pulse blew through its chest. He swiveled left, going for the other threat. As he curled his finger around the trigger, plasma bolts tore through its side, and it fell out of his sights. He lowered his aim, saw a stump where a head should be, and turned to the other beast.

Strangely, incredibly, the demon rat still moved, still scrabbling across the tiles, reaching for Ghazan. Li Ming fired again, this time taking it in its skull. And now it went still.

And fell.

Ghazan thrust upwards, catching the beast's chest. Swiveling, he slashed straight down, dumping the corpse on the road. And looked up.

"Thanks," Ghazan said,

"You're welcome," Li Ming replied.

Shots thundered in the neighboring street.

"Two yaoshu down," Kang the Elder said.

"We took out three more over here," Song Huizhong said.

"I don't sense any more beast qi in the area," Cai Yan said.

"Roger that. And Ghazan?"

"Yes?"

"Yaoshu hunt in packs. You should know that by now."

"I sensed the yaoshu were above me."

"You didn't act."

"I didn't have to."

Li Ming stared for a moment, dumbfounded.

"You're impossible," he said at last.

Ghazan dragged his kill out of the alley. It was a huge specimen, large and muscular as a boar. It seemed perfectly intact, until Li Ming saw the blood flowing from its punctured left eye. The bayonet had punched clean into its brain. Death would have been instant.

An amazing thrust. Li Ming didn't think *he* would have been able to do that, not under combat circumstances. Yet Ghazan had pulled it off with casual panache.

The biaohang lined up the corpses by the road. Song Huizhong took plenty of photos with his helmet cameras and dictated notes. Cai Yan held out her hands and concentrated. An army of ice cubes flashed out of thin air and buried the bodies.

"What are you doing?" Li Ming asked.

"The moment a beast dies, it begins to rot. If we don't preserve the meat, we'll just be paid compost," she replied.

"Compost?"

"Because that's all the beast will be good for if it's not processed and preserved."

Li Ming was once a soldier. He'd never had to worry about such things. He'd be paid the same no matter how many beasts he shot.

"What about the yaoshu we killed before we were deployed? We didn't ice those," Li Ming said.

"I photographed them and tagged them for you," Cai Yan said. "You'll still be paid."

"Was the scene secured?" Song Huizhong asked.

Li Ming and Cai Yan exchanged a look.

"I don't think so..." Li Ming said.

"I told Father about the engagement. I think he arranged for police protection," she said.

"But did you see the cops?" Song Huizhong asked.

Li Ming thought hard, trying to recall the minutes following his departure. He remembered the cops were out in force, but were they protecting the hutong? He hadn't noticed.

"If the scene isn't protected, scavengers will steal your kills. If there's no body, you won't get paid," Song Huizhong said.

"If the cops are corrupt, you won't get paid either," Kang the Younger added.

In life, beasts were the bane of mankind. In death, they could be turned into meat and medicine. They fetched premium prices on the gray and black markets. Buyers weren't too interested in the provenance of their raw materials, only their quality and quantity. A man could make a decent living, or at least secure a nice windfall, by selling beast bodies to the underworld.

The hunters did the killing and shouldered the risk. The scavengers stole part of their rewards. A mimicry of the food chain in the natural world.

"Too late to do anything about it," Li Ming said. "Let's move on."

"Not yet," Song Huizhong said.

"Not yet? Why?"

"The police are moving up to us."

"No time. We need to run down the beasts before—"

"If we move off now, the bodies won't be here when we get back."

"People are in danger, and you're worried about money?"

"We're not working for free," Ghazan said.

"Isn't our job to protect the people?"

"Our job is to hunt beasts."

Li Ming whirled in place, turning to Ghazan.

"You're serious?"

Ghazan stared back at Li Ming, and said nothing.

"We can't protect them if we can't afford the equipment we need," Song Huizhong said. "More importantly, you do *not* want yaoshu venom turning up on the black market."

"If you can't feed yourself, you can't protect people," Ghazan added.

Li Ming sighed.

"How long do we have to wait?"

"They're right around the corner."

As if on cue, a quartet of cops appeared at the mouth of the hutong, pistols in hand. Song Huizhong waved them over.

"Here's the scene," Song Huizhong said. "Make sure scavengers don't touch anything."

"Your harvest is safe with us," the senior cop said.

"It'd better. I've photographed the bodies. If anything goes missing, I'm holding all of you personally responsible."

"Don't worry. You can trust us."

Ghazan looked away. A strange sound escaped his lips, a cross between a chuckle and a grunt.

"Squad One, Command," Boss Cai radioed. "Eyewitnesses on Seventh and Xuanzhen have reported four to eight yaoshu in the area. Get over there and deal with them."

Song Huizhong patted Li Ming's shoulder.

"Back to work. Let's go."

Chapter Twenty

Evolved

A major advantage of hunting in a major city was that there were many eyes to look for beasts. Eyewitnesses, cameras, police, and now the Air Force.

Fixed-wing drones circled the skies above Luoyang District, training their high-powered sensors on the streets and hutong. A police airship joined them, filling gaps in their coverage. Dispatchers passed on vital information from callers.

But it was up to the biaohang to finish the job.

In the military, Li Ming would have had a wealth of information at his disposal. Live feeds from airborne sensors. Augmented reality callouts to identify points of interest. Friendly force tracker.

The jianghu had none of that.

Dayong's helmets might have been military-grade, but they didn't come bundled with military software. There was only so much the government would allow. Dayong installed commercial off the shelf software on the onboard computers instead. Software that couldn't cross-talk with the military's own software suite. Or the police, for that matter.

Instead, they called the Dayong command post. The command post in turn called the field squads. It was a step down from what Li Ming was used to. It was warfare from the previous decade, if not century.

On the other hand, it was still information. Enough information to work with.

The squad zipped from call to call, tearing down the roads in their cars. The Kangs brought their own vehicle, Song Huizhong lent his own to the cause. Li Ming and Ghazan, without cars of their own, followed Song.

"You really should get a personal car," Song Huizhong said. "You can't rely on public transport in times like this."

"Too expensive," Li Ming said.

"It's an investment."

"I can't afford one now."

"You will in the future. Car companies will fall all over themselves to offer favorable terms to biaohang and martial cultivators."

"I can understand why Li Ming doesn't have a car, but Ghazan, why don't you have one?" Cai Yan asked.

Ghazan grunted. "Too expensive."

"You've been with us for half a year already. You should be able to afford one by now."

Another grunt.

"You're a human, not a beast. I know you can talk!"

"Someday," Ghazan said.

That was all the time they had for conversation. They returned their focus to the job, to the world outside, ready to respond in an instant. Weapon held tight against his chest, muzzle pointed at the roof, Li Ming stared out the rear passenger window, watching houses and shops flash past.

Every callout was a five-step process. Deploy. Search. Kill. Secure. Move. It played out over and over again on the streets and in the alleys, among the hutong and the houses. It was repetitive, but Li Ming didn't dare allow himself to think the next call was like the last.

They filled a narrow hutong with fire and wiped out a pack of six demon rats.

They chased three yaoshu into a courtyard and Cai Yan finished them with firebolts.

They spotted yaoshu sneaking across rooftops and sniped them from a distance.

And now they were barreling down the city's southern highway, a six-lane road that connected Bao An to the southern half of the province. Rows of abandoned cars and trucks and bikes lined the sides of the roads, many of them flashing anti-collision lights and blaring loud music in the vain hope of scaring away beasts.

Every building here was designed for life at the edge of civilization. Security grilles defended every window and door. Tall walls topped with spikes surrounded high-value properties and neighborhoods. Locked gates blocked access to residential hutong. People patrolled rooftops, armed with long guns and shapers.

Li Ming prayed the locals wouldn't shoot them.

"The road ahead is blocked," Song Huizhong said. "We'll have to proceed on foot."

Up ahead, a semi-trailer truck lay on its side, blocking off three lanes out of six. Cars and bikes choked off the remaining lanes, so many there was no way to drive through. Doors hung open. Shattered glass twinkled in the late morning light. Bloody trails led deeper into the steel maze.

Within the warrens, something squeaked. Lots of somethings.

As the biaohang got out of their vehicles, six more cars rolled up behind them. More shooters spilled out. Cai Yong's team.

"How goes it?" Cai Yong asked.

"I think we wiped out most of the yaoshu in our area of operations," Song Huizhong said.

"Same here. All that's left is the highway and the surrounding neighborhoods."

"And the breach."

"The Special Military Police is on site, along with the engineers. They've established a cordon around the breach. Everywhere north of the cordon belongs to us."

"Do they know we're here?"

"They should, but—"

An infinity gun discharged.

Everyone hit the deck.

More shots. More plasma bolts screamed overhead.

Li Ming ducked behind the closest vehicle and spun towards the shooter. High on a nearby rooftop, a man with an infinity gun rained down fire on the choked road.

"HEY! WHAT THE DEVIL ARE YOU DOING?!" Li Ming yelled.

"YAOGUAI!" the shooter replied.

"IDIOT! YOU SHOULD HAVE WARNED US!"

"But the yaoguai—"

"We could have shot you!"

"THE YAOGUAI ARE COMING!"

"CONTACT FRONT!" Ghazan roared.

Li Ming spun around. A huge yaoshu darted around the crashed truck. A second leapt over the trailer. A third squeezed out from under it.

With a thunderous roar, Ghazan charged the pack. The yaoshu hissed, turning to him. The closest pounced. Ghazan stepped off-line, fast as lightning, and speared it in the throat.

The two attacked.

"LOOK OUT!" Li Ming called.

He snapped his sights to the nearest yaoshu. His world narrowed to the red dot in the glass window, hovering over gray flesh. He pressed the trigger and saw pink mist. He looked up, where was the other one—

Another flash—

The third yaoshu skittered to a halt right in front of him, missing its head.

Li Ming circled around it, reorienting on Ghazan. The Yue kicked the demon rat off his spear. The creature slammed against a car, flailing and shrieking, spraying blood in every direction—

A spray of plasma bolts destroyed its upper torso.

"Who fired?" Ghazan snarled.

"I did!" the civilian shouted. "And you're welcome!"

"IDIOT!" Ghazan roared. "It was dead already!"

"We gotta be sure!"

Ghazan stepped forward. Li Ming braced his hand on his shoulder.

"Not the time. We have beasts in front of us."

Ghazan grumbled and turned back around.

As the biaohang fanned out, Li Ming extended his senses down the road. Qi signatures popped up in his awareness. Clear and simple, bright and burning, they exuded an endless hunger mixed with anger and fear. Yaoshu, one and all. But somewhere deep in the maze, he sensed something... bigger.

Nearby, Song Huizhong whipped out his scroll, set it to speaker mode, and punched in a number. Cai Yong hovered nearby, listening in.

"Boss, we've reached the southern highway. Just took care of a pack of yaoshu, but I sense a lot more in the area. Do we have a way to contact the Special Military Police detachment at the breach?"

"I'll go get it," Cai Mengyang replied. "Give me a second."

Song Huizhong got on the radio.

"Squad Two, we will stay here and hold the line. Don't move just yet. I'm going to deconflict with the troops downrange."

A minute later, the scroll vibrated. Song Huizhong glanced at the screen and dialed another number.

"Lieutenant Chan, this is Song Biaohang from Dayong Biaoju. We got your number from your commanding officer. We are now at the southernmost tip of Bao An, about half a *li* from your position. What's the situation on your end?"

A young male voice, trembling but trying to suppress it, replied.

"We've fought off three waves of yaoshu since we arrived. Two from the wildlands, one from inside the city. We heard that your biaoju is in charge of clearing the area?"

"That's right. I'm calling you to deconflict our operations."

"One moment... Do you see a drone overhead?"

A buzzing sound filled the air. Looking up, Li Ming saw a small drone, a quadcopter the size of a man's head. Song Biaohang waved at it.

"I see it. Do you see us?"

"I see you," Lieutenant Chan confirmed. "You are awfully close to a large pack of yaoshu. They're hiding among the cars ahead."

"I can sense them, but I can't see them."

"Isn't the Air Force feeding you information?"

"Verbally. They can't livestream the drone feeds to us. Our computers can't talk to each other."

Lieutenant Chan sighed.

"I've pulled the streams on my visor. If you need it, we can talk you into the enemy."

"Much appreciated. Is your position defensible?"

"Affirmative. We've established a blocking position to intercept any yaoshu escaping down the highway."

"Understood. My biaohang and I will sweep the area and push the yaoshu to you. We'll be the hammer to your anvil."

"Solid plan. But give us a shout before you approach us. I've got some real nervous troopers and engineers with me."

"Roger that. Where are the yaoshu?"

"There are three packs. There's a pack hiding in the neighborhood to your left. There's another to your right. Each pack has about fifteen yaoshu. The main pack is dead ahead, hiding among the vehicles, about thirty strong.

"The main pack is rearranging the vehicles. It's like they're forming a nest or something. That's not typical yaoshu behavior. And, according to the sensors, there's an Evolved yaoshu in there."

Evolved beasts usually assumed leadership of a pack of their lesser brethren. They might not be as intelligent as humans, but they were certainly much more powerful—and cunning.

"This keeps getting better and better..." Song Huizhong muttered.

"Can we just call in a gunship and finish this?" Li Ming asked.

"You don't want to get paid?" Cai Yong asked.

"You really want to fight so many beasts at once?"

"Negative on the gunship," Lieutenant Chan sad. "The Air Force is not authorized to use lethal munitions within the city limits unless the beasts are threatening the breach."

"It's up to us, then," Song Huizhong said.

"We'll help however we can."

Song Huizhong rubbed his chin, surveying the chaotic pile-up before him.

"How do you want to do this?"

"We'll need three... no, four teams," Cai Yong said. "Two teams of three or four each to handle the small packs. A team of shapers and sharpshooters to engage the highway beasts from an elevated position. The last team will take blocking positions at ground level. And to manually clear the nest."

"Last team has the most dangerous job," Song Huizhong said. "We'll need our best shooters and fighters for that."

"I volunteer for blockade and clearing operations," Ghazan said.

The biaohang exchanged a frank look.

"I'd say you're crazy, but I also think you're the best man for the job," Cai Yong said.

"I volunteer too," Li Ming said.

"Rookie, you don't have to prove anything to us," Song Huizhong said.

"If we must clear the maze ourselves, it'll be extreme close quarters combat all the way. That's what I specialize in. And Ghazan needs backup."

Song Huizhong frowned. "Not that I don't trust you, but... it'll be dangerous."

"I've seen how he fights," Ghazan said. "He's perfect."

Cai Yong arched an eyebrow.

"Did you just... *praise* him?"

Ghazan scowled. "He's perfect for the mission. That's what I meant."

The other biaohang shuffled about, forming up in teams. Li Ming moved over to Ghazan, keeping his eyes on the cars ahead.

He'd seen a few pile-ups in Taiping, and this wasn't one. The beasts had dragged cars and trucks all over the road, following some deep-seated animal instinct, creating narrow channels and defensive walls.

"Clearing this will be a nightmare," Li Ming said.

"It'll be close work," Ghazan agreed. "We'll have to use our short weapons if we go in. I hope you brought more than your fan."

Li snorted. "I've got my knives. I could lend you one if all you've got is your bayonet."

"If they get that close, I can use my bare hands. Or my magic."

Each of Ghazan's shapers held a strange primordial crystal within their cages. The one on his right, a blazing red, bore a carving of the sun. The other, as blue as the deep sea, was engraved with a crescent moon. He had no idea what they were.

"I've never seen Yue magic before," Li Ming said.

"If you do, consider yourself lucky. Few people outside the Homelands will ever get a chance to witness it in person."

The yaoshu shrieked.

"Get ready!" Song Huizhong yelled. "Here they come!"

The yaoshu came.

Boiling out the metal maze, squeezing out from under trucks, leaping up and over cars, they charged headlong at the intruders in droves.

And they died in droves.

Li Ming didn't think. He aimed and fired, aimed and fired, over and over, his body moving of its own accord, dropping every target as it appeared. The moment gray hide appeared in his sights, he pressed the trigger, saw a white flash and red spray, and moved to the next. And the next. And the next.

And suddenly, silence.

Exhaling, Li Ming scanned. A line of fresh corpses lay across the highway, burned and blasted beyond recognition. The one intact kill he could readily identify belonged, unsurprisingly, to Ghazan, its eye skewered through to the brain.

"Good work," Lieutenant Chan said. "I count twenty yaoshu left in the main pack. They're retreating south and are concentrating in the middle of the nest."

Song Huizhong and Cai Yong barked orders. The hunters and shooters moved out, leaving the blocking team alone in the highway. It was just Li Ming, Ghazan, and two other biaohang Li Ming had never seen before.

"New guy, what's your name?" the closer of the two asked.

"Li Ming."

"Nice to meet you. I'm Zhang Xinhua, and this is Lan Yi."

"Wish we could have met under more pleasant circumstances."

"When this is all over, we're all going to have a drink together. You can tell us all about yourself later."

And that was all the time they had for pleasantries. The beasts were just seconds away, hiding in their nests.

The surrounding houses were mostly one- and two-story affairs. None exceeded three-stories. The shooters positioned themselves on the tallest buildings, while the hunters swept the neighborhoods. Infinity guns crackled, magic howled, monsters shrieked. A fresh round of fear and anger roiled from the maze. But no more demon rats emerged.

"Shooters in position," Song Huizhong radioed. "We're going to start picking off the beasts. Start with the northern end of the nest and work your way south. Blocking team, prepare to intercept leakers."

A disjointed fusillade of plasma fire hammered the road. Bolts slashed from up high, striking metal, asphalt, flesh. Steel scraped against steel. Yaoshu shrieked. Blood erupted. A severed limb flung high into the air and out of sight.

And claws scraped against asphalt.

Lots of them.

"Blocking team, they're coming your way!" Song Huizhong called.

Li Ming breathed. In. Out. In. Out. In.

A yaoshu clambered over the fallen trailer, its beady eyes wide and furious.

Li Ming shot it in the head.

A second yaoshu appeared, darting around the hood of the truck. Li Ming aimed—

Ghazan stepped up.

"You're in my line of fire!" Li Ming warned.

Ghazan charged the beast. The beast pounced. Ghazan deftly stepped away, spearing it in the throat. He snapped his weapon down, spinning as he went, dumping it on the road. Another thrust, and it spasmed uncontrollably.

More shots to his left. Li Ming turned, saw the other two biaohang burn down two more yaoshu. He continued his scan, saw nothing else.

And suddenly the world fell silent again.

"Clear!" Li Ming called.

"Clear here!" Zhang Xinhua agreed.

Li Ming whirled to Ghazan.

"You stepped into my sector of fire!" Li Ming shouted. "What were you thinking?"

"And where was your sector?" Ghazan asked.

Li Ming spread out his arms, indicating his left and right limits. "Here!"

"It's too wide."

"What?"

"A sector of fire covers a ninety-degree angle. Yours is more like a hundred and twenty."

"I don't know where you got that number from, but in the military, we set up interlocking fields of fire. I could have shot you in the back!"

"But you didn't."

"There's a time for *qiang*, and a time for *wuji qiang*. This is the latter."

Ghazan shrugged. "We shall see."

Li Ming sighed. That man was impossible. Just when he thought he had a handle on him, when he was starting to warm up to him, he had to pull a stunt like this. The Special Military Police wouldn't have tolerated a prima donna like him.

The shooters continued their grim work. Plasma pounded the nest. Single shots rang out from the neighborhood. Monsters shrieked and guns answered. Metal screamed, more urgently this time. Twice more beasts slipped through the killing fields, twice more the biaohang stood firm.

It wasn't combat. It was butchery. The biaohang were less a blocking team, more a firing squad. The yaoshu didn't have a chance to resist. The biaohang gunned them down the second they appeared.

Li Ming didn't mind. It was safer that way. But both times Ghazan insisted on spearing a beast by himself. At least he didn't wander into Li Ming's sights again.

And just like that, the guns went silent.

"Shooters, can anybody see the... the truck fortress in the middle of the highway?" Song Huizhong asked.

"I see it," Cai Yong replied. "It wasn't there just now, was it?"

"It wasn't. They must have... The cars. They're moving around by themselves. Something's dragging them across the road, but I don't see any yaoshu around."

"Magic?" Kang the Elder suggested.

Li Ming's blood went cold.

"Possibly," Song Huizhong said. "Does anyone have a good angle on the Evolved?"

"Negative over here," Cai Yong said. "They are using the trucks as shields. They're smarter than they look."

One by one, the other shooters chimed in. They had no clear shot. They could see the trucks, but not what lay beyond them.

"Lieutenant Chan says the rest of the pack is sheltering inside the fortress," Song Huizhong said. "Six yaoshu, including a huge Evolved. He thinks it's the brood mother."

"Can we just drop a bomb on them and call it a day?" Li Ming asked.

"Air Force isn't authorized to do that." Song Huizhong sighed. "Blocking team, move up and clear the rat fortress."

"This is going to suck," Zhang Xinhua muttered.

"Roger," Li Ming said. "We're moving out. Cover us."

"If we're going to do this, we need to coordinate," Lan said.

Ghazan cracked his neck.

"You two take your side of the highway, we'll take ours. We move in a skirmish line and push towards the fortress. Easy enough."

"Let's move along the roofs of the cars," Li Ming suggested. "Last thing we want is to be trapped in between them if something goes wrong."

"I was thinking of that too," Zhang Xinhua agreed.

"Watch your fire," Lan Yi added. "Set your weapons to half-power and single shot if you haven't already. At this range, a full-power shot might blow through a yaoshu, penetrate an engine and detonate a cosmic tap."

Li Ming checked his weapon. The safety was on, the fire mode set to half power.

"Infinity guns are too powerful for such close work," Ghazan said. "I'll use my bayonet when I can."

Zhang Xinhua shook his head.

"You and your spear."

"It works, doesn't it?" Ghazan replied.

"I'll back you up," Li Ming said. "But stay behind me, and *out* of my arc of fire. Understand?"

Ghazan's eyes twinkled.

"Roger that."

With a running jump, Li Ming hauled himself up the side of the fallen trailer. The metal was slick with blood and gore. Instinctively he crouched, rooting himself. Ghazan planted himself next to Li Ming, sinking into a low stance of his own.

Now he saw the fort. Cars and trailer trucks lay piled atop each other, forming a rough circle. A small passageway between two stacks of cars served as the only entrance and exit. And as he watched, a strange rectangular object drifted across the street, as if it were a windblown leaf, creeping towards the passage. Li Ming zoomed in with his sights.

It was a car door.

"Do you see the door floating across the road?" Zhang Xinhua asked.

"I see it," Li Ming said. "I don't see the caster."

"Me neither."

"The beast has field effect magic. It doesn't need line of sight," Lan Yi said. "This is going to suck."

"You have non-line of sight magic too, don't you?" Zhang Xinhua asked.

"I'll need to get close to use it," Lan Yi said. "Twenty *chi* out."

"As close as the door was to the nest," Li Ming said.

"Yes. The second the nest is in range, I am too."

"How long do you need to cast your spell?" Ghazan asked.

"Five seconds. Maybe less."

"I shall charge into the nest and distract the beast long enough for you to cast your spell."

"I'm going too," Li Ming said.

"It's dangerous work," Zhang Xinhua said.

"I'm ready," Li Ming said. "I've got shields and countermeasures."

"I don't need backup," Ghazan said.

"If it has to split its attention between two targets, we'll buy a few extra moments."

"I should go instead," Zhang Xinhua said. "I've five thousand more qi points than you."

"We're just the distraction. Lan Biaohang will do the killing work. We need someone to go around the back and cut off the enemy's escape."

"He's got a point," Lan Yi said.

Zhang Xinhua sighed. "Very well. But don't be a hero, you hear? Enough people have died today."

They didn't rush. They had all the time in the world to do this. They stayed where they were for a minute, scanning the highway of death before them. Li Ming switched his sights back to 1X, scanning for movement in his peripheral vision.

He saw snaking lines of cars crushed together. Motorbikes squashed between vans and buses. Lakes of broken glass and rivers of dried blood. Dead yaoshu.

No sign of humans. Or human remains.

Cautiously they advanced down the highway. Hopping from roof to roof, hood to hood, they navigated the labyrinth of crushed steel and broken glass. Li Ming scanned near and far, watching for threats, while Ghazan prodded the bodies with his bayonet.

There was so much, too much, to see before him, a chaotic crush of smashed vehicles and debris. Li Ming kept his vision soft, using his peripheral vision, watching for movement, his breathing smooth and slender.

Death hung heavy in the air. Li Ming scented metallic blood, waste, fresh soap, sweet roasted meat. The yaoshu reeked of dirt and decay, of musk and mold, of a lifetime in the wilds. None of the bodies harbored any more than trace qi. Still he expanded his senses, feeling the world before him, hunting for souls.

Distant gunshots rang out. He'd learned from hard experience what incoming and outgoing fire sounded like. This was outgoing fire, too far away to matter. The hunters kept the remaining yaoshu from the highway, leaving the clearing team free to concentrate on their job.

Closer, closer, closer they drew to the yaoshu fortress. The military drone buzzed overhead, a silent guardian observing their progress. Its sensors were no less powerful than theirs, but it wasn't omniscient. It wasn't sentient, for that matter, and so it couldn't sense qi fields the way humans and living beings could.

Now they were eighty *chi* out. Fifty. Thirty.

And they halted.

"Do you feel it?" Song Huizhong whispered.

Li Ming did.

A large qi field emanated from the center of the fortress. Wild and chaotic, primal and starving, it pulled on his aura, seeking to draw everything around it into itself. Yet it was also pure and uncomplicated, easier to read than the human soul.

"The beast has an earth qi field," Li Ming said. "It has the power to draw anything in its area of influence into itself. If it's skilled enough, it can feed off fire-type magic to make itself stronger. We need wood to counter it."

"I use the eight trigrams system," Lan Yi said. "That means thunder or wind."

"Use thunder. Rain down lightning bolts on the nest."

"Works for me. Give me a sec."

Lan Yi set down his backpack and unzipped it. The interior was festooned with pouches mounted on hook-and-loop panels. He peeled off a large pouch and opened it to reveal a row of primordial crystals. Lan carefully detached the crystal from his shaper and swapped it for another.

"What are you doing?" Li Ming asked.

"Changing to a thunder crystal."

"Isn't an eight trigrams crystal good enough?"

"Only for general purpose use. For the spell I have in mind, I need a specialist crystal."

An eight trigram crystal could express eight kinds of energy. But it had one-eighth the qi output of a dedicated trigram crystal of equivalent size. Each kind of energy required specific crystalline structures and arrangements to store and manifest. Eight trigram magicians carried specialist crystals with them or toted oversized shapers with huge crystals to make up the difference. Or else they spent much more time charging up their shapers than others.

The eight trigram method was the most flexible magic system Li Ming knew, but that flexibility carried a price. The Special Military Police favored the yinyang system, a yin crystal on one arm and a yang crystal on the other, but it was lavishly funded and well-equipped, and there were things Li Ming could do with the other systems that the yinyang method couldn't.

The five element system offered the best compromise between flexibility and power. A five element crystal might have one-fifth the qi output of a single element crystal but made up for it by having the ability to deploy a hard counter to any kind of magic Li Ming might encounter. And if his magic failed, Li Ming could count on his guns and blades.

"Shapers up," Lan Yi said.

"Finally," Ghazan growled.

"Zhang Biaohang, move up first," Li Ming said. "See if there's an exit on the other side of the nest."

Zhang Xinhua deftly hopped from car to car. It was as if he were a fairy dancing in the wind, every move light and effortless. Li Ming covered his advance, sweeping the world, senses cranked to the max, ready to respond to the slightest hint of beasts and magic.

Zhang Xinhua shot past the fort and kept on going. He perched himself atop a bus and rotated through a small circle.

"All clear," Zhang Xinhua radioed. "There's a small passageway on the northern end, small enough for a yaoshu to squeeze through. I'll keep them from escaping."

"Roger," Li Ming said. "Ghazan, on me. We're going in."

The men bounded forward, two men covering, one man advancing. They communicated with hand signals, unwilling to risk being heard. Metal roofs creaked under the weight of their boots. Broken glass tinkled. The stench grew stronger with every step. Li Ming kept on eye on the automobile maze, another on the nest.

Inside the fortress, beasts skittered past windows and doors. Soft black forms, quick as cobras, fading from view as soon as he took up the aim. Their qi presence grew stronger, clearer, more distinct.

There were six of them. Five ordinary yaoshu, each as large as a scooter. And a gigantic demon rat, large as a minibus, seething with bestial malice.

Li Ming held up a hand. Pointed at Lan Yi. Held up a fist and spread out his fingers like a star. And pointed at the nest.

Lan Yi closed his eyes. Gathered qi into his being. And shook his head. He pointed at his face, then at a nearby car, brought his hand to his hip, and mimicked a quick scooping action.

Lan Yi was out of range. He had to move closer to use his magic.

Li Ming touched his thumb to forefinger. He turned to Ghazan—

Who was already on the move.

The Yue treaded carefully across the roof of a passenger bus, approaching the entrance to the nest from the right. Li Ming studied the world before him, plotted a route to the left side of the passage, and skipped over to a nearby car. And the next. And the next. And the next.

The beasts' pungent odor overpowered Li Ming's senses. His eyes threatened to tear. He'd never smelled anything as terrible as that in his life. And beneath that was another scent. Blood and death. Heedless of the olfactory assault, Li Ming pushed on.

As he approached the nest, he spotted the discarded door. It lay in between two towers of stacked and crushed cars, a roof that defined the entrance of the nest. For a moment Li Ming wondered how it had managed to get there.

Then he felt the pull.

An invisible force lifted him off the ground, hurtling him through the air. Suddenly down was sideways and sideways was somewhere else. The center of the planet shifted this way and that, dragging him with it, pulling him towards the opening.

Ghazan shrieked in fury. Tumbling about in mid-air, he glowed blazing white, as blinding as the sun. He uttered something in his native tongue, and suddenly he righted himself, just in time to catch the door-roof against his helmet.

The door went flying. Ghazan brought his weapon to bear, howling a war cry, and vanished into the narrow passage.

And then it was Li Ming's turn.

Metal. Window. Glass. Metal. Glass. Window. Sharp corners and jagged edges ripped at his clothes. Something cracked against his helmet. He touched his shaper, felt the stored qi there, ready for use.

And he plowed into the nest.

In a fraction of a second his senses captured everything important. The five yaoshu arrayed around him singing at a high pitch. Gnawed bones and entrails scattered around like a mat. Ghazan aiming his bayonet like a spear, shining as bright as a celestial spirit.

The brood mother, looming tall over him.

The Evolved yaoshu glared at him with bright yellow eyes. A jewel inset into its forehead pulsed with ethereal light. Standing on its hindlegs, it dug its claws into the ground, holding itself firm. It opened its jaws, revealing teeth the size of sabers.

A part of Li Ming screamed to resist the magic, to make right what was wrong, to plant himself back down. But he recognized instantly it would be suicide. He would tangle himself up with the other yaoshu, and he would abandon Ghazan to his fate. He could not, *must not*, resist the magic.

He had to yield into it.

And in yielding, he conquered.

Wood conquered earth. Wood parted earth, the roots of a great tree digging into the ground, yet simultaneously holding it together. He flashed the stored energy in his crystals to wood qi, wrapping himself in a cloak of wood.

And accelerated.

Suddenly the gravitational wave fell apart. He could still feel it buffeting his body, an unseen force trying to draw him into the beast's mouth. But he was like an arrow shooting through the air, the steel head parting all before it. Now, instead of rising into the beast's maw, he simply shot forward in a straight line, rocketing to its breast.

In a single, fluid stroke, he drew his swordbreaker with his left hand and brought it to his right hip. Aimed the weapon. Thrust.

Impact.

The swordbreaker punched through bone, fat, muscle, sinking all the way to the hilt.

A heartbeat later, Ghazan slammed into the beast, his bayonet driving deep into its throat.

"THUNDER CRASH!" Lan Yi yelled.

Lightning bolts screamed from the heavens, shattering everything on impact. Concussive booms ripped through Li Ming, bounced off the walls of the nest, struck him again and again. The successive shock waves drove the air from his lungs and battered his organs. His ear and eye protection cut in, blinding and deafening him. Yaoshu shrieked. Blood splashed. Debris scored his clothes and armor.

The world returned to sanity.

Now Li Ming saw a huge smoking hole in the brood mother's upper torso, next to its right shoulder. The thunderbolt had blasted clean through the beast. But it wasn't a fatal wound. Li Ming's cameras reported its qi score. 12891 points and falling fast.

Not fast enough.

And the brood mother toppled.

It fell away from Li Ming, pulling him down to the earth. He held on to dear life, breathing deep, sending qi to his depleted crystals. Ghazan gripped his weapon with one hand, punched the monster's jaw with the other. Something broke, something else shattered, then a river of cracking sounds filled Li Ming's ears, and the brood mother hit the road with a colossal boom.

With both hands, Li Ming tugged at the swordbreaker. It was buried so deep, it barely budged. The brood mother writhed and flailed, clawing and scratching at the air. It twisted to the right, trying to roll over. Li Ming levered to the left, trying to counteract and control the colossal beast's movements, expanding the wound.

"Ghazan!" Li Ming shouted. "We have to get off this beast!"

Ghazan fired.

A geyser of vaporized blood gushed into the air. Ghazan rode the force of the explosion, leaping clear from its half-severed throat.

Gurgling in pain, the beast twisted to the left, away from the wound. Li Ming yanked to the right, jiggling and stirring, trying to—

The beast tipped over.

Li Ming let go and jumped away. Contorting in mid-air, he infused himself with the power of earth. He landed softly but awkwardly, falling on his butt.

The brood mother hauled itself upright. Bright red blood gushed from its enormous wounds. In the chaos, its spiny tail had broken off. Even so, it wagged its bloody stump, trying to whip at the biaohang.

Li Ming scrambled to his feet, taking up his infinity gun, scanning around him. The other yaomo were dead. Definitively, gorily, dead. Only the brood mother was left.

Ghazan hustled over, weapon at port arms, maneuvering for a better shot. The brood mother lumbered around on unsteady feet, orienting towards Li Ming. It loosed an ear-splitting shriek, a shriek he felt in his hair and skin and bones. Its forehead jewel flashed, and a powerful gravitational force yanked him towards its yawning mouth.

Li Ming fired.

Ghazan fired.

Twin plasma bursts detonated in the depths of the creature's maw. Gore gushed from its orifices. The magic cut out suddenly. The creature slumped over, now completely and definitively dead.

"It's dead," Ghazan said.

"At last," Li Ming said.

Chapter Twenty-One

Harvest

Li Ming and Ghazan huffed and heaved and pushed, rolling the enormous Evolved beast over on its side. Li Ming braced one foot against its enormous chest, strengthened his arms and legs with fire, grabbed the swordbreaker.

And pulled.

And pulled.

And *pulled*.

And now the long blade that wasn't a blade freed itself from dead flesh. Li Ming held it up to the light, inspecting it. Somehow, between the magic, the plasma, and the sheer weight of the creature falling on it as the yaoshu turned around, the weapon had survived practically unscathed.

A miracle.

Wiping off his swordbreaker on the monster's thick hide, Li Ming asked, "How did your bayonet fare?"

Ghazan held his up to the light, and sighed.

"Blasted."

The blade had warped and broken under the intense heat of a point-blank plasma shot. Now it was a broken stump of jagged steel, coated in thick red blood.

"During bayonet training, my instructors advised us never to shoot a threat off our bayonet unless we absolutely had to," Li Ming said.

"I think the situation counted," Ghazan said, and shrugged. "Bayonets are replaceable."

"Why not get a fixed bayonet?"

"On occasions where it isn't appropriate to use one, it is troublesome to put it on and take it off. A folding bayonet can be mounted permanently and deployed when needed."

"Folders are weaker than fixed blades."

"Immaterial in this case. The fixed bayonets I've tried also break after one or two point-blank shots. Kicking the enemy off or dumping him remains the best solution where feasible."

Song Huizhong's voice cut into the radio net.

"Special Military Police reports all beasts in the area are down. We'll regroup and continue to patrol towards their position."

Li Ming felt no more beast qi traces around him. But it always paid to be sure.

The biaohang rallied south of the nest. Li Ming counted them as they approached. They were all alive, all relatively well, though a few of them had picked up small cuts and bruises. Cai Yan looked him up and down, and her eyes widened.

"Your throat's been cut."

Li Ming breathed in.

Gulped.

Breathed out.

"But it's just a scratch," she added hastily. "It's not even bleeding anymore."

Li Ming touched the delicate skin of his throat. A twinge of pain passed through him. But his gloved hand came away dry and cool.

"Do you feel any burning sensations? Any chills or fever? Nausea? Dizziness?" she asked.

"I'm fine. Must be shrapnel. Nothing to worry about."

Just in case, Li Ming patted himself down. He found small cuts across his uniform, one of them wet—A claw? A tooth?—but none had penetrated the tough reinforced fabric.

She pursed her lips. "Keep monitoring your wound. If you feel anything, *anything* out of the ordinary, take the antivenin immediately."

"Roger that."

The group made their way south, following the highway. It was jammed all the way to the city's edge, a pile-up to end all pile-ups, so many cars and buses and trucks and bikes Li Ming stopped counting. He'd never seen so many vehicles crammed in one place before. Yet the biaohang acted as if it were a perfectly ordinary sight.

In the big city, maybe it was.

The traffic jam finally ended at the toll plaza. Six automated gates, one to a lane, controlled access to the highway, and with it, the city. There were no humans here, only cameras and sensors and electronic payment machines.

Long rows of high poles, each as tall as a man, marched from the outskirts of the plaza into the distance, encircling the city. Six retractable bollards rose from the road, sealing off the perimeter. Blazing blue energies emanated from the posts, forming an impenetrable wall of crackling thunder qi.

Here was the Bao An City Barrier. The slightest brush would produce a painful electric shock, sufficient to scare off a wandering beast. Li Ming had read rumors that a determined attacker hell-bent on running through the barrier would be fatally electrocuted, though the authorities steadfastly denied such rumors.

Even this far out, he could hear the constant hum of their emitters, taste the ozone in the air, feel stray sparks dancing across his exposed skin. Li Ming had thought the plaza itself had been breached. But, no, it was still standing, the barrier still intact.

The actual breach was off to the southwest, a hundred *chi* from the toll plaza proper. Eight stumps jutted from the ground like broken teeth. Large enough to admit a horde of yaoshu.

A platoon of Special Military Police troopers guarded both sides of the breach. They'd come loaded for dragons, their defensive lines bristling with infinity cannons. Military engineers equipped with exoskeletons and specialist tools delicately extracted the damaged machinery from the posts and lowered fresh poles into place. Past the breach, a squadron of Bear armored vehicles formed an echelon, their weapons trained at the grasslands and forests past the boundaries of Bao An.

Torn-up beast corpses surrounded the troopers on both sides of the breach.

"Tewujing, hello!" Song Huizhong yelled, waving.

"Dayong, is that you?" a trooper shouted.

"That's us! Can we come over?"

"Go ahead!"

Lieutenant Chen was a short man, coming up to Li Ming's nose. His uniform, helmet, armor, everything on his person seemed a tad too big for him. Yet somehow, as the biaohang approached, he seemed to expand outwards, filling out his kit.

"We finally meet!" Lieutenant Chan said.

Song Huizhong shook his hand. "Pleasure to meet you. Thank you for the support."

"Least I could do. I'm sorry the Air Force wouldn't help. We could have ended it early if the gunships were authorized to fire."

"Rules of engagement are a beast," Li Ming said.

"True, true. We saw your fight with the Evolved yaoshu. That was incredible," Lieutenant Chan said.

"I'm just lucky to be alive."

"You're a martial immortal. It must be easy for you."

"I'm no immortal. In fact, it hasn't even been a year since I was discharged from the military."

"Really? Where did you serve?"

"Tewujing. Capital Region Battalion."

"*Wo...* A brother trooper!"

"I'm out of the Army."

"Once Tewujing, always Tewujing."

Li Ming smiled tightly. "You got that right."

"Are there any more beasts in the area?" Song Huizhong asked.

Lieutenant Chen danced his fingers through the air, consulting his augmented reality visor.

"You got them all. Air Force reports that the district is clear, and that there are no signs of dangerous beasts in a thirty-*li* radius around the breach. There's a few out there, but they are keeping their distance from the breach."

"How did the beasts breach the barrier anyway?" Li Ming asked. "I thought the posts are reinforced."

"Bao An is a third class city," Song Huizhong said. "The government gives enough money to build and maintain the barrier, not enough to reinforce them. It costs the city less to deploy biaohang to respond to beast hordes than to build a sturdier barrier."

"But that places people at risk!"

"The city thinks it's an acceptable risk. Besides, the barrier does nothing against beasts that can jump or fly. There'll still be a need for biaohang."

"This would never happen in Taiping."

"If beasts invade the capital, someone's head will roll. If they invade Bao An, everyone gets a chance to make money."

"Unbelievable..."

"On the bright side, we'll always have a job," Ghazan said.

Li Ming shook his head. He didn't, couldn't, say anything. If he opened his mouth, he feared he would lose control.

Song Huizhong turned to Lieutenant Chan.

"If there's nothing else for us, we'll back clear the city and call in the clean-up crews."

"Go ahead. We'll stay here and protect the breach."

"Nimen xinku le."

You've worked hard.

"Bu, bu, bu, nimen cai shi xinku le."

No, no, no, you're the ones who worked hard.

"We get to go home after this. We'll get paid well too. You... you're stuck with this until you're done, and you'll only get chickenfeed," Li Ming said.

"Tell the men that. I'm a regular."

The biaohang and the trooper chuckled.

Now came the part Li Ming hated the most: recovery, security and consolidation.

The next two hours passed in brutal tedium. Cleanup crews from the Jianghu Association roamed the city, collecting the scattered beast parts and cadavers, cataloging their findings, bundling everything into large body bags and hauling them aboard refrigerated trucks.

The Dayong biaohang escorted the workers from place to place. At secured scenes, the workers compared the biaohang's notes and photos with the cops'. At unsecured locations, they scoured the scene thoroughly, scooping up every last scrap of flesh and bone.

Inevitably, there were discrepancies.

"What the devil happened to my kill?" Cai Yong exclaimed.

"I do not see any kills," the foreman said. "I see bloodstains. I see a photograph of a dead yaoshu. I do not see the yaoshu itself."

Cai Yong sighed in frustration. "Someone must have carted it off. You see the drag marks. See how it ends so abruptly? Someone must have wrapped it up in a tarp or something."

"Nonetheless, I don't see a body, and none of my workers have found a body. I'll mark this spot for follow-up investigation. If a claims investigator from the Association finds eyewitnesses who can corroborate your account, you will be credited with the kill. But without a body, we can't issue a bounty. You know how this works."

Similar scenes repeated all over the neighborhoods adjacent to the highway. Five yaoshu bodies had mysteriously vanished from the scenes. Biaohang argued with civilian shooters over who had killed what and where, and who was entitled to what kind of compensation.

Mere anarchy descended on the highway. Civilians returned to their vehicles. Rescue crews attempted to extricate stuck vehicles. Traffic police tried to maintain a semblance of order. Off to the side, the cleanup crew and the biaohang struggled to work out the timeline of combat.

Li Ming couldn't remember how many yaoshu he'd killed. Was it three? Four? He wasn't sure. He didn't keep track, and the workers had moved the corpses before he could jog his memories. But there was one thing he was sure of.

"The bayoneted ones are Ghazan's work," Li Ming said. "All of them. Solo kills."

The foreman seemed impressed. "You hunt beasts with bayonets?"

"Most challenging," Ghazan said. "Most rewarding too."

"What about the brood mother? Who took that one?"

"Myself, Li Ming, and Lan Yi. Joint kill."

"No, no, that was you and Li Ming," Lan Yi said.

"You hit it with your lightning bolt," Li Ming said.

"From what you told me, it barely slowed it down. You two risked your lives. You should reap the rewards."

"How much is the bounty for that anyway?" Li Ming asked.

The foreman shrugged. "You'll have to ask the assessor. I just collect the dead."

Li Ming found the assessor in the outer garden of the Dayong compound. Seated next to Cai Mengyang, the assessor scrolled through multiple galleries on his slate, comparing the photos the biaohang took to the cleanup workers' imagery.

"Everything checks out," the assessor said. "A shame about the stolen kills, but in a site as chaotic as this, it can't be helped. I'll deploy investigators to the areas you mentioned to follow up with the locals. I can't promise you that they'll recover the bodies, but they'll do their best to at least get your biaohang credited for the kills."

"Thank you." Boss Cai looked up at Li Ming. "Li Ming, good timing. This is Assessor Meng from the Jianghu Association, one of the most experienced assessors in Bao An. The Association usually sends him to handle major hunts like this."

Li nodded. "Good afternoon, Assessor Meng."

"Afternoon, Li Biaohang. You're new here?"

"I entered the jianghu barely three weeks ago."

Assessor Meng chuckled.

"A hunt like this is an exciting debut, yes?"

"Absolutely. The yaoshu were right at our doorstep."

"I saw the bodies. Dangerous work. Are you all right? Yaoshu venom is deadly."

Li Ming nodded. "I'm fine. Kept my distance."

"Good, good. I don't care what people say about how valuable yaoshu venom is. You can't cash it in if you're dead."

"It's a rough business all round," Boss Cai said.

"But a necessary one. Keeps all of us fed."

"What's next on the timeline?" Li Ming asked. "Do you need anything else from us?"

"I will need preliminary statements by tomorrow, and then a full report in the next thirty days. You don't have to do into detail for your preliminary statements. Save it for the report. In your statements, I just need to know what you killed, with what weapon, and where. That way I know who to credit with each kill."

"How are kills assessed?"

"You don't know?"

"This is his first beast hunt," Boss Cai said. "We haven't had time to explain how everything works."

"Been busy?"

"Every day," Li Ming affirmed.

"*Ni xinku le.* Anyway, to answer your question, we use a point deduction scoring system to grade your kills.

"It starts at a hundred points. From there, we take away points based on the quantity and quality of harvested meat, organs and bones. This system has three main point bands.

"The first and lowest band is for chunks. These are bits and pieces blown off from the body. Usually they are bruised, cooked, bleeding... all this reduces their value. It only pays compost, but it's better than nothing, and in a situation like this, it all adds up.

"The next band is for partials. Whole limbs severed from the body, or beasts missing significant chunks of flesh. With infinity guns and destructive magic in play, this is the most common grade of recovered beasts. Once again, battle damage will reduce the value of the harvest, but quantity makes up for it.

"The highest band is for whole animals. A clean kill, minimal damage to the hide, meat and internals. Many companies will pay a premium for wholes, and the Association will pass it on to you. This is why many beast hunters prefer to use old-fashioned weapons. Slug guns, crossbows, bows, spears, that sort of thing."

"Isn't that dangerous?"

"Absolutely. But reward is commensurate with risk."

"As with everything in the jianghu," Boss Cai said.

"True, true."

"What can harvested beasts be used for?" Li Ming asked.

"Lots of things. Chunks are composted and used as fertilizer. Agricultural companies claim that fertilizer made from beasts is nutrient-rich. They'll buy chunks from us, compost them, then sell it to farmers. Higher-grade chunks can be also used for meat and bone meal, either for animal consumption or for biomass power generators, but given the condition we find chunks in, this tends to be the exception.

"Partials have more uses. We can recover hide and turn it into leather scraps. Bones are used for medicines, plastics, music instruments, tools, and so on. Depending on their condition, meat and organs can be used for animal feed, human consumption, or pharmaceutical use. If, however, the meat's been left out for too long, we compost it.

"As for whole animals, our first priority is to recover valuable but sensitive tissue from harvested beasts, such as nerves, eyes, and tongues. They can be used for medicines, industrial research and the like. Yaoshu venom, in particular, can be used for manufacturing antivenin and for treating cancers and nerve diseases. Then we'll harvest the hide, meat, organs, bone and marrow.

"The more uses we can find for your harvest, the more we will pay you for it. The actual payout will also depend on the age, sex, and threat level of the beast you bring in. It's complicated enough that you need to complete a six-week training course and a three-month apprenticeship program before you're licensed to assess beast kills."

"What about the yaoshu we destroyed with fire or lightning?" Li Ming asked.

"Compost. Or bone meal. That's all they're good for. That's we can pay you for. Sorry."

"I understand. What about an Evolved? How do you assess one?"

"An Evolved beast is formally defined as a beast that possesses an unusually high concentration of primordial crystalline structures in its body. That's how they can cultivate and use magic. In addition to the standard scoring method, we use another system to assess the recovered beast crystals. This one is an additive system: the higher the quantity and quality of crystals you recover, the more you'll be paid.

"Take the brood mother. Its forehead crystal alone is easily worth fifty thousand yuan. And that's not counting other crystals we may recover from the spines, organs and bloodstream."

Li Ming's eyes goggled.

"Fifty *thousand*?"

"Sure. It's intact, it's clear, it's the size of a child's fist, it's easily worth that much. I'll need to send it in for a lab analysis, of course, but fifty thousand yuan is a good estimate."

Boss Cai slapped Li Ming's shoulder. "You've just earned yourself a nice payday."

"That was you?" Assessor Meng asked.

"And another biaohang. We shared the kill."

"Not bad. But to manage your expectations a little, we can't pay you top-tier bounties for your harvest. Not today, anyway."

"Most of them were chunks?"

"Yes. That, and they've been left out for a long time."

"Spoilage?"

"Precisely. The freshness of recovered meat is an important scoring criterion. Freshly harvested and preserved tissue can be used for many purposes. Spoiled or unsafe tissue can only be composted or burned.

"We use the 1-2-3 rule to grade the freshness of meat. One hour for chunks, two hours for partials, three for whole animals. If the harvest has been lying around longer than that without being preserved or processed, or if we see identify signs of spoilage, it's automatically given the lowest score and composted."

"And this hunt lasted for the morning and most of the afternoon," Li Ming mused.

"Exactly. The second you kill a beast, it starts to spoil. Your colleagues had the foresight to chill the harvest with ice. But since the beasts you slaughtered during the first wave was left lying around, well... we can only pay you for compost."

"I see..."

"Don't be so disappointed. The sheer number of beasts you destroyed makes up for it. And you protected the city from a yaoshu horde. Never forget that."

"Money isn't important," Boss Cai added. "There'll always be opportunities to make money. If the tactical situation doesn't allow you to chill meat before recovery, don't do it. Your life, and the lives of those around you, must come first."

"Roger that."

"Even though you didn't have time to chill some of the bodies, you'll still make a lot of money from this hunt," Assessor Meng said. "One of your biaohang brought in eleven whole yaoshu. He killed them with a single spear thrust. Amazing work. Whoever he is, I'd like to shake his hand."

"That must be Ghazan," Li Ming said.

"You're working with some of the finest biaohang in the business," Assessor Meng said. "Your boss sure knows how to pick talent."

Boss Cai chuffed. "It's why Dayong is the best biaoju in the province."

"I killed a yaoshu with a swordbreaker. How much is that worth?"

"Swordbreaker?" Assessor Meng said.

"This one," Li Ming said, patting the weapon.

"Let me see it."

Slowly but smoothly, Li Ming drew the swordbreaker from his sheath. Assessor Meng stared at the blade for a long while.

"I've been in this business for twenty years. This is the first time I've seen a biaohang carry a swordbreaker for a hunt."

"It's my only long cold weapon."

"Most biaohang prefer edged weapons. Why do you carry a swordbreaker?"

"Family heirloom."

"I never thought you were the sentimental type," Boss Cai said.

"Also, it's the only weapon I could take from the town armory."

"That sounds more like it."

"A swordbreaker is an impact weapon, isn't it? I'd advise you not to use it for hunts. It'll damage hide, bruise muscle, break bones. It'll reduce the value of the harvest," Assessor Meng said.

"The tip is sharp. I used it to kill a yaoshu with a single thrust."

"You mean the brood mother?"

"No, the one I killed in the house across the street."

"You did? I didn't see that body."

"What do you mean?"

"Your swordbreaker has a very distinctive blade profile. It'll create a cross-shaped wound. Except for the brood mother, none of the recovered bodies have a wound like that."

"What the devil?"

Boss Cai's face hardened. "How about we go through the photos of the harvest one more time?"

They did. Photo after photo, dozens of them, taken from multiple angles and positions across the district. Other biaohang buzzed around them. Li Ming barely noticed. He scrutinized every body, looking for the beast he had slain with his swordbreaker.

"It's not here," Li Ming said.

"Someone must have stolen it," Assessor Meng said.

Li Ming's voice dropped to a cold, murderous whisper.

"I think I know where it is."

"You should go recover it before it disappears into the black market," Assessor Meng said.

Li Ming rose to his feet. "I'll be back."

"Wait!" Boss Cai said. "Xiao Yan!"

And suddenly she was standing next to Li Ming.

"Yes?" she said.

"Li Ming is going to recover a missing body. I want you to accompany him and represent the company."

Her eyes narrowed.

"Do you expect trouble?"

"If scavengers took it, yes."

She nodded and checked her Avenger.

"I'm ready."

"Let's go," Li Ming said.

L i Ming marched across the street, Cai Yan three steps behind.

Cold fury radiated from every pore. With every step, he discharged fire into the earth. His hands bunched into fists.

He saved two lives and this was how he was repaid for it? Madness. He would not stand for this.

The hutong was slowly returning to normal. Police watched the cleaner spray down bloodstains with high-pressure hoses. Biaohang lingered around, waiting for future instructions. Civilians crept out of their houses, reopened their shops, unlocked the hutong gate.

All of them gave Li Ming a wide berth.

Li Ming counted the doors down the street. He replayed the memory of that kill in his mind. He identified his objective by the claw marks the yaoshu had left on the window frame. He planted himself at the entrance. Breathed. And pounded the door three times.

"Dayong Biaoju! Open up!"

"Coming!" a girl called.

Li Ming waited. Breathed. Waited some more.

The door slid open, revealing the little girl he had seen hours ago.

"I need to speak to your grandmother."

She whipped her head around.

"*Nainai!* The Dayong biaohang are here!"

The grandmother shuffled into view. He locked his eyes on hers, searching for the slightest hint of guilt.

Her face brightened into a huge smile.

"Ah! You're the one who saved us! Come, come! I have something for you!"

Li Ming blinked.

Breathed.

And entered the building, hand on his pistol.

The first floor was a small sundries shop. The shelves were crammed with a dizzying array of goods. Candy, snacks, jars of preserved fruits, household goods, toys, scattered at random around the place. Long ceiling-mounted hooks suspended brooms, balls, dustpans, feather dusters. The elderly woman squeezed through the shelves and made her way through the back door.

Here was a tiny indoor courtyard. An open-air kitchen, a small fridge, a plastic table and some chairs, laundry hung out to dry. A flight of steps led up to the second floor. The grandmother beckoned Li Ming onwards, up the stairs and through a small door.

Li Ming extended his senses, feeling the qi of the world around him. The girl's qi, young and small and filled with potential. Cai Yan's qi, blindingly bright and powerful. The grandmother's qi, shrunken and wrinkled. That was all. No surprises lying in wait.

The moment he stepped through the door, a familiar scent hit him. Blood. Diluted and thin, but blood nonetheless. A soft trickling sound came from the bathroom.

"Come, come," the elderly woman gestured, pulling aside the bathroom curtains. "Take a look."

A large yaoshu lay in a bathtub, buried under a mound of half-melted ice and submerged in pink water. A hose ran into the tub, bubbling away. Its limbs were carefully folded, its eyes closed, but for the cross-shaped hole in its forehead and its missing tail, it could have been simply sleeping.

Li Ming blinked. Blinked again. Blinked a third time. He knew what was looking at, but he wasn't sure if he could comprehend it.

"I read about how biaohang are paid by the freshness, quantity and quality of their kills," she said. "Once we heard the all-clear, I dragged the yaoshu into the tub and poured ice and cold water over it to keep it fresh. Now you can sell it at the best price."

Li Ming's jaw dropped. The fire within dispersed. His hands unclenched.

"I... thank you."

"No problem. Thank you for saving us. It's the least we could do."

Cai Yan bowed.

"On behalf of Dayong, we thank you for your kindness and your service."

"*Aiya*, it's nothing. You've protected our city for generations. Now we can repay the favor."

"You didn't have to do this for us. Let me pay for you for—"

"No no no no no! You did all the hard work! You put your life at risk for us! I just cooled it down, that's all!"

"Ice and water isn't cheap. We can help you—"

"No need to worry about that. It's a small matter."

"You helped us earn a lot of money with this. We can share some of it with you."

"*Aiya*, what is money? I already have enough."

"You did right by us. If we don't pay you back, we're not showing you face."

"Okay, okay, okay. You don't have to give us a lot."

Cai Yan drew her wallet from her pocket and pulled out a sheath of banknotes. The elderly woman recoiled.

"It's too much! Too much!"

Cai Yan gently pressed the money into her hand.

"You've helped us make ten times that amount. Call it a token of our appreciation."

"Thank you, Miss Cai!"

Li Ming and Cai Yan carried the still-dripping carcass out the building. This time, everyone stared as they left. Together they brought it to the gate of the hutong. A cleanup crew hung around, chatting and relaxing. As the biaohang approached, they rose to attention.

"We've recovered a missing beast!" Li Ming called.

A worker sighed. "We've already packed everything."

Cai Yan smiled sweetly.

"*Shuaige, qing bangbang yi xia!*"

Hey handsome, please help us for a while!

The foreman laughed.

"Come on, guys. Let's go."

The workers wrapped the beast in clear plastic and loaded it on the truck. The biaohang and the foreman filled out the necessary paperwork.

"Keep up the good work," Cai Yan said.

"You too," the foreman said. "We appreciate you protecting the city from beasts."

"Hey, you do an important job too. You clean up after we're done and you help us get paid. Thanks for helping."

"No problem."

Li Ming and Cai Yan strolled leisurely down the hutong. The police were leaving. The biaohang were returning to the compound. Life was restarting.

"Back to the compound?" she asked.

"Yes, I—"

His stomach announced its existence. Loudly.

She laughed.

"When was the last time you ate?"

"Last night."

"No time for breakfast?"

"And lunch."

"Me too. I'm famished."

"Let's go wash up and have lunch together."

Her eyes sparkled.

"Sure!"

Chapter Twenty-Two

A Man and A Woman

The days and weeks rushed past like a flood. Li Ming was always on the go, doing something somewhere in the city or its outskirts.

Every job was different. Escorting a wealthy foreigner and his family as they toured the city on vacation. Protecting a high-risk witness to and from the courthouse. Supporting a neighbourhood watch in patrolling the streets following a rash of break-ins.

Sometimes he worked alone. Usually he was part of a larger group. He partnered with Song Huizhong to conduct a security audit at a corporate office. He worked with Ghazan and the Cais to put together a training workshop for the Police Tactical Unit, focusing on dealing with criminal cultivators. When beasts invaded a scrapyard just past the city's limits, he rolled heavy with a team of biaohang—and spent the night manning a blocking position while they hunted monsters.

At least he would be paid a share of the bounty.

For the next three nights, nightmares haunted him. Visions of fire and smoke, blood and screams, shapeless nightmares with claws and teeth. The things he'd seen, the things he'd done, they all came back to haunt him.

He'd done everything he could. Everything Duty had demanded of him. A foster family without children of their own had adopted the baby he and Cai Yan had rescued. Surely that had to count for something in the grand scheme of things.

Finally the nightmares faded—if only because he was too tired to dream.

The workload was intense. Cai Mengyang hadn't been kidding when he described life as a biaohang. If anything, he'd downplayed it. Most people enjoyed three days off every week. He had two—in a month. The rest of the time, he was working one job or other. There were so many different kinds of jobs, he figured it was deliberate. His seniors must have wanted him to gain as much experience in as many fields as humanly possible in such a short time.

With every job, Li Ming tallied up his job points. A hundred points for protecting Dong Hai, eighty for another job, fifty for a third. Then one day he woke up to discover that the Jianghu Association had poured eight hundred points into his account.

The Bao An job. He'd slain many beasts, protected the city, felled an Evolved. Just like that, some five weeks after entering the jianghu, he'd already cleared one of the major obstacles to promotion. Now all he needed was six months of experience in a biaoju, and he'd become a bronze ranker.

And after that... the jianghu lay open to him.

Everything in his life was ever-changing. Except his training.

Every morning, he trained. Zhan zhuang. Five Elements. Twelve Animals. No exceptions. Some days he moved on to physical training, with weights and long runs and other exercises he remembered from his military days. On others he worked with dummy weapons. Sometimes he sparred with Ghazan, or practiced yizhang with Cai Yan. But always, *always*, he made time for the fist and the swordbreaker.

He knew the forms by heart. He could perform them in his sleep. But the sum of his knowledge of the applications, follow-ups and principles of the art was but a drop of water in an endless ocean. With every step of every form, he thought about what he could do with them. What was the intended purpose of that movement, and what else he could do from there.

Ghazan was quite happy to test Li Ming's knowledge. The Yue wasn't content to simply be a practice dummy. As soon as Li Ming thought he had a movement down, they banged through a scenario at full speed, zero compliance. As close to combat as they could mimic. In these situations Li Ming discovered the flaws in his strategy, the chinks in his defenses, the errors in his techniques, and constantly refined them.

Li Ming in turn did the same for Ghazan, helping him sharpen his own fighting skills—and, along the way, learning some shifangquan by osmosis. Their yaoshu hunt had further broken down the barriers between them, and now he was comfortable discussing and transmitting some of the basic techniques of the art.

Still, Ghazan always trained alone in the morning.

Cai Yan was less combative-minded. She understood the need for resistance testing, but she didn't *like* it. Between running through a two-man set and outright sparring, she always chose the former. She didn't say why, but Li Ming sensed she was uncomfortable up close and personal, at the range where the fiercest fighting took place.

But then, she wasn't a fighter. She was a magician. If she had to go hands-on with someone, things would have gone terribly wrong.

Dayong understood the value of training too. On the sixth week after Li Ming's arrival, Boss Cai sent half of its staff to a three-day combat training package. At a ranch in the middle of the forests fifty *li* northeast of Bao An, they worked with former military and police special operations veterans to hone their skills and install new ones.

Training was intense. More intense than what he'd experienced in the military. From the moment they arrived, they worked an astonishing range of scenarios. Close quarters battle. Dignitary protection. Field combat. Sweeping for beasts. The most intense situations a biaohang would find himself in. They began at dawn and worked late into the evening, then stayed up even longer to discuss finer technical points.

They returned to Dayong late that night. The moment Li Ming trudged through the gate, he saw Cai Mengyang waiting for them in the garden.

"You've trained hard, did you?" Boss Cai said.

"They really put us through our paces," Li said, stifling a yawn. "My brain feels like it's been stretched and kneaded like dough."

"Take the weekend off. All of you. You need the rest, and I cleared your schedule. Come back to work on Jia-Day."

Sweeter words Li had not heard since his arrival in Bao An.

He cleaned his kit. He showered. He collapsed into bed.

Habit pulled him awake at his accustomed time. He was groggy, fatigued, aching. Part of him wanted to go back to bed and wake up when he was feeling more human. But, through the window, he heard a distant, rhythmic stomping.

Ghazan.

He'd never met a man more obsessed with the martial arts. But that was what it took to be the best in the jianghu.

Li Ming dragged himself to the washroom and cleaned up. He splashed ice-cold water on his face over and over, but it failed to revitalize him. That was all right. After morning cultivation, he would be wide awake.

In the courtyard, he stood stock-still for long ke, frozen in the three powers stance, bringing mind and body and spirit in line with Heaven and Earth. He punched his way up and down the courtyard, splitting and drilling and crushing and blasting and crossing. Sweat gathered in his armpits and thighs, clean and honest, the sweat that came from hard labor.

Sure enough, he felt the qi flow through him. But it was weak, the slow trickle of a lazy brook, a languid tingling in his muscles. No massive energy surges, no sudden eruptions, no heavy qi fields.

That was all right. Personal feeling didn't matter. Smooth qi circulation was far more important.

His daily routine completed, he shifted to the second phase of training. With empty hand and swordbreaker, he revisited the techniques and principles he had learned at the camp.

The instructors had come from a wide range of backgrounds. The techniques came from all over the world. He hunted for the universals, for the principles that bridged his art and theirs. He sought to adapt these new techniques to the wuxingquan framework, to the Five Elements and the Twelve Animals.

Some techniques were easy. A straight punch was a straight punch, after all, the force simple and easy to perceive. But grappling and counter-grappling, little tricks and set-ups, those needed brain sweat, more than he could summon at this time.

Presently he grew aware of someone staring at him. But it was a friendly gaze, light as a feather, carrying no ill intent. He slashed and stabbed at the air a few more times with his swordbreaker, transitioning to a takedown or a lock wherever possible, and at last turned around.

"Good morning," Cai Yan said.

She was dressed for training. Loose white jacket and comfortable red pants, gleaming in the pale light.

"Morning," he said.

"You're revising what you learned at the camp?"

"Yup."

"You're a hard worker, aren't you?"

"Through constant practice, you reach the pinnacle of gongfu."

"Are you planning to be the leader of the jianghu?"

"First I'll need to be a martial immortal. And it's a long way up a distant mountain."

"I'm sure you'll get there someday."

A voice, calm and quiet, whispered in his mind.

But if you do, what then?

He had no answer.

"I see you were working takedowns and grapples," she said.

"Yes, I'm trying to see how I can integrate what we learned with what I know."

"I don't know if it'll work with wuxingquan, but yizhang smoothly integrates grappling and striking. We should see if it works in that context."

"Sure. Do you need to warm up?"

She smiled. "Sure. Let's do two man sets."

They assumed their stances. Hands outstretched, torsos twisted to face each other, feet and legs oriented to the left, ready for instant motion. He nodded. She nodded.

They flowed.

By now he knew her touch. Her qi. Soft and yielding, evasive and fluid, she smoothly swirled through posture after posture, technique after technique, the energies manifesting in a moment and suddenly fading away.

She was air and water, swift and elusive; he was fire and earth, explosive and grounded. They switched roles, over and over, and yet expressed their moves as only their bodies and personalities could.

A strange feeling came over him. Similar to the first time they had walked the circle, but deeper, more profound, touching him at the depths of his being. She was the yin to his yang, softness to his hardness. Yet in every touch he felt steel encased in silk, fire submerged in water. Within himself, he sensed the stillness in his motion, the serenity of focused chaos. Their energies blended, a harmonious dance of action and reaction, every step containing a movement that led to utter domination or swift change.

Round and round they went, stepping through circles large and small, finding the lines in the circles and the circles in the lines. All at once, as though a veil had fallen away, he saw strikes and grapples becoming one and the same, palms and feet shaping themselves to targets and timing, feet taking him simultaneously towards and away from danger, and... something more. Something real. Something that hinted at a wider existence beyond this mortal plane, beyond the present reality of a man and a woman and the two man set.

He chased it. But the more he chased it the more it slipped away from it. The more energy he threw into the techniques the easier she moved and countered, and the faster she went, forcing him to keep pace. When he turned his attention back to her the feeling faded, there but not there, creeping at the edges of his mind.

And then, just like that, the set was over.

They stepped back from each other, back in their starting positions. Energy flowed through him, his and hers, rivers of ethereal fire spiraling around his limbs and through his spine and into his mind. He stayed where he was a moment later, feeling the energy, *becoming* the energy, letting it permeate through him to concentrate in his dantian, in his organs, in every cell of his being.

"Warmed up?" he asked.

She smiled. Her eyes blazed, her fingertips crackled, her heart opened, and for a moment he felt like he was staring at the sun.

"Yup!"

And then, just like that, the magic dissolved. Now it was him and her in an empty courtyard under a brightening sky. The fleeting, subtle, incomprehensible *thing* he had sighted, he had felt, melted in the light of the dawn.

Maybe he was tired. Maybe he had slept too little, trained too hard. All he knew was that if he chased it now, whatever *it* was, he'd just be burning daylight.

So they trained. Not hard and fast the way he did with Ghazan, but slow and technical and precise, drilling down to the fundamentals of motion. They practiced the grappling and the striking they had learned and compared them to the closest wuxingquan and yizhang analogues. They were fellow seekers walking the Way, looking for the simplest, swiftest, surest movements, the golden moves that would end a confrontation in as few steps as possible.

Other biaohang stepped out into the courtyard. Some were reporting to work. Others emerged from rented rooms. Most of them let Cai and Lan train in peace. A couple practiced their own routines in different corners. Jiang Long watched for a few moments, then stepped in and offered some advice. How to position the feet, where and when to shift weight, the right angle to hold an arm and leg, the little details that would make or break a particularly tricky technique.

Finally, an hour after awakening, Li Ming and Cai Yan mutually agreed to end the session.

"Thank you for coming out to train with me," Li Ming said.

"Pleasure is all mine. I should thank you for showing me things from wuxingquan."

"You showed me your yizhang. It's only right to show you my wuxingquan."

"But in the end, we are part of the same family."

Li Min raised an eyebrow.

She giggled, looking away.

"Sorry, I meant to say, our styles are part of the An Family Gongfu."

"Thought so."

"Anyway... are you busy today?"

"No. Why?"

"Would you like to go shopping with me at the Cultivator Quarter?"

Li Ming blinked. Blinked again.

Did she just…?

"*En*, ah, I mean, Father wanted me to introduce you to our suppliers, and since we've been paid, I thought it would be a good time to go gear shopping."

"Wait. We were paid?"

"Yes. On the fifteenth. Five days ago. You didn't notice?"

"I was too busy."

She shook her head.

"Your salary is paid on the fifteenth of every month. It's in your contract. But not the bounties. The Jianghu Association takes between thirty to forty-five days to process payments."

"So long?"

"They have their own paperwork and banks to deal with. We make sure to pay on time. And I'm sure you have an equipment shopping list."

"A *long* list."

"Exactly. We can go shopping today."

"Let's go."

"I need to go wash up first. I'll meet you at the gates in three ke?"

"Sure."

"Great! It's a date!"

She skipped away, swinging her arms high and against her sides, her hair bouncing with every step.

Li Ming stared at her back, processing what she'd just said.

A date.

Yes.

She'd said that. She definitely had.

⚫

Li Ming spent a little extra time in the shower. He scrubbed himself down, thoroughly washed every square *cun* of his body, shaved off the beginnings of a beard and the hair that threatened to join his eyebrows. When he was finished, he mused that the military had taught him to bathe as quickly as humanly possible, to use as little water as he could get away with to ensure a minimum baseline of hygiene, but the jianghu had pulled him in the opposite direction.

Not the jianghu. A girl.

He dressed his best too. Or, rather, he chose the only clothes he had left for a day out in the town. Half-length blue tunic and matching pants. Wide belt. Swordbreaker on his left hip, folding knives clipped to his pocket. Blue jacket over the shirt. Raptor smartglasses.

He checked himself in the mirror, saw a gentleman-warrior properly armed and accoutered to escort a young lady down the daylight streets of Bao An.

He chuckled. He was dressing up as if he were going on an escort mission in a formal setting. But it never hurt to be overdressed, at least for something as casual as a date. He reached for his pack...

The military patterns and colorations stared at him.

He stared back.

They wouldn't do. The rucksack was too huge. The assault pack was too martial, even among martial cultivators. As with his swordbreaker, he'd look out of place on the streets.

He added a backpack to his to-buy list. A pack tough enough to stand up to the harshness of biaohang duty, yet non-tactical looking. A gray man pack.

Maybe multiple packs. One when out and about, one to lug around huge loads. A third, also, a messenger bag, to better blend in with urbanites...

He shook his head. There truly was no end of things to buy.

Out in the living room, he found Ghazan lounging on the sofa, his scroll stretched out on the table before him.

Scroll. Did he need a scroll? All his life, he'd only needed one device, but now that he was a biaohang...

Ghazan cut off his train of thoughts.

"Good training today?"

"Yup," Li Ming said.

"I wanted to join you, but you seemed to be enjoying yourself with Ms. Cai."

"We're not like that."

"Sure, sure."

"Really!"

"I totally believe you."

"*Wei.*"

"Whatever you do, don't forget: we work for her father."

"I won't."

"Good. And speaking of work..."

He lifted his device.

"We're on the Jianghu Times."

Li Ming startled.

"What?"

Ghazan handed the scroll over.

"Here."

A huge photograph splashed across half the screen. An aerial image of the highway of death. The shot centered on the yaoshu nest. The brood mother rearing up, teeth bared and claws out. Its lesser brethren, ready to swoop in. And two tiny figures flying towards the brood mother, the light glinting off their cold steel weapons.

Li Ming and Ghazan.

"What... How... I didn't see any media around!" Li Ming exclaimed.

"They must have had a news drone in the area."

"Wasn't the district locked down?"

"The police and the jianghu have a special arrangement. This extends to the jianghu news services. Go on, read the article."

Shaking his head, Li Ming accepted the device.

RISING STAR ENTERS THE JIANGHU!

War hero Li Ming and martial cultivator Ga San destroy ferocious yaoshu in Bao An!

On the 6th day of the 4th month, a horde of yaoshu breached the Bao An Barrier and invaded the history Luoyang District. Tearing down the streets and highways, they overpowered the police and charged to the heart of the city. Dayong Biaoju mobilized in minutes, checking the horde's advance. Collaborating with the Civil Police and the Special Military Police, the biaoju launched a counterattack, sweeping the beasts from the district.

Among the biaohang who responded to the horde was Li Ming (qi score: 13618, iron rank). Hailing from the small farming village of Fuyang, Li Ming served with distinction in the Special Military Police, where he earned a Medal of Valor during the Battle of Shanxia. Half a year after his military service, Li Biaohang entered the jianghu, signing up with Dayong as a biaohang...

The rest of the article breathlessly recounted the operation blow by blow, from the monsters swarming the hutong to the sweep through the district and the final assault on the yaoshu nest. The reporter peppered the article with quotes from police and civilian bystanders, and photographs of the aftermath.

Li Ming's incredible performance marks a strong entry to the world of the rivers and lakes, consistent with his military record. While he is only an iron ranked cultivator, the Jianghu Times *expects Li Biaohang to go far.*

Neither Dayong Biaoju nor Li Biaohang could be reached for comment at press time.

"The Jianghu Times didn't contact me before writing this!" Li Ming sputtered.

"Did you check your spam folder?" Ghazan asked.

"En..."

"If they ever tried reaching out to you, their email might be in there. I heard Boss Cai grumbling about some reporter blowing up his inbox. That might have been the Jianghu Times."

"He didn't talk about it."

"Our policy is to never comment on our operations, not without clearing it with the relevant authorities, our lawyer and the Jianghu Association. Besides, I think the boss did you a favor."

"What do you mean?"

"Would you like the Jianghu Times hounding you day and night?"

"No."

"There you go. Nothing good comes from talking to *gouzidui.*"

"I thought life in the jianghu was all about the fame and the glamour."

Ghazan laughed.

"You're just an iron rank. It's more trouble than it's worth."

"So I hear. But anyway, I need to go."

"Wait."

"Yes?"

"I never heard anything about you being a war hero. What's that about?"

"Another story from another life."

Li Ming's flinty eyes shifted ever so slightly. His face settled into a neutral expression.

"Is that so?" Ghazan said mildly.

"I did my job. I got lucky. That's all there is to it. And I'm running late."

"Have fun on your date."

Li Ming didn't bother replying to that.

At the door, he donned his shoes. Black zero drop slip-on shoes, the soles light and flexible, the toebox wide and roomy, custom-made to fit his feet. The only part of his attire that was old and worn, but it was comfortable and it had served him for years. And it fit well with the rest of his outfit.

He hoped.

Cai Yan was waiting at the main gate, an amused expression on her face.

"Right on time," she said.

Her tone suggested something else.

"Thanks for waiting," he said.

She'd cleaned up well. Very well.

She tied up her long black hair into a pair of neat buns, holding them in place with chopsticks, letting pigtails swish down to her shoulders. Her Eight Eyes headset rested on her head, the visor lifted to expose her clear, soft eyes.

She wore a sleeveless white silk blouse, revealing muscled arms and silver reality shapers with delicate golden etchings, pairing it with a deep blue skirt that flowed down to her ankles.

Over her right shoulder, she wore a large handbag. A thick dark sash encircled her narrow waist, almost hiding the thin handles of a pair of knives on her hips.

She had applied makeup as well. Bright red lipstick, a touch of powder and rouge, brightening her face and widening her eyes. It was the first time he'd seen her with makeup.

Arms held behind her back, she leaned into him, tilted her head just so, and smiled.

"You dressed up nicely today," she said.

"Same for you."

Her smile turned into a pout.

"What's wrong?" he asked.

"Nothing."

He knew that tone of voice. Mother and Sister used it all the time. He suspected he knew what she really wanted, but he thought this was professional. It was a little too late to go back now.

"Have you had breakfast?" Li Ming asked.

"Not yet."

"Let's go then."

"Sure!"

He held out his arm, as though ready to escort her. She smiled, huffed in mock-annoyance, and brushed past him. He shook his head.

Women.

Chapter Twenty-Three

Cultivator Quarter

The Cultivator Quarter was a city within a city. The laws of mortal rulers ended at its borders. Here there was only the law of the jianghu, a law older and harsher and swifter than that of the Zhongxia Republic. The high walls that once sealed off the district from Bao An had been torn down long ago, replaced by skyscrapers and apartments, their placement cunningly designed to isolate the neighborhood.

The paifang remained. Huge arched gateways, standing at every entrance to the Quarter, their signs proudly proclaiming the words *Xiuzhe Quyu* in huge golden characters against a deep black background. Past the gates, asphalt road turned to brick. Buried bollards lay ready to spring up and close off the district. Cameras peered down from lamp posts and walls. Quadcopters buzzed through the air. Two guards manned every gate, armed with infinity guns and reality shapers and augmented reality headsets, wearing the black and white uniforms and shoulder patches of White Tiger Security.

The Civil Police did not dare come here. Mere mortals were powerless in a district populated by the most powerful cultivators in the city, in the province, in the nation. The government of Bao An, as their ancestors had done in the days of the Celestial Empire and the Yue Dynasty, elected to allow the jianghu to police itself.

Within the Zhongxia Republic, White Tiger was the foremost private military company. Not a biaoju like Dayong, which focused on security, but an army for hire, its activities strictly regulated by the laws of the Zhongxia Republic, the world, and the jianghu. When the government of Bao An ceded control of the Quarter to the jianghu, it hired White Tiger to carry out the duties of the Civil Police in its stead.

Li Ming didn't know if it were a good thing. Only that no mortal cop would risk the wrath of a cultivator who walked the way of devils, and no immortal would tangle with one without suitable compensation.

The air pulsed with qi. Li Ming felt it the second he stepped out the taxi. Six dragon lines, natural rivers of qi crisscrossing the world, intersected here, forming an immense energy vortex. The district was built upon this dragon grid, its layout carefully designed to maximize and harness qi flow. Here, it felt like he was standing at the mouth of a roaring river, a torrent of pure qi rushing into and through him.

"Intense, isn't it?" Cai Yan said.

"That's saying something."

"Is it too much for you?"

"I can cope."

Drawing on the abundant qi flow, he created a shield around himself, a round shell covering him from head to toe. The qi flowed harmlessly around him, wearing away the edges of the shield. He sent the excess qi within him deep into the earth, where it could be renewed and recycled.

The White Tiger guards paced from side to side, chatting with each other, yet keeping an eye on incoming visitors. They stayed at the sides of the gate, at the edges of the dragon line. As Li Ming and Cai Yan passed, they turned to scan them, their cameras studying their faces and gaits. An instant later, the White Tigers relaxed, resuming their conversation.

Inside the district, Li Ming had the uncanny sensation of stepping into a different world, a world that meshed the past and the present to reflect a vision of a timeless future. Rows of narrow tenements lined the streets, retaining the arched roofs and decorative urns and balustrades of the previous eras. The ground floor was for commerce, the upper levels for residents—or more commerce. Forests of signs announced a dizzying array of products and services, brands and outlets, franchises and private businesses. Here and there, pagodas towered over the district, local landmarks announcing the presence of temples, shrines, major businesses.

There were no cars or motorbikes on the streets. Bicycles and rickshaws abounded, mingling freely with pedestrians. Laborers, some equipped with exoskeletons, ferried bulky goods from vehicles parked outside the Quarter to establishments within. Delivery drones carried smaller packages. Security drones buzzed through the air, following the grid of the Quarter.

Hawkers shouted out their wares. Street food and fresh fruits, elixirs and pills, crystals and jewelry, deals and discounts. The wealthier among them worked from carts and stands, the rest made do by spreading out their goods on blankets and tarps on the road.

"Don't buy anything other than food and drink from the hawkers," Cai Yan advised. "Most of the stuff here is low-quality or cheap imitations. We can afford much better than this."

"What about the food and drink?"

"It's delicious. You should try it."

There were so many options. A hundred scents drew him in every direction: barbecued meats, roasted sweet potatoes, candied fruits, deep-fried flatbreads. Chefs and barkers beckoned to passers-by, holding up samples of their wares. Music blared, screens played videos, signs shouted menus and prices and discounts.

He chose a huge steamed bun, stuffed with pork and eggs. She enjoyed a deep-fried jianbing, loaded with peanuts and beans and lettuce.

As they ate and walked, she pointed out landmarks and places of interest. Here was the sole surviving remnant of the outer wall that once surrounded the district. There was the oldest apothecary in Bao An, run by the same family for ten generations. This street specialized in cultivator-friendly fashions, that one had nothing but weapon shops.

"And this is the Sanjie Baihuo Shangchang."

The Three Worlds Emporium stood alone, occupying an entire block all to itself, a three-story square-based pagoda. Its green roofs were like petals of ceramic tile, sweeping upwards to face the sky, contrasting with the vivid red walls. A golden finial stood atop the highest roof, shaped like a jingang, a double-headed scepter symbolizing the indestructibility of a diamond and the irresistibility of a thunderbolt.

Surrounded by a tall steel fence, a single gate controlled access to the building. Two White Tigers stood at the entrance, scanning everyone who entered. Two more stood at the main entrance to the Emporium. They were all armed to the teeth and kitted with full body armor.

"Sanjie is one of the largest cultivator-centric retail chains in Xiazhou. Dayong has secured a partnership with them. You'll get a ten percent discount off all purchases from Sanjie, more if you buy in bulk."

Anything a cultivator wanted, he could get at Sanjie. Apparel, weapons, shapers, crystals, supplements, everything he needed to walk the Way of the Xia. He had visited the main Taiping outlet a few times, mostly when looking for upgrades for his military-issue kit. The Bao An outlet was only slightly smaller. He'd spotted this place during his initial exploration of the district, but he hadn't entered. He hadn't had time for shopping, or a need to.

Until now.

"Are you looking for anything?" Li Ming asked.

"No, not really," she said. "Go on ahead and pick what you need first. Present your biaohang card to the cashier to enjoy your discount. Just call me when you're done."

Li Ming cracked his neck.

"It's going to take a while."

She laughed.

The ground floor was dedicated to general goods. Cultivator-friendly fashions from top brands, elegant tunics and dresses and pants, many of them boasting hidden pockets, reinforced seams, temperature- and cut-resistant fabrics. Tactical apparel and armor, everything from simple chest rigs and battle belts to elaborate sets of full body armor. Bags and backpacks, the kind that could fit in high society and the kind that would stand up to the rigors of the battlefield. Blades and tools for every occasion. The entire floor was split in half, one for civilian goods, the other for combat.

Sights and sounds pulled his eyes in a thousand directions. There was so much to see, so much to examine, so many wonders from the finest brands. Screens played advertisements of a dizzying range of products, from multitools to clothing, bags to shoes, trying to capture his attention.

There were lots of things he wanted. But first he had to get the things he needed.

He checked the floor directory, hunting for categories and listings. And grinned. And climbed the escalator to the second floor.

Guns.

Lots of guns.

Racks of infinity guns. Display cases of handguns. Shelves stocked with accessories, cleaning supplies, weapon parts. Racks stocked with local and foreign publications dedicated to tactics and weaponry. Signs on the walls declared that none of the infinity guns on display had live crystals.

For every use case, the Emporium stocked a dozen makes and models. Military-grade infinity guns. Precision weapons. Hideout handguns. Bulky repeaters for sustained fire. Concealed carry pistols. Ultra-high-powered hunting guns when you absolutely, positively, needed something to die. He was almost disappointed not to find infinity cannons on display.

Behind him, the other half of the store was dedicated to cold weapons. Every conceivable type of cold weapon. Spears and swords, knives and needles, more exotic implements he had seen only in movies, all of them neatly mounted inside display cabinets and enclosed shelves.

Posters on the walls showed celebrity cultivators showing off the latest in wargear. Videos played on a dozen screens, advertisements for guns, swords, brands, crystals, all of them approved and endorsed by the biggest names in the jianghu. They were all men, men dressed in military and police uniforms, men in hunting jackets and outdoor apparel, their grizzled faces and hardened eyes speaking of countless battles, praising every sponsored product, painting them all as cranes standing amongst chickens.

Staff circulated the floor, tending to a range of customers. A young man painstakingly assembled a long infinity gun at a counter, discussing the merits and drawbacks of various parts. A pair of customers, each gripping an enormously long spear, scrutinized a heavy crossbow. An enthusiast compared performance charts and price tags, pacing among the shelves. An old man waited patiently as a cashier rang up an even older slug gun. Scattered around the room, dozens more customers perused the wares, nine in ten of them men.

Li Ming didn't care for archaic weaponry. Customers had their own reasons for buying them, and the Three Worlds Emporium accommodated them wherever they could. Re-enactors sought to keep the past alive. Collectors enjoyed looking at objects from the past. Hobbyists found pleasure in using these ancient weapons. Beast hunters needed firearms that would stop a beast in its tracks with minimal excess damage.

Li Ming needed a weapon that would stop a threat immediately, and there were no weapons as widely available or as deadly as the infinity gun.

He wandered the infinity gun section, looking at products and prices. Every reputable company was represented here, plus some ultra-specialty brands he'd never heard of. There were no bad guns here. Plenty of good options too.

But which was best?

He went back to his needs. If he needed an infinity gun for a job, he could draw it from the armory. What he really needed was a gun he could draw when he wasn't on duty. And a gun for specialist assignments, the kind that needed a concealable weapon smaller than his Golden Legion. A compact self-defense handgun.

But there were so many, so *many* choices...

A staff member walked up to him. His nametag read 'Tao Zhong'.

"Hi! How can I help?"

Irritation flashed through Li Ming. Tao Zhong had broken his train of thought. He breathed it out and decided to roll with it.

"I'm looking for a very specific type of handgun," Li Ming replied.

"What kind?"

"A compact or micro-compact infinity handgun, for self-defense. *Discreet* self-defense, in environments that don't allow for larger weapons."

"Self-defense against beasts or humans?"

"Cultivators. Human and otherwise."

"Are you a biaohang?"

"Yes. I work for Dayong."

"I'll need to see your..." Tao Zhong's eyes widened. Are you Li Ming?"

"Yes."

"I read about you in the *Jianghu Times*! Thanks for saving the city."

"No problem."

Li Ming fished out his biaohang card. Tao Zhong squinted at it and nodded.

"Please follow me."

Tao Zhong led him to a display counter. Here there was nothing but compact handguns. The largest wasn't much bigger than his hand. The smallest could fit comfortably up a sleeve.

"May I see your hand?" Tao Zhong asked.

Perplexed, Li Ming held it out. Tao Zhong produced a measuring tape and measured his palm.

"Thank you. Based on your parameters, and the size of your hand, I have two choices for you."

"Let me see their specs."

"Of course."

Tao Zhong pulled out his scroll from a pocket and unfurled it to its full length. He tapped the screen for a few moments, then flipped it around.

Two guns sat side-by-side on the screen. Photo galleries filled with close-up images dominated the upper half of the screen. Numbers and words filled the lower half. With his finger, Li Ming scrolled through the display.

Kaiser 26

Sustained rate of fire: 3 shots / second

Maximum rate of fire: 5 shots / second

Heat capacity: 10 shots

Overheat cooldown time: 30 seconds

Weight: 1 jin *1* liang

Overall length: 16 fen
Overall height: 1 cun *1* fen
Width: 1.2 cun
Price: 3997 yuan
Hellion 360
Sustained rate of fire: 4 shots / second
Maximum rate of fire: 6 shots / second
Heat capacity: 12 shots
Overheat cooldown time: 25 seconds
Weight: 1 *jin 4 qian*
Overall length: 15 fen
Overall height: 1 *cun*
Width: 1 cun
Price: 4197 yuan

They were solid choices. Imported from overseas, they had won raving reviews from police officers, soldiers and shooters across the world. But every way he looked at it, the Hellion was the superior option. Except cooldown time and price.

Did money matter that much? Not really. Better to be alive and poor than rich but dead. And besides, a measly 200-yuan difference was nothing. He'd earn it back and then some tonight, just by sleeping.

He paused.

Nothing?

Two hundred yuan was... nothing? With that kind of money, and some careful choices, he could feed himself for a week. When did he reach this point?

Well, it didn't matter now. He was here, and he needed a gun, and there were two before him.

"I'd like to see the Hellion," Li Ming said.

Tao Zhong fished out a huge bunch of keys, unlocked the case, and carefully handed the weapon over butt-first.

The Hellion fit his hands perfectly. The aggressively-textured grip bit deep into his palms. Pointing it at a blank wall, finger off the trigger, he peered through the reflex sight. Located at the rear of the weapon, it was shaped like the viewfinder of a camera. Buttons on the side allowed him to adjust the point of aim, the reticle, the lighting, so many options, but lacking a firing crystal and a cosmic tap, the display was blank.

"The Hellion is best in class among micro-compact infinity handguns," Tao Zhong said. "For an iron ranker like yourself, you can't go wrong with the Hellion. When you rank up, you can upgrade every major component. It's an excellent investment for the future."

The Hellion reviews said the same. But...

"The grip isn't *quite* perfect," Li Ming said.

"We could 3D print a grip module sized exactly for your hands."

"Nice. How much for that?"

"One hundred yuan. But since you work for Dayong, ninety yuan."

"I'll take The Hellion and the grip module."

"Wonderful. Is there anything else you need from your weapon?"

"It's pretty good as it is."

"What's your worst case scenario with this weapon?"

"Facing down a charging tietou, an Evolved one with the ability to harden its entire body."

Tao Zhong winced.

"*He*... you need a long gun."

Most beasts *probably* wouldn't be able to resist a full-power plasma bolt from a long gun. The kind that could demanded a military response. Even so...

"You *did* say worst case scenario."

"You also said it's for self-defense. Do you plan on defending against a criminal cultivator too?"

"Yes. Someone with a qi score at least ten thousand points higher than mine, with an energy shield."

Tao Zhong shook his head.

"You shouldn't use a handgun. It will not be able to overload his shield."

"I'm not planning to. I want to blind him so I can run away. Or engage with cold weapons."

"Ah, I see. I would recommend replacing the charging module with one designed for rapid fire. We stock premade modules, but you could choose to put together one for yourself. We could also change the output crystal, but could mean sacrificing power, or paying a bit more."

"Let's see what you have available," Li Ming said.

For the next two ke they did just that. At the accessories corner, Li examined cosmic taps, heatsinks, charging modules that combined both, output crystals. The Emporium stocked every possible weapon part in existence, but Li Ming focused only on those.

With an infinity gun, if the first hit didn't stop the target, the second would. But in combat, one or two extra shots per second spelled the difference between life and death. So did a heat sink that could soak up two or three extra bolts. The yaoshu hunt had shown him that. The last thing he needed was to burn out his guns right when he needed them most.

For his intended use case, he really needed a heavy handgun, one capable of multiple fire modes and continuous fire. But, as Tao Zhong regretfully informed him, such hardware was restricted to silver-ranked biaohang or higher. Nonetheless, Li Ming pressed on, attempting to replicate the performance of a larger and more powerful weapon in a tiny package.

At last Li Ming made his choice. Oversized cosmic tap, aftermarket heat sinks, and output crystal optimized for rapid fire. And a holster. Tao Zhong's scroll updated the spec sheet, calculating the effect of the upgrades. Li Ming looked only at the most important changes.

Sustained rate of fire: 5 shots / second (+1)
Maximum rate of fire: 8 shots / second (+2)
Heat capacity: 20 shots (+8)
Overheat cooldown time: 20 seconds (-5)
Weight: 1 jin 12 qian (+8 qian)
Price: 5617 yuan (+1420)

It was an improvement in almost every aspect. He could handle the weight increase. But the price...

Li Ming winced. It was almost half of his budget, and he still had more stuff to buy.

On the other hand, no amount of money could buy a life.

"If you buy this, we'll throw in the custom grip module for free," Tao Zhong said.

"Sold."

Li Ming paid using his Aitan mobile wallet. Tao cast a mold of his hand and sent it to a backroom. He promised that the gun would be assembled and ready for collection in two ke. In the meantime, Li Ming would be free to explore the Emporium further.

He wandered through the cold weapon collection for a few minutes. Long enough to know that there was nothing he needed here. Plenty he *wanted*, sure, but nothing that was on his essential shopping list. So he headed upstairs.

The third floor was a cultivators' paradise. Reality shapers of all possible configurations—and more than a few he had never seen before—rested in high-security racks, enough shapers to equip an army of cultivators. On the other side of the room, primordial crystals rested in reinforced display cases under lock and key and armed guard. Shelves of supplements, elixirs, pills, magazines and manuals occupied the rest of the retail space.

The air crackled with qi. Cultivators circulated around the floor, small bands of youths on a collective shopping trip, veteran solos examining the highest-grade products, security staff keeping an eye on the merchandise. Even with his shield up, his pulse quickened, his lungs electrified, his skin tingled, just by standing in the midst of so many crystals and qi sources.

As he navigated the shelves, he spotted Cai Yan in the crowd. He slipped behind a knot of cultivators, drifted past a shelf of meal replacements, ducked behind a rack of cultivation magazines, and approached her from behind.

"*Wei*," she said, looking at a pill bottle, her back to him.

Li Ming's heart fell. How had she sensed him?

"Busy shopping?" he asked.

"Just checking prices and products."

"Found anything interesting?"

"The Emporium stocks a huge range of products. Everything you see here comes highly recommended."

Li Ming didn't doubt that. Where the ads below showed battle-hardened male veterans, the ones on this floor were paragons of female beauty. Delicate, elegant, slim, dressed in tasteful robes and dresses and sportswear, highlighting soft curves and long hair and wide eyes. The few men in sight were uniformly boyish and youthful, their faces painted pale, their lips full and glossy, their hair thick and full. They were all immortals, celebrities signed to some entertainment company or other. He didn't know their faces, much less their names, but enough people did that their word must carry weight with the crowd.

Cai Yan glanced to her sides, as if looking for witnesses, then tiptoed and leaned into his ear.

"If you buy supplements in bulk here, I can get you a steeper discount."

Her breath was warm against his skin, her voice low and intimate. It took his brain a second to register her words.

"Thanks, but I'm looking for a reality shaper," he said.

"In that case, you're in the right place. There's someone who can help."

She bounced on her heels, waving her arms. Bright gold qi flashed past his eyes.

"Manager Xu! Over here!"

A portly gentleman approached, hands resting on his ample belly.

"Lady Boss Cai! Pleasure to meet you again!"

"Pleasure is all mine," she said.

"I trust this gentleman is your companion?"

"Yes," they said at the same time.

Manager Xu laughed merrily. "May I dare ask your honorable name?"

"Li Ming."

Manager Xu snapped into a salute, punching his palm over his heart.

"Li Biaohang! In my store! I've read about your exploits! Thank you for your service!"

Li Ming returned the salute.

"You're most welcome."

"Is there anything I could help you with?" Manager Xu asked.

"I'm looking for a new reality shaper."

"We stock the finest shapers in all of Bao An. Is there anything you are looking..."

His eyes drifted to Li Ming's left hip. His voice trailed off.

"What's wrong?" Li Ming asked.

"May I see your weapon?"

Li Ming carefully lifted his sheathed swordbreaker from his belt and handed it to Manager Xu. He held it up to the light, his face scrunched in total concentration.

And his lips parted in a perfect O.

"What is it?" Cai Yan prodded.

"Li Biaohang, is this what I think it is?"

"It's a swordbreaker," Li Ming said.

"Yes, but what kind of swordbreaker?"

"I don't understand. It's just a swordbreaker."

"Just a swordbreaker, you say? Interesting..."

"What is it?"

"I have a hunch about this weapon, but I need to examine it further. May I?"

"Sure."

"Please follow me."

He took them past the counters, past the staff access door, and into a workshop. Here the air hung thick with the scent of oil and steel. Well-used workbenches stood ready in neat rows. Tool boards hung from every well. Technicians occupied most of the benches, working over infinity guns, swords, and other exotic weapons.

The trio found an unoccupied workbench. Manager Xu set the swordbreaker down on the table, and reverently drew the weapon from its sheath. Holding it lightly in both hands, he tested the weight and balance, inspected the swirling patterns running down the blade, checked the tip, scrutinized the hilt and handle.

"The wrap is falling apart," Manager Xu said at last. "See?"

He rolled the weapon around, holding up the hilt to the light. Squinting, Li Ming saw frayed cords and cracked leather, barely held together by threads.

"I could remove it and replace the wrap for you," Manager Xu said.

"Go ahead."

Manager Xu produced a small folding knife. Slowly, delicately, he cut the frayed cords, using just enough pressure to part the leather without scraping the handle beneath.

The wrapping fell apart like a split cocoon, revealing a plain grip fashioned from the same meteorite steel as the rest of the weapon.

"Amazing..." Manager Xu whispered.

"What is it?"

Manager Xu ignored him, peering intently at the pommel.

"May I disassemble it?"

Li Ming blinked. "It can be disassembled?"

"You never tried?"

"...No."

"The pommel is screwed into place and holds the grip panels together. Do you see these fine seams running down the grip?"

Li Ming leaned in close. Now he saw the seams, almost invisible, revealing two curved plates, a shell that covered an inner grip.

"I see them."

"This swordbreaker is hiding a secret. May I take it apart?"

"Sure."

Manager Xu grabbed a bottle of oil from a drawer. He squeezed a few drops over the pommel, the seams, the hilt, working them over with a buffing cloth. Then, slowly, gingerly, he began to unscrew the sphere-shaped pommel.

It was hard work. The passage of decades had fused pommel and thread together. Abandoning all notions of delicacy, Manager Xu grunted heavily, muscled the sphere, and applied even more oil. One last twist and the pommel came off, revealing a mysterious three-pronged structure at the end of the handle.

Manager Xu held up the pommel. And grinned.

"Look! It's hollow!"

Li Ming blinked.

"Okay..."

"You don't get it?"

"I don't."

Manager Xu's grin grew brighter.

With his fingertips, he slid the grip panels off the handle, producing a cloud of ancient dust. Then he lay the panels down next to the grip.

"What do you see now?" Manager Xu asked.

Circuits.

They were ancient and corroded, but undeniably circuits. Fine golden threads ran down the length of the tang, joining round islands of tarnished silver, terminating in the three claws at the end of the handle.

"What *is* this?" Li Ming asked.

Manager Xu looked around. The technicians were engrossed in their work, paying them no mind. Cai Yan looked in on surprised silence.

"Li Biaohang, you don't know what you're carrying?"

"I've never seen it before."

Manager Xu glanced around again. And hurriedly reassembled the weapon.

"Let's go to someplace quiet."

Manager Xu brought them to a private office in the corner of the workroom. It was an afterthought, a tiny room as small as a monk's cell. There was a table, a computer, a chair, two smaller guest chairs. As the biaohang sat, Manager Xu closed the door and locked it behind him.

Manager Xu cleared a space on the table and set the weapon down between them. Now his face grew cold and serious. His hands dropped below the surface of the table. He peered at Li Ming through the lenses of his smartglasses. In that gaze, Li Ming understood Manager Xu was running a qi assessment app.

"I am going to ask you again. You don't know what this is?"

"I don't," Li Ming replied.

"Why not? You've never used it?"

"Only as a training weapon. And for emergency self-defense."

"And you never thought to inspect it?"

"Manager Xu, what's going on?" Cai Yan asked.

Manager Xu looked at her. At him. At the weapon. Back at Li Ming.

"This is a magic weapon."

Li Ming gaped.

A magic weapon. A cold weapon capable of mounting a primordial crystal. It could be used like a reality shaper, but a skilled user could use the crystal to transform the weapon. He'd fought a criminal cultivator with a magic weapon once, and he didn't care to repeat the experience.

"How did you get your hands on this?" Manager Xu asked.

Li Ming understood Manager Xu's real question. Li Ming was just an iron-ranked cultivator, a newcomer to the world of the rivers and lakes. Magic weapons were rarely sold on the open market. Usually they were made to order by the finest artisans in the industry. Equipment like this was the domain of gold-ranked cultivators with qi scores in the twenty and thirty thousands.

But only in the daylight world.

"It's a family heirloom. My father gave it to me. He, in turn, received it from his father, who received it from *his* father."

"Who is your father?"

"Li Guo An."

"*Colonel* Li Guo An? The gold-ranked martial cultivator Li Guo An?"

Father hadn't hidden his past from him, but he never made a big deal about it either. Manager Xu's reaction seemed melodramatic. But, he supposed, Manager Xu had never grown up with him either.

"Yes," Li Ming said.

"Who is your great-grandfather?"

"Li Yan Shun."

Now it was Manager Xu's turn to gape.

"Li Yan Shun? Tiger of Qingfeng? Liberator of Taihang? Hero of the Republic? *That* Li Yan Shun?!"

"Yes."

Manager Xu lowered his head.

"Forgive me. I didn't know I was in the presence of Li Yan Shun's descendant."

Li Ming shook his head.

"It's nothing. The glory of the ancestor does not pass to his descendant."

"I didn't know you were related to Li Yan Shun," Cai Yan said, her eyes sparkling in wonder.

"It's not something I like to spread around. I want to make my own way in life, not depend on a famous name. All the name meant to me was a standard to live up to," Li Ming replied.

"How did your honored ancestor obtain this weapon?" Manager Xu asked.

"Generalissimo Jiang gifted him this swordbreaker after the Summer Revolution."

"The Generalissimo himself! Do you have proof of this?"

"We have records in the family home. But I don't have them with me now."

"Is that so..." Manager Xu sucked in a breath. "I knew there was more to this swordbreaker than met the eye. I recognized the design immediately."

"What *is* it, anyway?" Li Ming asked.

"It's a relic of the late Celestial Empire. Not a reproduction weapon. A relic. This was the standard-issue cold weapon of the Imperial Bodyguards. Their mission was to protect the Celestial Emperor, his household, and the Purple Heavenly Palace.

"At that time, the mass manufacture of primordial crystals led to a revolution in the military arts. The greatest threat the Imperial Bodyguards faced was an assassin who could deflect energy bolts and harden his skin to resist swords and spears. They adopted the swordbreaker in response. Even if they couldn't pierce his flesh, they could break his weapon and batter him into submission.

"Later, the Imperial Bodyguards armed themselves with magic swordbreakers. These could mount primordial crystals and be used like modern-day reality shapers. With the right training and magic, an Imperial Bodyguard could shatter a shield and break bones with a single blow.

"This pattern of swordbreaker became the symbol of the Imperial Bodyguards. Everywhere they went, it was the badge of their office. They need but show it, and everyone short of the Emperor himself had to bow to their will.

"*This* swordbreaker is astonishingly well-preserved. The Imperial artisans used secret techniques to forge it. Even a hundred years later, we still don't know how to reproduce it. Legend holds that the blade will never rust, that the tip will never blunt. Is it true?"

"Well... I've never performed anything but basic maintenance on it. Hasn't anyone used a swordbreaker like this in combat?"

"Not in the past hundred years, not in major engagements. When the Imperial Bodyguards were destroyed, their weapons were lost alongside them. The few surviving specimens are locked away in museums and private collections. You're the only martial cultivator I know who carries a swordbreaker like this into battle. And for good reason."

"Why?"

"A swordbreaker like this will be valued on the open market at no less than one million yuan."

"One *million?!*"

Absurd. Unbelievable. Impossible. He couldn't even begin to imagine possessing even a tenth of such an astronomical sum. A number like that belonged to the lives of the super-rich, not some dirt bun from the middle of nowhere.

"Are you sure you want to carry it around?" Manager Xu asked gently.

"It's the only belt-worn cold weapon I have."

"A weapon like this should be honored in a museum, or at least in the family home. You should get a cheap, replaceable blade instead. One you can afford to lose."

"My budget doesn't extend to a new cold weapon right now."

"We have plenty of cold weapons in the Dayong armory," Cai Yan said. "We could loan you one."

"If it were meant to be locked away, my father would never have allowed me to carry it. Besides... Manager Xu, you said this is a magic weapon?"

"You never tried casting magic with it?"

"Never."

"Good thing you didn't. The circuits are all corroded. If you tried casting magic, if you're lucky, the working would merely fizzle. If not... the weapon could explode in your hands."

Li Ming winced.

"Your father never told you that this is a magic weapon?" Cai Yan asked.

Li Ming shook his head. "We've only ever used it for training."

"Which explains its condition," Manager Xu mused.

"Are you able to restore it?"

"Yes, but..."

"But?"

"It's a delicate process. I will need to send it to a restorer. He could strip out the circuitry and the prongs and replace them with modern circuits compatible with modern crystals. He does excellent work, but it doesn't come cheap."

"How much does he charge?"

"For a restoration and update package like this, fifteen thousand yuan. But since it's a commission, and not a product or service, your Dayong discount doesn't apply. Sorry."

Never mind his budget, that consumed the greater part of his earnings for the month. If he'd dropped that kind of cash, he wouldn't have money for rent.

"Don't bankrupt yourself if you can't afford it," Cai Yan said.

"She's right," Manager Xu said. "You're an iron ranked cultivator. You're going to need to buy a lot of things to survive in the jianghu. You shouldn't splurge on this one item."

Li Ming needed a gun and a shaper. Everything else could wait. Still...

"You said a magic weapon could be used as a shaper?" Li Ming asked.

"Yes. This swordbreaker should be no different."

Li Ming leaned back and calculated more sums in his head.

"Do you accept an installment plan?" Li Ming asked.

"Half up front, half on delivery. Best I can do. If we could do this in-house, we could work something out, but we have to commission an outside expert for this."

That worked out to seven thousand five hundred yuan per installment. Pretty much what he'd expect to pay for a high-end shaper available to iron-ranked cultivators. But he'd have to pay twice.

"I take it a magic weapon doesn't care about rank restrictions?" Li Ming asked.

"This swordbreaker predates the Jianghu Association, never mind the ranking system. The restorer will lay down circuits compatible with all kinds of primordial crystals. So long as it fits in the crystal holder, you can use it."

Manager Xu paused, and leaned in.

"As an iron-ranker, you can only *purchase* iron-ranked equipment. But this swordbreaker, as you said, already belongs to you. All we are doing is *restoring* the weapon to its original function. You understand what I mean?"

The restoration would transform the swordbreaker into an *unrestricted* reality shaper. It would be as powerful as any crystal he could slot inside it. It would become a weapon that could fell a cultivator with a single blow. A cultivator like the tietou he'd met on the road to Bao An. *That* was worth paying fifteen thousand yuan for. Even *fifty* thousand yuan would be a bargain.

"Absolutely," Li Ming said.

Manager Xu relaxed. "Good."

"How long will the restoration process take?" Li Ming asked.

"The restorer lives in the north. I ship it to him, he does the work, and he ships it back. The process will take about a month."

A month. Could he go for a month without the swordbreaker?

He could. If he rearranged his gear, drew more kit from the armory to replace it...

"If you take this option, we could re-wrap the handle for you and deliver it to Dayong for free," Manager Xu said. "A token of our appreciation for protecting the city."

"Let's do it. Half-half payment option."

"You *sure* you can afford it?" Cai Yan asked. "It's a lot of money for you."

"It's a long-term investment. It's worth it."

Manager Xu laughed.

"That's the right mindset for success!"

"Thank you."

"How would you like to pay? Cash or credit?"

"Smart contract," Cai Yan interjected.

"A what?" Li Ming asked.

"Smart contract. Never heard of it?"

"Haven't used one before."

"You're really a... I don't know what to say."

"The term you're looking for is 'dirt bun'."

Everyone laughed.

"A smart contract is a digital contract stored on the blockchain. An electronic public ledger that nobody controls but everyone can see, and therefore everyone can trust. It ensures automated execution of payment terms and shipping of goods without human interaction—and therefore, human interference."

"A smart move," Manager Xu said. "With a weapon as valuable as the swordbreaker, you don't want to risk it. You should think about getting insurance too."

"Our insurance plan covers loss of equipment in transit." Cai Yan turned to Li Ming. "You *did* opt into our insurance scheme, yes?"

"Yes."

"Excellent. Now we just need to set up the smart contract and we're all set."

Cai Yan lowered the visor of her headset and shared her display with the men. Together, they crafted the contract.

"That's it," Cai Yan said, lifting the visor. "It's done."

"Thank you for doing business with us," Manager Xu said.

"Thank you for the offer," Li Ming said.

"It's the least we could do for a descendant of a Hero of the Republic."

"I am not my great-grandfather."

"Indeed. But the jianghu will expect much from you."

And Li Ming knew it.

Chapter Twenty-Four

Arms Race With No End

Back in the retail space, Li Ming wandered the supplement aisles, marveling at the huge range of products on sale. Vitamins, antibiotics, meal replacements, snacks, mints, herbs, pre-workout powders, broths, potions. He hadn't even known people even *needed* some of these things.

Every item on sale promised to take the consumer to the peak of human potential, and beyond. Some required long-term consumption, others promised quick results, all claimed they would revitalize the qi, rebuild the body, nourish the brain and wash the marrow.

A few boasted exotic effects. Superior night vision. Superhuman muscle and bone strength. Blockage dissolution. Accelerated healing. And that was just for starters.

Anyone who wished to climb the ranks of the jianghu had to supplement their diets. Those at the top maintained peak performance through a careful regimen of cultivation, training, pills, beast broth, elixirs, and rejuvenation treatments. To catch up, those below them needed to do the same. Those who refused, out of conviction or a simple lack of wealth and connections, would be left behind by those who relentlessly pursued perfection. The logic was undeniable.

It was an arms race with no end.

Was this what he wanted?

Li Ming shook his head. It didn't matter what *he* wanted. If he stayed in the world of cultivators, he would inevitably come into conflict with cultivators more powerful and accomplished than himself. He already had. He needed an edge. He needed to *survive*. And that meant becoming more powerful. More than he already was.

His own cultivation practice could only go so far. He logged an average qi growth of one thousand points a year, and that was with a strict cultivation and training regimen. In the military, with access to potions and pills, it had shot up to twelve hundred and fifty points. A cultivator who followed a customized diet specific to his needs and body could double, triple, even *quintuple* that.

Even the cheapest and lowest grade of supplements helped. While they may only boost his qi cultivation by a small amount, it added up over the months and years. Even wuxingquan, one of the most powerful martial cultivation methods in existence, could only do so much. To catch up with others, he either had to spend an impossible amount of time training every day, or he had to take supplements.

"See anything you like?" Cai Yan asked.

She had filled a large basket with goodies, a mind-boggling array of bottles and boxes. Combined he guessed he guessed they were worth at least one-fifth of his income. But to the Cais, it would be nothing.

Li Ming thought of the beast broth. He could start with that at the least. But his wallet was already lighter than it should be, and he had to survive the coming month. He'd already broken Father's rule of saving half his income. Digging himself deeper wouldn't serve any purpose.

He had to become stronger. But it was a journey without end. He had to pace himself or destroy himself.

"I'm good for now," he said.

But he could, at least, add items to his wish list. He wasn't spending any money, and he could compare them later. That much he could do.

As he made his way to the exit, he sensed a powerful presence. A tall man with a powerful, confident stride, his qi blazing like a beacon, stepping into the aisles. Li Ming saw dusky skin and platinum hair and amber eyes and—

"Ghazan?"

"Li Ming," Ghazan said. "Ms. Cai."

"Shopping for supplements?" she asked.

"Yes. I'm looking for beast broth."

"I haven't seen you drink any before," Li Ming said.

Ghazan smiled. "Excellent."

Ghazan was seriously old fashioned. He trained in secret, cultivated in secret, he even drank beast broth in secret.

"Where do you do it? Your room?" Li Ming asked.

"That's for me to know and you to find out," Ghazan replied.

"Even paranoia has its limits," Cai Yan said.

"It's only paranoia if no one is out to get you."

Ghazan tried to inject a humorous tone to his words. Cai Yan tried to laugh it off. Li Ming knew they were only pretending.

"Are you two out on a date?" Ghazan asked.

"No!" Li Ming and Cai Yan protested as one.

"Really."

"Really!" they declared.

"You two seemed so in sync, I thought—"

"No!" she said.

Li Ming just shook his head.

Ghazan's lips spread into a shark-like grin.

"Ah. My mistake."

Downstairs, Li Ming picked up his pistol and holster. He stripped, examined and reassembled the weapon, confirming it met his specs. He clipped the holster to the outside of his belt, inserted the handgun, and covered it with his jacket.

"You bought a micro-compact pistol?" Cai Yan asked, amused.

"Why not?"

"I carry a larger gun than that!"

"And?"

"I thought a gun nut like you would get something... bigger."

"This weapon is for self-defense and assignments requiring deep concealment. If I need to go tactical, I already have the Golden Legion."

She shook her head. "That's... unorthodox."

"Of course."

The weapon came with additional accessories. Carrying case, owner's manual, cleaning kit. He arranged to ship them all to Dayong. An extra cost, but a trifling compared to what he'd spent today, and well worth the convenience.

They strolled through the exit. A couple of veterans glanced at them. First at Cai Yan, then at Li Ming, as though trying to figure them out. She smiled at a few she recognized. But they were all strangers to him.

"You're famous around here?" Li Ming asked.

"I represent Father when making company purchases sometimes."

"People recognize you everywhere you go."

"Part and parcel of being part of the family."

"It felt like they were sizing you up."

"It's a jianghu thing. Alpha males trying to see who's the biggest dog on the street."

"I wouldn't know how to deal with that."

"Start learning. Everywhere you go in the jianghu, you'll meet people like that."

"Any pointers?"

"Don't go out of your way to make enemies. You'll make plenty as is if you stay here."

"Roger that."

"You know, I'm surprised you didn't mention you were related to Li Yan Zhong."

"Does it matter?"

"Lineage goes a long way in the jianghu."

Li Ming exhaled sharply.

"You heard what Manager Xu said. If they knew who my ancestor was, people would expect a lot from me. They think I'm him. But I'm not. I'm me."

"They expect you to be another Hero of the Republic."

"These expectations are nothing but burdens."

"I sympathize. People expect me to be like Father too. But I'm not. I can't be him."

"Who would you rather be?"

She exhaled sharply.

"I'm still finding my way in this world. But until I find answers, being part of the jianghu and helping people is as good a way as any other."

"Better than some, too."

"Yes..."

Her voice trailed into nothingness. He knew the myriad ways a cultivator could lose himself to the way of devils. Surely she'd have seen them too. It was impossible to explain them all to a non-cultivator, and to a martial cultivator, there was no need to.

"What's next on the agenda?" Li Ming asked.

"I need to go off soon. I have an appointment at the rejuvenation clinic."

The words hung in the air for a frozen moment.

Li Ming looked at Cai Yan again with fresh eyes. Her lustrous hair. Her fair skin. Her soft curves. Her youth and beauty. He looked at them all, piece by piece, then reassembled them in a fresh understanding of her.

"You're an immortal?"

"Everyone in the Cai family is immortal."

The evidence was right there, in front of his eyes, under his nose. And he hadn't noticed it, hadn't thought to notice it, until now.

"Ah," Li Ming managed. "*Ganwen xiaojie fangling?*"

May I dare ask for this miss' fragrant age?

Cai Yan chuckled.

"*Wei*, don't you know it's impolite to ask a woman her age?"

"Apologies, Grandmother Cai."

Hands balled into fists, she bent her wrists parallel to the ground, straightened her arms, and pouted.

"*Tao yan!*" *Annoying!* "You really enjoy making fun of me!"

He bowed. "Thank you."

"*TAO YAN!*"

She broke into unrestrained laughter. So did he.

"Do you treat all women like this?" Cai Yan demanded.

"Only my younger sister."

She humphed.

"I pity her for having an elder brother as cheeky as you."

"I'll be sure to pass on your feelings."

"*Zhen shi de!*"

"I take it I'll have to address you as Grandmother Cai from now on?"

"*Tao yan!* I'm not that old!"

"How old are you?"

"We're close enough in age that you don't have to use honorifics."

"I see you still haven't answered the question."

She sniffed.

"And I see I have to go."

"I won't keep you then. Shall I wait for you?"

"The treatment will last the whole day. You don't have to wait for me."

"All right. I'll head back first, then."

"See you."

He headed outside and sucked down a deep breath of clean air. He hated to lie to someone, especially someone like Cai Yan. But here, it was necessary.

In some ways, he, too, was old fashioned.

Li Ming spent the rest of the morning wandering the Cultivator Quarter, taking in the sights and sounds. When lunchtime came, he found a restaurant with a rooftop garden. His biaohang card earned him access to a secluded corner overlooking the street. He placed his order, glanced around, saw no witnesses, and touched the control button on his smartglasses.

"Call Father," he said.

A dial tone echoed in his head. Li Ming maintained his vigil, watching for passers-by who came too close.

"Hello?" Father asked.

"It's me," Li Ming said. "It's been a while."

"This is a pleasant surprise. Or did something happen?"

"A bit of both."

"Is it something I need to tell your mother about?"

"No. It's about the swordbreaker."

"Ah. What about it?"

"Did you know it's a magic weapon?"

"You finally noticed?"

"...You *knew* it was a magic weapon?"

"It was in our family for generations. Of course I knew."

"But you didn't tell me! You just said it was a training weapon!"

"If I told you it was a magic weapon, would you have dared to take it out of the armory?"

Li Ming couldn't say anything.

"There's your answer. Besides, consider it part of your training," Father said.

"What do you mean?"

"Always know your equipment. Even something as innocuous as a swordbreaker may hold a secret."

"Yes, Father."

"Don't give me that tone. This is not just about your equipment. It's about what lies in front of you, beside you, and right under your nose. The jianghu is a world of lies and deception. Forget the romance of the big screen. It is a world inhabited by powerful men who are always seeking to take advantage of others.

"You didn't notice that your swordbreaker is a magic weapon. What else are you not seeing about the things, people and organizations around you? What do you not know about the people you've met?"

Li Ming thought about Cai Yan's revelation that her family were all immortals. About Ghazan reveling in how he had hidden his consumption of beast broth—and how he continued to hide his training and cultivation from everyone around him.

What *did* he know about the world of the rivers and lakes?

"I guess there's a lot I don't know," Li Ming admitted.

"What you don't know can kill you. There's a huge gap between what you know and what you *think* you know. You must close it. Never see what people want you to see about them and about others. Learn to see the world exactly as it is."

"How do I do that?"

"Insight. Awareness. Wisdom. You must cultivate these alongside your qi. Pay attention to the people and things around you. See what is being presented, then look for what else might be hidden. Never be satisfied by surface appearances and explanations."

"That sounds tough."

"It is also necessary if you wish to survive the rivers and lakes."

"Why didn't you tell me about this before I left?"

"Some lessons can only be learned through experience."

Father was right, again. Better he learn about this principle through minor and pleasant revelations than on the battlefield.

"How did you learn that the swordbreaker was a magic weapon?" Father asked.

Li Ming described the events at the Three Worlds Emporium.

"You didn't ask about the restorer?" his father said, his voice stern.

"His name was listed on the smart contract. Chen Zhong Hua, from Jinsu."

"But you didn't look him up?"

"Just his website."

And only on the way to the restaurant.

"You shouldn't rush into such contracts. Always know who and what you're dealing with, especially when handling high value goods like a magical weapon. At least Cai Yan has a good head on her shoulders."

"She does."

"Pay attention to how she conducts business. Learn from her. The Cai family has been doing business in the jianghu for generations. They can show you the ins and outs of the trade."

"Got it."

"Be sure to monitor the contract and check in on the performance milestones. It is your money, and our heirloom. You need to make sure you're getting what you paid for."

"Yes, Father."

"Good."

Father sure liked to nag a lot. Unfortunately, he was also right a lot of the time.

"Have you ever used the swordbreaker in combat before?" Li Ming asked.

"Yes. Many times."

"When?"

"First in the Special Forces, and later when I entered the jianghu. I was the only man I know who carried a swordbreaker into battle."

"Any pointers on how to use it?"

"Which form are you using to train it?"

"Short stick, primarily, with some straight sword."

"Good. The swordbreaker has the properties of both. The short stick form shows how to use it as an impact weapon. The straight sword teaches you how to use the point. But do not focus only on body mechanics and strikes. Seek the intention behind the form, and see the tactics and strategy."

"I've been working on that."

"Keep at it. Each form may only be a minute long, but it covers a huge scope. It is not enough to memorize the form. You must be able to break it down, know how and why each step works, and apply the right move at the right time."

"Under what circumstances did you use the swordbreaker?"

"In close quarters, when the enemy was shielded, had heavy armor, or both. A single well-placed blow can take out his hand. Or his weapon, if you're lucky. Done properly, it will neutralize the enemy and position you for a finishing blow if he insists on resisting. It's in the form, if you can find it."

"What about magic? Have you used the swordbreaker to cast magic?"

"Yes. Sometimes as a substitute for a reality shaper. Especially useful in non-permissive environments where reality shapers are forbidden but cold weapons are not. If you wear your swordbreaker close to you and behind your hip, if people try to scan you, your own qi will mask the qi stored in your primordial crystal. But only if your crystal isn't more powerful than your qi field, of course."

Li Ming frowned. Not quite the answer he wanted, but he supposed he'd asked the wrong question.

"How do you use the swordbreaker as a magic weapon?" Li Ming asked.

"The swordbreaker can be enhanced with magical energies. The blade will take on the properties of the qi you infuse it with. At the most basic level, a qi-charged swordbreaker will strike much harder than an ordinary impact weapon. The shock of the impact may knock a weapon out of the opponent's hands. Useful for disarming someone without killing him."

"What about higher levels?"

A slight pause.

"You have to see for yourself. Fortunately, our honored ancestors left behind a manual for us."

"A magic swordbreaker manual?"

"More than that. Li Yan Shun wrote it along with his son, your grandfather, Li Bai. They were both experts in An Family Gongfu. Together they formulated the Li Family Magic Weapon Style, a style that draws on An Family Gongfu principles and combines their investigations into the properties of magic weaponry."

"You never told me about this manual."

"You never asked. Besides, you already know the foundations."

"I do?"

"The weapon forms. The five elements and the eight trigrams. They are the foundations. But *only* the foundations. Actually using magic requires in-depth study and intense research. It is a challenging road, but a rewarding one."

"I am ready."

Father chuckled.

"I have with me a digitized copy of the manual. Shortly after your grandfather passed, I scanned the manual as an ebook and encrypted it. I can email the manual and the decryption key to you. But on one condition."

"What is it?"

"You must never show the art to anyone outside the Li family. Do not allow any outsiders to see you train the magic weapon techniques. You can only show them the basic weapon forms, but not the magic. This is the Li family treasure, used in combat all over Xiazhou to protect the people and the nation. Do not use it in vain. Do not allow devil cultivators to study it and learn how to defend against it."

"What if I have to use it in combat? Does that count as 'showing'?"

"Don't be ridiculous. Of course it does. Always assume someone is watching you when you fight. Train until you are so proficient no one can see the hidden principles of the art."

"How do I do that?"

"Have you seen videos of An Shigong demonstrating the art?"

"Yes."

"Emulate him. Watch how he moves. You will see that he moves so smoothly, so subtly, yet so powerfully, that he expresses the power of the art without revealing its internal dynamics to outside observers."

Li understood what he meant. When looking at other practitioners from other lineages perform the Five Element Linking Form, Li could, with time, pick out the five elements hidden in the moves. But Shigong... Other than the most obvious fists, Li couldn't tell which element a move belonged to, if it were a transition or a strike or something else. Not until after the execution. His movements were so fluid, so subtle, so *effortless*, it was as though he were a force of nature, the cosmos incarnate.

"How did he do it?"

"*Hengxian cang quxian, daquan cang xiaoquan, mingjin cang anjin.*"

The line conceals the curve, the large circle conceals the small, the obvious power conceals the hidden.

"You want me to be like Shigong?"

"Be the best you can be. Climb to the peak of your martial powers, and beyond.

"All right. I will."

"Good."

"When was the last time you cast magic with the swordbreaker?"

Li Guo An sighed. Just like that, he sounded like a weary old man.

"Twenty-two years ago. My final year in the jianghu. My final mission as a biaohang."

"What happened?"

"I was tracking a group of bandits operating in the province. My party and I had located their hideout. We called in the Special Military Police. They, in turn, requested our assistance to apprehend the leader. He was a fearsome cultivator in his own right, with a score of twenty-five thousand points. The Tewujing were afraid that they didn't have anyone who could defeat him.

"We accepted the mission.

"The raid began as planned. But when my party made entry, the bandit chief leapt up and ran to his safe room. His family delayed us just long enough for him to grab his gear. He cast a shield on himself and opened fire. We suppressed him, and I closed in. I drew my swordbreaker and charged it with qi.

"But nothing happened.

"I didn't know it then, but the circuits had finally fried. It was my fault. I thought it never needed maintenance. It never occurred to me to inspect it, to figure out how it worked, to check the circuits often.

"Fortunately for everyone, I neutralized the bandit. But it was a sign. I was getting old, slow, complacent. I'd made a mistake I would never have made when I was younger. We survived that one, but what about the future? What else could happen?

"It is better to retire gracefully than to be the cause of someone else's death, a death that could have been prevented. I washed my hands in the golden basin and returned to Fuyang."

"You didn't have to do that. You could have learned from it, carried on—"

"Also, your mother had you."

Li Ming fell silent.

"We'd been trying for years to have children. At last, after I returned from that job, your mother discovered she was pregnant. I saw it as a sign from Heaven. It was time to retire and find another way of life.

"I didn't need the swordbreaker anymore. I left in storage, took it out only for training, not for real combat. Even during my other missions, when I was called away to defend the province from beasts and bandits, the swordbreaker remained at home. But when you started talking about joining the military, and later, the jianghu, I thought it was time to pass it on."

"But you didn't restore it?"

"Some lessons must be learned through experience."

"You always say that."

"Doesn't make it any less true."

"Fine... Anyway, the swordbreaker is on its way to the restorer. There's not much I can do with it now."

"You can practice the forms. You can study the theory. There's a lot you can do. But before I send the manual to you, there is one more thing I must tell you."

"What is it?"

"The swordbreaker was the weapon of the finest bodyguards in the history of the Xia people. It is a weapon for protection and defense. Not a weapon of aggression and oppression. You must use it well, use it the right way, or not at all."

"Understood."

"Good. And now, there's one more thing."

"There's always one more thing."

"This one isn't related to gongfu."

"What is it?"

"This is the first time you've called me since you reached Bao An. Have you been busy?"

Li Ming exhaled sharply. Guilt gnawed at his heart.

"This is my third day off since I signed up with Dayong."

"Understandable. Still, your mother and sister miss you. At this rate, they're going to forget your face."

Li Ming didn't say anything. Even in the Special Military Police, he'd made a point to call his family at least once a week. But here, when they were only two hours away by bus...

"Call us more often. They need to know how you're doing."

"I'll try my best."

"Don't try. Do."

Chapter Twenty-Five

Foundations

The manual was indecipherable.

It was a slim volume, exactly one hundred and eight pages long. The original copy was written and illustrated by a sure hand, every stroke clean and confident, every word bleeding through the page to leave faint shadows and deep impressions on the reverse side. The version Li Ming received was an album of one hundred and eight images, each image a high-quality scan of a single page—without touch-ups or cleaning.

Written entirely in traditional script, the script that came before the language reforms seventy years ago, every page hosted an army of mysterious words marching from top to bottom, right to left, each of them a dense synthesis of strange radicals and inscrutable dots. Platoons of smaller characters formed sidebars parallel to the gutter. Illustrations filled many pages, demonstrating the intricacies of footwork and body mechanics, the interactions of the elements, the dynamics of an ever-changing universe. Tiny captions and footers offered additional elaboration.

Li Ming could barely read it.

This script was the ancestor of the script he knew. To promote literacy and fast-track modernization, the early Zhongxia Republic sought to simplify and standardize the written language across the nation. The pronunciation had remained the same, but the simplified characters were so pared-down, they became a different species of writing. Some characters he recognized by their resemblance to the words he knew; too many were completely alien to him.

That problem he solved by purchasing a simplified-traditional script dictionary. Then he discovered a deeper problem.

Every line was a couplet, every page a poem, every chapter a song. His ancestors had disguised every key concept with literary allusions and beautiful language, expecting the true knowledge to be passed on by oral transmission and learned by personal experience.

He understood a few key phrases. Seven Stars referred to the head, hands, elbows, shoulders, feet, knees and hips. Three Powers meant heaven, man and earth, and also the head, arms and legs. The Twelve Shapes meant the Twelve Animals.

But the rest?

Thunder Voice? Death Touch? Mind Freeze? He had no idea what these were. And what was this about the No-Fist, the Final Shape, the Harmony of Five Elements and Eight Trigrams?

There was only one way to understand the manual, and that was to consult Father regularly over the phone.

And that, Li Ming realized, might have been what he, and the rest of the family, wanted as well.

Strategy within strategy, small within large, circles within lines. Li Ming had to remember that.

In the evening, he called his family for a brief chat, then read a page or two of the manual alongside his father, taking copious notes and clarifying ideas. The following morning, he practiced the weapon forms after his daily cultivation—and tried to incorporate the extra information he had learned.

This time, he charged his practice weapons with his own qi. Simple on the surface, enormously difficult in practice. The flow of qi had to be smooth and even, filling the weapon from grip to tip. The weapon had to retain the charge while in motion. When it was no longer needed, he had to return the energy to his body.

It took him a full minute to completely fill a weapon with qi. The manual demanded the practitioner to charge his weapon in the space between heartbeats. With every swing and every thrust, he shed a bit of energy. The manual insisted that though a swordsman might cut a thousand times, the weapon would lose not a single drop of elixir. When he ended a form, he needed half a minute to retract the energy into himself. The manual required this to be done faster than an eyeblink.

Father didn't reveal much. He preferred depth over breadth, moving on to the next concept only when he was satisfied that his son understood exactly what his ancestors were trying to communicate. Of the ideas hidden further in the text—the terms Li Ming had no knowledge of—Father remained silent.

"These are advanced concepts," Father said. "Until you have perfected the basics, you won't understand them."

Twelve years. Li Ming studied the art for twelve years and still he didn't have a perfect grasp of the basics. His heart roared in frustration. His mind understood that the martial path had no end, that every summit revealed yet higher peaks.

The next five days passed like this. On the evening of the fifth day, after their daily discussion, Father closed with a question.

"Have you been training the other aspects of wuxingquan and yizhang?"

"A little," Li Ming replied.

"Don't neglect them. It's good that you're focused on studying the manual, but never forget it is built upon a foundation of An Family Gongfu. If you do not practice them, you will not understand the entirety of the art.

"From now until the end of next month, I want you to focus on the foundations, and learn how to integrate them with everything I've taught you so far. Consolidate everything you know. Until then, further progress is pointless."

When Wu-Day arrived, Li Ming tried a different tack.

After his morning routine, he worked with the fan form. First he did it slowly, paying extra attention to his body mechanics, his posture, his footwork. Every subtle motion, every shift in weight, every last detail, he examined in depth. He worked the form over and over, until he was certain he came close to perfection.

Then he charged it with qi.

And this time, it was nearly instant.

Not as fast as the manual demanded, but faster than a staff or sword.

Of course it was, he realized. It was a short weapon. Less mass to infuse with qi. More to the point, how could he hope to instantly charge a swordbreaker with qi if he couldn't do it with a fan?

He flowed through the fan form over and over and over again. Slowly. Carefully. Precisely.

He still lost qi with every major movement. But not as much. And then he saw.

If he overextended a movement, the qi burst out into the great unknown. If a swing were anything else than clean, he lost qi to muscular tension. If his footwork were off, if he took himself out of alignment with heaven and earth, the qi would not flow smoothly.

But that meant...

His weapon. He was treating it as a tool, separate from his body. But that was wrong. It had to *be* part of his body, utterly inseparable from his hands, his qi, his intent. Without that deep connection, the qi would not flow smoothly, and if would not flow smoothly it would not be fast.

One last set. A sip of water. And a new weapon.

Two weapons.

They were called judge's pens. Imitating the pens used by officials of the ancient eras, each pen was a thick steel rod slightly larger than a man's fist, with a pointed tip on either end. It looked like an archaic weapon, an implement from bygone days. But the form could be applied to knives, pocket sticks, and other improvised weapons.

And, more importantly, he was training to work with a *metal* weapon.

The manual noted complex interactions between different kinds of qi and matter. Qi behaved differently in wood than metal. It didn't matter for basic techniques. But at the higher end, the realm of combat magic, these subtle differences spelt the difference between a glorious success and an ignoble death.

Already he felt the difference. In a fan the qi felt warm and solid. In the pens, the qi was lively and electric. He flowed through the form, once again with extreme attention to detail. This was yizhang, not wuxingquan, and the circles and weight shifts were different enough that he had to work with them consciously, to remind himself that he was working with a different art.

As he spun through a tight circle, he saw the Cais at the edge of the courtyard. Sister, bother, father. They were all watching him, watching his—

He pulled the qi into himself.

Electricity charged down his meridians and into his dantian. A spin, a double thrust, and the excess qi was now safely stored within him. A few more steps and the set reached its end.

"Not bad," Cai Yan said. "I think it's the first time I've seen you do it."

"It's the first time I've done the form in months."

"I can tell," Cai Mengyang said.

So could Li Ming. He'd felt the hesitations, the tensions, the disconnections, breaks in the flow of qi and intent.

"I need more practice," Li Ming said.

"Yes, but don't be so focused on training you forget to go to work."

"Yes boss."

Chapter Twenty-Six

Breakfast

The hutong was healing.

The desperate defense against the yaoshu swarm had left the alley blasted and blackened and bruised. Cai Yan's flames had slagged everything they touched, leaving behind fire-seared walls, melted glass, silhouettes scorched into the stone setts. Li Ming's plasma fire had blown deep pits into buildings and the earth.

Li Ming would have paid for the damages. It was what his father would have done in Fuyang. But the city covered the bill. The city hired the workers, purchased the materials, organized the repair efforts. The city officials told him he didn't have to worry about it. He was defending Bao An, the violence was necessary, and no innocents were hurt. He had nothing to feel guilty about.

Even so, Cai Mengyang personally visited every home and business his shooters had damaged, offered profuse apologies, and handed the owners red packets stuffed with banknotes.

The biaohang had contributed to the pot. Li Ming, too. Ten percent of his cut of the bounty. He hadn't been paid for the hunt yet, no one had, so Dayong would claim it from his share later. A man had to set right what he made wrong. It wasn't just the way of the jianghu. It was the way of being human.

Now, four weeks after the hunt, repairs were finally complete. The laborers, long used to cleaning up after martial cultivators, had worked with delicacy and precision. They had replaced the blasted stones with fresh ones, carefully treated and artificially aged to blend into their neighbors. They had installed new windows, reproducing them to the owners' exact specifications and respecting the aesthetics of the larger building. They had filled in the pits, smoothed them over, then painted and aged them so convincingly it was as if they had never existed at all.

By the time they were done, there was no outward trace of the yaoshu attack, or the violence that followed. Not to a stranger.

But Li Ming saw the lingering signs of trauma. Fresh coats of paint, still brilliant in the morning light. Brand new bikes, purchased with compensation money, after the biaohang had destroyed their predecessors. New items on the shelves or shrunken menus, replacing the goods lost to beasts and fire.

He had, in his own way, contributed to this. The guilt still hung heavy on him, a leaden coat draped across his shoulders. If he had moved faster, shot more accurately, kept his cool, maybe he wouldn't have inflicted so much damage on his neighbors.

Yet they didn't seem to mind. If anything, they were grateful. The children smiled and waved at him on the street, the storekeepers hurried to offer special rates and discounts, adults addressed him as *nin* or as Li Biaohang, never his name in isolation.

The people looked up to him. To Dayong. He didn't feel that he deserved such respect. He'd only done his job, and imperfectly. All he could do was become worthy of it.

Today was a laundry day. Before leaving Fuyang, he'd told himself he would do his laundry himself. He'd done it in his military days, and he was prepared to do it again. But the life of a biaohang had left him little time for anything but the most basic and essential of chores. Laundry was not one of them.

He didn't want to burden the housekeepers any further. Instead he favored the neighborhood laundry service. Every time he visited, he chose the same-day service. Dry cleaning for his formal wear, cold water wash for his tactical uniforms and low-pro clothing. Expensive, but it was an investment. He could always make more money, but time was priceless.

Besides, the laundry offered free delivery to Dayong.

After dropping off his load, he wandered down the alley. He still had two ke before Dayong officially opened for business. Enough time for a slow breakfast.

There were so many choices. A street cart selling fresh-cooked jianbing, thin flatbread stuffed with eggs and beans and vegetables and other fillings, so renowned it attracted a long queue. A newly-opened store specializing in fruit smoothies and juices. A traditional coffee shop that served traditional breakfast staples...

Ghazan.

The Yue sat in the far corner of the coffee shop. Back straight, head erect, he ate like a king, deftly manipulating his chopsticks. Plates and bowls lay arrayed before him, occupying half of the table. Ghazan dipped a spoon into a bowl, lifted it to his lips, and raised an eyebrow at Li Ming.

Li Ming entered the cramped shop. A no-nonsense establishment, it existed only to serve hot beverages and hotter snacks from dawn to dusk. Mr. and Mrs. Zhang, the ageless couple that ran the shop, worked tirelessly behind the stainless steel counter, expertly measuring and pouring coffee and tea into time-worn cups, never stopping, always in motion. They greeted Li Ming by name as he approached, and he did the same.

Rows of circular tables and cheap plastic chairs cut through the length of the shop, packed so tightly there was barely room to move. This place attracted a predominantly elderly crowd, lounging in tight, noisy knots scattered across the floor, yapping at the top of their lungs. What few younger customers here preferred takeout.

But there was a young man in a loose jacket at the far side of the room, sitting with a half-empty cup of coffee, intently watching the world through a set of smartglasses.

Near the back, cardboard boxes stacked high in the corners, next to a tiny altar. Dedicated to the gods of the five directions, the Zhangs had laid out five cups of tea, five types of fruits and flowers, and five incense sticks.

Ghazan sat at the table closest to the altar, his back to the corner, his eyes at the road, feet planted on the floor. He tracked Li Ming as he approached.

So did the young man.

"Is this seat taken?" Li Ming asked.

"Go ahead," Ghazan said.

Li Ming drew up a chair.

"What are you having?"

Ghazan gestured at the plates.

"*Tsagaan idee.* You call it white food."

Everything was white. A bowl of white milk tea that smelled of toasted grains and salt. A plate of white doufu. Another plate of fried dough sticks, sliced up into small bite-sized pieces, to expose their white hearts. A second bowl of thick creamy yoghurt.

"Is it a traditional Yue breakfast?"

"Almost, but no. The Zhangs use condensed milk in the tea, but the Yue favor fresh, whole milk. Doufu is made of soybeans, while we prefer dried curd made of coagulated and fermented milk. Our *boortsog* is served with honey, butter or cheese, and is denser and sweeter than youtiao. Instead of yoghurt, I grew up drinking airag, fermented mare's milk."

"I'd like to try that someday."

"If you ever visit the Homelands, you should. It's much different from this... this... approximation."

"You don't like it?"

"The Zhangs mean well, and they do their best, but there's nothing like real milk and honey. On the other hand, this is the closest I've come to recreating the breakfast food of my people in this place."

Ghazan dipped a slice of youtiao into the milk tea with his chopsticks, stirred it around, then fished it out with a spoon and brought the mix to his mouth. As Ghazan chewed, Li composed a private message with eyeblinks and subtle hand gestures.

The man next to us is staring hard at me.

Ghazan swallowed. Soaked a piece of youtiao in his tea. And blinked out another message.

He's still looking at you out the corner of his mouth. Fan of yours?

I don't know him. Is he a threat?

He was here since I came in. He glanced at me and passed over me when I sat down. He didn't show any signs of suspicious behavior until now.

Keep an eye out.

Out loud, Li Ming said, "I'm going to get my own breakfast."

Ghazan grunted.

Li Ming stood. Out the corner of his eye, he saw the man take a sip, turning his face from Li Ming's gaze.

Stalker? Spotter? Or just a jianghu fanatic? Li Ming didn't know yet.

His heart jolted in his chest. Heat rushed to his hands. Li Ming breathed it out. This wasn't time for a fight, not yet anyway.

Li Ming casually ambled up to the counter. Mrs. Zhang smiled at him, revealing perfect teeth.

"Li Biaohang, what would you like?"

"*Laoban niang*, what kind of buns do you have today?"

"Lots! We have red bean buns, lotus paste buns, pork buns, vegetable buns."

"They smell delicious. Give me two pork buns and a cup of hot coffee."

The young man looked up at Li Ming again. And looked away.

"How much for everything?" Li Ming asked.

"Twenty yuan."

Li Ming drew his wallet and shook out a handful of coins. Large denomination coins. He angled his hand towards Mrs. Zhang, letting her see them, and pressed them into her waiting palm.

Her eyes boggled. Before she could speak, Li Ming leaned in.

"Did you see the young man seated in front of the Yue?"

Mrs. Zhang nodded.

"Do you know him?"

"No."

"How long has he been there?"

"Two ke."

"Did he do anything strange?"

"No. He just sat there and quietly drink his coffee."

"Thanks. Keep the change."

"Is something happening?"

"I don't know. But I'd appreciate it if you could hurry the coffee and send the buns with it."

Li Ming returned to the table. Now the young man studiously avoided looking at him altogether, looking at everything *but* him, while keeping him in his peripheral vision.

Maybe it was nothing. He'd seen many people act like that with cultivators, overawed by their presence, unable to look at them but unable to look away. But this guy... he was nervous, but he was trying not to show it. Why?

Li Ming made small talk with Ghazan, asking about the origins of white food. On his smartglasses, he sent a single message.

Keep an eye out on the subject. Could be nothing, but let's not take any chances.

His instincts screamed at him to walk away. But he was committed. If the man had hostile intentions, if Ghazan and Li Ming left now, in the middle of breakfast, it would tell him that he'd been blown. He might escalate. Or, if he had an organization, they'd replace him with a fresh face, someone who might be more skilled.

I'll tell the boss, Ghazan replied. *Just in case.*

Li Ming nodded. *Good idea.*

Ghazan dunked his tofu and youtiao without eating them, instead pretending to sip from his tea, and left his yoghurt alone.

The coffee arrived with Li Ming's buns. Wisps of fragrant steam wafted from the deep black liquid. The buns came soon after. Li Ming blew on his coffee and—

A hard gaze swept over Li MIng.

Keeping his eyes fixed on the coffee, he drew his attention to his peripheral vision.

Three young men strode into the coffee shop. Dark shirts and jackets, tough jeans and work boots. Hard lines bulged out from the sleeves, revealing the unmistakable profile of reality shapers.

Looking up, Ghazan sipped at his tea.

Cultivators. Qi score between 1600 to 1800.

The man in the middle spoke.

"Li Ming?"

"Who wants to know?" Li Ming replied, rising to his feet.

The stranger ignored him.

"And you're Ga San, right? The undefeated champion of the Taiping circuit?"

Undefeated champion? Circuit? What was that about?

Ghazan stood, hands low, voice calm.

"We don't know you," Ghazan said.

The man smiled unpleasantly.

"We do. The Hong Shun Tang sends their regards."

The Hong Shun Tang! The secret society that ran Shanxia! Was this a revenge hit? It had to be!

Li Ming's hand swept to his hip—

His bare hip.

His gun! He had left his gun in his room!

His knives, his shaper, *everything* was in his locker!

He'd expected a laundry day and a quick breakfast. Not this. He hadn't brought any live weapons to training, he stowed his dummy weapons in the storeroom, he'd showered and changed and *left his weapons in the locker!*

Quarter-brained idiot! Had water leaked into his brain? What was the point of buying weapons if he didn't wear them when he went out?!

The gangsters caught the movement. Their jaws dropped. Their eyes widened. Their boss stepped in.

"GUN!" the boss yelled.

As one, they swept their jackets aside, reaching for their waistbands—

Ghazan drew.

He was *fast*, faster than lightning, his hands a blur, reaching for his belt and coming up with a handgun, extending the pistol out in both hands, firing one two three bolts.

The shots splashed against the jackets, dispersing in a shower of sparks.

"SHIELDS!" Ghazan shouted.

"DOWN! DOWN! EVERYBODY DOWN!" Li Ming ordered.

Ghazan rocketed forward, pistol blasting in a rapid cadence, moving around the table. He shot at faces, at bellies, at exposed shirts, but every bolt struck an invisible shield. The civilians screamed, ducking and covering. The gangsters brought up their own pistols, their qi flaring to fill the world, and hammered away. Li Ming ducked, covering his head, staying under the line of fire.

Ghazan turned *black*.

He was man of shadow, of pure nothingness. He drank in the bolts, absorbing them into his being, swallowing them into a void. Only his palms and fingers remained whole, retaining enough tangible mass to fire, and fire, and fire again—

Steam burst from the overloaded pistol.

More smoke erupted from the gangsters' guns.

Ghazan turned *white*.

A shockwave of pure white light burst forth. It smashed into tables and chairs, cups and plates, the gangsters, blasting them all out into the street.

Next to Li Ming, the young man swore, rose, reached for his beltline—

Li Ming grabbed his coffee and flung it into his face.

The threat screamed, clawing at his scalded face and neck, desperately wiping down his lenses, his weapon forgotten. Li Ming seized the edge of the man's table and flipped it over. The table smashed into the threat, knocking him down, pinning him under its mass. Li circled around the table, hands high, legs grounded, shuffling for a better—

The table blasted off the ground.

Yelling, Li sank into the floor and cannoned his palms outwards. His qi screamed forth, hot and furious, surging from his dantian and down his arms. The table split in half. Shrapnel whistled past his ears, tugged at his sleeves, scraped against his Raptors.

The young man scrabbled to his feet, sucking down deep breaths, pulling qi into his left forearm, into a low-profile shaper under his sleeve. Li stepped in and blasted a straight punch to the head.

The threat slipped the shot, covering with his left arm, answering with a cross. Li chopped his left fist down, deflecting the punch, then bounced off and launched at his head again. Another slip. Li twitched high, the man jerked to cover, then Li went low and rocketed his fist into his gut.

A horrible retching sound spewed from the man's throat. He doubled over into the blow, all resistance gone. Li coiled in like a snake, elbow slashing, smashing through his temple. Down the threat went, falling on shattered wood, bouncing his head off the floor, and went still.

Outside, Ghazan advanced on the threats, his body returning to the material world. He was meat and matter again, his magic spent, his gun still smoking. He returned his weapon to his appendix holster, smoothly and confidently, scanning left and right.

The gangsters were all down, shaken but still in the fight, trying to pick themselves up. One of them had lost his weapon, but the other two retained death grips on their guns.

Ghazan rushed up to the closer of the armed men and kicked him in the head. He bowled over, gun flying from his hand, blood spurting from his nose, and went still.

The second man rose unsteadily to his feet, shaking his head, pistol twitching and quivering, but relentlessly rising towards Ghazan.

Leaping towards the threat, Ghazan spun around, arms whipping ferociously through the air, so fast and so violently the air itself split apart with a tremendous whoosh. His hand flattened into a palm and smashed into the man's crown.

Wet *POPs* echoed in the street. His neck collapsed. His head folded down. He ragdolled instantly, sprawling over the stone.

The last man was back on his feet. A long kitchen knife flashed in his hand. With a bestial scream, he charged at Ghazan.

Ghazan stood.

Glared.

Killing qi blasted from his eyes, piercing the gangster's own, punching through his qi field to bore deep into his soul.

The gangster hesitated.

Ghazan exploded.

He slapped the knife hand away with his left hand and blasted his right forearm into the gangster's neck. Quick as a flash, he cycled his right arm, twisted the other way and speared his elbow into his jaw.

The gangster collapsed into the double blows, struck his skull a third time against a lamp post, and fell limp to the floor.

Ghazan clenched his fists. His qi blazed high and bright, a leaping pillar of ethereal flame. He threw his head and back and roared at the sky.

"Ghazan!" Li Ming said.

Ghazan blinked. Relaxed. And opened his hands.

"Are you okay?" Li Ming asked.

Ghazan patted himself down. "I'm all right. You?"

"Yes. They never had a chance."

"What was that all about? A revenge hit?"

"I—"

A squad of heavily-armed biaohang rushed out the gates of Dayong. Cai Yong, Cai Yan, a half-dozen others.

"Li Ming! Ga San! What happened?!" Cai Yong demanded.

"The Hong Shun Tang just tried to hit us," Li Ming said. "Three fighters, one spotter. We took them down. The situation is under control."

"*Xie tian xie di.*"

"Is anyone injured?" Cai Yan asked.

"Let's find out."

By some minor miracle, the worst injuries among the civilians were merely bumps and bruises. The Zhangs had taken cover the second they saw the guns. Ghazan had soaked up all the incoming fire into himself; there was no damage to the shop. Just furniture damage.

The spotter was out cold. But at least he was still breathing.

The others...

"You broke his neck with one blow?!" Cai Yong exclaimed.

"Yes," Ghazan said calmly.

Li stared at the body of the second fighter. He'd thought he'd seen the myriad ways a man could die, but this was new. It was as if his neck had completely liquified. His head flopped about bonelessly. One look at him and Cai Yan just shook her head.

The knife man was completely insensate, but his chest heaved up and down. The last one had gone completely still, his qi pouring out of his body. If he weren't dead yet, he soon would be.

"They attacked us in broad daylight, right in front of our compound," Cai Yong said, shaking his head. "*Tamen danzi zhen da.*"

They've got huge guts.

"At least no one else got hurt," Li Ming said.

"The Hong Shun Tang will have to answer for that. But why did they attack you?"

Li Ming sighed.

"It's a long story."

Chapter Twenty-Seven

Absolution

The police investigation took up the rest of the morning. A ke after the Civil Police arrived, they confirmed that Li Ming and Ghazan were the defenders, and treated them as partners in the investigation.

At the scene of the crime, they walked the cops through the fight. In the station, they gave their statements. The investigators did their thing, and by lunchtime the prosecutor announced that they were free to go.

Boss Cai released both men from the day's duties, promising to pay them the regular day rate. Any other time and Li Ming would have jumped at the chance to explore the city further. But he was unarmed and had a bullseye on his back.

Instead, he returned to the hutong.

The cops had taken everything they needed. But the shattered table remained outside the coffee shop, fit only for kindling.

Li drew his tactical shaper, returned to the coffee shop, and gathered the scrap wood. With great precision, he pieced the pieces back the best he could. Then he pressed his hands to the table and touched his mind to the shapers.

Wood qi, to repair and reconnect the broken pieces. Earth qi, to strengthen the bonds. Careful manipulation of both kinds of energy, so that the wood would hold the earth together instead of parting it. Piece by piece, bit by bit, the broken table reassembled itself.

It wouldn't be perfect. He couldn't restore sawdust, lost splinters, any tiny bits missing from the whole. But he could salvage it, return it to its original purpose, save the Zhangs some money. And himself.

"You don't have to do this for us," Mrs. Zhang said.

"I want to do it. It is good practice," Li Ming insisted.

Indeed it was. It demanded precision and concentration, the same precision and concentration needed to wield a magic weapon. He worked on each piece slowly and methodically, moving on only when he was satisfied it was restored, as close to restored as he could make it.

After two hours, the table was *almost* as good as new. Small scars marred its surface, but it was just cosmetic damage.

The Zhangs thanked him profusely, offering him tea and coffee on the house. Li insisted on paying for them, for the privilege of allowing him to hone his art at their establishment. After long, long minutes of back and forth, they reluctantly accepted his money.

Li spent the rest of the afternoon and evening inside the Dayong compound, training and cultivating. He lost himself to the movements, flowing through countless repetitions of forms and fists, tracking time only by the passage of the sun across the sky. Moments after he begun, powerful stomps echoed within the secret courtyard.

Most people would take the time to unwind. He couldn't. The Hong Shun Tang would make another run at him. He'd have to be ready for them. When he was sure no one was looking, he took up the dummy weapons and ran through the qi exercises in the Li Family manual.

He paused only for dinner and a short break. Long enough to re-read key sections of the manual. Then he went out to train again.

Finally, at the close of the eleventh hour, he ended training. He had, finally, wrung himself dry. His muscles ached, sweat soaked through his clothes, and his qi was spent. He'd done everything he could today. Now he just needed to relax.

He enjoyed a long cold shower. When he stepped out, he saw Ghazan in the living room, looking up from a scroll. Next to the device was a half-filled glass and a bottle of clear liquid.

"Enjoying a drink?" Li Ming asked.

"We're off-duty. After a day like ours, we need one."

"Mind if I try it?"

A dark expression flitted across Ghazan's face. And, just as quickly, vanished.

"Get a glass."

Li Ming grabbed one from the kitchen and returned. Sitting next to Ghazan, he studied the bottle. This close to it, he felt the chill radiating from it, promising icy oblivion. Drops of water dripped down the side, ending their brief existence trapped in a cork coaster. The spirit within the bottle was so pure and clean and clear, it looked like water. The label was written in the Yue script, a collection of vertical lines and stylized curls and occasional dots, at once mocking and seductive.

"What is this?" Li Ming asked.

Disbelief crossed Ghazan's face.

"You wanted to try a drink you don't know?"

"It seemed like a good idea at the time."

Ghazan shook his head.

"Futejia."

Ghazan might as well have spoken in an alien tongue.

Li Ming poured out a small measure for himself. Just a finger. And lifted his glass.

"Ganbei."

They clinked glasses.

Li Ming took a tiny sip.

Liquid fire rushed down his throat, igniting a sun in his chest and a star in his belly. The taste of medicine lingered in his mouth. Blood rushed to his face and hands. Li Ming winced, setting down his glass, trying not to cough.

"It's strong," Li Ming gasped.

"It is eighty percent pure alcohol. It ought to be."

He had no idea why people drank this stuff. But the fire settled into a smooth golden lake. His muscles relaxed. His tongue loosened. His mind wavered.

Careful. Let's not go overboard with this.

Another sip, larger this time. And now he felt like he were floating on clouds.

"You sure you can hold your liquor?" Ghazan asked.

"No one in my family drinks," Li Ming admitted.

"Go easy. Futejia isn't a beginner's drink."

"I can tell."

Somehow he found that to be the height of hilarity. A grin spread across his face.

"What's so funny?"

Li Ming didn't know how to put it in words. There was *something* that provoked his sudden good humor, but whatever it was, it drifted away on a sea of spirits, leaving only warmth and radiance behind.

"It's nothing," Li Ming said.

"It's getting to you. Take it easy."

Li Ming eased the glass aside. The remaining futejia looked so deceptively little, not much more than a mouthful, but it was a mouthful of liquid obliteration.

Ghazan mumbled something.

"Eh?" Li Ming asked.

"Thanks."

"What for?"

"Dealing with the spotter. You kept him from taking me from behind."

"No problem. I should be the one thanking you. You dealt with the hitters. I didn't have the hardware for that."

"Why not?"

"I was just going out for laundry and breakfast. I didn't think I'd need weapons."

"Careless. It could have been a fatal mistake."

Li Ming exhaled sharply. "Yes. I won't do that again. If the hitmen failed once, they could try again."

"I don't think they were hitmen."

"What do you mean?"

"They wouldn't have announced themselves. Pros wouldn't, at least. They'd just draw their guns and start blasting."

"Who were they, then?"

"Probably low-level thugs sending a message. Telling you to be on your toes, that they are watching you. Secret societies do it to martial cultivators and biaohang all the time."

"But why did they draw?"

"They must have thought you were going for a gun."

The floor fell out of Li Ming's stomach.

Ghazan was right. Li Ming went to for his gun, but he realized he wasn't carrying one. The gangsters must have thought he was about to draw down on them, so they drew their own guns. Then Ghazan did what he did and...

Li Ming whispered a curse, dark and bitter.

"I wasn't armed."

"But they thought you were."

"I started it."

"No. They did. They chose to come after us. They chose to act in a suspicious manner. They chose to draw their weapons. They chose to fight us."

Li Ming pressed his palms against his forehead. "I don't..."

"If you're worried about the police, don't. They'll side with Dayong over gangsters. The official story is that we fought off an assassination attempt, and no one will believe anything the Hong Shun Tang has to say about it."

"We *killed* them!"

"They tried to kill us. We stopped them. That's all."

"But—"

"No buts. They'll just eat away at you. Stick to the story. The Hong Shun Tang targeted us, and we dealt with them."

Li Ming took another sip.

"They had a spotter. He recognized us and called in his friends. It looked exactly like a set up for a hit. We had to assume it was," Li Ming said.

"Exactly. Don't worry about it. The more important question is why they came after you."

Li Ming sighed. Stared into his drink. At the bottom of the glass lay a promise of relief, of acceptance, of absolution, if only he had the courage to speak.

He sipped.

And spoke.

He spoke of the days of fire. Of the Hong Shun Tang and his campaign in Shanxia. Of how he had fought four Hong Shun Tang cultivators and leaders, one on one, and won.

"You've been through a lot, haven't you?" Ghazan said.

Li Ming looked away.

"Yes."

"You made it. You won. That's what matters."

"And maybe that's why the Hong Shun Tang was after me."

"Revenge?"

"Yes. The Jianghu Times told the world where I was and who I worked for. It wouldn't take a genius to find Dayong. The Hong Shun Tang sent spotters to the hutong to identify my patterns of life. When the spotter identified me, he called in the hatchet men."

"Or messengers."

"Why would they spend that kind of time and energy just to send a message? They would have wanted something from me. It might have been a warning to back off. Or just a prelude to a kill. Whatever it was, it was nothing good."

It felt like a rationalization. Maybe it was. All the same, Li Ming's actions had led to the deaths of two men, possibly more. It wasn't something he wanted to be proud of, especially if it wasn't necessary.

Next time, he vowed, he would refrain from such carelessness. And he would always, *always*, carry a weapon whenever he was out. Even on laundry runs.

And...

And he would have to avoid unnecessary escalation.

Violence was an inevitability in this job. The power to save a life and the power to end a life were opposite edges of the same sword. And yet, his hands were sullied enough. Every kill came with a terrible cost and certain retribution. He didn't want to burden his soul more than it already was.

Was this what it meant to stay in the jianghu?

"Something good came out of it," Ghazan said, interrupting his reverie.

"What is it?"

"We showed them they should never mess with us again."

"Let's hope they learn their lesson this time."

Ghazan threw back a slug and exhaled sharply. Without a word, he refilled his glass. They sat in silence for a while.

A minute passed. Two. Then Li Ming spoke again.

"How did the Hong Shun Tang know who you were?"

"What do you mean?"

"They called you an undefeated champion. What was that about?"

"It's a long story."

"We have time."

"I don't know where to begin."

"From the start."

Ghazan's lips bunched together. His shoulders tensed. He sighed. And drank. And stared into his glass.

"I grew up in the western steppes of the Yue Homelands. As far west as you could go while still remaining in Yue territory. Past the steppes, there was nothing but barren desert. It's the second-largest desert in the world. We called it the Place of Ruin.

"Life was... harsh. This close to the Place of Ruin, the land was poor. It could barely support agriculture of any kind. Dust storms regularly blow in from the west. Anyone foolish enough to start a farm would wake up to find their crops buried overnight. We had no choice but to live the way of our ancestors.

"We lived in a small... 'Village' isn't the right word for it. The word implies a permanent settlement. What we had was more like a... market. An open-air market where people could meet to exchange goods and perform services. Only a handful of people lived there permanently.

"Nine in ten of the inhabitants lived nomadic lives. They herded livestock across the steppes, moving their gers once they've exhausted the land. A nomad can move up to a hundred times a year, chasing the best grasses and cleanest water.

"Horses, sheep, cattle, goats, camels, yaks, they were our meat and bones. The nomads made money by selling milk, meat and fleece—but they had no connections to the outside world.

"Hence, the market. The town people. They bought the goods the nomads had to offer. They processed milk into cheese, cream, butter, and other dairy products. They wove clothing and blankets and other goods from fleece. They traded these goods for medicines, technology and other essentials from traveling merchants.

"It was an arrangement as old as the Yue Dynasty. Life followed the same patterns, the same cycles. Entire generations lived their lives without ever leaving the town. Life was... It's not as comfortable as it is in the city, but we had everything we needed. However, if you wanted more out of life, the town was too small for you. You had to leave.

"My father came from a nomad clan. My mother was the daughter of town merchants. Their marriage benefited both their houses. The merchants bought goods at preferential rates from my father's clan. In turn, the nomads enjoyed high-end outside goods from my mother's side of the family. I spent half my childhood wandering the steppes, the other half in the streets of the town. I had everything I needed, but... It wasn't enough. The world was wide, and I wanted to see it all.

"There were only two ways out of town. The way of the book, or the way of the spear. I had no talent for the book. Few people in town did.

"The town was tiny. Perhaps two hundred permanent residents at most. It wasn't large enough to support a school. We couldn't even afford to pay for a full-time teacher.

"Instead, twice a week, a traveling teacher visited the town. She held classes in the town square for the children, and any teenager who wanted to attend. She taught us how to read and write, the fundamentals of math and science, the history of our people, even the basics of magic theory. Most importantly, she showed us that there was a wider world outside the village.

"For all that, she could only visit twice a week. Nowhere near enough for a proper education. The town shaman helped however he can, but his was the knowledge of our ancestors and of the spirit world. Not the knowledge of the present day. And our parents and grandparents had even less of an education than we did.

"Education, paper degrees, was not important to us. Not like for your people. Every academic qualification was a massive expense. The town was too small and too remote for the examiners to come to us. To earn a certificate, we had to travel to the city and sit for exams as private candidates. Every hour we spend studying is an hour away from work.

"The knowledge and traditions of our ancestors could feed us, if only we apply them. We don't need paper to survive. But we all need to eat, and that meant we all needed to work. For most of us, there was no reason to study more than what was necessary.

"Instead of formal education, I turned to weapons. From my paternal uncles, I learned wrestling, horse riding, archery. From my maternal grandfather, I studied the art of the spear. My grandfather was the only one among us who had lived, for a time, in the cities. He had learned shifangquan before retiring to his hometown, and he passed on that knowledge to me.

"When I came of age, I joined the military. I barely met the educational requirements, but I scraped through. After basic training, they assigned me to an armored cavalry unit. We were the descendants of the hordes that had conquered the lands to the east and west. We were the inheritors of a proud heritage. We reveled in it.

"At that time, I felt this was where I wanted to be, what I wanted to do. The Army offered me a chance to continue my education through night classes. This was how I learned the Xia language. In the Army, we traveled across the homeland on maneuvers and operations. Once we even traveled to Barate on a joint exercise. I was... I thought this was my ticket out of the steppes.

"In my fifth year of service, disaster struck. The nomads reported strange sightings from the Place of Ruin. Unexplained dust storms swept over the steppes. Herds vanished into the wilderness, leaving only humongous holes. Strange cries echoed from the desert. The village sent a team of volunteers to investigate. A week later, they returned with a message.

"They had sighted a death worm.

"Death worms are the bane of our people. They are titanic monsters, large as dragons. They burrow through the sands and strike from ambush. Their skin is coated with powerful toxins. A single touch will kill you.

"The village reported the sightings to the military. The military, however, was reluctant to respond. Death worms resided deep in the deserts, away from the abodes of men. They said that so long as we didn't enter the Place of Ruin, or did anything to provoke it, we would be fine.

"But we weren't. The storms grew stronger, burying the townspeople in their homes. The death worm grew more brazen, snatching livestock in broad daylight. The people lodged another complaint. Again, the military said the monster didn't pose a threat to human life, and they couldn't act. But the village could hire beast hunters.

"Any other place and it would be the time-honored solution. But my village was a poor village. The dust storms wrecked our dairy stockpile and sheds. The amount of money we could scrape together wasn't sufficient compensation for hunters powerful enough to take on a death worm. The kind of hunters we could afford were too green or too shady.

"Finally we hired a party of hunters from the city. They went out into the Place of Ruin. They never came back.

"The following day, the death worm visited its wrath upon the village.

"The military finally responded. I was the first to return. I... There was nothing left. Nothing but sand and ruin.

"We found the death worm in the desert. We destroyed it. But it was small comfort. The village was gone. The only survivors were those who weren't in the village when the worm struck. The nomads tried to rebuild as best as they could, but...

"The worm struck on market day. It took both sides of my family. I had nothing and no one left."

Ghazan drank and looked away.

"I'm sorry," Li Ming said.

Ghazan shook his head. Gulped down a shot. And carried on.

"The military had failed my people. They had failed *me*. I realized they were just for show. They talked a lot about being the descendants of conquerors, but when it was time for them to defend the people, they turned into rabbits afraid of their shadows.

"When I completed my eight-year contract, I walked away from the military. I burned my uniforms and sold my kit. I was done with them. I was going to live my life on my terms. I bought a plane ticket to Taiping and never looked back.

"I had a plan. Taiping is the capital of the martial world. If there was anywhere in the world a man could make a living through the spear, Taiping was that place. I would enter the jianghu and become a martial immortal.

"When I landed, the first thing I did was to rent a pod in a capsule hotel. The unit was tiny. Barely larger than a coffin. But it was cheap, it had a bathroom and clean water, and it had a courtyard where I could train and cultivate.

"For the first two weeks, I studied Taiping. I trained in the morning, researched the jianghu in the day, trained again in the evening. I decided I would break into the combat sports circuit.

"Every other day, the Martial Arts Stadium holds lei tai matches. The rules were simple. Two men step up on the platform, one man walks away. No lethal or crippling techniques, no weapons, no time limits. The contestants fight until someone is knocked out, surrenders, or is thrown off the lei tai.

"These were sanctioned matches. There was a referee and a panel of three judges. Any of them had the power to stop a match if someone broke the rules. Even so, it was full contact gongfu, the closest you could get to real-life combat.

"The lei tai circuit is the most violent circuit in Taiping. But also the most prestigious of the amateur circuits. Matches were aired live on the Net. Corporations advertised their products during the matches and sent scouts to observe fighters. Viewers could place bets on the fights, amounting to hundreds of thousands of yuan per match. Winners would earn a share of the pot. The best were offered sponsorships.

"I signed up as a free fighter. I trained three days a week, fought one day, rested the next, then trained again and fought again. I fought at least two matches a week. Sometimes, if the fights ended too early for the organizers, I could fight the winners of other matches.

"I won forty-two matches, twenty-one by knockout. I never lost.

"A year after I joined the lei tai circuit, I was scouted. Western Honor Fight Club wanted to sign me on as a professional fighter. For five fights a year, they would pay me two hundred and fifty thousand yuan, plus sponsorship and advertising money. I would only have to fight every other month, and I could spend the rest of the time training and cultivating.

"I signed up straight away.

"I won the first two fights. As I geared up for the third fight, I was asked to participate in an exhibition fight with Huang Ji Ke, an up-and-coming pro fighter. I was fine with it; it meant more money for me. The club would pay me a bonus of fifty thousand yuan for this fight. But on one condition.

"I had to lose."

"*What*?" Li Ming sputtered.

"Huang Ji Ke was sponsored by one of the Ten Corporations. Rumor held that he was also backed by the Hong Shun Tang. He brought in hundreds of millions of yuan in revenue for them. If he fought an undefeated fighter and won, even in an exhibition match, his star would rise to the heavens.

"The club told me it was just an exhibition match. It wouldn't go into my fight record. I would remain undefeated. I just had to put up a show for the first few minutes, then let him throw me off the stage. Everyone wins.

"Except me.

"I told them where they could stuff it. They demanded that I participate in the fight, or they would break my contract. Worse, they would blacken my name and prevent me from ever finding sponsorship anywhere else. But in the jianghu, some things are important than money.

"On the day of the match, I fought. Fought for real, fought hard. In the first few minutes Huang Ji Ke was taken aback. He'd probably been told that I was supposed to throw the fight. Too bad for him. Finally he rallied and fought back.

"He used every dirty trick in the book. He 'accidentally' jabbed his fingers into my eyes. He aimed punches and kicks at the back of my head. Once, when he threw me down, he tried stomping my face. He was desperate to get the win.

"I got mad.

"I pounded him with everything I had. I forced him to the edge of the lei tai. I cornered him, kept him from escaping. Then I slammed him with an elbow and flung him off the platform.

". There were safety mats all around the lei tai. But the blow was so powerful, he shot past the mats and struck the back of his head against the floor.

"He died an hour later in hospital.

"The police ruled it as misadventure. I was cleared of all wrongdoing. But it didn't matter to the jianghu.

"The club canceled my contract and blacklisted me, claiming I was too violent. My manager abandoned me. I got death threats from the Hong Shun Tang in the mail, warning me to never step on the lei tai again.

"I tried looking for another job. But what else could I do? My paper qualifications were unimpressive. The spear was my only teacher. All I had going for me was my martial arts.

"Finally, just when I thought of returning to the Yue Homelands, I saw an advertisement. Dayong Biaoju was recruiting. I packed my bags and headed to Bao An.

"That was half a year ago. I'm sure you can figure out the rest."

Ghazan slammed down the rest of his drink and went quiet.

"You've been through a lot," Li Ming said.

Ghazan grunted.

It was the most Li Ming had ever heard him speak. Now he withdrew into a sullen silence, as if compensating for his sudden garrulousness.

"For what it's worth, you did the right thing. It is easier to earn money than to regain lost honor," Li Ming said.

Ghazan grunted, refilled his glass, gulped down a third of its contents in a single pull, and went quiet again.

"I appreciate you sharing your story with me. It frames things in a new light," Li Ming said.

Ghazan frowned. "Like what?"

"The way you see things."

Ghazan snorted and said nothing more.

Li Ming swirled his drink around. Listening to the long talk had drained him dry. Now he felt like Ghazan, unwilling to speak. He had no energy left for conversation. He just wanted to finish his drink. And yet, though it seemed so little...

"We've got a long day tomorrow, and it's getting late," Ghazan said. "Let's finish our drinks and head to bed."

Li Ming lifted his glass.

"*Ganbei.*"

Ghazan clinked.

"*Ganbei.*"

Chapter Twenty-Eight

Yinguo

Every cause had an effect, every action a consequence. It was the iron law of the universe. There was no running from it. All a man could do was allow the consequences to run their course—and mitigate the undesirable ones as best as he could.

Li Ming had tasted it yesterday at the coffee shop. In Boss Cai's office the following morning, Li Ming saw it again.

A dour mood filled the air. Behind his desk, Boss Cai wore a somber expression, his fingers laced together into an enormous fist. Ghazan sat at attention, posture perfectly upright, perfectly settled, a tiger lying in repose—or in ambush.

"We have a delicate situation on our hands," Boss Cai said.

"What is it?" Li Ming asked.

"The spotter you knocked out woke up. The police interrogated him all through the night. He revealed that their job was to send a message. To warn you to refrain from acting against Hong Shun Tang interests. They had no intention of killing you—unless you reacted violently."

"They had guns. I didn't."

Frowning, Boss Cai crossed his arms. "Why didn't you?"

"A mistake. It won't happen again."

"It'd better not. As a biaohang, as a member of the jianghu, you must be ready to defend others, and yourself, at any moment."

"Understood."

"The gangsters you met were outlaws. They're always on a hair trigger. When they saw you move, they thought you were going to shoot them."

"It was the perfect set-up for a hit. A spotter to identify the targets. Three men to cut off the only exit, armed with reality shapers and guns. If they were hitters, if we had waited for them to draw, it would be too late."

The words rang hollow, leaving a bitter taste in his mouth. Hadn't he kicked things off by reaching for a gun that wasn't there? What if he'd kept his cool? What if he'd listened to what the gangsters had to say? What if he'd waited for just a few seconds more? What if—

Boss Cai held up his hand, cutting off his thoughts..

"The police agree. The Hong Shun Tang are becoming increasingly brazen. An act like this is a throwback to the bad old days, when the secret societies ruled the city. Until recently, they didn't dare to step into a biaoju's territory.

"Privately the police are pleased that you removed four Hong Shun Tang members off the board. In public, they must run a full investigation. But that isn't what you need to worry about."

"Retaliation," Ghazan said.

"Yes, exactly. The Hong Shun Tang holds a grudge against you for what you did in Shanxia. They understood that what you did then was from another time. You were a soldier, you had your orders, you carried them out. Now that you are a biaohang, with more freedom of action, the freedom to choose jobs, they wanted to influence you, to choose jobs that would not interfere with their interests.

"Every member of the Hong Shun Tang is honor-bound to support and avenge his brothers. At the same time, if they tried to kill you, they'd risk waging war against us. That isn't something they are willing to stomach. If they persuade you to leave them alone, it is as good as a victory, at least among the cooler heads in the organization. But now that you fought and killed them in Bao An too, that calculus may change."

"They may make another run at me. At Ghazan. And this time, they'll shoot first," Li Ming said.

"Exactly."

The jianghu never forgets what you've done. Everything you do always comes back to you. Every action creates a consequence, and every consequence sets other consequences in motion, and so on until they ripple across the world and come back at you with the weight and fury of an avalanche. The priests called it yinguo, the law of cause and effect.

There was no outrunning yinguo. All a man could do was allow it to exhaust itself.

"Will they attack Dayong?" Li asked.

"In my time, secret societies attempted retaliation attacks against us. We beat them all back. They know better than to strike us at our stronghold. But out on the street, in the field... you must watch your back."

"Let them come," Ghazan said. "I'm ready."

"Don't be so confident, young man. Skilled you may be, but there is no defense against a sniper shot from half a *li* away."

"Then we take the offensive against them."

"Cool off. We're biaohang, not vigilantes. Without sanction from the civil authorities, we cannot act against the Hong Shun Tang. If we do, we'll be declared an illegal organization and shut down."

"They won't sanction us?"

"They used to, once. When the secret societies ran this city, the government gave us broad powers to combat crime. They were revoked five years ago, after we'd driven the underworld back into the shadows."

"We can only defend ourselves against them?" Li Ming asked.

"Yes, unless the Civil Police explicitly requests for our help to suppress them."

"The world of cultivators must bow to the laws of men."

"Men and cultivators alike live in the same world."

"No war was ever won through defense," Ghazan said.

Boss Cai shook his head. "This is no war. Not yet. But until they have something else to worry about, you two are now at the top of their to-do list.

"We don't know what the Hong Shun Tang is thinking. If we're lucky, they'll acknowledge the situation as the cost of doing business and move on to other matters. If not, they'll send more hatchet men. But we do not rely on luck."

"We act," Ghazan said.

"Yes. Until the Hong Shun Tang calms down, or unless the situation changes, I will deploy the two of you on jobs outside of Bao An. Outside of Hong Shun Tang territory."

Disappointment crept into Ghazan's voice. "We're running away?"

"They outnumber us a hundred to one in this city alone. We do not want a war with them. We *cannot* afford a war with them. If you stay out of sight and out of mind, they may forget about this in time."

"If they don't?"

"We are ready for combat against secret societies at any time. But we do not seek it out."

It was the rational thing to do. The only thing to do. The biaohang in Li Ming agreed that it was the best course of action at this time. But the warrior in him resonated with Ghazan.

"This is not exile," Boss Cai added hastily. "There are many jobs you can do outside Bao An. Necessary jobs, well-paid jobs. Besides, it's high time you two gained more experience working elsewhere in the province, not just Bao An."

"What kind of jobs?" Li Ming asked.

"Convoy security. We hold contracts with the Ten Corporations to protect shipments of high-risk high-value goods across the province. It's straightforward work. Just ride alongside the truckers and protect them from beasts and bandits."

Aircraft were the preferred method of hauling goods across long distances. Up in the sky, neither beasts nor bandits could threaten the cargo. But trucks remained the preferred last-mile transport solution for most bulk goods. They were cheaper to operate than airships, and profit margins were the top priority of the Ten Corporations.

"We get to play security guard?" Ghazan said.

"Well-paid security guards at that. There's a possibility you might encounter bandits or beasts on the highways."

That seemed to mollify Ghazan. Li Ming wasn't sure if it were the promise of payment, or the prospect of combat. Or both.

"What do we do if we encounter bandits?" Li Ming asked.

"Standard use of force policy and laws apply."

"What about beasts?" Ghazan asked.

"Do with them as you see fit. But you'll only be paid a bounty if you find a way to turn them in. Otherwise, you'll just be paid air.

"Remember: the convoy must meet the timetable. Your priority is to get the convoy to its destination on time and in one piece. If we delay the convoy without an acceptable reason, we'll have to pay a late fee. It'll come out of your paycheck. You hear me?"

A wolfish grin spread across Ghazan's face. "I hear you."

"Are there any other contracts available outside Bao An?" Li Ming asked.

"There are reports of increased beast activity to the south and southwest. We may be called upon to carry out beast hunts out in the towns and villages. If so, you two will be the first biaohang I'll send."

"Understood."

"You'll have to live on the road for a while. Depending on the routes and jobs, you might bounce around every corner of the province. Pack only what you need. You'll need to move light, fast and far. But it's good experience and easy money."

"I didn't enter the jianghu to make easy money," Li Ming said.

Boss Cai frowned. His aura blossomed like a flame feeding on a powerful gust.

"If you stay in the jianghu, this won't be your last time dealing with secret societies. You can't take them all head-on. If you make too many enemies, you'll find yourself with no friends. Don't pick a battle you don't have to fight. You'll live longer that way."

Li Ming should have kept his mouth shut. Too late now.

"When do we leave?" Ghazan asked.

"Once you're done packing."

Back in the main hall, Li Ming saw Cai Yan tapping away at an invisible keyboard, her headset locked over her eyes. Ghazan brushed past her and left the building. Li Ming wanted to join him too, but...

This might be the last time he'd see her for a while.

As he approached, she lifted the visor, a concerned expression on her face.

"Are you alright?" she asked.

"Yes," he said.

"Father said he'll send you and Ghazan to the countryside for a while."

"Better than provoking a war with the Hong Shun Tang."

"True, true. But this will be the last time we'll see each other for a while."

"Missing me already?"

She pouted, folding her arms across her chest.

"*Tao yan!*"

They chuckled. Briefly.

"I wish I could join you," she said.

"Really. Why?"

"Father has me cooped up in the compound all day. Just in case the Hong Shun Tang retaliates against the rest of Dayong."

"He cares about you."

Yes, I know, but... I didn't enter the jianghu so I could become a secretary."

"And I didn't enter the jianghu so I could be a glorified postman's assistant."

Another laugh, longer this time.

"This will pass," she said. "The Hong Shun Tang will move on to other things, and we can get on with our lives."

"Yes. Until then we just do what we got to do."

She patted his shoulder.

Her touch held the pressure of a feature, no more, but in that instant, a circuit closed, sending an electric current through him and her, connecting their hearts and spirits for the space of a heartbeat.

And then the sensation was gone.

"Stay safe out there, okay?" Cai Yan said.

"Always."

Chapter Twenty-Nine

Logistics and Capitalism

For the rest of the week, and the week after, Li Ming and Ghazan shuttled from town to town, riding in an array of big rigs. The trucks were the lifeblood of civilization, ferrying food, medicines, precious metals, supplements, high tech goods, everything needed to sustain society. Where airships would not economically go, the truckers answered the call.

Guided by the unseen hand of logistics computers and AIs, Li Ming and Ghazan tracked a winding circuit around the province, occasionally straying into border towns and cities. Their days followed the same unchanging routine. Get up in the morning, drive for hours on end, stop in a town, repeat. At the end of the contract, the truckers and the biaohang split ways, the former to pick up new cargo, the latter to join up with a new convoy.

Sometimes they worked with other Dayong biaohang. Occasionally they joined biaohang from other biaoju. Twice Li Ming and Ghazan worked by themselves. Like the convoys, they were constantly in motion, pushing ever onwards into the unknown, balancing value against cost, time and distance against profits and losses.

Neither beast nor bandit bothered the convoys. At every stop, Li Ming or Ghazan or both stood guard. With tactical gear and infinity guns, reality shapers and cold weapons, they were a powerful deterrent against thieves and robbers. On the go, the truckers rushed along the highways at top speed, too fast for beasts to catch up, too massive for bandits to blockade.

It was easy money, but it was also boring money.

At last, at the end of Xin-day, the twin forces of logistics and capitalism drew them back to Bao An. There were, for now, no more contracts on the horizon.

Li had intended to spend the weekend at Fuyang. To study the Li Family Magic Weapon Style. Instead, shortly after he submitted his report, Boss Cai deployed him, Ghazan, and a small team of biaohang, to a remote village to the south.

Yaoshu had been spotted in the region. They hadn't threatened anyone yet, but they were encroaching on farmland and pasture. The villagers filed a report with the provincial government, and the provincial government in turn sent Dayong.

The government would pay the bounty. It was the only way the villagers could afford to hire biaohang, never mind Dayong. It was a poor town, its inhabitants entirely reliant on the sweat of their brow and the yield of their farms, so poor they didn't have regular electricity and piped water.

Their main defenses were ancient walls of rammed earth whose origins were lost to the mists of time, the enduring legacy of their ancestors. They had no guns, not even slug guns, and the only reality shapers they had were for utility tasks. The village arsenal held only spears, staffs and homemade repeating crossbows. Adequate for fending off bandits and taking small game. Useless against yaoshu.

Yaoshu were cathemeral. They had no fixed activity patterns and were known to be active throughout the day and night. Dayong needed someone to guard the village, in case the yaoshu swarmed the village while the other hunters were away. It wasn't glamorous, the guard wouldn't be paid for personal beast kills unless the yaoshu attacked, but it had to be done.

Li Ming volunteered. He was the junior man in the group, and therefore the man who was least mission critical and could be spared to do the grunt work.

Besides, it was a great opportunity to cultivate and exercise.

The town watch had the day shift. Li Ming walked the walls at night. It was his idea. With his helmet-mounted fusion goggles he could see further and better than any of the villagers at night. If the monsters attacked in the morning, the watch could simply wake him up. The watch agreed.

They also left him alone.

As he patrolled the battlements, he practiced his art. The Five Fists, the Twelve Animals, the myriad sets and energy exercises of wuxingquan. Over and over and over again, countless reps over long hours. The only drills he skipped were those that needed more room than the narrow walkway allowed.

As he practiced, he kept his attention on the outside world. He pricked his ears, listening for the slightest sound that betrayed an intruder. He kept his eyes soft and his vision wide, constantly watching for movement. If he spotted even the slightest hint of movement in the wilds, he aborted his training immediately, fired up his goggles and scanned the night.

He saw no beasts.

In the moments between sets, he thought about the fight in the coffee shop. About *every* fight he had participated in or witnessed. About how things could have gone terribly wrong. About what he could have done to end it fast—or, in the case of the coffee shop, what he could have done to prevent an outbreak of violence.

He tested techniques. He hunted for applications in forms. He sought commonalities between bare hands and weapons.

He cultivated.

The work left him tired. Switching suddenly to the night shift was hard on the body. Even with deep meditation exercises, breathing, coffee and other tricks he'd learned in the military, he existed in a state of chronic exhaustion. Without his gongfu, he knew he would surely have nodded off on watch.

For their part, the villagers were grateful for his presence. The village chief fed and sheltered him, letting him stay in the upper story of his barn. The town watch marveled over his equipment and offered advice on the surrounding terrain. He, in turn, taught the town watch basic spear, staff and fist techniques in the daylight hours. He would have paid for food and housing too, but the chief insisted on refusing. He was the village guest, after all, the man who protected them from ravenous beasts. It was the least they could do.

Three days after arrival, Li received an email. His swordbreaker was finally ready for collection. He made a mental note to pick it up after he returned to Bao An, whenever that was.

On the fifth day, the hunters returned in triumph. They'd cleared out the yaoshu nest, claiming twelve kills. They had processed the bodies and left them in a stream to cool. As proof, they had taken the yaoshu's ears.

"Don't worry, Li Ming," the detail leader said. "This is a group effort. You'll still be paid a share of the bounty."

Li Ming wasn't too worried. Doing nothing but practicing gongfu for half a week was reward enough. Being paid was a bonus.

In mid-afternoon, the collectors and assessor from the Jianghu Association arrived in an airship. The group led them to the bodies in the stream. As the collectors went to work, the assessor confirmed the kills. They returned to Bao An by air in the early evening.

Li Ming joined the team for a celebratory dinner. He forced himself to stay awake just long enough to digest his meal. Then he returned to his room and crashed.

He almost couldn't wake up in the morning.

In the end, between his screaming alarm and the stomping from the secret courtyard, he found the energy to rouse himself from bed. Or, more precisely, to prevent himself from drifting off again.

Today would be a light day, he decided. Mostly neigong, replenishing the energy he had expended over the last five days, as well as stretching and mobility drills. After his morning fists, he did just that.

Cai Yan made her courtyard appearance early. She seemed amused by today's less-combative approach. Even so, she indulged him, and they spent their training time on two-man drills. Not combat drills, but sensitivity and flow drills—with hidden combat applications.

As they trained, more people entered the compound. Every biaohang he recognized, including the hunters. Ghazan, too. Li Ming needed a few minutes more to figure out what was going on.

"Is there a general summons?" Li Ming asked.

"Yes," Cai Yan said. "Meeting in the main hall in three ke."

"You should have mentioned it earlier."

She giggled.

"Sorry! Lost track of time."

Li Ming powered through a hot and cold shower, chasing the fatigue from his bones. He changed into the only clean clothing he had left, chowed down on a pair of protein bars, and headed out just in time to see the biaohang stream into the main hall.

Everyone was here. Every biaohang currently contracted to Dayong, plus the Cai family. They arranged themselves around the furniture in the waiting area, orienting on Cai Mengyang.

"The provincial government has declared a state of emergency," Boss Cai said.

A cold wind sucked the heat from the room.

"Over the weekend, the Central Plains reported a surge in beast activity. Many of those beasts have leaked across the borders of the Zhongxia Republic and are now ravaging the south and southwest of Dongshan Province," he continued.

"Does this explain why we've seen so many beasts lately?" Jiang Long asked.

"Yes. We think the ones that invaded Bao An and the surrounding areas are the vanguard of the horde. The main body has finally arrived."

"Or the surge happened much earlier, and the Central Plains has only gotten around to reporting it," Song Huizhong said.

"*Gaishi zhongyuan,*" someone muttered.

"We can worry about casting blame later," Boss Cai said. "As one of the leading biaoju of the nation, we've been tasked with neutralizing the beasts. We are going on a beast hunting expedition."

"Who's paying the bill?" Kang the Elder asked.

"The province. No need to worry about payment issues this time."

Ghazan smirked.

"This expedition will be a joint effort between the government and the jianghu," Boss Cai continued. "The military will mobilize to defend the towns, sweep the roads, and patrol the skies. Our job is to engage and destroy the beasts wherever they appear in the wilds.

"White Tiger Security will front the expedition. They will set up shop at the border town of Lianghe, and liaise with the military, the local militia, the provincial government, and what passes for a government in the Central Plains. They will take care of the admin, logistics and other heavy work for us.

"White Tiger and the provincial government have invited the leading biaoju in Dongshan Province to send hunters to Lianghe. That includes us. Other biaoju and freelancers are also welcome to participate in the expedition if they can pay their own way.

"A variety of beasts have been spotted in the region. Yaoshu, tietou and yugou are among them. There are unconfirmed reports of nuhou as well. The military estimates at least a thousand beasts in the area of operations. Go loaded for dragons. A horde of dragons."

Li Ming had never encountered nuhou before, but within the jianghu and the military, they carried a fearsome reputation. He made a note to read up on them.

"This expedition will last until it's over," Boss Cai continued. "We don't know how long that will take. One week, two weeks, months, even. Until the government lifts the state of emergency, we will be operating out of Lianghe and the surrounding villages.

"I've canceled all our nonessential contracts. The only contracts still on our books are the ones we've signed with the government, emergency services, and the Ten Corporations. I will lead a team to Lianghe. The rest will stay in Bao An to service these contracts, and to respond to emergencies. Ah Yong will remain here take charge of the company while I'm away. Depending on the situation, we may boost our numbers with temporary staff or freelancers."

Cai Yong tensed. His eyes narrowed, his lips flattened, his muscles stiffened. Li Ming guessed that he'd rather go hunting. But whatever disagreements he might have had with his father would have been hashed out behind closed doors. In public, the Cais had to maintain a united front.

Boss Cai handed out assignments. First for the Bao An team, then the expedition members.

Cai Yan was going to Lianghe.

So was Ghazan.

And Li Ming.

"Expedition members, we will have two days to prepare," Boss Cai said. "White Tiger has arranged a flight from Bao An to Liangshan. We leave tomorrow evening. Meet up at the airport at the eleventh hour with your kit. Be sure to prepare all the necessary paperwork before then. If you don't know how to do it, look us up and we will walk you through."

Boss Cai paused. Looked around the room. Looked at every biaohang in the eye.

"This expedition will be a major operation. We may encounter many dangerous beasts, including beasts capable of magic. The rewards are great, but so are the risks. If you haven't already, prepare your wills.

"Your loved ones may just need them."

Chapter Thirty

Xi Nan

Li Ming had anticipated many things before he joined the jianghu. The long hours. The danger. The never-ending quest for cultivation and martial perfection.

He had not anticipated the paperwork.

He understood its necessity. The last thing anyone wanted was to be mistaken for bandits, terrorists or criminal cultivators. But health insurance information? Criminal record? Qi assessment? What did the bureaucrats need all this for?

The deeper he delved into the paperwork, the more ridiculous it got. Every agency involved in the expedition had their own sets of forms, many of which demanded duplicated information. The Jianghu Association wanted to know what kind of hardware he would bring to the expedition. White Tiger insisted on asking what kind of hardware *everyone* would bring, plus their weight and dimensions. The military demanded a detailed breakdown of weapons, tools, supplies, items, supplements...

"Why the devil do they need so much information anyway?!" Li Ming exclaimed.

"They're afraid we'll bring in illegal or black market items," Cai Yan said.

"Why would a criminal cultivator declare them on his manifest?"

"If Customs inspects his equipment and finds undeclared contraband, they can slap on extra charges for making a false declaration."

Li Ming shook his head. "I'm using company gear. Gear that should normally be sold only to gold-ranked cultivators. Is the military or the Jianghu Association going to penalize me for that?"

"We'll take care of that on our end. But we do need to know which company gear you're taking into the field."

"I don't know. I haven't packed yet."

"Why not?"

"Because I won't know what I'm allowed to carry until I do the paperwork and read the regulations and restrictions."

"But you won't be able to complete the paperwork until you pack your stuff."

Li Ming threw up his hands in mock-exasperation. Cai Yan laughed.

"Come on, let's leave the office for a while. I need to go on a supply run. I won't be able to finish the paperwork until we get the items."

Li Ming raised an eyebrow.

"You need someone to escort you?"

She batted her eyelids.

"And there is a strong young man in front of me right now."

"You need someone to carry stuff for you?"

"Yup!"

Li's Ming eyebrows floated as high as they would go.

"I need to go get new kit anyway. And pick up my swordbreaker," he said.

"Your *magic* swordbreaker."

"Let's not go spreading that around."

"Why not? A weapon like that is a signature weapon. Many martial immortals based their reputations on signature weapons."

"It also attracts a lot of attention. Until I know how to use it, it's more trouble than it's worth."

"I thought you spent twelve years practicing An Family Gongfu?"

He almost, *almost*, told her about the Li Family Magic Weapon Style. The words died on his tongue and took rebirth in new sounds and ideas.

"The quest for martial perfection is never-ending," he said.

"Is that why you like to train with me?"

"Yup!"

"That's it?"

"Let's go. The clock won't stop for us."

"*Wei!* You haven't answered my question!"

"What's the first stop? The Three Worlds Emporium?"

She pouted.

"*Zhen shi de!*"

The state of emergency didn't extend to Bao An. The Cultivator Quarter didn't care.

Martial cultivators filled the streets and hopped along roofs. Stores laid out advertisements for discounts and special offers on tools, supplements, pills, potions, weapons, crystals. Shoppers haggled aggressively with shopkeepers. The qi of the district was a river of flame roaring through Li Ming, forcing him to shell up.

"Everybody's stocking up for the state of emergency," Cai Yan said.

"They can't all be headed to Lianghe."

"Some are. Everyone else is kitting up to take over the contracts they're leaving behind."

"Or taking advantage of the discounts."

"That too."

Their first stop wasn't the Three Worlds Emporium. Instead, they wound their way to the northeastern end of the district. Here, the crowds thinned out. Low-rise houses gave way to ten and fifteen-story complexes. Signboards pointed to lawyers, doctors, accountants, insurance agencies, other specialist services. The people here were a higher class of being. Their clothes were well-fitted, their gear polished and elegant, their auras huge and powerful.

Which was how Li Ming spotted the street sharks.

There were four of them, slouching against the walls of a nearby alley. Their clothes were rough, their vibes hot, their eyes hungry. One of them saw the couple. Through his headset, he stared at Li Ming, then glimpsed at Cai Yan, and stared at Li Ming again.

He was reading Li Ming's aura.

The man nudged his buddies. Together they stepped off and approached Li Ming and Cai Yan, fanning out to fill the street.

"Got a minute?" the starer asked.

"No, sorry," Cai Yan said. "We're on an errand."

"Really? We're just here to greet our elder brother."

"I don't know any of you," Li Ming said.

The starer smiled unpleasantly.

"We've read all about you. Li Ming, a biaohang from Dayong, a rising star in the Jianghu. You took down the Evolved yaoshu that invaded Bao An. We want to thank you for your service."

"You're welcome. Now please, step aside."

"We were wondering if Elder Brother Li were willing to give us a lesson in his esteemed martial art."

Li Ming knew the game. He was a name maker. People like that hoped to gain social standing by defeating cultivators more powerful than them. If they were registered members in the Jianghu Association and both sides agreed to an official challenge match, the victor would climb the leaderboards while the loser would fall.

But only people with nothing to lose and everything to gain would play a game like this. The real boss would hang back and watch his underling.

Li Ming activated his qi assessment app. Sure enough, the man in front of him had a qi score of merely eleven thousand points. He was just small vegetables. Behind him, to the right, was the true leader of the gang, an older male with a qi score of thirteen thousand five hundred points.

Li Ming addressed the leader.

"We're busy preparing for an expedition. We don't have time for a lesson."

"You don't have time for your juniors?" the name maker sneered.

"Sorry, no," Cai Yan said. "We're really busy. If you could step aside—"

"I wasn't talking to you, *xiaoji.*"

He'd called her a chick. It was a near-homonym for *whore.*

Heat flashed through Li Ming's heart. His fists clenched.

DON'T!

He exhaled.

Relaxed.

"Let us pass, and we won't have to do anything we'll regret," Li Ming said.

"And what do you—"

"*WEI!* What are you doing?!"

A pair of White Tiger security officers trooped over, their infinity guns held at port arms.

"These... *gentlemen* were obstructing us," Cai Yan said.

"We just wanted a lesson from our elder brother," the name maker wheedled.

"Shut up," the senior White Tiger said. "You know the rules. The only legal challenge matches are those held in the Arena."

"Yes, we were just about to invite him to the Arena."

"I must respectfully decline," Li Ming said.

The name maker opened his mouth. The White Tiger cut him off.

"There you have it. He declined, and that is that. Now get lost."

The name maker spat on the ground.

"You got lucky this time."

The quartet slunk away. The White Tigers and the biaohang stood their ground until their shadows disappeared.

"*Xianzhai de haizi zhen mei limao,*" the White Tiger muttered.

Kids these days have no manners.

"Thanks for your help," Li Ming said.

"No problem. You did the right thing, turning them down."

"I don't plan on accepting any challenge matches."

"A wise choice."

As they left, Cai Yan smiled to herself.

"What is it?" he asked.

"Nothing," she replied.

And her smile grew brighter.

Xi Nan Logistics and Services occupied a small corner office in a bland high-rise office complex. It drew no attention to itself. Its sole signboard was perfectly ordinary, it had no exterior decorations, it did not place ads or signs out on the street.

It was the premier biaohang support company in Bao An.

The staff ushered them into a tastefully-decorated private room and served them tea and biscuits. A minute later, a woman who appeared to be in her early twenties entered with a wide smile.

"Ms. Cai! A pleasure to meet you again."

"Manager Chan! It's been a while. How have you been?"

"I'm now in charge of handling senior accounts, such as Dayong."

"Congratulations!"

"Thank you. And the gentlemen is..."

"Li Ming," he said.

Her eyes lit up.

"Ah! Li Biaohang! I read about you. You saved the city from the yaoshu. Thank you for your service!"

"I only did my job."

"Someone's getting popular," Cai Yan said.

Li Ming shrugged. He had no idea how to handle attention like this. The only option he knew was to stay silent.

The women exchanged pleasantries for a while longer. Li Ming sipped his tea. It was fresh and fragrant, carrying a subtle flavor he couldn't quite place. Was it a foreign tea? A high-class tea? Perhaps both.

"How can we help you today?" Manager Chan asked.

"We're looking for logistics support to handle a high volume of beasts and beast parts," Cai Yan replied.

"Ah. You're participating in the Lianghe Expedition?"

"How did you know?"

"I just put two and two together."

"You're really astute."

"Thank you."

It was more social dancing. Cai Yan was simply letting Manager Chan display her prowess. Li Ming understood the game when he saw it, but had little idea how to do it in real life.

"What would you recommend?" Cai Yan asked.

"Let's start by talking a bit more about your needs," Manager Chan replied.

"There'll be ten of us in this expedition. We'll be ranging far from Lianghe and other towns and cities. We'll need to process beasts on site and pursue hordes across long distances. We need to preserve bodies and beast parts for an extended period."

"We'll also be operating in austere terrain," Li Ming added. "We'll need to sustain high-intensity operations for at least one week with minimal to no support."

"How many beasts do you expect to encounter?" Manager Chan asked.

"It's a target-rich environment, with dangerous and mobile beasts," Li Ming said. "Worst case scenario, we might have to deal with a horde of yaoshu."

"I see. How much meat, hide and organs do you plan to preserve?" Manager Chan asked.

"As much as possible," Li Ming said.

Everyone laughed.

"Given your requirements, I would recommend Dongbing Mobile Meat Coolers," Manager Chan said. "Each cooler is a walk-unit, able to hold up to four whole deer, or about seven hundred and fifty *jin*. Each cooler comes with its own cosmic tap, so you don't have to worry about power. It only takes five minutes to assemble and keeps meat below freezing temperatures even in summer."

"Can I see the specifications?" Li Ming asked.

"Sure."

Manager Chan slipped her scroll out of her pocket and unfurled it into its full size. With a few swipes and touches, she displayed the cooler as a hologram, with a call-out listing its full technical specifications.

"One mobile meat cooler per biaohang should be sufficient for your needs," Manager Chan said. "I could recommend a larger centralized cooler if you prefer, but with the mobile meat coolers you have the flexibility of rearranging your team to suit different tactical situations without sacrificing your ability to process large numbers of beasts. I also recommend at least two carts to transport carcasses."

"Agreed. What do you think?" Cai Yan asked.

"The specs check out. Do we really have to process the meat in the field, though?" Li Ming asked.

"The collectors and assessors are civilians. They won't go out into the field with us, not without an armed escort," Cai Yan replied.

"We can't just chuck the meat inside the cooler?"

"Not if you want to cool it down quickly," Manager Chan said. "If you process the meat, you can remove a lot of heat without risking spoilage. This is especially important if you're hunting large beasts the size of elk."

"I see. But how are we going to haul it around? Each cooler is the size of a large closet," Li Ming said.

"Man-portable interspatial storage devices."

Li had heard of such things. He'd never seen them before. Not even in the Army, outside of exhibitions by special operations troops.

"Would you like us to make a recommendation for you, or would you like to browse our catalog?" Manager Chan asked.

"Catalog," Li Ming said.

"Recommendation," Cai Yan said.

Chan laughed. "We can do both. Just tell us what you need."

"It needs to be large enough to fit the cooler, plus all our gear," Li Ming said.

"It should be small enough that we can wear it all day without compromising mobility or flexibility," Cai Yan said.

"It needs to have a constant and integrated power source."

"It should be easily accessible."

"It should have anti-theft protection."

"And a tracker."

Manager Chan worked her device, steadily narrowing down their options.

"Rent or buy?"

"Rent," Cai Yan said.

"How much to buy one?" Li Ming asked.

"Our entry model starts at five million yuan."

"Five *million?* I could buy a mansion for that kind of money!"

"Not a mansion," Cai Yan said. "Maybe a one bedroom apartment."

"In Bao An, maybe. But in Fuyang, you could live like an emperor with that kind of money."

"Li Biaohang, you came from Fuyang?"

"Yes."

"Ah."

Her face flattened. Her eyes narrowed. Her nose turned up. Her voice cooled.

"Our entry model has a cubic capacity of thirty-three cubic *chi*, and a payload capacity of twenty-five thousand dun. Large enough to fit the contents of a one bedroom apartment."

"Ninety-nine out of a hundred jobs, Dayong doesn't need such huge storage capacity," Cai Yan said. "For the remainder, we can rent an interspatial storage unit."

"Do you have meat coolers fitted with interspatial storage?" Li Ming asked.

"We do, for large-scale meat harvesting operations. It's not meant for expeditions. And, before you ask, if you attempt to place an interspatial storage unit inside another, it will create a hazardous space-time anomaly."

"They will implode and crush themselves into a tiny cube," Cai Yan clarified.

"An interspatial storage unit will also self-destruct if you attempt to move a living being into the pocket dimension. Their qi disrupts the boundaries of the pocket dimension, causing it to catastrophically collapse."

"Sounds like a great way to kill someone and hide the body," Li Ming mused.

"An extremely expensive way, too. Reality shapers and infinity guns are cheaper and more common," Cai Yan said.

"Can we stuff carcasses inside the interspatial storage unit?" Li Ming asked.

"Time doesn't stop inside an interspatial storage unit," Manager Chan replied. "Neither does bacterial activity. The meat will spoil without proper processing. You could harvest the carcass, pack the meat in ice, and place it inside a storage unit. But this is suboptimal. It's not recommended for long-duration hunts. A mobile meat cooler allows safe and convenient processing operations for an expedition like yours."

"You really know your stuff," Li Ming said.

"We aim to please."

Li Ming and Cai Yan scrolled through the catalog. The man-portable storage units came in many form factors. Backpacks, handbags, pouches, duffle bags. They discussed the potential candidates among themselves, occasionally with Manager Chan's input and advice.

This time, Li Ming had the final say.

"We need something small, lightweight and portable. Something that can be mounted on a belt or rucksack and is readily accessible with either hand. It should not be our primary load carriage system."

"Why not? Many of our customers prefer the convenience of carrying a single backpack, or even a small belt-mounted pack," Manager Chan said.

"An interspatial storage unit requires a constant supply of power to maintain the pocket dimension. If the power is interrupted, the pocket dimension will collapse and everything inside will be destroyed. While some of these models have emergency batteries, we can't guarantee that we'll be able to replace the cosmic tap or perform field repairs before they run down. Even Special Forces units never use interspatial storage units to hold first line kit."

"You sound like you're going into combat, not a hunting expedition."

"We expect to face nuhou."

Manager Chan pursed her lips.

"*En...* In that case, I think I know the best model for you."

She flipped through the online catalog, settling on a product.

"This is the Shanbang Belt Bag. Small and lightweight, it can be mounted on a belt, worn as a standalone shoulder bag, or attached to a larger pack."

Inspired by military-issue gear, it looked like a fanny pack. It had the dimensions of a fanny pack. But it had the storage capacity of a large shipping container, one large enough to store the contents of a one-bedroom apartment.

"I like it," Li Ming said.

"Me too," Cai Yan said.

"Shall we place an order to rent ten Belt Bags?" Manager Chan asked.

"Sure," Cai Yan said.

"Wonderful. What else do you need? Exoskeletons, perhaps?"

Cai Yan turned to Li Ming. "What do you think?"

"It would be nice, but not necessary."

"On the other hand, if you'll be pursuing large hordes of beasts cross-country, you'll appreciate the ability to move freely and weightlessly," Manager Chan said.

"That's true," Cai Yan said.

"It's nice to have, if the budget has room for it," Li Ming said. "But we need to sort out the essentials first."

Cai Yan nodded. "We'll come back to it later."

There were so many other things to buy. Camping supplies. Hunting clothing. Utility blades. Water purification methods. Rations...

"We're buying Special Warfare rations?" Li Ming asked.

"Sure," Cai Yan replied.

"Why?"

"Why not? Military-grade rations are superior to civilian ones in every respect but price. If we're going to be mobile, the Special Warfare rations allow us to eat on the go. Plus, they are lightweight and low-bulk. Haven't you eaten them before?"

"I have."

"Then you also know they taste good too."

"They... What?"

"They taste good."

"Ni zai kaiwan xiao ma?"

Are you kidding?

"You don't like them?"

He sighed.

"Could you do me a favor and not buy Menu 1?"

"But I *like* Menu 1."

He shook his head.

"Unbelievable..."

"Wei, if you don't like it so much, you can give them to me."

"You said it..."

There was, just barely, enough room in the budget to rent exoskeletons. These were civilian-grade, but military exoskeletons were restricted tech, and the model Manager Chan recommended were used by rural emergency service workers. They were close enough to military specs that it didn't matter. Cai Yan locked in the order, with a promise to deliver everyone sizes later.

Now, at last, they moved on to the most difficult subject of all: cost.

"As you're a repeat customer, I can offer you a special discount," Manager Chan said. "One hundred and sixty yuan per day per mobile cooler. Two hundred yuan per day per Belt Bag. Two hundred and fifty yuan per day for the exoskeletons."

"That's expensive, if you put everything together."

"You might get cheaper elsewhere, but you won't get better."

"We've also placed a very large order."

"True. I could give you a special price of thirty thousand yuan in total for the perishable goods. And free delivery for everything. Fair?"

Cai Yan ran through a bunch of calculations.

"Done," she said.

Manager Chan drew up an agreement. Cai Yan signed it. Li Ming witnessed everything.

"Pleasure doing business with you again," Manager Chan said.

"Same here."

Outside, back on street level, Cai Yan stretched. Li Ming looked away.

"That went well," she said. "Shall we have lunch? There's an excellent restaurant around the corner."

"Sure. And after that, Three Worlds?"

"And one more place."

"Which is?"

"You'll see."

Chapter Thirty-One

Ready for War

The Three Worlds Emporium was packed to bursting. A low-grade roar filled the shops. The air conditioners struggled to keep the place cool. Cai Yan headed off to negotiate with the management. Li Ming went shopping for his own gear.

The dirt bun in him shrank away from the ever-escalating prices. The biaohang reassured him that he could afford everything.

The bounty had come through. Nearly a hundred and eighty thousand yuan. The most money he had ever seen in his entire life. He could buy everything he wanted.

Almost everything, anyway.

Even so, his father's advice echoed in his head. He set a strict budget for himself and kept to it.

There were many things he wanted. But he focused on the things he needed. A headlamp for hands-free illumination, a pocket light, a backup light. Hunting multitool. First aid supplies. Scent control hunting clothing. Poncho. Protein bars. Items on his checklist that weren't covered at Xi Nan.

The guns on the second floor tempted him. He could buy any weapon he wanted. Even another Sima Clan weapon, or at least one an iron-ranked cultivator could get. But... not today. Today he needed to reserve his funds for something else.

On the third floor, he found Manager Xu. Manager Xu brought him to an unused counter and disappeared into a back room. Minutes later, he returned with a heavily wrapped package, and carefully handed it to Li Ming with both hands.

"Li Biaohang, your swordbreaker," Manager Xu said gravely. "Please check it for defects."

Slowly, carefully, Li Ming unwrapped it. He savored every moment, running his eyes and hands over every revealed segment of the weapon.

A handwritten note fluttered out on the counter. Every word was written in the classical script, running top to bottom, right to left. Li Ming needed a moment to mentally translate the letter.

Dear Li Biaohang,

Thank you for the opportunity to work on such a magnificent weapon. I trust you will be pleased by our efforts to revitalize and modernize it.

Your magic weapon has a saturation point of 5000 points, a recharge rate of 2500 points per second, and a discharge time of 0.01 second. It can use any primordial crystal from any system. This swordbreaker is now the equal of the ones used by the Imperial Bodyguards of the previous era.

I regret that I am unable to bring out the weapon's full potential. While capable of even greater performance, the law only allows me to restore it. Should you desire to upgrade it further, the law demands that you must become a gold-ranked cultivator.

I beg your indulgence in this matter, and I pray this will be adequate for you. Should you earn a promotion to gold rank, you need merely send your swordbreaker back to my humble workshop, and I shall be pleased to work on it again.

Chen Zhong Hua was seriously old-fashioned. Instead of a signature, he stamped his personal seal in red ink.

The weapon's stats boggled his mind. Performance like this was high silver, even gold. Li Ming wouldn't be able to use it to its full potential, not for a long time. He was barely able to manipulate a thousand points of qi at once, never mind *five* thousand. If he wished for even greater performance, he had to become worthy of his weapon.

He stowed the letter and drew the swordbreaker from its sheath.

It was the same weapon as before, now restored to its former glory. The new handle wrapping bit deep into his hand and would not let go. The hilt and handle were brand new, yet still a respectful copy of their predecessors. The cross-shaped blade gleamed in the light. A faint scent of oil wafted into his nose.

Holding it up to the light, a powerful sensation overcame him. It was as if he had stepped back centuries into the past, back to the glory days of the Celestial Empire, where might made right and the righteous were mighty. In that moment, he saw what the Imperial Bodyguards had seen in this weapon, what his honored ancestors had seen.

Now the swordbreaker was ready for war.

"Li Ming?" a voice called out from behind.

"Ghazan," Li Ming said, lowering his weapon.

Ghazan slid up next to him.

"I'd recognize that swordbreaker anywhere," Ghazan said.

"Distinctive, isn't it?" Manager Xu said.

"Yes. I've never seen anything like it before."

Li Ming sheathed the swordbreaker and mounted it on his hip. It felt *right*, as if it had always belonged there, ready for instant action.

"I noticed you hadn't worn your swordbreaker for a month," Ghazan said. "Was this where it went?"

"Yes."

"What did you do to it?"

Li Ming didn't want to lie to him. But if Ghazan knew it were a magic weapon... if *anyone* knew what it was...

"I sent it for restoration," Li Ming replied.

"Ah. What did you restore?"

"The wrap. The handle and pommel. The grip panels."

"It took so long?"

"I sent the swordbreaker to the finest restorer in the Zhongxia Republic," Manager Xu said. "He does *everything* by hand. It's time-consuming, but it's worth it."

"Fascinating... Personally I prefer a spear. Or perhaps a bayonet."

"Could I interest you in a new bayonet?"

"Thanks, but I already bought one downstairs. I'm here to get magical equipment."

"So soon?"

"We're going on an expedition. We need the best gear possible."

"Of course, of course. Do you have anything in mind?"

"Primordial crystals. Sky and Night. The most powerful I'm qualified to buy."

"Apologies. We're out of stock."

"You told me you had some the last time I asked."

"True, but here in Bao An, there isn't much demand for Sky and Night crystals. You are one of the handful of regulars who buy them. We don't keep many such crystals in stock. I regret to inform you that other customers snatched up the crystals before you. We still have a few Sky and Night crystals left, but they are only fit for utility work. Would you like yinyang crystals instead?"

"No thanks. If it's not Sky and Night, I'm not interested."

"What's the difference between Sky and Night and yin and yang?" Li Ming asked.

Ghazan drummed his fingers against the glass, his brows furrowed in concentration.

"Yin and yang... They are the foundational principles of the cosmos, yes? Feminine and masculine, passive and active, dark and bright. They are opposite forces, yet complementary and interdependent. Together they create the universe. Yinyang crystals express and rearrange the balance of these forces to create effects.

"Sky and Night goes *beyond* the cosmos. Sky touches the highest heavens, the realm of gods, far beyond this mortal realm, far beyond human understanding. Night reaches into the deepest shadows and beyond, beyond the world of men and into the realm of the great unknown. We, as mere mortals, cannot normally touch them. Sky and Night crystals allow us to bring forth fragments of these powers into this realm."

"Sky and Night sounds powerful," Li Ming said.

"Powerful beyond measure. There are no limits to this system but the users' own. It is how the Yue conquered Xiazhou."

"I see. Is there anything else you need?"

Ghazan exhaled. "No, not really. You?"

"I need to upgrade my crystals. And get a new shaper. I need the best iron-ranked stuff I can buy."

"That I can help you with," Manger Xu said. "Please hold still for a moment."

Looking at Li Ming, Manager Xu clicked a button on his headset. And gaped.

"What's wrong?" Li Ming asked.

"You have a qi score of fourteen thousand and eighteen points. High bronze, almost silver. It is a waste to buy iron-ranked gear."

Li gaped too. He'd felt his energy increase, sure, but he hadn't expected it to rise this much, this fast. Still...

"I can't wait until I rank up," Li Ming said.

"A pity. But I will show you our finest iron-ranked goods."

Manager Xu brought the men to a set of shelves. Li Ming and Ghazan discussed the pros and cons of the products on display. In the end, it boiled down to two choices.

Chang An Model 32

Qi saturation point: 800 points

Qi recharge rate: 300 points / second

Discharge time: 0.08 seconds

Crystal optimization: Eight Trigrams (+150 qi saturation, +100 recharge rate, -0.03 discharge time)

Five Mountains Type 12

Qi saturation point: 700 points

Qi recharge rate: 350 points / second

Discharge time: 0.05 seconds

Crystal optimization: Five Elements (+50 qi saturation, +50 recharge rate, -0.02 discharge time)

There were more powerful models on display. There were others that offered faster recharge rates and shorter discharge times. But only these two models had the right balance of all three factors. The question, as always, was which.

"The Chang An can cast more powerful spells, but the Five Mountains will recharge my crystal much more quickly," Li Ming said. "And since I use the five elements, the difference between them is only fifty points."

"Two hundred points, if you use an eight trigrams crystal with the Chang An," Ghazan said. "Also, if you're maintaining a shield, even fifty points will be critical."

"If I need a shield, I need it fast. The Five Mountains is faster."

"I prefer casting shields before I need them."

"That's you, I guess."

"Have you considered output per second?" Manager Xu asked.

"If I cast magic, I want as much power as possible from the start," Ghazan said. "Output per second doesn't need much."

"If *I* need magic, I'll need to sustain it, or repeat if needed," Li Ming said, and opened his calculator app. "Let's say I have a thousand-point qi crystal, and I need three thousand points' worth of output. With a five element crystal, I can use two hundred points of qi per second, while with an eight trigram crystal, I can only use one hundred and twenty-five points of qi per second.

"With the Chang An fitted with an eight trigrams crystal, it will take 7.68 seconds to completely discharge the shaper. That leaves a surplus of fifty qi points in the crystal. It will take another 2.25 seconds to completely recharge the shaper. And I'll need three complete cycles, plus a partial cycle, to discharge three thousand qi points. It works out to... about thirty seconds.

"With the Five Mountains and a five element crystal, it will take 3.8 seconds to completely discharge the shaper, leaving behind two hundred and fifty qi points in the crystal. I can make a second follow-up shot of two hundred qi points immediately after that, so we'll call it 3.85 seconds, leaving behind a surplus of fifty points. It will take 1.75 seconds to recharge. The shaper will take four complete cycles to hit the target. That means... 22.4 seconds."

"It sounds like a significant difference," Ghazan said. "However, you have your own crystal charging breath techniques, don't you?"

Primordial crystals, once depleted, recharged naturally but slowly on their own. A reality shaper accelerated the process, its internal mechanisms and circuits drawing qi from the world into the crystal, cutting down the charging cycle from hours to second.

Every serious martial art had its own secret breathing techniques, empowering the cultivator to absorb qi from the cosmos. More advanced techniques allowed him to drink in qi using specific meridian points. From there it was only a short hop away to transferring qi into a crystal, further accelerating the recharge time.

"Yes, but with a higher recharge rate, coupled with crystal charging breath, an optimised five element shaper would be replenished even faster," Manager Xu said.

It wasn't enough to be powerful. Li Ming had to sustain that power, to repeat it when needed, until every enemy in sight was defeated.

"I'll take the Five Mountains, as well as two thousand-point five element primordial crystals," Li Ming said.

One thousand points sounded like a lot. But he could only pour out two hundred points' worth of power per second. It was a hard limit, imposed by the internal structure of the crystal, and no amount of technology or qigong could change that.

If he needed more power, he had to concentrate more qi within the shaper, until it hit the saturation point. Or fire another working. In the military, he'd learned that you should always carry a crystal with a higher capacity than the saturation point of your shaper, in case you need to service multiple targets, or fire at the same one again.

"A wise choice," Manager Xu said.

"Why do you need two crystals? You don't have to replace our company-issue crystal," Ghazan said.

Li blinked.

"*En...* I was thinking of sending my utility shaper home. I tried fighting a tietou with it before. My firebolt barely burnt its skull. It's no good for combat. But since I'm here, I might as well upgrade the crystal while I'm at it."

"But why? It's only for utility work. With such a low qi saturation point, a larger crystal won't do much."

"The crystal is old and weak. With a larger crystal, the user can cast more magic with it before it needs to be recharged."

Ghazan shrugged. "Well, it's your money."

Only later, after making payment, did Li Ming realize something amazing.

The prices of his purchases hadn't registered with him. He'd glanced at the price tags, just long enough to know that they were within budget, before carrying on. After all, he had plenty of money now. He wasn't constrained by lack of wealth anymore.

For now, anyway.

The men gathered their purchases and met Cai Yan at the entrance. She wore a smile on her face.

"What a coincidence!" she said.

"Every cultivator who's somebody will come through here at some point," Ghazan said.

"Did you get what you were looking for?" Li Ming asked.

"Yes. Now there's one more stop."

"Which is?"

"The temple."

Chapter Thirty-Two

Red Dust

The Temple of the Crescent Moon was the only temple in the Cultivator Quarter. It was a temple not for mere mortals, but for martial immortals. Though it venerated the Fo, the main sacred personage was a god of war.

An enormous statue of General Yun stood front and center in the courtyard. In life he was a giant among men; as a god, he stood as tall as a mighty oak tree. Resplendent in golden armor, his enormous beard flowing down to his belly, he held a titanic reclining moon blade in his right hand, a polearm with a heavy curved blade and spikes on the spine. In his left hand he held a bow. On his belt he wore a quiver of arrows on his right hip, a broadsword on his left. He glared through thick clouds of sweet incense, his face red as lava, challenging the demons and the beasts that walked the world.

Lesser protectors flanked him. Warrior deities one and all, dressed as soldiers from history, they were General Yun's subordinates in life and the afterlife. They stared out at the world, ready to carry out their commander's bidding.

Ghazan stayed outside. Li Ming followed Cai Yan inside, through the thronging masses.

"Traditionally, before a major expedition, we pray and make offerings here for safety and protection," Cai Yan said.

"General Yun very popular here, isn't he?"

"Of course. He is protector of police officers, soldiers, and members of the jianghu, and the patron god of martial arts."

The offertory tables overflowed. Fruits, flowers, water, buns, candies, oil lamps, an overabundance of everything that would please the protectors. Devotees burned incense sticks by the dozens, planting them deep within ash-filled troughs. Monks wended through the crowds, clearing the offerings and the joss sticks at regular intervals. Prayers resounded from loudspeakers mounted on the eaves, lost in the noise. Dozens of martial cultivators conspicuously dropped large banknotes into the donation box at the General's feet. The incense was so thick, Li Ming's eyes watered and his nose itched.

Past General Yun, past a small gate, stood the worship hall. Here resided dozens of Fo and Pusa. They were the Protectors of the Law, enlightened beings taken wrathful multi-armed forms to defend the faithful and the teachings. Wreathed in skulls and fire, they trampled upon the bodies of sinners and monsters, every hand carrying a weapon, their faces locked in furious grimaces. But the main Fo, the Taifo, he who brought the teachings to this realm, sat placidly upon a golden lotus in the center of the sacred army, smiling in radiant joy. A priest chanted in a corner of the prayer hall, head lowered, palms pressed before his chest.

There were only two dozen visitors here. Many of them ignored the priest, bowed perfunctorily at the Fo and left behind coins and incense. A time of war was coming, and everyone's energies were focused on the warrior god.

"It's a shame," Cai Yan said.

"What is?"

"These warriors serve a noble purpose, but that purpose is to protect the faithful and the teachings, so that followers of the Way would find peace. The protectors stand guard not just against the monsters of the world, but also the demons of the heart. The weapons they wield are not just to slay the wicked, but to cut through delusions and achieve liberation. The final victory lies not in the destruction of enemies on the battlefield, but the destruction of delusions.

"This is why the temple is arranged like this. General Yun and the Protectors of the Law guard the Taifo against evil, and lead the faithful to him. And yet..."

"Everyone chases the red dust of the mortal world."

She cocked her head.

"I thought you were a dirt bun. When did you start speaking like a scholar?"

"I thought you were a hard-nosed biaohang. When did you start speaking like a nun?"

They bought incense and flowers from temple staff, leaving the offerings at the ritual troughs. They dropped banknotes into the donation boxes. They prayed. Li Ming didn't know about Cai Yan, but his prayer for the General and the Fo were one and the same.

Thank you for watching over us. We will soon depart on a mission to protect the innocent from beasts roaming the wilds. Please protect us and ensure our safety. Please help us cultivate the courage, the strength, and the discipline to carry out our mission. Thank you.

They regrouped at the main entrance, reeking of incense. Ghazan was waiting, sipping from a freshly-cut whole coconut.

"Are you done?" Ghazan asked.

"Yes," Li Ming said. "You don't pray?"

"I have nothing here to pray to."

"'Nothing here'? What do you mean?"

"The Celestial Empire tore down many Yue altars and shrines. Outside the Yue Homelands, you will not find them in cities and towns. Here, in Zhongxia, there are only a few surviving places of worship for the Yue people, hidden away in the mountains and valleys."

"That's... sad," Cai Yan said.

"Could you tell us about the Yue faith?" Li Ming asked.

"It's a complex system, covering medicine, philosophy, reverence of nature, and worship of ancestors, spirits, and gods."

"Not too different from ours, isn't it?" Cai Yan remarked.

"In a manner of speaking. The key difference is that the spirits and gods are divided into Sky and Night, White and Black, Earth and Clan, and others. It's not a strict division, though. Many spirits occupy different positions in different hierarchies."

"But no Fo?"

"They're not native to the Yue religion. They're not even native to Xiazhou. Your people imported them from Barate. We never adopted the Fo as part of our own practices."

Li Ming noticed the use of 'your people' and 'we'. Even after everything they'd been through, Ghazan still maintained his distance from them.

Ghazan was Ghazan, he supposed. He couldn't do anything about that. He just had to be the best he could be.

"What else is there left to do?" Li Ming asked.

"Lots," Cai Yan replied.

Chapter Thirty-Three

The Bridge Between Them

Lianghe was a city divided by the river that gave it its name. The northern half fell squarely in the territory of the Zhongxia Republic. The southern half belonged to the Central Plains. So far as Li Ming could tell, the only difference was that the north had a functioning national government, while the southerners proudly maintained their tradition of local rule.

Among Lianghe's many landmarks was the Heping Lianhe Hotel. A joint effort by both halves of the city, the builders had hoped it would promote peace and harmony after the fires of the Summer Revolution. Like the city, the hotel divided into a northern and southern wing. On the sixth floor, a massive bridge spanned the Liang River, a combination of courtyard and connector.

The bridge was packed.

At the northern end, a group of young men and women in training uniforms flowed through the twelve forms of the Yijin Jing. To the south, a solo male who carried himself with a timeless dignity floated through the Eight Silken Movements, his movements at once totally serene and undeniably martial. In the space in between, martial cultivators practiced their arts.

A team of hard gongfu practitioners burned through a lengthy routine, punching and stomping, kicking and jumping, shouting with every step. Pairs of cultivators performed intricate two-man sets, their energies entwining and expanding as they cycled through offense and defense. An isolated knot of people practiced with steel weapons, their blades gleaming in the dawn light.

In the exact center of the courtyard, two blocs of cultivators, one dressed in tactical attire, the other in a myriad of civilian clothes, saluted and bowed and shook hands, following a timeless script composed and transmitted over countless generations by the inhabitants of the rivers and lakes, a script that ended either in a friendly exchange of greetings or a not-so-friendly exchange of blows. Or both.

Li Ming, in his hotel room, watched them in bemusement. Why were they training so openly? What benefit was there in showing off their skills and exposing themselves to challenge matches? Why were they letting the whole world spy on them?

More to the point, what *else* weren't they showing?

Li Ming wondered if it was simple pride, or if there were some deep psychological game unfolding before his eyes. Or both. All he knew was that he wasn't going to get involved in it. Calmness and clarity came from remaining free from worldly entanglements.

In his room, he trained.

Zhan zhuang. One hundred fists. Energy exercises. The drills he could perform in such a tiny space. When he was warmed up, he drew the swordbreaker from its sheath, stood by the window, and assumed his battle stance.

Yesterday, he hadn't had a chance to practice the Li Family Magic Weapon Style. In the morning, Ghazan and Cai Yan had insisted on cross-training with him, specifically in the art of the spear and in close quarters combatives. For the rest of day, he was either running errands in the city or surrounded by strangers.

Here and now, he was alone.

There was little space to move. Not with a weapon. As is, the tip of his swordbreaker came perilously close to the balcony. He had enough room for maybe one or two steps before he reached the guardrail. But it would be enough.

He breathed. Touched his mind to the five element primordial crystal he had installed in the pommel. Tuned in to the element of earth. Raised his swordbreaker.

Swung.

Heavy yellow qi rushed down the length of the weapon, merging with and reinforcing the meteorite steel blade. Suddenly the weapon grew weighty, as though it had taken on extra heft mid-swing.

He thrust. The weapon was heavy, fighting against him, but at last it overcome its inertia and blew forward with irresistible force, until it came to a reluctant halt when his arms reached the limits of their extension.

He blinked.

Grinned.

It had worked!

If anything, it was easier than with wooden swords and steel pens. But of course it was. Instead of drawing entirely on his bodily qi, he had a primordial crystal, one hooked up to magic circuits, just like a reality shaper.

He retreated into the room and dispersed the qi into the world, taking care to express every last point. His ancestors had warned against the perils of mixing different elements together, especially at such an early stage in training. When the blade was once again nothing more than steel engraved with impressions of flowing water, he filled it with metal qi.

A steel-gray blade encased the length of the weapon, a sword sheathing a swordbreaker. The points and edges were so sharp just looking it made his eyes tingle. The weapon grew light and lively, contracting and shooting out as quick as a cobra.

He cycled through the rest of the elements. With water, the swordbreaker gained a blue tint, flowing freely through the air. Wood concentrated power in the weapon's green-tinged heart and shot outwards like an arrow. Fire wreathed the swordbreaker in a red glow, always rising and expanding.

Li Ming thought about how the energies felt. How they affected the weapon. Then flowed through the five element short staff movements.

This time, with every move, he activated the corresponding elemental qi. He infused the swordbreaker with metal qi, then lifted it high and split the air. He changed the qi to water, then drilled the weapon through a parry and riposte. Next came wood in the form of a powerful thrust. Then came fire, a rising diagonal stroke. Last was earth, coiling through an arc to cover his flank, then slashing horizontally across.

He smiled.

The elemental energies didn't just infuse the weapon with special properties. They also facilitated certain movements, movements expressed in the five elements.

The classics stated that earth was the mother of all elements, and the ten thousand things returned to the earth. Thus the Li Family made the earth element the foundation of its style. To understand the style, he had to master the earth element.

And there was only one path to mastery.

He swung the swordbreaker. Over and over and over again, repeating the earth stroke. He drew his attention into himself, into the subtleties of weight transfer and impulse and timing, the little details that would make or break a technique. A little voice whispered that he should let gravity do the work for him, allow the swordbreaker to rotate like the rotation of the planet.

But how?

Charged with earth qi, the swordbreaker was heavier, clumsier, more awkward than usual. With every repetition, he tried to realize the most efficient movement possible. Yet the weapon fought him, its augmented mass and inertia resisting every spiral and the rotation.

Minutes passed. Ke passed. Sweat dripped from his brow and arms. And still he was no closer to understanding the secret of the earth strike.

That was all right. He had the rest of his life to learn. Already it was the hour of the dragon, and he had other things to do.

He secured his swordbreaker, grabbed his towel, and headed down to the gym.

As expected, it was packed. Burly men in tank tops and athletic women in sportswear competed to use the limited weights and machines. He joined the crowd and worked the gym equipment when his turn came, doing bodyweight exercises in between sets to keep the blood going.

Three ke later, he strode out, drenched in sweat and drained of qi. Being around so many people wasn't good for him. But he'd survived, and that was the important part.

He took the lift to the rooftop garden. Fifteen stories above the ground, it offered a commanding view of the cityscape, rivaled only by its twin to the south. Here, under the sun and in the open air, he could cool down and regenerate his qi. And breakfast at the roof restaurant and bar was just a few short steps away.

He stretched, swung his arms, twisted from side to side, pacing the perimeter. At the southeastern corner, facing the river, he saw a familiar female silhouette walking through a circle, her arms outstretched.

"Good morning," he said.

"Morning!" Cai Yan replied. "Done with training?"

"Yes. And you?"

"Just cooling down a bit."

Today was a new look. She had on a dark T-shirt and leggings, sneakers and her headset. Her face was flushed, her skin shiny with sweat.

"Want to practice some yizhang?" she asked.

"Here?"

"Why not?"

He gestured all around him.

Cultivators populated the garden, performing qigong in the sun. To the north, two men worked pad drills, every strike resounding like thunder. A woman faced the river, locked in her art's version of zhan zhuang. At the restaurant, more cultivators sat and spied on everyone around them.

"So?" she asked.

"Lots of people around here."

She grinned. "Are you shy?"

"I don't like people looking at us when we train."

"Oh, come on. Everybody knows what yizhang looks like. They won't learn anything from us."

"I..."

"This is our last chance to train before we go out into the wilds. You sure you don't want to?"

Li Ming sighed.

"Let's go."

"All right! What do you want to do?"

"Two man sets."

"I knew it. Which sets?"

"All of them."

They began with wuxingquan. It had been a while since Li Ming had performed any of the two-man sets with a partner. He had to go slow, shake off the cobwebs, consciously dig out every step from memory. He was rusty, but he just needed a jolt. She knew the forms too, but matched his pace and energy.

Together they explored the conquering and producing cycles, Cut the Root, Baby Catching the Butterfly. Their bodies moved in a sluggish symphony, two engines revving up to speed. The movements came back to him, and together they flowed faster and faster, smoother and subtler, each matching the other.

They stepped back. Circled their arms, bringing their fists to rest by their dantian. Relaxed. Stood for a moment, looking at each other.

She wore a neutral expression. Her hair drifted gently in a slight breeze. Her soft eyes peered into him, through him, drilling into the depths of his being. An electric current built up between them, bridging their eyes, concentrating into an unbearable tension.

He nodded. She nodded.

And they extended their arms.

And shifted their feet.

And moved.

Spiraling and circling, twisting and torquing, they flowed around and crashed into each other. Attack and defense, evade and counter, smoothly changing from posture to posture, role to role. Bone slid against bone, skin glued to skin, qi entwined with qi.

A serene expression fell over her face, something between a smile and a stare. Her gaze softened, taking him in, all of him, *and* the world around. Qi sheathed her arms, her legs, the entirety of her being. Her touch was soft but sticky, sticky yet fleeting, fleeting and firm, shifting to meet the situation and the set. A cool wave washed over him, the qi expressed from her movements, blending with his own, a front of flame that rose from his toes and up to his fingers.

Something nibbled at the edge of his consciousness. He could feel it, taste it, see it. It was a silk veil, a velvet curtain, a misty wall, something that obscured the shape of something greater, something true. He reached for it and it crumbled in his mental grasp.

He'd felt it before. He shouldn't chase it. He should just let it come.

They flowed through the eight palms, combining them into sixty-four palms, express-ing them as ten thousand palms. Heaven and Earth, Marsh and Mountain, Fire and Water, Thunder and Wind, joining them in myriad ways and breaking apart into solo palms. They moved in straight lines and circles and the countless variations between.

Fatigue weighed down his muscles. Thirst gnawed at his throat. The growing heat and high humidity glued his sweaty clothes to his body. He acknowledged the sensations and let them go. He let *himself* go, ceasing all thought, allowing the energy to flow.

Expansion and contraction, rise and fall, seizing and releasing, firm and flowing, eight powers, eight trigrams. The energies flowed through them, expressed in the postures, the steps, the adaptations they made for the shapes of their bodies, and in that flow, they were yin and yang, positive and negative, the created and the unborn, the primordial emptiness and the supreme ultimate.

All at once the veil dropped and the universe rushed into his mind.

Everything was qi. He, she, the plants, the planet, the cosmos, everything. Qi combined and expressed in countless forms, ever-changing into new forms, falling apart and recom-bining to make new ones, expressing the grand cycles that defined all of creation.

He saw her now. Saw everything about her. Her qi rushed into his eyes, sweet and fiery and electric. His fingertips tasted the fluidity of her movements, as clean and mutable and free as pure water. His feet danced around her every step, the grounded foot as firm and solid as a mountain, the moving leg as swift and weightless as the wind. His joints torqued and opened and closed in synchrony with her own, as regular as a heartbeat. In this moment, in this exchange of information, they registered each other as separate beings, yet also part of something greater, united by the subtle forces that governed all things, joined in the moment through the mediums of touch and movement.

He and she, they and the world, they were all part of a grand tapestry, integral elements of all creation, interconnected and interdependent, entwined and entangled, with no barriers between them and no limits to govern them.

They were free.

They were one.

They were all.

And then the set ended and they circled away and they beheld each other.

He was a man. She was a woman. This was the language that joined them, the bridge between them. And yet...

And yet, she was his boss' daughter, and that would always define her. And them.

And that was how the world was, and there was nothing he could do about it. Nothing but to accept it and to flow with it and to carry on.

So he brought his feet together and punched his palm over his heart.

"Thank you," he said.

"I should thank you," she said.

Eyes burned into his back. He stepped through a circle and saw a tall young man staring at them.

"What was that? Yizhang?" he asked.

"Yes," Li Ming said.

"It doesn't look like it. Yizhang is all about the circle. All about the spiral. You must keep moving round and round. Those linear movements are not yizhang at all."

"Is that so?" Li Ming said, trying to keep the fire from rising in his chest.

"It sounds like you have some experience with yizhang," Cai Yan said.

"Yes. Five years."

"Ah. Which style?"

He puffed his chest.

"Shang style."

"That explains it," Li Ming said.

"Explains what?"

"We practice the An Family style."

"Never heard of it."

"It's a very old, very obscure style. It draws movements from wuxingquan. That's why you see the linear movements."

"That kind of power isn't yizhang."

"It was how we were trained."

"Is that so? I'd like to request a lesson in An Family yizhang from you."

Li checked his qi score. 13823 points. High enough to be concerning, low enough that the challenger had nothing to lose and everything to gain by dueling with either of them.

"Sorry," Cai Yan said. "We're out of time. We have to go."

"Really? You can't even spare a ke? I promise I won't take long."

"We're leaving," Li Ming said.

"I was talking to you, not her."

"Let's go," she said.

Li Ming turned away.

"Come on! You're hiding behind a woman?"

Li Ming twitched.

Breathed.

Turned.

Smiled.

"She's my boss. If she says we're out of time, we're out of time."

"That's right," Cai Yan said. "We have to meet White Tiger and Colonel Zhou."

The interloper blinked.

"You two are biaohang?"

She smiled sweetly.

"Yes. We're from Dayong. Where are you from?"

"I... *an... en...* Don't you need to go?"

"After you tell us who you are and where you're from."

"Nobody important. Just a tourist. That's all."

Everyone knew he was lying. But it wasn't worth pressing the issue.

"Then we should both go, yes?" Cai Yan asked.

"Yes, yes, I'm sure you're very busy," the stranger said.

Inside the elevator, Li Ming caught Cai Yan smiling.

"What's so funny?"

"Nothing."

"Really."

"Really!"

"You're thinking about the other guy, and how handsome he is."

"No! No way!"

She huffed and crossed her arms.

"So?"

She pouted.

"It's nothing important!"

"So you can tell me."

"*Tao yan!*"

"Oh, you're annoying?"

"No, you are!"

"Thank you. So what is it?"

"*Zhen shi de!*"

"So?"

She turned away and looked in the corner.

"I just thought it's nice that you don't go around picking fights you don't have to. That's all."

"Sounds like a rare trait."

"Ghazan would have thrown down right away. He wouldn't even give the other guy a chance to react. And the others... only the older biaohang don't do silly stunts like this."

"I see. Does that mean you think I'm more mature?"

She humphed.

"Think what you like!"

And they laughed.

Chapter Thirty-Four

Open Season

The ballroom of the Heping Lianhe Hotel was the largest in the city. Under more regular circumstances, it hosted dinners, speeches, seminars, industry events. Today, it was configured for war.

Tables filled the rear of the room. Technicians hooked up machines and routers. Specialists tested the screens, apps, connections. Tea makers, coffee machines and water dispensers stood at strategic intervals.

At the front, rows upon rows of chairs formed islands and blocs, oriented towards the stage. Biaohang and hunters from all over Xiazhou filled every seat. Many wore the uniforms of biaoju and private military and security companies. The rest attired themselves in everything from suits to hunting gear to casual streetwear.

On the stage, a short pudgy man in a shiny suit stood at the podium, waxing lyrical into the mic. He praised the biaohang for their courage and honor, thanked them for coming to this fair city on such short notice, offered the gratitude of the city, wished them the best of luck.

Li Ming tuned him out. He might be the mayor of the city, but Boss Cai said that he was just a puppet of the Central Plains Merchant Association. He had no voice to speak but what the merchants saw leave to grant him.

"We're cleaning up his mess but he won't even acknowledge it," Ghazan grumbled.

"It happened across the border, so it's not technically his mess," Jiang Long whispered.

"There's no sense of responsibility. This is what you get when you don't have a government," Song Huizhong muttered.

During the Summer Revolution, the Central Plains Merchant Association offered to bankroll the revolutionaries. But their price was the right to carve out an autonomous zone from the Central Plains. Lacking better options, the rebels agreed.

After the war, after the borders were drawn up, the merchants set out to create their own country. Or what passed for one. The only semblance of government was the Central Plains Merchants Association, which was far more interested in commerce and business than the mundane matters of day-to-day governance or national defense. Cities became city-states, their surrounding towns and villages their satellites and protectorates. There was no unified military, only militias and local defense forces with sharply defined jurisdictions.

The merchants claimed they had created the freest society in Xiazhou. A society so free and individualistic it saw little need to prevent homegrown beasts from invading its neighbors.

The mayor finally left the stage to minimal applause. Up next came the man they were all here to listen to: Commander Ouyang of White Tiger Security.

A man in magnificent dress whites strode on the stage. His black leather shoes, polished to a high gloss, clicked with every step. A chestful of medals glittered in the light. Gold bars rested on his shoulder epaulets. Gold buttons marched down his uniform jacket. A black tie slashed down his centerline. High on either arm he wore the distinct logo of White Tiger, necessary to distinguish him from the military. On his left hip he wore an elegant straight sword, the scabbard, hilt and pommel adorned with fine gold detailing.

He was no mere man. His hands were large and pale, his fingers long and elegant. His hair swept down in a dark wing. Smooth and clean-shaven, he appeared to be in the flower of youth. But his eyes were cold, hard stones that swallowed all light and revealed nothing.

He was a martial immortal.

"On behalf of White Tiger, I thank you for your commitment to the collective defense of the people," Commander Ouyang said. "We have a lot of work ahead of us, so please forgive me for skipping the pleasantries."

Appreciate chuckles rippled through the crowd.

A holographic screen appeared behind Ouyang, high as the wall, displaying a map.

"Here is a map of Lianghe and the surrounding region. Our operational charter extends from the border with the Central Plains, all the way across the southern half of Dongshan Province, and ends at the outskirts of Bao An. Within this zone, our mission is to identify and destroy all dangerous beasts—especially those who have leaked across the border.

"At last count, there are about two thousand eight hundred beasts now roaming the province. Many more beasts have crossed the border since you received the initial notification. The provincial government has declared open season on all beasts. You will be paid for every beast you bring in to the Jianghu Association, per standard rates."

Symbols appeared on the map. Dotted lines crisscrossed the land, denoting dozens of tiny territories.

"The Air Force has airships and drones monitoring the area. They've identified many beast herds and their territories. Identified species include yaoshu, tietou, bashe, yugou and nuhou. You may also see exotic species more usually found in the Central Plains, so keep an eye out.

"We have divided the area of operations among the participants in this expedition. Each zone will be anchored and secured by an established biaoju. Freelancers, you may hunt in any zone you wish, but you must first obtain the permission of the biaoju in charge of the area.

"As for White Tiger, we will patrol the border alongside the Army and prevent further beast infiltration. We will also maintain a Quick Reaction Force stationed here in Lianghe. If you ever get into trouble, call for help, and we will fly at once to your aid.

"We have authority for cross-border operations. If you find yourself chasing beasts across the border, you are free to pursue them and claim them. However, you must keep us updated. We'll help coordinate with the relevant authorities. When you've finished the hunt, you must return to our side of the border.

"Likewise, hunters from the Central Plains are also authorized to cross the border in pursuit of beasts. Please be careful of your targets and watch your fire. They are fellow members of the jianghu, so treat them with the respect they deserve.

"We have reports of scavengers and bandits taking advantage of the state of emergency. We don't expect much trouble on *our* side of the border. But if you encounter someone suspicious, check their identification. Jianghu members from the Central Plains carry the same cards we do. When in doubt, call us for assistance. If you *do* have to detain someone, secure the area and call us.

"In addition to the jianghu, government forces will be participating in this mission, mainly in a defensive and support role. In the Zhongxia Republic, the Military Police will defend the towns and secure the roads. If you need to resupply or take a break, just head for the nearest town. The Air Force will find targets for us and walk you into the closest targets. The Special Military Police will secure the border alongside White Tiger.

"As for the Central Plains... Their Border Force will *try* to secure their side of the border. Local militias will *try* to protect their homes. That's all I will say about them."

The audience laughed.

"If you stick to your area of operations, you shouldn't run into Central Plains forces. Just in case you do, we've briefed our counterparts. You shouldn't encounter any hassles if you happen to meet their military units. Probably."

Another round of laughter, this time dark and bitter and sardonic.

"Medical support will be limited. Lianghe has the best hospitals in the region. The major towns also have one hospital each, and the villages have their own doctors. If any of you are injured in the field, White Tiger will evacuate you to Lianghe. If we're not available at the time, the backup plan is to move the casualties to the nearest urban area and seek medical help. We will move you to higher care the moment we can.

"The terrain here is rough and austere. There are roads linking the major inhabited areas, but until the military declares they are secure, do not count on safe road travel. The smaller villages and towns don't have proper roads at all, just dirt tracks. Be sure to get off-road vehicles before you move out. When you're moving on foot, expect level plains and rolling hills. Nothing too difficult to traverse, but remember that if you can see the beasts, they can see you. Adjust your tactics accordingly.

"This expedition will last until it's over. It could take a few days. It could take a few months. Until the military gives the all-clear, we are committed to this operation. Of course, you will also be richly rewarded. The more effort you put in, the more money you'll make."

Ouyang scanned the room now, looking into everybody. His gaze rested on Li Ming for a moment, on his swordbreaker. Just as Li Ming thought Ouyang was paying him too much attention, his gaze lifted off.

"Ladies, gentlemen, the finest hunters and biaohang of the Zhongxia Republic are gathered in this room. If anyone can carry out this mission, it's us. We have the skills, the gear and experience for an expedition as lengthy and as dangerous as this. Neither beasts nor demons can stand against us. No matter what happens, we *will* prevail.

"Good luck, and good hunting."

Chapter Thirty-Five

A World of Science

Technology made hunts easier. Thermal vision and infrared sights to detect living beings by night. Infinity guns with unlimited ammo and stupendous power. Air Force drones on standby to locate targets. It was almost too easy.

But in the end, there was no substitute for boots on the ground.

In recognition of Dayong's reputation, they had been assigned one of the province's richest hunting grounds, and the most dangerous. The Air Force counted no less than five hundred beasts, spread out over a hundred square *li*. But, with the zone sited next to the border, that number could spike at any moment.

Dayong shared the zone with crews from two lesser biaoju and a mixed bag of assorted freelancers. After receiving their assignments from White Tiger, the biaohang had conferred to coordinate their operations, to negotiate a fine balance between risk and reward, duty and danger. There was plenty of room—and monsters—to go around, but out in the wilds, anything could happen. It was easier to break down the zone into smaller jurisdictions, areas where each crew could hunt freely without worrying about running into an unknown cultivator.

Dayong had the largest hunting ground—and therefore, the riskiest. It ran right up to the border, occupying the southwestern-most tip of the province. Here, the Air Force had reported many beasts, and many kinds of beasts.

Li Ming wasn't disappointed.

Shortly after lunchtime, Dayong arrived in four trucks at the edge of their area of operations. Here the asphalt roads transformed to gravel, and gravel melted into dirt. Verdant plains and rolling hills stretched to the horizon. Off to the north, fields of wheat painted the land in living sheets of rippling gold. To the south, the Liang River marked the border with the Central Plains.

Shortly after they'd arrived, the Air Force called in. A herd of tietou, two *li* northwest. Boss Cai stayed on the line with the drone pilot, guiding everyone into the target. Eight hundred *chi* away, they exited their vehicles and patrolled the rest of the distance on foot.

Ghazan spotted them first.

"Quarter-left from my position. Eight tietou in the open, four hundred *chi*. They are feeding."

He zoomed in to the limits of his helmet-mounted cameras. A group of ten large goats swam into his field of view. He counted their legs, saw six legs per beast, the surest sign of a tietou. Six tietou meandered around the foot of a hill, munching on shrubs, weeds and small trees. Two stood guard, head swiveling and ears raised, watching for hunters and predators.

The guards were males. They were larger, stronger, their horns more pronounced and developed. Within the herd there were Four females, recognizable by their smaller statures and lack of horns. Not that it mattered much. The females were only slightly less aggressive than the males—unless something threatened their young, in which they tended to fly into a berserker rage. And the two juveniles in the herd were on the cusp of maturity.

In truth, tietou weren't *that* dangerous to human life. If left alone, they were content to leave people alone. They were, however, fiercely territorial. Anyone who entered any land they claimed placed their lives at risk.

The true threat came from their voracious appetites. Left to their own devices, they could feed all day and night. If allowed to head north, they would make quick work of the farms. Only locusts posed a greater risk to the livelihoods of farmers.

Farmers might tolerate a small herd of tietou in their area, especially if they could be taken for meat. But now, with hundreds of them in the province alone, the biaohang were in a race against time to prevent an apocalyptic eco-disaster.

Li Ming scanned the foreheads, the bodies, the legs, looking for crystals or mutations, anything that signaled the presence of an Evolved. From this distance, his cameras couldn't assess their qi. He didn't *want* to be close enough for them to do their work either.

As Ghazan stood watch, the biaohang conferred. It only took them a minute to work out a plan. Then they set off, keeping downwind. Tietou had terrible vision but superb noses. Even with their scent control jackets, sprays and other measures, the last thing the biaohang needed was to spook them.

They climbed a nearby knoll. Li Ming treated it as a military maneuver, keeping his weapon close, his head on a swivel, his eyes and ears wide open. He was glad to see the others do the same, watching their respective sectors of fire.

They spread themselves out along the military crest, just below the topological crest, where they could fire down on the herd. Li Ming sat down on a comfortable patch of ground, crossing his ankles, braced his elbows against his knees, and shouldered his weapon.

He picked his target. One of the rams on guard duty, facing the knoll. Li Ming clicked a button on his optics, livestreaming his sight picture to the team net.

"Sights are hot," Li Ming reported. "I've got the ram closest to us."

One by one, the other biaohang checked in, reporting their targets, cross-checking with each other. Whenever two or more shooters found themselves aiming at the same tietou, one of them moved off to another available target. When in doubt, they checked each other's sight pictures, ensuring they were all aiming at separate beasts.

Finally, Boss Cai got on the radio.

"Shooters, ready. Fire on my mark."

Li Ming centered his crosshairs on the tietou's skull. He touched the fire mode wheel, felt the two indentations that marked a standard power shot. At this range, a half-power shot would disintegrate just shy of the target.

"Five. Four. Three."

Li Ming clicked off the safety.

"Two. One. Fire!"

Eight shooters fired as one. Eight plasma bolts flashed. Meat vaporized. Bone shattered. Blood boiled. As one, eight tietou dropped to the ground.

Li Ming tracked the target as it fell, watch it twitch and flail and spasm. He felt nothing. This was just the latest in so many beasts he'd personally slain. He knew it was just the final signals of a blasted brain going into permanent shutdown. Even so, he still felt the temptation to pull the trigger again, to end its suffering. Except that it wasn't actually suffering. Not anymore.

At last, the beast went still.

The biaohang waited a few minutes more, scanning the world. Satisfied that the beasts were truly dead, that there were no more threats in the area, the hunters moved up to break down their kills.

Now this was the part he hated the most. Li Ming knew how to do it. He'd learned it in the military, and he'd read a refresher on the flight to Lianghe. He'd done it a few times in his Special Military Police days. Enough to know that this was the least glamorous aspect of this profession.

The tietou lay crumpled on the ground. It was an adult male, the size of a deer, the size of a man. The earth drank up its lifeblood, leaving a large patch of soaked earth. Stray blood drops speckled its thick ivory coat. The shot had bored through its famously-hard head and blew out the other side. Even now, the wound was still leaking, surrounded by bone fragments.

He dragged the beast up the knoll, orienting its rear end to the bottom of the slope. His rented exoskeleton, while a far cry from the military-grade model he was used to, reduced what would have been hard labor into a job as effortless as a walk in a park.

He set down his backpack, slung his weapon, and grabbed a bunch of resealable plastic bags from the pack. Rolled the carcass on its back and spread out its legs. Pinned down the front legs with nearby rocks. Sat down next to it and drew his multitool.

Pulled out the knife.

Reflexively he looked around. The other hunters were already processing their kills. The remaining biaohang stood guard. No beasts would come disturb them today. Not without being noticed.

He returned his attention to the carcass. Probing below the left horn, he found the scent gland. He poked it lightly, and a musky fluid spurted over the blade. He carefully dug it loose and stowed it in a bag. He repeated the process on the other side, then dug out more glands from its legs.

Perfume companies turned tietou scent glands into sweet fragrances. He wasn't sure how, only that they paid a premium for wild-harvested glands. He placed the bag aside, then condensed water from the air and cleaned his blade.

That was the easy part done. Now came the hard work.

He found the sternum and cut into the skin, just deep enough to part the hide without harming muscle. He sliced down in a long, clean cut, sternum to anus. Then he peeled back the hide, revealing thick red muscle.

He washed the hair off his blade, then gently punctured the meat below the bone and made a small cut, just enough to separate the muscle and abdominal lining and reveal the milky white stomach. He inserted two fingers into the opening and lifted, pulling the lining away from the guts. He turned his blade edge up and placed it against the inside of the soft tissue. Then, one hand guiding the blade, the other holding up the lining, he cut his way down to the pelvis.

Gas, hot and stinking, wafted into his nose. He paused for a moment, inspecting the dark guts. They were all intact. He checked the knife and saw no signs of contamination.

He heaved a sigh of relief. He still had the touch. If he'd punctured the guts, it would taint the meat. And reduce the value of the kill.

Working delicately, he cut around the opening. The stench of death and waste wafted free. Reaching in, he cut the colon free. He retrieved a length of cord from his pack and tied the exposed anus closed.

He wiped the sweat from his brow, folded the knife and pulled out the bone saw, and steeled himself with a breath.

And grabbed the guts.

The viscera was warm. Wet. Soft. Blood spilled over his hands. Gently but firmly, he gathered up the innards and pushed them up and away from the pelvis. With his other hand, he sawed through the pelvic bone. One side, then the other. He splayed the legs apart and discarded the bony tube that used to house the anus, exposing the tietou's insides to the world.

He returned to the sternum and carved through the thick bone, working up and away from the organs. He rinsed down the saw, folded it back, drew the knife, and peeled the ribs apart.

The tietou's heart rested within the cavity. It was a huge muscle, the size of two fists put together, fed and drained by large blood vessels. He cut it loose and lifted it free. It was warm and wet and firm in his hand, once the organ that powered an enormous beast, now a lump of dead tissue. Even so, he felt residual qi within, qi that hadn't yet dispersed to the winds.

The ancients believed that by eating beast organs raw, they gained their strength. They were drinking in the qi, pure and unfiltered, taking their essence into themselves. But this was a world of science, not superstition. The benefit of such a practice was questionable at best. He stowed the heart in a clean plastic bag, then cut the windpipe and esophagus. He stowed the tubes away, then sliced through the delicate tissues of the diaphragm.

The carcass was completely opened now, the viscera held together in a soft, wet package. Grabbing the gut pile with both hands, he dragged it out and down the rear opening.

He felt his way around the bowels until he found the liver. He removed it from the pile and set it aside. Next came the lungs and spleen. Last of all, he removed the kidneys. He dragged the gut pile clear of the meat, then stowed the organs in separate plastic bags.

He was done. The carcass was clean and dressed, the valuable parts secured, the toxic guts discarded. A mostly perfect kill.

He had mounted his belt pack on his main pack. He touched the control button on the side, and a holographic screen emerged, displaying the bag's inventory. He scrolled through until he found a bottle of pure alcohol. He tapped the icon, and the screen dissolved into a circle of perfect dark. He reached in, grabbed the bottle, closed the portal.

He sanitized his hands and multitool, condensed water from the air with his shapers, and washed himself off. Then he dug out a book of beast tags from his backpack. He filled out the tags one by one, describing the kill and recovered organs, then he fastened the tags to the carcass and the organ bags.

This was standard procedure to document a kill in the field. Back in Bao An, the biaohang hadn't had time to do that, and the Jianghu Association had made a special exception. Here, with time on their side, the Association expected them to work by the book.

Back at the Belt Bag, he worked the controls, now setting it to eject selected items out into the open. Hidden cameras and holographic emitters winked to life, displaying a translucent three-dimensional image in the space before him. If the cameras sensed anything within the volume of the image, the interspatial storage device would refuse to work. He found the largest item in the inventory and hit it.

The screen became a black hole. A mote of white light rushed out. It leapt out into the real world and rapidly expanded into its full size. Suddenly the mobile meat cooler stood before him, its refrigeration unit humming merrily away.

He pulled the door. Freezing air blasted him in the face. The unit was new, clean, fully assembled and ready for use.

He retrieved an apron, gloves and boots from his interspatial storage device, and slipped them on. He placed the bags of organs in a corner of the meat cooler, then dragged the carcass inside. He hung it up by the front legs on a high rack. Blood spilled out, sloshing over his apron and overboots and the floor.

Back outside, he shouldered the door closed. Generated water from the air and washed his overgarments clean. Finally he laid them out to dry and rewarded himself with a hit of water.

The others were finishing up too. They cleaned themselves down, drank water, chatted softly. Cai Yan sauntered over, infinity gun held in both hands, a smile on her face.

"You've worked hard," she said.

"Thanks. It's been a while since I last dressed a beast."

"How long ago was that?"

He had to think about that.

"Over a year ago. Back when I was in the Army."

"Really? What about life in Fuyang? You don't slaughter your own meat?"

"My family doesn't rear livestock. We buy our meat from the butcher."

"Ah. It's been a long time since I dressed a beast too. Eight months I think."

"Do you think you remember how to do it?"

"Eh... Maybe..."

"But you'd rather get someone else to do it for you."

"Chuli yaoguai zhenshi exin."

Processing beasts is disgusting.

"And you're too much of a princess."

"Wei! Ni caishi exin!"

You're disgusting!

They chuckled.

"Just remember," he said, "if you shoot a beast, I'm not going to dress it for you."

"Tao yan! Zhen tao yan!"

"You're going to do your work yourself? Great."

She pouted.

"I'll show you."

"Fall in on me!" Boss Cai called. "Air Force has called in another target!"

"Looks like you'll get the chance sooner than we expect," Li Ming said.

She smiled.

"Just watch me."

Chapter Thirty-Six

Firelight

Cai Yan shot two beasts. Li Ming harvested two more. Ghazan killed four, filling out his cooler.

All told, the party had claimed thirty-two beasts. And that was just half a day's work.

In the evening, they made camp atop a gentle hill. They circled their trucks on a patch of flat land and set up tents within the enclosed space. Song Huizhong started a fire. The Kang brothers volunteered for first watch. The rest settled around the flickering flames for a quick dinner.

Li Ming didn't enjoy military rations. But they were quick, fuss-free, and could be eaten without heating. He had personally inspected every ration he carried in his interspatial bag, ensuring none of the menus he hated had sneaked into his inventory. Now he picked one at random and pulled it out into the material world.

Menu 7. He'd never tried that before. For that matter, he'd never even seen it before. The main course was a huge jianbing, stuffed with ham, eggs, beans and assorted vegetables. He tore open the retort pouch, squeezed out the jianbing and took a large bite.

Disgusting.

Jianbing was supposed to be crispy. This was *soft*. The alleged ham was chopped up into fine tasteless chunks. The vegetables were bitter. And the eggs... he had no idea what the dry crumbly yellowish-beige matter was, but eggs it wasn't.

He was half-tempted to spit it out. Instead he breathed. Centered himself. And connected his stomach qi to the energy of the food.

Is this food nutritious?

His belly, extremely reluctantly, pulled his body towards the meal.

He chewed the so-called food and forced it down. It left a chalky aftertaste on his tongue. He chased it down with water and grimaced.

He thought Menu 1 was bad. This was worse.

He scrolled through his inventory. He had twelve more specimens of Menu 7. The majority of his rations.

"Does anyone want to trade with me for Menu 7?" Li called.

Zhang Xinhua replied instantly.

"Qihao? Qu ah!"

Everyone laughed.

No one took him up on his offer.

Li Ming groaned.

"All right, all right, that's enough," Boss Cai said. "We've got to figure out what we're going to do tomorrow."

"Is the Air Force going to call in more targets?" Lan Yi asked.

"They've only got thirty-six drones to cover eighty-five thousand square li and support fifty teams. They're going to focus on early warning for the towns and cities. We're not going to have a drone on call forever, not out in the wilds."

"Shouldn't they bring in more drones?" Jiang Long asked.

"White Tiger just flew in ten more to cover the border. If they see any beasts, their teams will get the first call. We can't count on aerial support."

"We have to hunt the old-fashioned way," Ghazan said.

"Yes. Come the morning, I was thinking of going west. We'll patrol all the way to the border, then run a serpentine search pattern throughout our area of responsibility. We'll keep at it until otherwise directed."

"If our future harvest will be as rich as today's, we'll need to drop off the meat. My cooler is filled."

"Mine too," Song Huizhong said.

"Same," Boss Cai said. "There's a small town to the west, close to the border. Nanlin. We'll make our way there, drop off the meat, then resume the patrol."

"We shouldn't trust the locals to hang on to the meat," Li Ming said. "Once we arrive, we should call in the assessor and collectors. Actually, why don't we do it now?"

"They're civilians. They won't land out in the wilds. But they've got their own airship. I'll arrange to meet them at Nanlin. Once we hand over the harvest, we'll head off again."

"That'll take time from the hunt," Ghazan said.

"Plenty of beasts to go around in the wilds."

After dinner, the biaohang relaxed. Lan Yi produced a koudi from his backpack. He worked the tiny bamboo flute with practiced ease, playing traditional folk tunes from the north. Zhang Xinhua pulled out a pipa from his interspatial storage and joined his strings to the performance. A few biaohang sang along. Boss Cai walked a distance away, talking into his phone. Cai Yan worked her headset.

Li Ming and Ghazan stood watch.

At the edges of the firelight, Li Ming peered out to the west. In the darkness he saw the shapes of rugged hills and dense forests. Stars twinkled in the heavens, a universe of stars, bright and faint, huge and tiny, so many stars he would never see in the eternal light of the big city. Squinting, he just about made out a milky band of constellations, the Fire Wheel, the galaxy that encompassed the known cosmos, of which this planet was but an infinitesimally tiny yet integral part.

A half-moon hung high in the night, the reigning king of the heavens, its hidden half serving as its queen. Li Ming calibrated his helmet optics, adjusting them to the light. It was a delicate balance of gain and contrast, one only the user could strike.

One by one, the biaohang retreated into their sleeping bags. The Cais continued working by firelight. Li Ming paced the perimeter, keeping his night-adjusted eyes oriented towards the darkness. Ghazan did the same.

Li Ming still had another half-hour on watch. His monkey mind whispered about the things he would do once he was off duty. Brush teeth, drink water, meditate, most of all, sleep. His sleep schedule was shot, and he needed to regularize it before...

He shook his head. Sipped water. Turned his attention to the forest.

He was still on duty. He had to—

Movement.

He couldn't tell what it was. When he looked directly at it, it faded away. He turned his eyes to the right, away from the source. Softened his gaze.

There it was again.

He turned on his fusion vision.

Black and white and yellow and orange splashed across his visor. A combination of image intensification and thermal vision to meet every tactical situation. If it were in the open—

He was in the open.

He hustled behind a truck, crouching behind the wheel and the hood.

"What's wrong?" Cai Yan asked.

"I thought I saw something. Stand by."

Back to the forest. He scanned left to right, up and down, near to far, looking for...

Orange.

A tiny orange figure emerged from the tree line. It crawled along the grass, steadily approaching the camp.

Among the woods, a half-dozen orange figures appeared.

"Stand to! Stand to!" Li Ming whispered.

The biaohang sprang into action. They rolled out of their sleeping bags, awoke their comrades, grabbed their weapons, donned helmets and armor, scrambled to defensive positions. Boss Cai duck-walked over.

"What are you seeing?"

"Unknown contacts emerging from the forest. One out in the open. Six among the trees."

"I see them," Boss Cai said. "Anybody see anything else?"

One by one, the biaohang reported in the negative. The contact continued its approach. It was the size of a man, but it was... *wrong*. Its arms were too long, its legs too short, its torso too large. It wasn't so much crawling as walking, its feet and palms flat against the ground.

"Nuhou," Li whispered.

The bane of forest dwellers, nuhou were among the most dangerous species of beasts in the province. Their enormous muscles could shatter rocks, their tusks could pierce soft armor, their fangs could tear through the toughest hides. When provoked, or when engaged in combat, they flew into a berserker rage, lashing out at everything around them, giving them their name. But their most dangerous weapon lay in their brains and opposable thumbs.

They could use tools.

They could use weapons.

"Kill it," Boss Cai ordered.

"Roger."

Li Ming brought the weapon to bear. He couldn't aim down the sights. The helmet-mounted goggles could not be aligned with the optics. Instead, he pointed it in the beast's general direction and thumbed on his infrared aiming laser. A solid beam of white light slashed across the world—

The nuhou howled.

The laser bloomed in a brilliant circle against the beast's chest. It stood upright, screaming at the top of its lungs, arms pointing at him—

He fired.

The bolt caught the beast center of mass. A white cloud blossomed across his visor. As the body toppled, he followed it down. Strangely, incredibly, the beast was still moving. He fired again—

And bright balls of flame volleyed from the forest.

"What the devil...?"

"INCOMING!" Boss Cai screamed.

The biaohang lit up the forest. A storm of focused thunderbolts raked the trees. Lasers played across the darkness. Wherever they rested, death followed. Li lashed the tree line, pumping out bolts at a steady two shots per second. More fireballs flew out from the woods. He fired at the light sources, working them over with tight strings of fire. The sun-hot plasma fused soil to glass, shattered ancient trees, set the woods alight.

The hostile barrage landed.

The fireballs crashed against the hill, exploding with the force of a thunderbolt, erupting in waves of fire, detonating in ground-shaking blasts. They marched up the slope, zeroing in on the biaohang.

"SHIELDS!"

Cai Yan dashed to the trucks, raised her arms to the heavens, and shouted.

A huge energy shield of deep green qi materialized in mid-air, covering the trucks. The incoming projectiles splashed in blinding bursts against the shield, their energies rapidly dissipating.

Li Ming noticed this only in his peripheral vision. He stared through the flames, through the forest, hunting for more targets. In his fusion goggles he saw only a solid wall of red and orange. Bolts blasted into the dark, single and desultory, chasing targets he couldn't see.

And suddenly it was over.

The last of the fireballs disintegrated. The shield dissipated. The shooting stopped.

The nuhou were gone.

"What the devil was that?" Lan Yi called. "Nuhou using magic?!"

"They have infrared vision too!" Li Ming replied. "The scout saw my laser!"

"*What?!* Nuhou can't do that!"

"Is it an Evolved?" Ghazan asked.

"A troop of Evolved," Cai Yan replied, her voice trembling. "Too many fireballs for there to be just one or two."

"Maybe they're *all* Evolved..." Li Ming muttered.

The biaohang swore softly. Nuhou were bad enough. But nuhou that could see infrared lasers? Nuhou that could fling fireballs? He'd rather hunt a dragon.

"What are we going to do?" Li Ming asked.

"We dig in and defend our perimeter," Boss Cai said. "We are not going to chase them in the dark."

"And the forest?"

"Let it burn."

Chapter Thirty-Seven

Dead Silence

The fires raged through the night and well into the morning. Thin clouds of soot and smoke drifted in a stiff breeze like wandering ghosts. The flames stripped the branches and leaves from the forest and consumed the undergrowth, leaving only the blackened and bare trunks of dead trees. The winding hills and gentle depressions had finally starved the fires, leaving behind a desolate wasteland the size of four football fields.

"We're going to have to write an environmental impact assessment when this is over," Boss Cai muttered.

"That sounds tedious," Li Ming said.

"That's the least of it. If the government or the Jianghu Association finds against us, we'll have to pay compensation."

"Seriously? They will penalize us for defending ourselves against magic-using monsters?"

"We need proof that our actions were justified. We need the bodies."

The beast Li Ming had shot was once a male in its prime. In life it would have loomed large over a man, its enormous frame packed with iron thews and concrete bones. Now it was fit only for compost and worm food.

The nuhou lay on its belly, limbs splayed out. The plasma bolts had sawed it nearly in half. Flies swarmed the stinking carcass, attacking its fine silver coat. Waste matter mingled with dried blood surrounding the massive wounds. In the morning light, the back of its hands glittered.

Wrinkling his nose, Li Ming approached the beast, weapon at the ready. The other biaohang spread through the charred forest, looking for signs of death. He scanned the world around him, ensuring the biaohang had set flankers and a rearguard, then chased away the flies and checked the carcass.

Crystals.

Dozens of tiny violet nodules lay buried on the creature's forearms, scattered randomly across the thick muscle.

Li Ming photographed the body with his helmet cameras. Then, slowly, gingerly, he rolled it over on its back.

Skin tore. Decayed muscle ripped. Hot stinking gas wafted free. The upper torso tumbled over. Everything below the massive wound remained. Li Ming grimaced.

And gaped.

Violet crystals sprouted from his forehead, forming a crown of horns. Its tusks were colored not the dull off-white of ivory, but the hard gray of steel. Even in death, its eyes burned a brilliant crimson.

Li Ming rolled the other half-torso over. More matter spilled out the wound. More crystals glittered in the light, running up its calves and quads, hidden among its fur.

And, nestled in the gore pile, something gleamed.

Li Ming snapped on a pair of disposable rubber gloves. Breathed through his mouth. And pulled the object from the pile.

A large violet crystal, the size of a child's palm.

He inspected the wound cavities and the bloated viscera. But that was the only crystal he found.

"Found anything?" Boss Cai asked.

Li Ming gestured at the crystals.

"Have you seen an Evolved nuhou like this before?"

"A couple of times. But not one with so many crystals. And... are its tasks made of *steel*?"

"Looks like it."

"Impossible. Nuhou don't use metal like this."

Li Ming tapped the closest tusk with the toe of his boot.

"Feels like metal."

"Impossible," Boss Cai repeated.

"What do we do with this?"

"We need to preserve what's left of the body for the assessors. The Jianghu Association needs to look at this."

"It's already decaying. I can't mix it with the meat in my cooler."

Boss Cai bunched his lips together.

"Take photographs. Lots of photographs. Then bury the body and the crystals. We'll mark the site and call in the assessors when this is over. If this is a new subspecies... you've just earned yourself a huge payday."

He returned the crystal to the gut pile. Photographed the remains from every angle. Rearranged the torso, piecing it together as best as he could. Checked the ground. Then fired his shapers.

The earth beneath the carcass parted. The nuhou fell into a deep pit. Li Ming stepped away for a moment, breathing deep, recharging his qi and crystals. Then he turned to the grave once more and poured dirt over the corpse until it vanished from view.

Boss Cai clapped his hands together and lowered his head.

"You're praying for it?" Li Ming asked.

"It was once a living being."

"It's a beast."

"So?"

"It tried to kill us."

"It's not trying to kill us now. And it was once alive. That alone is enough reason to pray for it."

"I... I don't understand."

"This is a hard line of work. You cannot let your heart grow hard."

The biaohang found only three more corpses. Far too few for the sheer volume of fireballs flung their way. But, like the nuhou Li Ming had slain, these were also studded with violet crystals and steel tusks.

"Are those primordial crystals?" Cai Yan asked.

"They've got to be," Jiang Long said. "How else would they cast magic?"

"But what kind of magic? I've never seen crystals like these before..."

Ghazan's face hardened. His eyebrows furrowed.

"Know anything about this?" Li Ming asked.

Ghazan shook his head.

"I've never seen anything like this before."

"I've found a trail!" the elder Kang called.

Large drag marks carved through the scorched earth, leading around a hill and into a copse of trees.

"Was it dragging away a dead body?" Li Ming asked.

"Got to be. But would they carry away their own dead?"

"Nuhou don't do that," Jiang Long said.

"We're not dealing with ordinary nuhou."

"What do we do next?"

Everyone turned to Boss Cai. He frowned at the trail, at the woods, at the men.

"We follow them."

The retreating nuhou had left plenty of sign behind. Drag marks running across leaf litter. Broken twigs. Claw marks across stumps and logs. Though the tracks of fleeing animals cut through the spoor, their heavy, wide-spaced footprints gave them away. The biaohang counted four separate but parallel tracks, cutting deeper into the forest.

The biaohang proceeded warily, penetrating the woods in a modified staggered column. With the Cais in the middle, the biaohang formed two wedges, forward and rear. They walked in each other's footsteps, obscuring their true numbers. They stayed close, close enough to create interlocking fields of fire, not so close that a single fireball would wipe out two men.

Old instincts and training came back to Li Ming. He moved lightly through the forest, walking on stone and dry earth where he could, staying clear of roots and trunks and broken leaves. His boots found clear paths through tall grass. He followed animal trails, troughs carved into the forest floor, void of vegetation. He shied away from open spaces, never straying more than three steps from cover. Weapon at the ready, he scanned left to right, near to far, up and down.

Animals revealed themselves. Birds high up on the branches sang and chirped. Rabbits peeked through shrubs. Squirrels scampered across the forest floor and up tree trunks. A snake coiled lazily on a fallen log. Li Ming gave them plenty of distance, keeping them from spooking, and continued scanning for signs.

There were plenty. Discarded fruit peels. Holes dug into the earth. Bones of birds and small animals, blasted and pulverized and charred.

The last was especially disturbing. Nuhou ate their food raw. They might feed off animals burned in wildfires, but this far from the blasted forest, there were no opportunistic fires. These nuhou had learned to cook with magic.

Not only that, they hadn't abandoned their dead. They had dropped the bodies to feed, then picked them up and continued moving along when they were done. The tracks dragged through the leaf litter, rubbings against trees, snapped-off twigs, the trail continued to point north by northwest, speaking of a troop of nuhou evacuating the bodies of their fallen.

Men did this. Not monsters.

What the devil was going on?

Suddenly a dead silence fell over the forest. The birds went quiet. Herbivores hid. All he heard was the wind whistling through the leaves.

There were predators in the woods, and the prey were keeping their heads down.

The biaohang took turns on point and rear, rotating every hour. The Cais remained in the middle, he to command the unit, she to respond to an attack from any direction. Li Ming floated steadily towards the front of the formation, senses on high alert.

Everything left tracks and signs. Man or beast or animal, there was always a trace of passage. He just had to stay alert, to keep his eyes peeled to see...

There.

At the base of a nearby tree, he saw a collection of large dark clumps. As he approached, he sniffed a familiar stink.

Droppings.

Long, large, tubular, and most of all, *fresh* droppings.

The nuhou were close. No other forest animals known to inhabit the area produced scat like this. Moreover, nuhou marked their territory with their waste. It was where they felt safe, where they called home, where they would fight to the death to defend.

And now, it was Li Ming's turn on point.

He stalked through the forest, a tiger on the prowl. He'd been raised in the country, where he'd learned firsthand how to read the land, to track game, to hunt man-eating beasts. The Army had augmented his hard-won experience with the skills that came from centuries of battle. He might have learned to adapt to life in the city, but he'd never left the wilds.

The odor of musk and scat mingled with the rich organic scent of fertile earth. Leaves rustled and branches swayed, but the air was still. Qi crackled and gathered in the air. Li Ming ghosted from tree to tree, root to root, minimizing his exposure and signature.

Behind him, the city-bred biaohang did their best to keep up. The undergrowth crackled beneath careless boots. A twig snapped. Someone sniffed. Li Ming could hear them from half a *li* away. So would their prey.

Ordinary nuhou would investigate suspicious sounds in their territory. But these weren't ordinary nuhou. They acted too much like men. Like *soldiers*. And if they were like soldiers, then...

Li Ming slowed. Braced himself against a tree. Scanned.

Black.

A flash of black, high in the trees, dead ahead. It was no larger than his thumbnail. But its shape was unmistakable.

Nuhou.

Li Ming held up a fist.

The hunters froze.

Li Ming scanned. Left to right. Close to far. Up and down. Where there was one nuhou, there was more. But he only spotted one—for now.

He glanced over his shoulder. Boss Cai stared intently at him, crouched beside a shrub. Li Ming pointed two fingers at his eyes, curled his hand into a tiger's mouth in front of his chest, and pointed at the threat.

Boss Cai touched thumb to forefinger and shot the remaining fingers into the sky.

Blue icons appeared on his visor. Movement orders, issued in augmented reality. The biaohang fanned out, forming a skirmish line. Li Ming stayed where he was, anchoring the formation.

The nuhou stayed still. Zooming in, he saw dark fur against green leaves, gangly limbs and a squat torso, a dome-shaped head and small tasks. It was a juvenile, but no less dangerous for its youth.

He zoomed out, scanning at ground level. And now a second nuhou appeared, walking on all fours across the forest floor. He estimated it was a hundred and fifty *chi* away, a deceptively thin stick figure. He brought his optics to maximum zoom.

This one was an adult male. Not as large and muscular as the one he had shot, which meant it was probably his height and a mere one and a quarter times his mass.

Back to normal vision. He monitored the beasts in his peripheral vision, tracking their movement. The juvenile fidgeted but remained locked in its perch. The male lumbered out in the open, going about his business, closing in on his position.

Nuhou had superb eyesight, as sharp as a hawk's. But it was one thing to see something, another to understand what you were looking at. In his camouflage clothing, exposing only his muzzle and half his face, his body resting in perfect stillness, Li Ming's silhouette melted against the tree trunk.

"Everyone's in position," Boss Cai said. "Pick a target."

Li Ming chose the male he had spotted. He streamed his sight picture to the team net. Other windows appeared, one, three, five, eight of them.

This must be the main troop.

"Initiate on my mark," Boss Cai said. "Three."

Li Ming exhaled.

"Two."

He thumbed off the safety.

"One."

Finger to trigger.

"Fire!"

The finger closed. The trigger clicked. The muzzle howled. A bright actinic bolt ripped through the air, blowing the beast down. More bolts seared through the forest to erupt in blasts of pink steam. Li Ming swiveled to the juvenile, just in time to see it throw its head back and shriek.

He blasted it in the chest, obliterating its lungs, cutting off its voice. But it was too late. Dozens of nuhou whooped and screamed, louder and fiercer by the second, bringing their blood to a boil.

"Moving up!" Ghazan called to his left.

"Covering!" Li Ming replied.

Infinity guns chattered. Bolts slashed into the forest. Vegetation exploded. Li Ming whipped his head around, saw no sign of shooters and targets. His world shrank down, becoming a narrow lane dead ahead, a lane of trees and roots and depressions. Even as he scanned, his brain went into overdrive, plotting a route—

A nuhou burst from the undergrowth. Li Ming snap-fired, catching it low in the belly. It tumbled away and out of sight but continued to scream at the top of its lungs.

"Set!" Ghazan yelled.

Now Li Ming saw Ghazan, crouching behind a tree, shooting at something only he could see.

"Moving!" Li Ming called.

"Covering!" Ghazan replied.

Li Ming sprinted across the undergrowth. Two steps out and fireballs arced down from the treetops. Ducking, he widened his gait. A ball hissed past his head, exploding behind him. He went low, sliding down to his knees, bringing up his gun.

"Set!" Li Ming yelled.

"TARGETS HIGH! ON THE BRANCHES!" Song Huizhong shouted.

Li Ming swiveled to the source of the fireballs. A juvenile nuhou clung to a thick branch with one hand, concentrating qi in its other hand. Bright red light flared from its many crystals. It raised its hand.

He fired.

Down it went, falling apart in two pieces, the upper half still screaming in pain. He didn't watch, couldn't watch. He returned his attention to the forest, to the world, to the sounds of beasts crashing through the undergrowth ahead of him.

"Moving!" Ghazan called.

"Covering!"

Li Ming kept his weapon at the compressed ready, ready to snap up in an instant. Breathing smoothly and deeply, he swept left to right, up and down, softening his gaze, looking for—

Fireballs.

Li Ming flung up his left arm. Qi flashed through the shaper, becoming a thick gray shield. The fireballs burst against the shield, blowing it apart. Raw heat washed over his body. Qi thundered through him, shaking his organs. Wincing, Li Ming took up his weapon in both hands, turned to the caster—

And three nuhou vaulted over a fallen log and charged at him.

Gun up. Red dot on leftmost beast. Fire. The second he saw the flash, he swiveled right, fired, swiveled again, fired again. Gun down. Scan.

The first beast he'd shot was still up, still howling. The plasma bolt had blown off its left arm. The rest of it was still charging at him, right arm cocked back to expose pointed fingernails, its lips peeled back to reveal yellow knives for teeth and steel sabers for tusks, and as he turned it pounced.

He leapt to his right. Drilled his infinity gun to the left. The muzzle crashed into its breast. Its arm smashed into the receiver. The humongous beast hung suspended in mid-air, defying gravity for an immeasurably long split second. In that moment, Li thought he saw its crown of violet crystals turn *white*.

Then physics reasserted itself and the beast fell on its enormous back. A blinding white ray blasted from its forehead, searing through the leaves and branches. Li flinched. Blood gushed from its stump, splashing over his visor. The beast tried to pick itself up, tried to kick out at him, tried—

Li shot it in the head.

He wiped down his visor and checked the other two beasts. They'd gone still, their qi dissipating rapidly in the woods.

"SET!" Ghazan yelled.

"Moving!" Li Ming replied.

Li Ming pressed on again, bounding to the next tree. He planted himself by a solid trunk and scanned. He extended his qi field, sensing for signs of life. But all he felt were the biaohang behind him and to the sides.

Movement up ahead. A nuhou was fleeing, rushing from branch to branch. He snap-fired. Missed. Fired. *Missed*. Fired.

The beast fell.

Hit the ground with a heavy *thump*.

And got up.

"No way!"

Li Ming aimed and—

It loped away.

And vanished.

The biaohang advanced, bounding forward in pairs, sweeping the forest. But the shooting stopped. The howling stopped. The shouting stopped. A tense silence fell over the forest.

"Cease fire! Cease fire!" Boss Cai ordered.

It was just a formality. Even so, Li Ming relaxed.

"Is everybody okay? Anyone injured?" Boss Cai called.

One by one, the biaohang checked in. They were all okay.

"I saw a wounded nuhou run away," Li Ming said. "Want me to pursue it?"

"Go ahead. We're right behind you," Boss Cai said.

Li Ming moved up, warily scanning all around him. A dark shape rested on the forest floor amidst a shroud of decaying leaves and fallen twigs. It took him a few moments to realize he was looking at a severed leg.

And spatters of blood leading into the woods.

"I've got a blood trail," Li Ming called.

"Chase it down. Don't let it escape!" Boss Cai called.

There was no rush. The blood was bright red, arterial blood, loaded with oxygen. Even a monster as large as a nuhou would bleed out soon. On the other hand, if it knew first aid, or first aid magic, or if it could get help...

He didn't want to risk it.

Li Ming moved as fast as he dared yet maintained total alertness. There might be an ambush up ahead, maybe another troop of nuhou, other beasts or predators sharing this patch of land.

The blood trail wended through the woods. It remained strong and thick, a broken crimson line splashing across leaves and roots, rocks and logs. Soon, Li Ming knew, the nuhou would weaken, tire, lie down, die.

No, wait. That was the nuhou he thought he knew. This one might not obey the laws of nature.

A trail opened in the forest. A wide road, cutting straight through the forest floor, empty of vegetation. Pinpoints of blood tracked towards the road and veered to the left.

This was not right. Few things in nature traveled in straight lines. This appeared to be an animal track, but it was completely, perfectly, straight. Most living things would follow the lay of the land, treading down a path. But this, it was as if a magician had commanded the earth to reshape itself to his whims.

To his right, the road led deeper into the forest, disappearing into the distance, a straight line where nothing lived. To his left, it fed into an opening in a nearby hill. He thought it was a cave, but... No cave he knew had a perfectly rectangular opening.

And the blood trail led into the opening.

"What the devil is this?"

"What do you mean?" Ghazan asked, behind him and to his left.

Li Ming pointed. "Look."

Ghazan looked. Blinked. Blinked again.

"What the devil...?"

"Exactly."

The rest of the biaohang caught up. Li Ming described his findings to Boss Cai. Boss Cai frowned deeply.

"The map doesn't show a cave around here. On the other hand, this forest hasn't been surveyed since the founding of the Zhongxia Republic. Maybe even the Celestial Empire. Proceed with extreme caution."

Li Ming led the way. Patrolling down the road, he kept one eye on the opening, another on the world around. Threats could come from anywhere, and he didn't want to fixate on the obvious avenue of attack.

As he approached, he felt a strange pulling sensation, tugging at the edges of his qi field. Deep within the earth, a black hole sucked in qi, converting and transforming it into useful energy. Cosmic taps operated using similar principles, but... this couldn't be one.

Could it?

The cave was no cave at all. It was a huge gateway carved into the hill, heavy doors swung inwards to reveal a dark antechamber. The odor of musk and droppings wafted from the opening.

And, right above the opening, he saw a logo.

And words.

"What the devil is this?!"

The logo was carved deep into the alloy, showing the head of a stylized wolf, its teeth bared, snarling at him. Twin thunderbolts slashed through its skull and out its neck, forming a cross. Backing the head was a double helix.

Engraved words ran across a banner underneath the logo. Above the opening, more words marched across in horizontal line.

Every word was alien to him. They began their existence as a straight vertical line. More lines branched out from the head, the tail, the shaft, becoming angular strokes and soft curves. Most of the strokes faced the left, but occasionally they doubled back to point to the right. Some words sported a crescent moon, dividing the main line in half. Others featured dots placed at precise positions in patterns he could not divine.

It was the Yue script.

"Ghazan," Li Ming said, "I need you over here."

Ghazan stepped up next to him. And went stock still.

"Is this...?" he whispered.

"Yes."

"How...?"

"I don't know. Can you read it?"

Ghazan breathed deeply.

"It's the old script. There's been some linguistic drift and changes over the centuries. Give me a moment..."

The rest of the biaohang gathered around Li Ming. Everyone stopped to stare at the logo. At the words. At the mouth of a bunker untouched by the passage of centuries.

"What does it say?" Cai Yan prodded.

Ghazan muttered to himself in the Yue tongue. Shook his head. Tried a few more variations. And nodded.

"The banner on the logo reads, 'Strategic Beast Corps'. The main text says, 'Thirty-Eighth Strategic Beast Spawning and Research Center.'"

Li Ming sucked in a breath. And turned to face the team.

"This is a relic of the Yue Dynasty. And it is operational."

Chapter Thirty-Eight

Long Watch

"Operational?" Song Huizhong asked. "How?"

"You can feel it, can't you? That source of power deep in the earth? That's a cosmic tap," Ghazan replied.

"But... that would mean it's over three hundred and fifty years old!"

"At least."

"How is it possible?"

"The Yue Dynasty developed the cosmic tap. It was among their final major innovations. The taps we use today were reverse-engineered from Yue designs."

"But our taps don't last nearly that long!"

"A cosmic tap—a *Yue* cosmic tap—is a solid state device. No moving parts. They were designed to last forever."

"Ten years ago, archaeologists discovered a Yue bunker over five hundred years old with a perfectly functional cosmic tap. Compared to that, this is nothing," Li Ming said.

Song Huizhong sucked in a breath and shook his head. "This is... I'm seeing it, but I'm not believing it."

"Believe it," Ghazan harshly. "It is in front of your eyes. This is a Yue relic whether you like it or not."

"It is also the nuhou's nest," Cai Yan said. "The tracks clearly lead into the bunker."

"Then we must clear it out."

"No," Boss Cai said.

"Why not? Their base is right in front of us!"

"There are only ten of us, and we don't know how large the base is. If we go in, we won't have rear security. If there are other nuhou in the forest, if the bunker has a sally port, the nuhou could trap us inside."

"Then we'll leave a couple of men up top and proceed deeper into the bunker."

"Subterranean combat is nothing like combat on the surface," Li Ming said. "We are not equipped for it. We need breathing devices, gas masks, chemical and biological threat detectors—"

"This base is a spawning center. It is designed to grow and deploy beasts. Rapidly. If we don't shut it down, we'll be drowning in nuhou."

"It takes years for nuhou to mature," Jiang Long said.

"Have you heard of bioprinting?"

"What?"

"Bioprinting. 3D-printing biological tissue."

"Didn't we recover that tech from the Celestial Empire?" Li Ming asked.

"*They* got it from reverse-engineered Yue technology. During the fall of the Yue Dynasty, the Celestials destroyed many key research facilities, including those dedicated to biological research. What we know today is but a shadow of what the Yue Dynasty knew.

"Bioprinting was a lost technology. We use it for medical treatments. They used it to rapidly clone beasts."

"Clone *beasts*? Then you mean—"

"Yes. A spawning center prints beasts from raw materials. It can also modify genes to create superior beasts, adapted to different environments and threats. Left unchecked, this place will spawn an army in days, even hours."

"If that's true, then why hasn't the province been overrun yet?"

"Maybe the base has a hard limit on how many beasts it can create at any time. Maybe it just restarted operations. The point is, this is not a nest. This is a spawning center. Until we go in there and shut it down, there will be no end of nuhou."

"Like Li Ming said, we're not equipped for this," Boss Cai said. "I appreciate where you're coming from. Believe me, I want to destroy the threat too. But if we rush in there and succumb to toxic gases or mold, or if the nuhou trap us deep inside, we are not going to accomplish our mission."

Ghazan clenched his fists. His eyes burned into Boss Cai's.

"The air is safe. The nuhou can breathe perfectly well."

"Or maybe they've been genetically modified to resist toxic gases and survive in low-oxygen environments. The point is, we cannot take chances with *our* lives."

Ghazan exhaled sharply.

"What do you plan to do?"

"A place like this is out of our depth. I'm going to call White Tiger and the Jianghu Association for support," Boss Cai said.

"We're not going to clear the base?"

"Are you in a hurry to be reincarnated?" Kang the Elder asked.

"A single Yue artifact is worth a fortune. Salvaging an intact facility like this would be the find of a lifetime. If we allow White Tiger to participate, they will claim the credit."

"I'll inform the Association first. I'll make sure they know our situation," Boss Cai said. "But until and unless we get the equipment we need, we cannot go in there."

"Can we at least clear and secure the surface level? I don't want to deal with nuhou flooding out the entrance," Ghazan said.

Boss Cai pressed his lips together.

"Very well. But do *not* go underground. Find and hold choke points, stairwells, and other access points. Bottle up any remaining nuhou in the lower levels. That is all you will do. Understand?"

"Roger."

"Li Ming and Kang brothers, go with Ghazan. Jiang Long, take charge of the penetration team. The rest of us will cordon the area."

The teams formed up. Li Ming positioned himself at the edge of the entrance, peering into the gloom beyond. There was nothing but a empty space, a short tunnel bored through the hill. Musk and waste invaded Li Ming's nose.

Li Ming twisted the lens cap of his weapon-mounted light. He had configured it to produce a high-intensity spotlight at long range. While excellent for outdoor use, it would only blind him in close quarters. He retracted the lens back into the shaft, converting the light into a wide-angle flood beam, tapped through the side switch to set it to half-brightness, and thumbed the light switch.

Bright light filled the tunnel, revealing an open doorway at the far end. Dried droppings littered the corners. Dark streaks covered the walls.

The nuhou had marked this place as their territory.

"If you've brought scarves or bandannas, tie them around your nose and mouth," Jiang Long said. "Droppings carry dangerous bacteria."

Li Ming retrieved his scarf from his pack and wrapped it around his face. It wasn't as good as a respirator, but it was the closest he had.

"Set your guns to half power," Jiang Long said.

Li Ming had almost forgotten about that. Standard power at this range was overkill. Li Ming clicked through the fire mode wheel.

"Enter and clear," Jiang Long ordered.

"Moving," Li Ming said.

Li Ming and Ghazan rushed through the entrance. Lights and weapons trained on the far doorway, they advanced down the length of the chamber. The odor grew thicker, stronger, fouler. Li Ming wished for a gas mask, if only to block out the stench.

The men stacked on the open door. Li Ming peeked into the room beyond and saw only a slice of wall. But something hummed softly beyond.

Jiang Long tapped his shoulder again.

"Limited penetration. Go."

Li Ming sliced the pie, edging through a counterclockwise circle, minimizing his exposure. He went slow, taking his time, watching for signs of ambush.

First he saw the guard room. It *had* to be a guard room, with its long clear windows and security doors and two tall booths that could only be security scanners.

One step. Two steps. And past the scanners he saw a door. A green sign above it showed a flight of steps.

Third step. Fourth. Now he was almost in front of the doorway. And past the scanners he saw a pair of wide open shafts. The source of the humming.

Elevators?

He stepped into the room. Button-hooked left. Ghazan went in right after him, going right. The rest of the stack stayed outside, pulling security.

The flood lights confirmed Li Ming's suspicions. This place was once a security checkpoint. Each scanner was a fully-enclosed booth, but an open metal gate bypassed them. A console controlled the door to the guard booth. Past the gates, the shafts were elevators. But not the kind of elevators he knew.

There were no doors. No cars. Just an empty shaft. But bright lights and words glowed above the openings. The one on the right displayed green downward-pointing triangles. The other showed a hollow red circle, divided by a horizontal line.

"Clear," Li Ming said.

"Clear," Ghazan echoed.

"What do the words above the elevator say?"

"The one on the right goes down to the first level. The other one says... 'No Entry'."

A trail of drying blood led to the right-hand elevator... and vanished.

"How does it work?" Li Ming asked.

"I don't know. There might be a clue in the guard booth."

"Check it out. I'll cover you."

Ghazan strode over to the door and tried the handle.

"Locked. I need a breacher."

Jiang Long entered the room.

"Fast or quiet?" Jiang Long asked.

"Minimal collateral damage," Ghazan said.

"Make room."

Ghazan scooted away. Jiang Long stepped up and booted the door.

Again.

And again.

And again.

"It's too strong," Jiang Long muttered. "Switching to thermal."

Jiang Long aimed his reality shaper at the lock. A thin jet of white flame bored into the metal. Sparks flew in every direction. Metal dripped on the floor. Jiang Long breathed audibly, deep and fast, replenishing his crystal with his own qi to keep the magic going.

Finally the shaper went dark. The biaohang stacked on the door again. Ghazan tried the handle.

The door swung in.

The men poured into the room. Jiang opened the far door. Ghazan bent over, inspecting something just below the window.

"Found anything?" Li Ming asked.

By way of response, Ghazan streamed his helmet video camera into Li Ming's visor.

Ghazan was looking at a computer screen. The logo of the Strategic Beast Corps splashed across the display. Below it was a text box crawling with Yue script.

"The text says, 'Failsafe mode activated. Please provide valid user identification or contact a system administrator'," Ghazan said.

"How is the computer still working?" Jiang marveled.

"Yue technology was designed to last. It remains the most advanced technology in the world."

"How can we unlock the computer?" Li Ming asked.

Ghazan scanned. Right in front of the screen there was a large silvery pad and an ancient cup, coated in the dust of centuries. An empty weapons rack stood in a corner. At the other corner, there was a four-tiered file cabinet, protected by a thick security bar and a heavy padlock.

Jiang Long burned through the lock and set the bar aside. Taking a deep breath, he pulled the first drawer open. A cloud of dust blew out. He shut the drawer and moved on to the next. And the next. And the next.

"Nothing here," Jiang Long said.

Ghazan muttered something under his breath.

"Move up and secure the door and elevators," Jiang Long ordered.

The team piled into the room. Li Ming vaulted over the metal gate and made his way to the right-hand elevator. Ghazan positioned himself by the other shaft. As the Kangs piled in, Jiang Long tested the stairwell door.

It opened.

Jiang Long stepped in.

"*Wa...* You have to see this."

Jiang Long's video feed showed a set of stairs spiraling down a deep, dark shaft. He trained his weapon light down the stairwell. Far, far below, a small patch of light shone back.

"Kang brothers, I need you here to cover the stairs."

Jiang stepped out. The brothers moved in. Li shone his light into his shaft. Nothing but four smooth walls, untouched by the passage of time. Deep below, something hummed.

Something shifted.

"Any idea how the elevator works? Or if it's even an elevator?" Jiang Long asked.

"No," Ghazan said.

"You're a Yue. Don't you know?"

Ghazan twitched.

"Your people destroyed much Yue technology during your rebellion. What we know is what you left us."

Jiang Long shrugged. "Stay here. I've got an idea."

He left the room. Ghazan rolled his eyes and stood his watch.

A soft *tap-tap-tap* echoed up the shaft.

"Hear that?" Li Ming whispered.

"Hear what?"

"That tapping sound."

Ghazan closed his eyes.

A second string of taps drifted up the shaft.

"I hear it."

"Beasts?"

"Maybe."

Jiang Long returned, holding a pair of stones in his hands.

"Let's see if this works," Jiang Long said.

He tossed a stone into Li Ming's shaft. It arced through the air, passed through the opening—

An unseen force grabbed the stone and flung it straight down.

"What was that? Gravity?" Li Ming asked.

"Maybe."

Jiang Long tossed the stone into the other elevator.

It bounced off an invisible wall.

And struck him in his helmet.

Ghazan looked away, his chest and arms shaking in silence.

"So that's why entry isn't allowed," Jiang Long said, unperturbed. "That shaft is for going up."

"Are these gravity elevators?" Li Ming wondered. "I heard they're being tested in a lab, but..."

"The Yue invented them first," Ghazan said.

"They're still working," Jiang Long said, awe creeping into his voice.

"We built things to last."

A bestial shriek echoed from the depths of the facility.

A chorus of screams replied.

"And now the nuhou can use them," Li Ming said.

"Stand to! Stand to!" Jiang Long warned.

Ghazan's bayonet deployed with a loud *CLICK*. Jiang Long positioned himself next to Ghazan. Li Ming pulled his weapon into himself and stepped towards—

The opening spat out a large dark shape. It unfolded into a nuhou, fully grown, crystals gleaming in the flashlight. Howling, it turned to the biaohang, hooking its arm around.

Ghazan drew his weapon through a tight circle, smacking its arm aside, then lunged in with a powerful thrust. His bayonet sank deep into its throat and ripped out. The beast backed up, its voice dissolving into a liquid gurgling.

And crashed into Li Ming.

Li staggered back. The dying beast whirled around, arm swinging, blood spraying. Li got his weapon up, shielding his head. Bone slammed into metal with colossal force. Li Ming rode the energy, deflecting it down and to his left, guiding its massive fist into the wall.

The beast continued turning, its other arm swinging around, splashing blood over Li's visor, its crystals glowing white. Li dropped to a knee and snapped his weapon up and fired.

Its head dissolved in red steam.

Momentum carried its arm forward, missing Li Ming by a hair's breadth. The carcass fell.

Right into the path of another nuhou.

The newcomer bulled the body aside. But it lost its balance, staggering for a moment. Ghazan thrust again, punching into the back of his knee. The nuhou stumbled, falling on its face.

Jiang Long shot it in the head.

Shots flashed and thundered from the stairwell. Something erupted deep below. The Kang brothers shouted. Li Ming stepped up to the elevator entrance and another nuhou emerged. He angled up and fired, taking off the top of its head. Ghazan chopped his weapon down, catching the back of its neck with his bayonet, guiding it down.

And another nuhou stepped out the tube and stumbled on the corpse and Jiang Long shot it in the head.

Li Ming moved to the shaft and aimed—

Gravity grabbed the gun and smacked it into his face.

He swore. Stepped back. Just in time to see another nuhou appear, catching itself on all fours.

Ghazan stabbed it in the leg. It stumbled onto its weakened side. Li Ming blasted it in the head.

"Ghazan, why don't you just shoot them?!" Li Ming exclaimed.

"You're in my line of fire!" Ghazan retorted. "A shot would go through them and hit you!"

"Clear the doorway!" Jiang Long shouted.

Ghazan and Li Ming stepped back.

Jiang extended his arms. Bright white qi swirled around him, coiling up his arms, and exploded out his hands.

Unseen hands grabbed a corpse lying on the floor, shoving it against the elevator. It bounced off the opening and crumpled on the floor. Then a second cadaver landed atop it. A third.

And another nuhou burst through the opening, roaring at the top of its lungs, its crystals afire with white light—

And Li Ming and Ghazan fired.

Its head vanished in a pink cloud. Its body flung back into the shaft, piling atop the dead.

Jiang Long continued his work, stacking the carcasses one atop the other. The elevator buzzed furiously. Words ran across the display.

"'Exit blocked. Please clear obstruction'," Ghazan translated.

More nuhou howled from deep below. But their voices fell away, fading out with distance.

"I think we did it," Li Ming said.

Jiang Long nodded. "I don't sense any more coming up—"

A bomb exploded in the stairwell.

A second. A third. A fourth. The world shook, sending dust flying in thick clouds. The Kang brothers screamed, loosing a furious fusillade.

"What happened?!" Jiang shouted.

A single shot. A second. A third. And then, silence.

"Stairwell clear!" Kang the Elder called.

"What was that explosion?" Jiang demanded.

"Magic balls! We're okay! But they cut the stairs!" Kang the Younger replied.

"How?"

An image appeared on Li's visor. Columns of thick smoke spiraled up the stairwell. The Kangs shone their weapon lights down the shaft, revealing huge gaps in the stairs and rubble at the bottom.

"They threw magic balls at us," the elder Kang said. "I got a shield up. A few missed and hit the stairs instead."

"At least it's harder for them to come up that way," Ghazan said.

"Their shots weren't *this* powerful," the elder Kang insisted. "Not in the forest."

"What color was the balls they threw at you?" Li Ming asked.

"White."

"One of the nuhou almost got me with a white ray back in the forest," Li Ming said. "Must be some kind of ultra-destructive spell."

Ghazan tensed.

"Do you know anything about it?" Li Ming probed.

Ghazan's eyes narrowed.

"I have a theory. But only a theory," Ghazan said.

"Let's hear it."

"The Yue Dynasty created what they called cosmic crystals. These combined the powers of Sky and Night, much like your yinyang crystals. But unlike a yinyang crystal, a cosmic crystal is as powerful as a single-element crystal of equivalent size and quality. Cosmic crystals do not exist in nature. The art of creating such crystals was lost when the Dynasty fell."

"Did the nuhou use Yue magic?"

"Their magic is similar to high-level Yue magic, but more destructive and more diffuse. It is either unique to their kind or recreations of lost arts."

"You didn't think to tell us earlier?" Jiang Long asked.

"It didn't occur to me until just now."

Jiang Long grunted. "Kang-Ge, how many nuhou did you kill?"

"Five? Six? Wasn't counting. But I saw them drag off their casualties. Ga San, any idea why they did that?" the elder Kang asked.

"No idea," Ghazan snapped. "I'm not—"

Boss Cai's voice crackled into their earpieces.

"Entry team, what happened? Are you all right?"

"Lead, entry team," Jiang Long said. "We just fought off an attack. No casualties. But the nuhou destroyed some of the stairs."

"Copy that. White Tiger and the Jianghu Association will be arriving in one hour. Hold what you've got until then."

"Understood."

A nuhou shrieked furiously in the deep. Then another, another, yet another, until an army of nuhou were screaming at the top of their lungs, drowning out the world in noise.

This is going to be a long watch, Li Ming thought.

Chapter Thirty-Nine

Underground Warfare

White Tiger knew how to make an entrance.

A Phoenix airship swooped silently down from the heavens. It was a huge, ungainly machine, a barely aerodynamic box with a pair of short stubby wings. But for its twin thrusters, one on each wingtip, it couldn't possibly fly. Flaring, it decelerated sharply, dropping beneath tree level. With a soft bump, it landed in the exact middle of the dirt road outside the bunker, its wings a finger length away from shrubs and treetops.

The rear cargo door dropped. Twenty White Tiger shooters, heavily armored and armored, filed out and formed a security perimeter around the airship. Commander Ouyang, now dressed in a combat uniform, strode down the ramp, one hand resting on his sword, the other on the grip of the pistol holstered on his hip. He glanced left and right, nodded, and made a gesture.

Eight more people filed out the airship. Seven were dressed in rough workmen's clothing carrying backpacks laden with gear. The last was a woman in an elegant red robe and black trousers, distinctly overdressed for this environment.

"Commander Ouyang," Boss Cai said. "We are honored by your presence."

"You called, we answered. That is all," Ouyang said.

"*We* should be honored you chose to call us instead of keeping this finding to yourself," the woman said.

"Madam, I do not believe we have met. May I have your honored name?" Boss Cai asked.

Her frosty eyes twinkled.

"Rao Xin Yan, Senior Operations Manager of the Jianghu Association, Lianghe office." They shook hands.

"Pleasure to meet you, Rao Xian."

"Miss will do. I am no immortal."

"Ah, but soon, you will be."

She smiled, shaking her head, and gestured at a nearby colleague.

"Immortal Cai, this is Foreman Hu. He's in charge of the collector team."

Foreman Hu saluted Boss Cai, smacking his fist against his palm. Boss Cai returned it, quick and crisp and precise.

"I heard you encountered a novel subspecies of nuhou," Ms. Rao said. "Could you please tell us more?"

Boss Cai gestured behind him. A half-dozen nuhou bodies lay in a neat line.

"These nuhou, as you can see, have strange crystals embedded in their arms, legs and foreheads. My man thinks the crystals are ancient Yue crystals, allowing them to use lost magic. Every single nuhou we've fought in this forest have these crystals, and used them to cast destructive energy balls or rays."

Ouyang pursed his lips.

"Strange. Rare enough that a nuhou becomes an Evolved. But an entire troop?"

"Not only that, they've displayed unusual intelligence and empathy towards their own kind. They laid ambushes, sent scouts, collected their wounded and dead. No nuhou I've seen does this."

"Same here."

Ms. Rao rested her hands on her hips, gazing down on the torn-up bodies.

"I'll need to send them in for a complete autopsy to make a proper determination. But in all my years in the Association, I have never, ever, seen anything like this."

"This is just the start," Boss Cai said. "That bunker you see behind me is a Yue relic. A spawning center from their Strategic Beast Corps."

Ms. Rao gasped. "A military base?"

"Yes."

Ouyang's face settled into a perfectly flat expression.

"You believe this place is the source of these novel nuhou?" Ouyang asked.

"Yes. My men fought off a wave of nuhou an hour ago. We don't know if a large troop of novel nuhou took up residence in the base, or..." Boss Cai exhaled sharply. "Or if the base is spawning nuhou."

"Impossible!" Ms. Rao said.

"The computers still work. The gravity elevators still work. Why not the bioprinter too?"

"It appears you've stumbled across a highly dangerous relic," Ouyang said.

"Yes. We will be thankful for any advice and assistance you can offer."

"None of us here have any experience with Yue Dynasty military tech. Fortunately, we've managed to acquire the specialist equipment you've requested. Although... there is one minor problem."

"What is it?"

"The kit you've asked for is extremely specialized. Even we don't stock them in great numbers, not in our provincial supply cache. I'm sorry to say we only have enough gear to outfit a squad. Ten men, no more."

"A squad is better than nothing."

"True enough. Allow me to make this proposal. My men and I will provide topside security and support, and sweep the forest for alternate exits. Should we find any, we will block them off and prevent the nuhou from escaping. Your men will penetrate and clear the base. Dayong, of course, will receive all the credit and rewards."

"You will also be entitled to ownership rights of any artifacts you may find," Ms. Rao added. "Should you choose to sell them, the Jianghu Association will auction them for you at highly favorable rates."

"A sound plan," Boss Cai said. "Thank you for your generous offer."

"Good luck, and good hunting," Ouyang said.

The White Tigers had brought an interspatial storage machine with them. They muscled it out of the airship, set it down at the entrance of the bunker, and emptied its contents.

Self-contained breathing apparatus. Air tanks and compressor. Chemical lights. Stun grenades. Man-portable radar. Oxygen sensor. Chemical and biological threat sensor. Breaching tools. Robot. All the equipment a modern infantry unit needed for underground warfare.

Everyone shucked their packs and mounted their interspatial bags on their plate carriers. They transferred critical equipment to their belts, pouches, bags, and donned their breathing apparatus. They tested their electronics and devices, checked their respirators and air tanks, refamiliarized themselves with the tools of war.

It felt like it had been a lifetime since Li Ming's last underground warfare training course. It *had* been a lifetime. Yet the old knowledge rushed back in an instant. Some brands were different, others had unfamiliar user interfaces, but the principles and use cases remained the same.

As the biaohang kitted up, they talked tactics among themselves. Formations, immediate actions, who would carry which gear, contingency plans in case of chemical or biological or other threats. Cai Yan hung back, listening to everything, saying little. She was the outsider, the female, the non-soldier. She might be a biaohang, but every man in the squad was once a soldier. They had all undergone underground warfare training. She hadn't.

Which was why she volunteered to take point.

"You're kidding," Jiang Long exclaimed.

"You were talking about using shields and other defensive magics to lead the way. That's my area of specialty," she said.

"You weren't trained in underground warfare."

"That's true. But I have undergone the same urban warfare training as you guys. It's mostly the same, right?"

"No. Underground is a whole different ball game. It's going to be dark and cramped. Little to no cover. The main base is deep underground, so there might not be much air. Our air tanks will only last us for a half hour at most, less if we exert ourselves. There might be chemical, biological or explosive hazards. Nuhou droppings are toxic, and there's plenty of them. There's so many things to consider."

"Other than the time limit and explosive hazards, does the shield operator need to worry about those considerations?"

The men looked at each other.

"I don't think so," Li Ming said.

"Right. So I'll lead with the shield and lock down hallways and choke points. That frees you underground warfare experts to do your thing."

Now everyone looked at Boss Cai.

"Do what you think is best," he said, "but don't take unnecessary risks."

She grinned. "Understood!"

"I'm running a shield too," Li Ming said. "Doctrine is to have at least two shields where possible. If I see something that is underground warfare specific, I'll let you know. We'll work the situation."

"No problem."

"I'll cover Li Ming," Ghazan said.

"*I* will protect our lady boss," Zhang Xinhua said.

"Let's do this!" Cai Yan said.

"Don't rush," her father scowled. "The more you rush, the less time you have down there."

The team formed up at the mouth of the bunker. Two teams of five, five pairs standing side by side. As one, they donned their respirators, checked the seals and opened the valves of their air tanks.

"Shields up!" Li called.

He held out his left forearm and touched the element of earth. A thick plate floated before him, covering his face and upper body, leaving two cutouts at head height. Straps grew from the rear of the shield, securing it to his forearm.

He infused the shield with metal qi. Earth produced metal, and this combination would create a reinforced shield that would stop even double power plasma shots. It left him feeling fatigued, but the extra protection was worth it.

"Shield ready," Li Ming said.

"Me too," Cai Yan confirmed.

"Moving up!"

They plunged into the chamber. Li Ming rested his infinity gun on the right-hand cutout. Ghazan aimed over his left shoulder, weapon braced against the shield. Li peeked over the top of the shield, maintaining his field of view.

Back in the security room, they gathered around the elevators. The incoming tube continued to buzz angrily at the biaohang, its mouth still blocked with beast carcasses. Song Huizhong waved his biochem threat detector about.

"Fecal and bacteriological contaminants detected," he said.

"You don't say," Jiang Long said dryly, stepping around a pile of scat.

The biaohang cleared the mouth of the elevator. The buzzing finally, blessedly, stopped.

"Bringing out the bot," Boss Cai said.

He pulled it out of interspatial storage. Small but rugged, it was a flat box with rubberized tracks and a sensor dome. The biaohang fanned out around the downriding tube, giving him space. He laid the machine carefully on the floor, then took the controller in both hands.

The bot zipped into the unknown.

Artificial gravity grabbed the bot and plunged it into the great unknown.

The men waited.

Boss Cai fiddled with the controls.

The men waited some more.

Boss Cai mashed a button. Then some more buttons.

"Gaisi!" he swore. "We've lost the signal. The bot is too deep underground. We have to go in blind."

"Figured," Zhang Xinhua muttered. "Stairs or elevator?"

"The stairwell integrity has been compromised," Kang the Elder said. "If we take the stairs, they might collapse under us."

"There might be an ambush waiting for us," Kang the Younger said. "If we go down the elevator, we can't climb back up the same way."

"Then we go down in force," Boss Cai said. "Shield team first. Shooters in second wave."

"I'll take point," Li Ming said.

"You sure about that?" Cai Yan asked.

"I'm least mission critical. If something happens to me, you'll have warning time. I'll shout if I can."

With that, he stepped up to the shaft.

Cai Yan stacked behind him.

The rest of the biaohang lined up.

He waited. Breathed. Slowly, smoothly, calmly. Whatever happened, whatever was waiting down there, he would be ready for it.

"Wait," Boss Cai said.

He fished out a stun grenade from his pouch and pilled the pin.

"I sense living beings down there."

Li Ming sensed nothing but the cosmic tap. But the elder Cai was, after all, a martial immortal.

"Stun grenade out!'

He tossed the grenade down the shaft. Paused. And patted Li Ming's shoulder.

"Go!"

Li Ming stepped off into the shaft.

An invisible, irresistible force grabbed him, pulling him into the exact center of the tube. For a brief, heart-stopping moment, he was standing on nothing, suspended in mid-air, utterly weightless. Then another force seized him and yanked him straight down, down the shaft, a magnet drawing iron filings.

Hurtling through the bowels of the earth, stale air whipped past his ears and buffeted his skin. He was falling fast, *too* fast, plummeting into depths unknown. His weapon light revealed the floor rushing up to him. His muscles locked up, all of them, a sudden iron-hard tension that turned flesh to rock. His heart screamed in his chest.

He breathed out.

And his body relaxed.

And just as abruptly a third force pushed against him, gently, ever so gently, bleeding off his excess velocity, nudging him forward through a subtle arc, and abruptly ejected him out an opening and into the landing.

Nuhou.

Lots of nuhou.

"CONTACT!" he bellowed.

The beasts screeched back, an army of them, surging forward to tear him limb from limb. Crystals flashed red, green, blue, black, white.

And the stun grenade exploded.

Right at his boots.

A supernova ignited in the tiny space. Blinding white light flashed in the tiny space and kept on flashing, so monstrously brightly Li Ming *felt* each flash against his skin. Deafening bangs erupted, amplifying and reverberating in the chamber. His visor darkened, his earpieces canceled the sound, but he felt his eyes, lungs, heart tremble.

The nuhou staggered away, covering their eyes and ears, screaming in terror and rage and agony. He clicked the fire selector to continuous fire and held down the trigger.

Man-made lightning hurled from the gun's yawning mouth. There were so many of them, so close, he didn't have to aim. Hot pink steam exploded from every impact point. The still-bursting grenade filled the room with hellish illumination and thunder.

Strangely, incredibly, the nuhou rallied.

Their crystals glowed a deep shade of turquoise. Battered by the sensory assault, they gathered their wits, roared back at the grenade and the gun, and charged.

Li Ming pivoted on his heels, sidestepping left, clearing the entrance, shuffling left—

A nuhou collided into his shield. He shuddered, the force of the impact blowing through him, but he was rooted in a deep horse stance. He shuffled his right foot to the side, cocking and coiling dantian and muscles and sinews, and blasted to the left. His shield rammed into the beast, sending it tumbling and—

White flame arced through the air. He pivoted, catching it against his shield, gritting his teeth against a flash of furnace-hot flames, then extended his infinity gun in one hand and hosed down the caster's general area, and—

Cai Yan burst through the gravity elevator, screaming a ferocious war cry, and a shock wave of blinding white light blasted forth, knocking down everything in its path.

To his left, the nuhou swarmed again, piling up against him, battering the shield with fists like rams, trying to reach around or under it. He couldn't take them head-on; a single clean impact cracked the shield and sent reverberations up through his arm. He twisted, spiraled, intercepting and deflecting every blow, forcing the attackers off-balance however he could, barging his shield into and through them, making room for the men behind him, clicking the fire mode wheel, once, twice, thrice and—

Fired.

A cone of nova-hot plasma roared forth. Everything in its path simply ceased to exist, replaced by an expanding cloud of crimson steam. A huge gap opened in the enemy formation. But there were still many of them, too many. He aimed to the right and pressed the trigger—

BEEP

Overheat. The gun had shut down and the nuhou were forming fireballs in their hands and—

Ghazan emerged, yelling in the tongue of his people, Zhang Xinhua right behind him. Their infinity guns blazed bright, burning down the nuhou, giving Li Ming space to breathe, space to back up from the relentless horde of monsters to his left, to angle his shield and turn towards them and take their blows and hold them back. A fireball arched above the crowd. Li Ming caught it on his shield, a nuhou tried to sneak around him, he slammed the edge of his shield against its arm, bashed the battered shield into its face, knocking it back, and stepped into the gap, and a nuhou grabbed the shield, trying to wrestle it from him.

He braced himself, snatched the Hellion pistol from his holster, smashed the muzzle against flesh, fired, fired, fired, and then the nuhou fell away and he pointed at the next threat and fired and moved to the next and saw a crowd and loosed into the mob, working the trigger as fast as he could fire, shooting blindly, no time to turn on the weapon-mounted light, and continued shuffling left, making his way to the corner, and—

BEEP

And there were still nuhou pressed against him, swarming him. A heavy fist glanced against his helmet, slamming him against the wall. The helmet took the brunt of the blow, but it shook his vision, shook his brain, and the nuhou flowed around him—

And he detonated the shield.

The shield of earth-metal qi became a front of fire, blowing forward, converting completely to energy. The wall of flesh pressed against him suddenly vanished. He holstered the screaming weapon with his right hand, reached for his swordbreaker with his left—

And then there were none.

And the stun grenade had finally gone silent.

He inhaled.

And he kept moving, heading to the corner, taking up his point of domination. The firefight might be over but there might be more hostiles lying in wait. He took up his infinity gun, muzzle still spewing steam, and out the corner of his eye he counted three other biaohang, up and moving.

"Clear!" Li Ming called.

"Clear!" Cai Yan echoed.

This place might have been a rest area, a waiting area, a lobby, something like that. Metal benches lay buried under copious amounts of gore. Pots stood at the corners, whatever plants they'd once held reduced long ago to dark dirt. Light patches on the dark blood-streaked walls hinted at posters, pictures, now lost to the ravages of time.

And, at the far end, there was an opening.

"Trailers, move up!" Li Ming yelled.

Boss Cai's reply echoed down the long shaft.

"Moving!"

"Shield team, move and hold the opening!"

Splitting into buddy teams, they headed to the hallway. Li Ming carefully stepped over and around the bodies. Blood dripped from the ceiling and walls. He had no idea how many nuhou they'd fought, his brain registered only a lake of blood and churned meat, but he knew that there were way too many of them.

At the opening, Li Ming checked his infinity gun. Its optics showed a yellow crosshair. Smoke still issued from the cooling vents. He could shoot again, just not very many times. As Ghazan covered the hallway beyond, Li Ming crouched and regenerated his shield.

"*Tian ah...*" a voice muttered behind them.

"How many beasts did you kill?" Song Huizhong asked.

"All of them," Li Ming said.

Li Ming checked his infinity gun, realized it was still set to breach mode, and reset it to half power. On the other side of the opening, Cai Yan put a new shield up. Hers was strange, colored a deep brown, with more ragged cutouts on the side for increased aiming positions.

Li Ming leaned out, weapon ready. The hallway fed into a wider chamber at the far end. Halfway down the corridor, tunnels branched out to the left and right, forming a cross.

"Anyone see the robot?" Boss Cai asked.

Li blinked. In the madness of the firefight, he had lost track of the recon robot. For that matter, he didn't think he even saw it.

"Found it!" the younger Kang said.

"Shield team, hold position and continue covering. We're setting up here," Boss Cai said.

Fabric rustled. Plastic and metal tapped against each other. Green chemlights glowed. Li Ming strained his ears, listening for anything that might lie ahead.

"Oxygen sensor says the air is fifteen percent oxygen and five percent carbon dioxide. Barely breathable," Kang the Younger said.

"More fecal and bacterial contaminants floating around," Song Huizhong announced. "Hazardous concentrations."

"Keep your respirators on," the Cai patriarch said. "Deploying the robot."

The little machine rolled past Li's boots. Somehow it had survived the hellstorm with little more than a fresh coating of blood. It stopped in the middle of the crossroad and spun in a full circle. Then it ventured down the left turn.

Li Ming waited.

Long minutes later, it turned around and headed down the right hallway.

More waiting.

The robot reappeared. Now it ventured into the chamber at the far end.

Li Ming waited some more.

And at last, Boss Cai spoke.

"The hallways on the left and right lead to a number of rooms. Looks like living quarters, offices, a lab. Doors are all open. No immediate signs of threats, but we need to clear them just to be sure. The lift lobby at the end of the hallway is empty. But the gravity elevators are operational.

"Shields, and *only* the shields, move up and lock down the lobby. Cover the lifts and the stairs. Shooters, and this includes the cover team, clear the halls and rooms."

Li Ming and Cai Yan led the way. He advanced slowly down the passageway, shining a light at the left-hand bend, and the landing, alternating between the two. The walls showed the same eerie lack of wear. But for the urine streaks and lightened patches, they had stood the test of time.

They stopped at the cross-junction. Paused for a second. And, as one, stepped out and pivoted to cover the hallways.

Empty.

They shuffled to the side, turning as they went, reorienting on the landing, clearing the fatal funnel.

The rest of the biaohang flowed up behind them, splitting left and right. They whispered orders and movement calls and findings to each other, coordinating the dance.

"Move up," Li Ming said.

If another swarm of beasts rushed through the elevators, he wanted room to retreat. Or at least to maneuver.

They stopped at the entryway to the landing, far back just enough to keep their weapons from extending into the chamber beyond.

And waited.

Boots shuffled. Men whispered. More chemlights glowed. Fatigue built in Li Ming's tensed arms. He flexed, stretched, shaking off the worst of it, getting the blood moving—

A powerful qi presence flowed out the shaft.

"Incoming!" Cai Yan called.

And a nuhou stepped out, eyes burning red, a silvery giant in the weapon light.

It had four arms.

Li Ming blinked, trying to process the sight, and in that moment its crystals flashed black. A tower of perfect darkness appeared, covering its head and upper torso. Two arms and two eyes peeked out above the shield, glaring at the world.

Li Ming fired.

The shield swallowed his shot. No splash, no burn, no dispersal, it just... vanished.

And the two arms blasted blazing white.

A ray struck Li Ming's shield. The shield took it full on, spreading the energy across its mass. But it was too much to handle. The shield blew outwards, a last ditch attempt to neutralize the hellish burn.

Cai Yan's shield took the other ray. It, too, overloaded. But this one detonated into a screaming gale, sweeping the monster off its feet.

Li fired at its exposed legs. Its limbs blew apart in fountains of gore. He moved up to its other arm and—

And a second four-armed nuhou rushed out the lift, shield high and magic arms glowing.

Li Ming snap-fired, amputating its ankle. As it fell, a pair of blinding beams slashed into the ceiling.

Cai Yan extended her arm and shouted a word. A tongue of white-hot flame screamed forth, rushing over the bodies. The monsters spasmed, screamed, twitched—

A third nuhou stepped out into the flames. It, too, shrieked in pain and fury, stumbling aside, throwing away its shield, dropping and rolling.

The flame cut out.

And a *fourth* nuhou emerged from the lift tube, charging straight at the humans, power gathering in its palms.

Li fired.

Missed.

The plasma bolt erupted at its foot. It stumbled in the shock wave, falling forward. It blasted its palms out, catching itself against the floor.

Li shot it in the head.

Turned. Fired. Turned. Fired. Turned. Fired.

And then the beasts went still.

And the lift screamed its blockade alarm.

Li Ming exhaled.

"What the devil was that?" he muttered. "Were they learning from us?"

"I think so..." she whispered.

"Is everyone okay?" her father yelled.

Li Ming patted himself down.

"I'm good!"

"We're both okay!" Cai Yan reported. "Four novel nuhou down! These have four arms and use shields!"

"Shields?!"

The biaohang trooped over.

"Li Ming, did that shield absorb your shots?" Ghazan asked.

"Yes. Like the magic you used at the Zhangs' coffee shop."

Ghazan muttered something in his native tongue under his breath, then spoke in Xiayu.

"The nuhou have access to Sky and Night magic. High level magic. The shield you saw was pure Night."

"How do you counter it?"

"You cannot. Unlike your own shield, it cannot be overloaded or destroyed. Instead of absorbing the power of a shot, it shunts the energy into the Night. It has an unlimited energy absorption capability. You must shoot around it, use explosives or magic, or wait until the enemy runs out of qi."

"Gai si..." Li Ming sighed. "The spawning center must still be online, and the nuhou are networked. They're learning from our experiences against us. We have to shut it down before it creates beasts we can't fight."

"Agreed," Boss Cai said. "Let's hurry."

As they regrouped on the lift, Li Ming reviewed what he remembered of military anti-shield tactics. Flanking, but there might not be space. Fire. Force. Blinding. And...

"Thunderflash!" Li Ming called.

Ghazan produced a stun grenade. Pulled the pin. Threw.

The gravity lift greedily swallowed it down its gullet. As Li Ming waited, he regenerated his shield. He was *not* going to step in front of an exploding stun grenade again, not if he could help it.

One second. Two seconds. Half-second and the nine-banger exploded and kept on banging, throwing light and sound and fury through the shaft.

Something shrieked.

Li Ming entered the lift.

The gravity field seized him and threw him down. He exhaled, keeping his body loose and limber, still reinforcing his shield. The grenade continued detonating at the mouth of the lift. He pulled his infinity gun into himself and lowered his shield a tad and the gravity field spat him out into the landing.

Four four-armed nuhou, all of them carrying shields, all of them fanned out to face the lifts and the stairwell door.

All of them blinded, screaming, trying to cover their eyes and ears with their extra hands.

Li stepped right, clicked through the fire mode wheel, pressed the trigger.

A cone of sun-bright plasma washed over the closest nuhou. Its shield captured most of the blast, drinking it up in infinite darkness. But the rest spilled around its edges, incinerating flesh and bone. As the beast toppled, Li turned to the next target and fired again.

Light. Heat. Thunder. He'd caught it at an angle, and this one seemed to melt under in star-hot flames. The infinity gun screamed again, spilling smoke, its sights turning red. He released the weapon, going for his handgun, just in time to see Cai Yan step up and extend her hand.

A whip of white flame roared forth, lashing the surviving nuhou. It snaked over and around their shields, zipping across arms and skulls. Pink steam explosions rocked the room. And they fell.

And the cover team spilled out the tube, guns up and blasting, delivering the finishing shots.

"Move up!" Li Ming yelled.

The quartet pushed past the burning corpses, stacking up at an opening at the far side. The rest of the biaohang rushed down the gravity lift, one by one, splitting up to form two separate teams.

Ghazan patted Li Ming's shoulder. His infinity gun had cooled to orange. Three or four shots before overheating, no more. Even so, he rounded the corner, rushing down the passageway. Cai Yan ran beside him, keeping pace.

The tunnel split in two. One arm went left, the other went right. A light patch on the dark walls suggested there was once a sign. Li Ming didn't care. He was on the right, so he went right.

Four doors. Two on the left, two on the right. But the ones on the left had windows.

Li Ming peered through the closest window as he trooped past. Long walkways spanned a huge cavern. Below them, enormous vats held lakes of a bubbling, steaming red substance. Pale yellow lights lent the room a dim glow, leaving much of it in shadows.

"What the devil is this?"

Ghazan paused to read a sign by the door.

"Recycling vats."

"Recycling? For what?"

Even as he spoke, machines mounted on ceiling tracks hummed and whirred and descended into view. They had huge nozzles, gigantic grippers, articulated arms. They buzzed about the tanks, spraying more red fluid into the vats, reaching in to grab more unidentified solids, dropping dark shapes into the liquid.

Bodies.

Nuhou bodies.

They were recycling their dead.

The next set of windows looked into another enormous cavern. Columns of man-sized pods stood in perfect parade-ground formation, stretching to the far side, many of them filled with bright green fluid. Others were empty, their glass covers lifted, leaving dripping green trails towards the door. Dark misshapen forms floated within the filled pods, stretching and turning. Machines passed over the strange objects at blinding speed, extruding thick gels and substances, illuminating them in blue light, building the objects from bottom up.

Not objects. Nuhou.

"Bioprinters," Li Ming whispered.

"*Beast* bioprinters," Ghazan said. "This is the spawning room."

"How the devil do we shut this down? Shoot up everything inside?"

"The sign on our right says 'Control Room'. I'm going to check it out."

"Go!"

Ghazan and the Kang brothers peeled off from the train and barged into the room. Zhang Xinhua moved up, tapping Li Ming's shoulder.

"I don't think it's safe to go in there," the senior biaohang said.

"Me too," Li Ming said. "We'll set up a choke point here."

Li Ming planted himself by the open door. Zhang Xinhua slammed the butt of his weapon into the window. It bounced off as if it were rubber. He swore, struck it again. And again. Nothing happened. He pressed his palm against the window and concentrated. White light erupted from his shaper and fizzled against the glass.

"What's this window made of?" Zhang Xinhua wondered.

A monster growled.

"Cover the door!" Li Ming whispered.

Zhang Xinhua scrambled to the door.

Heavy feet pounded the floor. Glass trembled. Metal quivered. Something screamed, as loud as a freight train.

Li Ming braced himself.

And a... a *beast* stepped into view.

It was a nuhou. A four-armed one. But most of its enormous body was covered in glittering violet crystals. It held up an enormous Night shield in both lower hands, covering most of its legs, body, arms and neck, leaving only the eyes and upper hands exposed. It stood tall, towering over Li Ming.

Its upper hands flashed.

The shots blasted into Li Ming's shield. The shield held for a sliver of a second. Then it detonated abruptly, violently, rocking Li back and flinging Zhang Xinhua aside.

Li Ming brought up his weapon, blasting away. The apex beast crouched, hiding behind its magic bunker. Li Ming caught one exposed hand, blowing it apart. The other hid behind the shield.

The infinity gun traitorously beeped and steamed.

Roaring, the nuhou rose.

Li Ming transitioned to his pistol. Zhang Xinhua got up, groaning, shaking his head. The beast advanced, slowly, ponderously.

Li Ming fired low. But his aim was off by just a touch, missing its foot. The nuhou dropped to a deep crouch, again hiding behind the bunker, arcing its other free arm about—

Zhang Xinhua fired.

The limb flew off.

The monster roared in rage. But remained still.

"Ghazan! HURRY UP!" Li Ming shouted.

"I'm trying!" Ghazan screamed back.

"Banger out!" Zhang Xinhua called.

Li Ming retreated. Zhang Xinhua tossed a stun grenade into the room. It exploded in thunder and fury, blasting again and again.

The nuhou didn't react. It just squatted there, still as a statue.

"BREACH THE SHIELD!" Li Ming ordered.

Zhang Xinhua's gun blasted a cone of pure white flame, larger and brighter and far more powerful than Li's own. The shield swallowed it all up without reaction. The rest of the plasma burst seared off fur, scoured exposed flesh, but left the nuhou's body untouched.

Suddenly the nuhou lunged, sprinting for the door. Stepping into the doorway, Li fired, fired, fired again, the shots disappearing into the darkness of the shield. The monster howled for blood, charging at him.

Li swiveled aside.

The monster bulled through the doorway, through empty space, and crashed into the wall.

Li Ming fired into its exposed back. A moment later, Zhang Xinhua joined in, his own sidearm flashing away. Flesh and blood evaporated under the high-energy hammer blows. The monster screeched, pushing itself off, trying to turn around. Li Ming fired and fired and fired, working his way up its back, taking it in the head—

It went down.

And went still.

Inside the control room, an infinity gun screamed. Something exploded.

The machines stopped. Alarms blared. A distorted voice mumbled gibberish through decayed speakers. The pods remained still.

Ghazan poked his head out the door.

"Did it work?"

"The spawning room has gone dark," Li Ming said.

"What happened?!" Boss Cai shouted.

"I blasted the control panel!" Ghazan replied.

"What's the voice saying?"

"Can't make it out!"

"Ga San, I need you over here! I think we found the cosmic tap and the life support system!" Boss Cai called.

"Moving over!"

Ghazan trotted over. The Kang brothers rejoined Li Ming.

"What *is* that thing?" Kang the Younger said, gesturing at the fallen beast.

"Nothing I want to fight again," Li Ming said. "Come on. We've got two more rooms to clear."

Chapter Forty

Duty and Money

The hard part was over.

Now came the hard*er* part.

They back cleared the entire bunker, re-checking every room, ever corner, every corpse. Halfway through the lowest floor, pneumatic alarms sounded. The air tanks were running low. They halted for a while, swapped out their tanks with fresh ones in interspatial storage, and carried on.

By the time they emerged into the surface, it was mid-afternoon. Li Ming's belly took the opportunity to remind him he hadn't eaten anything since the morning.

The men, and woman, of Dayong gathered by the bunker entrance. They stripped out of the bulky breathing apparatus and gear, downed copious amounts of water, and wound down from high alert. Fatigue sank into Li Ming's muscles and tendons, weighing him down. He yawned, shook his head, yawned again. Half of his brain wanted a nap, the other half wanted a meal.

But he still had work to do.

He checked himself, and others, for injuries. Inspected his gear. Scrubbed down his face and hands and armpits with wet wipes. Talked through the mission with the others, reconstructing the battle, figuring out who fought what and where. They cross-examined each others' actions, identified failings and mistakes, determined how to do the job better next time.

The collectors entered the bunker, kitted out in protective gear, interspatial storage bags clipped to their belts. There was no rush. By now the nuhou were good only for worm food. At least the crystals would fetch a high price on the market.

Or so Ms. Rao had promised.

The White Tiger demi-platoon was still on station, still pulling security. Half of them formed a circle around the bunker entrance. The other half patrolled the woods. Ouyang stationed himself by the airship. Li Ming wondered why the mercenaries were still here.

He was flattered to have the attention of a martial immortal, but surely the White Tiger quick response force had more important things to do.

Nonetheless, the biaohang delivered their report to White Tiger and Ms. Rao.

"According to Ga San, the cosmic tap was still operational, even after hundreds of years," Boss Cai said. "The status readouts were mostly in the yellows, but it was still capable of producing enough power to support critical operations. Including the spawning and recycling centers.

"The life support system was in the reds. The ventilation system was partially blocked and malfunctioning. Ga San thinks that the facility went into failsafe mode, opening all the doors to give the personnel a chance to escape, or at least to breathe.

"We found no trace of human remains. Not even bone fragments. We think the base was completely evacuated long ago. Perhaps it was supposed to be a temporary retreat. Maybe the former defenders thought they would return shortly. Whatever happened, the reasons are lost to time."

"Why did the base still produce nuhou?" Ouyang asked.

This time, Ghazan spoke.

"The Strategic Beast Corps of the Yue Dynasty were composed of beasts specially created for war. Perhaps when the facility's life support system was compromised, it spawned a troop of nuhou to summon help and protect the base.

"Instead, the nuhou found us. We opened fire. They assumed we were hostile. They defended their home base against our incursions. And failed."

"You're saying the base spawned beasts for *centuries?*" Ms. Rao exclaimed.

Ghazan shrugged. "Our people built things to last."

"Are nuhou intelligent enough to gather reinforcements?" Ouyang wondered.

"The Corps developed and implemented special technology to control their beasts. That's why they were called 'strategic' beasts. Perhaps they were like... organic robots. Controlled by an artificial intelligence, or just guided by orders programmed into their brains when they were spawned."

"There's so much we don't know about them," Boss Cai concluded. "The Yue and their beasts."

"There may be another reason there aren't any humans on site," Ouyang said.

"What's that?"

"The nuhou rebelled against their creators and threw them into the recycling centers. In the chaos of the uprising against the Yue Dynasty, no one noticed."

The biaohang pondered his words for a moment.

"Why isn't the forest overrun by nuhou?" Cai Yan asked. "For that matter, why hasn't anyone from the nearby towns noticed?"

"Perhaps the spawning center kept a strict limit on their population size. Perhaps the nuhou were forbidden from venturing beyond the forest. Or perhaps the base simply went into failsafe mode recently," Ghazan said.

"If not for the beast surge, we wouldn't have found this place at all," Ouyang said.

"At least, not until the nuhou raze a village or two," Li Ming said darkly.

"The only way to reconstruct the history of this place is to take it apart and study everything," Ms. Rao said. "Including and especially biological matter."

"Even the droppings?" Zhang Xinhua asked.

"Especially the droppings. We need to know how old they are to establish how long the nuhou have been around."

The veteran biaohang groaned. Ms. Rao continued, unperturbed.

"Now that the bunker is secure, we can proceed to the reclamation phase. We can bring in a crew of reclaimers to clear out the site. That will free you to continue your hunt. Or you can do it yourself."

"We're biaohang. Our place is out in the wilds," Boss Cai said.

"I understand where you're coming from. However, if you choose to participate in the reclamation process, you may lawfully claim ownership of any artifacts you recover from the site. If we send in reclaimers from the Jianghu Association, then artifacts will automatically become the property of the government and the Jianghu Association."

"How does claiming ownership work?" Li Ming asked.

"Under the laws of the Zhongxia Republic, any artifacts you recover must be logged and sent in to the Jianghu Association for tracking and study. Especially artifacts of unknown origin or purpose. Once these studies are complete, the Association will return these artifacts to you, to be disposed of as you see fit. Alternatively, we may offer to buy these artifacts from you. Especially if these artifacts are deemed too dangerous for personal use.

"If you choose to hand over the site to the Jianghu Association, you will automatically forgo any claims to anything recovered from the premises. This does not extend to the beasts, but it will encompass everything else. We will still pay you a bounty for ridding the world of dangerous beasts. If any recovered artifacts are later sold at auction or to private entities, you will receive a percentage of the proceeds. But that is all we can do."

There it was. The choice between duty and money. Li Ming was sure a reclamation job wouldn't take longer than a day or two. But it was time they weren't hunting beasts. Time the beasts could use to mount an attack on civilization.

"Please give us time to discuss this," Boss Cai said.

"Of course," Ms. Rao said agreeably. "Regardless of your decision, we will be ready to assist."

The biaohang sat by the road in a loose circle and broke out snacks and water. For a few minutes, they simply ate and drank, recuperating from the stresses of battle.

Finally, Boss Cai spoke.

"You heard Ms. Rao. What do you think?"

"I'm fine either way," Cai Yan said.

"I saw a lot of interesting tech on the way down, especially on the second floor," Jiang Long said. "We could be looking at a massive payday. Much, much larger than whatever we might earn from the expedition."

"Brother, I signed up to hunt beasts, not to do hard labor," Kang the Younger said.

"It's not that hard. We just shove things into our storage machines and pop them right out once we return to Bao An," Lan Yi said.

"This could be an opportunity for us to pick up Yue Dynasty gear," Ghazan said. "The nuhou were created using lost technology. There could be other lost tech in there. Maybe even weapons and armor. Kit we can use in the expedition."

"Li Ming, you're really quiet," Cai Yan probed.

Li Ming sighed. Swallowed more water. Gathered his thoughts.

"Sorry, just... Tired. But I have to say, we... *I* came here because of the beasts. Because they posed a threat to human life. This is an unexpected windfall, but it is also a distraction from the mission. We need to get back to it as soon as we can. Lives are counting on us."

"It's noble of you," Boss Cai said, "but I see we're all exhausted. *You* did the brunt of the fighting. I don't need to run a qi assessment to tell you're running on fumes."

"I can still carry on."

"Yes, but this expedition is a marathon, not a sprint. We won't do the world any good if we're so exhausted we can't battle the beasts if they come. We need to take a day off at least, long enough to recover our qi and hand off our harvested beasts. We could use that time reclaiming this site and setting us up for an even larger payday when this is over. As for the other beasts in the area of operations, there are many more hunters out there who can pick up the slack."

Li Ming nodded his assent. He didn't have to like it, but Boss Cai called the shots. More importantly, he was right. Fighting fatigued wasn't something you did if you could avoid it.

They spent the rest of the day and evening watching over the collectors, making sure they accounted for every carcass, washing away the blood and guts and gore sprayed over the area. At night, they camped in the open—but posted two guards at the entrance of the bunker. Alongside the White Tiger guards.

It wasn't that they didn't trust White Tiger, rather that in the jianghu, you could only trust your own people.

In the morning, Li Ming treated himself to a full breakfast. Menu 4, the menu everyone rejected out of long-standing superstition, the menu he found to be the least worst. Egg rolls with pork, a fruit bar, a packet of energy drink. Amazingly, it nearly tasted like real food.

Fortified for the task ahead, the biaohang stripped off their armor. Even with exoskeletons, they didn't need the extra weight, bulk, most of all, the heat. They stuffed their kit into storage, donned their breathing apparatuses, and headed into the darkness.

The collectors had done their best to clean up. Even so, dark, dirty streaks marked the spots where so many beasts had met their end. They had removed the droppings in the corners, sealing them in baggies for forensic analysis, and washed down the area with water and antiseptics, but the biochem detector still warned of aerosolized fecal matter floating around. Life support was still offline, so the biaohang carried extra air tanks.

The silence was eerie. Li's mind replayed the screams and shots, echoing in the shafts and hallways. His ears heard only the shuffling of boots. The biaohang dropped chemlights liberally across the main floor, lighting their path.

Inside the security office, Ghazan carefully disconnected the pads and screens from discreetly-hidden power points and swallowed them up into his bag. He recorded his loot on his smartglasses, and the biaohang moved on.

Those were the only artifacts on the first floor. The real treasure trove lay in the middle floor. The living quarters, the offices, the storage spaces, even the bathrooms were all intact. Or, at least, as intact as the passage of centuries would allow.

Li saw no signs of struggle. No blast points but what the biaohang had etched into the walls. No damage that could not be explained by the copious amounts of urine and droppings the nuhou had left behind.

His first stop was the barracks. There were other quarters in the base, narrower and more private, but this called out to him. This was the where the enlisted men lived. Men not too dissimilar from himself.

Double-decker bed frames filled the room. Enough beds to sleep a company of men, and still have room for gatherings and assemblies. There were no mattresses, not anymore. There used to be tables and chairs at the corners, but rust and rot had reduced them to wreckage.

But there was an intact locker at the foot of every bed.

Li examined the closest, carefully wiping away a thick layer of dust. Strange Yue script stared back at him, faded and broken. He found no lock, no hinge, nothing that could be opened.

But there was a control panel built into the locker.

A green button. A red button. A flat screen.

He touched the green button. An outline of a palm flashed across the screen, illuminating the room. Li blinked. Pressed the red button. And the palm disappeared.

"The lockers still have power!" Li declared.

"They must use a micro cosmic tap or something," Ghazan said.

Li concentrated. Now he felt it, a subtle tugging at the bottom of the locker, on the other side of the control panel.

Why would a locker need such a thing? Even an electronic lock wouldn't need constant power. Not unless...

"Are these interspatial storage machines?!" Li exclaimed.

"I think so," Ghazan replied.

"All of them?"

"Only one way to find out."

The lockers were *all* interspatial storage machines.

They were *all* functional.

"*Tian ah...*" Li whispered. "If I sold just one of these... I'd be able to buy out *all* of Fuyang!"

"There's a big payday for all of us right here," Lan Yi said.

"How the devil didn't the Yue lose any of these?" Song Huizhong asked.

"What do you mean?" Li Ming asked.

"Soldiers will be soldiers everywhere in the world. Sooner or later some idiot will try stuffing a locker into another. Wouldn't that create a space-time anomaly and destroy both lockers?"

"I imagine their soldiers were accountable for every bit of equipment and would be severely punished if they tried a stunt like that," Ghazan said. "I know I was, in my time in the military. Besides, in the time of the Yue Dynasty, interspatial storage was so cheap and so common, everybody had interspatial storage devices."

Unbelievable. Each of these lockers were worth a thousand times their weight in gold, maybe even *ten* thousand. To think that such things were so common back then...

Li Ming couldn't begin to comprehend the technological marvels of the Yue Dynasty. It was one thing to read about it, quite another to hear a descendant of that long-ago empire deliver such testimony so casually, as if he were describing something as mundane as breathing.

The biaohang hauled the lockers up to the ground floor. They were surprisingly heavy for their size, as though constructed of some unusually dense substance. A dozen trips later, Li Ming returned to find the barracks stripped bare.

And Ghazan poking around a much smaller room.

This was officer country. The single bed and roomy worktable gave it away. Next to the table, in place of a closet or locker, it had an interspatial storage machine, perhaps half the size of the one in Dayong. Ghazan rifled through the drawers, throwing up thick clouds of dust.

"Found anything interesting?" Li Ming asked.

"No. But it feels like something is stuck..."

He jiggled the drawers up and down, left and right, and pulled them clear of the frame. He knelt. Paused. Muttered something in Yue.

"Did you find something?"

Ghazan reached in and pulled out a long sheet of... something. It looked like paper, but no paper could possibly have survived the passage of centuries. It was as smooth and transparent as glass. Yet when Li held it up, it bent and curled as if it were parchment. It had a long tubular handle on either end, reminding him of a scroll.

And Li sensed a faint tugging sensation from the lower handle.

The tugging of a cosmic tap.

"Is that a *scroll*?" Li wondered.

"Yes. Thinner, lighter and more flexible than the scrolls of our era."

"Does it still work?"

Ghazan thumbed a hidden button on the upper handle.

The glassy screen glowed. Yue words flowed across the display in brilliant gold. A bright circle appeared under the text.

"What's it say?" Li asked.

Ghazan considered the words for a moment. Then he peeled off his glove and pressed his thumb to the circle.

The machine chimed.

And resolved into a series of icons.

A home screen.

"You unlocked it?! How?" Li exclaimed.

"The Yue exercised a policy of strict technology control. Non-Yue were only allowed the most basic of technologies. Even their servants were only allowed what tools they needed to carry out their duties, no more. To enforce this policy, many consumer-grade devices required proof of Yue ancestry to use. They could scan the user's blood from his skin."

"I... I can't believe the Yue were so... advanced."

Ghazan looked strangely at Li Ming for a moment.

"The Celestials tried to erase their legacy from the world. They almost succeeded," Ghazan said at last.

"Why isn't this device secured?"

"I don't know. It might be a civilian device. For personal use, not duty. The user must have been especially careless."

As he spoke, he touched an icon that looked like a book. A bookshelf filled the screen. Dozens of book covers appeared.

"The user must have been quite the bookworm," Li Ming said.

Ghazan grunted.

Paused.

Tapped a book.

The cover opened, revealing a black screen and white words scrolling down the length of the glass.

"What is it?" Li Ming asked.

Ghazan blinked.

"It's... an ancient classic. I can't believe there's something like this here."

Ghazan clicked the power button. The screen winked out. He activated his interspatial storage bag and dumped it into storage.

"We can figure it out later," Ghazan said. "Come on. We've got more work to do."

Chapter Forty-One

Windfall

Every room was a treasure trove. Interspatial storage machines, taken from almost everywhere. Computers and devices, lifted from offices and critical room. Sculptures and pottery, somehow untouched by centuries. Furniture, or what was left of them.

Li Ming wasn't sure what value there was in the latter two. Figurines he could appreciate as works of art. But vases and cups? Tables and chairs? Bare bedframes? Why would anyone want to buy them?

"They are artifacts of the Yue Dynasty, unearthed after hundreds of years," Ms. Rao explained. "The provenance alone gives them value."

"What do people want to do with them?" Li Ming wondered.

"Private collectors enjoy keeping specimens of Yue art. Museums want to show and preserve the remnants of previous ages. Research institutions want to study them. The artifacts you've recovered are in incredible shape. If the Yue can create things that can stand the test of time, we can learn how to do the same."

"A lot of it looks like junk to me."

"Wu zhi guijian, yin ren er yi."

One man's junk is another man's treasure.

Thus encouraged, the biaohang kept digging up more junk. Toolboxes filled with hand tools not dissimilar to the ones they knew. Large machines whose purpose no one could divine. Shelves and cabinets stuffed with dense cubes of strange material. Scrap metal frames and ceramic shards, probably once part of a larger assembly, their designs now lost to time.

Ms. Rao eagerly inspected them all, cataloging them on her scroll. The biaohang stacked the goods in the exit chamber, arranging and rearranging them by the walls. She insisted on logging and registering *everything* the biaohang recovered before taking them to a specialist facility.

She didn't say why, but Li Ming knew what accountability and loss prevention systems looked like.

Deeper and deeper the biaohang went, tearing every room apart, hunting in every nook and cranny. But there was so much they couldn't take with them. The vats in the recycling room, the pods in the spawning chamber, the cosmic tap.

In the power plant, Li Ming beheld the cosmic tap. A monolith of black steel, standing alone in a deep circular pit, covered by toughened glass. Computers and consoles radiated outwards from the central pit. Yue script and images flashed across every screen. Li Ming couldn't read any of them, but he inferred from the green and yellow words and the partially-empty status bar that the cosmic tap had defied the centuries, faithfully drawing the qi flowing through the pit and converting it to electricity.

What wonders had the Yue known? What secrets had they possessed? What inspired them to build everything—even the most mundane of furniture and containers—to sail across the gulfs of time untouched? The answers he knew not.

Even Ghazan, standing next to him, staring into the pit, his amber eyes wide in wonder, had no words to speak.

They could not take the advanced tech with them. They didn't know how to disconnect the computers, or what would happen if they did. If they tried to enter the pit while the tap was still running, the tap would leech their life essence and suck them dry before they could even touch the tap.

They had to leave this place, and the other complex facilities, to the specialists.

The loot Li Ming truly wanted was nowhere to be found. On the middle and bottom floors, there were two large rooms filled with nothing but interspatial storage machines and computers. Storerooms of some kind, maybe even armories. Once secured with card readers and retinal scanners, the doors now stood open to the world. But the machines were all secured with heavy-duty security devices, none of which had yielded to the needs of failsafe mode.

They found no weapons. No shapers. No magical tools. Nothing that would be of interest to a martial cultivator.

"Don't worry," Lan Yi said. "You'll get a huge payday out of this. After that, you can buy just about anything you want."

"Anything except bronze-ranked gear and higher," Li Ming said.

"You can always use company gear. For most work, iron-ranked gear is good enough."

For beasts and men, maybe. For cultivators... he wouldn't bet his life on it.

They took frequent breaks throughout the day, pausing to swap out and recharge their air tanks. They only had two tanks per man, and the air in the bunker remained as filthy and stale as ever. When afternoon came, they paused for a half hour for lunch.

Li Ming took his time, savoring his meal. Cai Yan had, very reluctantly, exchanged one of her Menu 4 rations for one of his Menu 7s—then ate something else. Ghazan scarfed his food down, then hustled back into the bunker.

"Back to work so soon?" Li Ming asked.

"Finders keepers," Ghazan said.

"Everybody gets the same share of the payout," Cai Yan called.

Ghazan disappeared into the gloom.

"If he wants to work, let him work," her father advised.

"Does he have enough air to work?" Li Ming wondered.

The biaohang looked at each other in silence.

"He'll come back up soon enough," Boss Cai said at last.

Sure enough, when the men got up from their meal, Ghazan returned. This time he clunked down his two empty air tanks and hooked up one of them to the air compressor.

Work continued well into the afternoon. The men cleaned up after themselves, rechecked the rooms and tubes, hunted for secret stashes, documented everything that they had to leave behind. At last, at the hour of the monkey, they finally called a halt.

The exit chamber was cramped. The biaohang had arranged piles of junk along the walls, leaving only a narrow aisle. The Dayong team waited outside, stripping off their air tanks and breathing apparatus, winding down from the day's labor. Ms. Rao and Boss Cai spoke with Ouyang. A team of five White Tiger commandos escorted the collectors to the airship.

The remaining fifteen stood watch at the bunker entrance.

Cold fingers brushed along Li's belly. Something was wrong here. But what?

The White Tiger guards stood in two neat blocs by the entrance, facing outwards, infinity guns held at port arms. Bayonets glittered in the afternoon sun.

Why hadn't they formed a defensive perimeter? If they were guarding against beasts, they should be stationed in a ring around the bunker. They would be down the road, by the airship, behind and among the hills. They wouldn't be standing here.

And why had they fixed bayonets?

Ghazan looked at Li Ming, then tilted his head slightly at the White Tiger guards, at their bayonets.

Li Ming shrugged, suspicion creeping down his lips.

Ghazan's face hardened.

Li Ming took his infinity gun in his hands.

Ghazan eased out his folding bayonet.

Boss Cai continued speaking with Ouyang.

"That's everything we've recovered," Boss Cai said. "Most of the artifacts we've left behind are in the power plant, the recycling vats and the spawning center. We're leaving those to the experts."

"A wise decision," Ouyang said. "We shouldn't mess around with things we don't know."

"I've marked the bunker on my map," Ms. Rao said. "Once we return to Lianghe, I'll call in a reclamation team."

"Have you called them yet?" Ouyang asked.

"I've alerted my bosses to the existence of this site. The Jianghu Association is assembling the team now. It'll take maybe two or three days."

"Wonderful. Thank you for your help," Ouyang said.

"My pleasure."

Ouyang shook Ms. Rao's hand. Then Boss Cai's.

"Congratulations on a successful expedition," Ouyang said.

"The expedition has only just begun. This is a windfall, but it is not our duty. Nonetheless, thank you for your assistance," Boss Cai said.

"You're very welcome. Now there is just one last thing left to do."

"What's that?"

Ouyang smiled.

"WANJIAN WANSUI!"

His voice thundered from his lungs, from his belly, from the depths of his being, a sonic shockwave deafening and disrupting and destabilizing everything in its path. Ms. Rao staggered away, into the arms of a waiting White Tiger trooper. Boss Cai flinched, arms high to cover his face.

Ouyang drew his infinity handgun and shot Cai Mengyang in the belly.

The plasma bolt vaporized everything in its path, tunneling through muscle and viscera and blowing out his spine.

Ouyang angled his gun up and fired again, destroying his head.

Time stopped.

The biaohang froze, staring at the sight. Li Ming watched the elder Cai fall, slowly, inexorably, his synapses strangely silent, a blankness where his brain should be, his muscles petrified.

"FATHER!" Cai Yan screamed.

And time shot forward and the biaohang swore in discordant symphony and Li Ming raised his weapon and saw the red dot on Ouyang's chest and clicked off the safety and placed his finger on the trigger—

Dark, dense, heavy qi surged out from Ouyang's shapers. A black mist, cold and sticky, spread outwards to fill the world, clinging to everything, pressing everything down, sucking everything into itself. It dimmed the light, chilled the bones, stole the breath.

Li Ming fired.

Nothing happened.

"KAN!" Cai Yan screamed. "He's using Kan magic!"

Kan was the Abyss, a bottomless pit that drowned all qi, the ultimate defensive ability of the eight trigrams system. Within the abyssal field, no magic would work, no guns would fire. Everyone caught inside would be reduced to bare hands and cold steel.

As Li Ming framed the thought, the White Tiger guards spun around smartly, leveled their glittering bayonets, and charged the biaohang.

Chapter Forty-Two

The Way of the Jianghu

The White Tigers marched like soldiers on parade, leaving no gaps between them, steel jaws closing on a trap. They merged into two lines, holding their bayoneted weapons like spears, advancing relentlessly on the Dayong biaohang.

"Wang ba dan!" Lan Yi swore, rushing at the White Tigers.

He slapped a bayonet aside with his infinity gun. Slipped past a second. Closed in with his own weapon—

A screen of bayonets stabbed into his thighs, belly, throat.

He shrieked, gurgling as he went down. The closest White Tiger kicked him down and trampled over him.

"FALL BACK!" Zhang Xinhua screamed.

Li Ming retreated. Ghazan, cursing under his breath, fell in line next to him. The Kang brothers grabbed Cai Yan and hustled her deeper into the chamber beyond.

Roaring a war cry, Zhang Xinhua threw himself into the incoming mass.

"DIE!" he screamed, lunging his bayoneted gun forward.

His target swiped his weapon through an arc, neatly deflecting the infinity gun.

And his buddies stabbed the biaohang, over and over and over again.

"Gaisi... pantu!" Zhang Xinhua spat.

Damned traitor!

Still impaled, he tried to wriggle free, stabbing at targets he could find. The men before him jinked and dodged, avoiding his blows, taking them on their armor when they couldn't. The White Tiger leader yelled a command, and the spear screen froze into two solid lines, refusing to open a break for Dayong to exploit.

The remaining biaohang fell back into the bunker.

"We need to break their formation!" Li Ming called.

"How?!" Ghazan replied.

Guns didn't work. Magic won't work. Charging head on was suicide. Attacking the flanks would cause the center line to roll up and envelop the attackers. That left—

"The footlockers!" Li Ming called.

Li Ming and Ghazan retreated deeper into the chamber. The dying man's scream reverberated in the hall. Li Ming hunted among the aisles, looking for the lockers, where the devil—

There.

He hefted the closest in both hands. Nice and heavy.

"What are you doing?" Cai Yan asked.

"Pick up something and throw it at them!" Li Ming replied.

Screaming war cries, the White Tigers flowed into the bunker, forming three lines of five men. They clambered around the artifacts, squeezed through the narrow aisle, closed in for the kill.

The right-most three-man file rushed towards Li Ming, in tandem with their comrades. He lifted his locker high above his head.

The lead White Tiger halted, his mouth falling open in surprise.

Li Ming grinned.

Threw.

The White Tiger flinched, shielding his head with his arms. The heavy footlocker ploughed into him, knocking him down, knocking all three men in the file down.

Another footlocker flew, another, another, and their lines crumbled.

Li Ming ran, left hand going for his swordbreaker—

A White Tiger rushed up, readying his infinity gun for a thrust.

Li Ming wasn't going to make it.

And Ghazan lunged in, smacking the gun aside, and thrust his bayonet into the man's mouth.

"GO!" Ghazan yelled.

Ghazan kicked the mercenary aside and took his place next to Li Ming. Li Ming drew the swordbreaker from its sheath, just as the White Tiger at his feet rolled off the footlocker. The mercenary snarled, thrusting at Li Ming. Li Ming deflected the clumsy blow, then stepped in and stomped him in the face, the mouth, trying to go for the throat.

The third man in the file scrambled out from under the pile. Yelling ferociously, his qi flaring, he leapt to the side, twisting in mid-air. His boots smashed into a closet. He sprang off, landed on the wall, ran through a tight arc, one two three steps, and jumped. Twisting about in mid-air, he flew at Li Ming, bayonet aimed for his face.

Li Ming ducked.

And held up his swordbreaker in both hands.

The man crashed crown-first into the blade. Gravity claimed him, slamming him down atop his buddies in a crumpled heap. Li Ming kicked him over, raised his weapon, reversed the blade, thrust.

The helmet was mil-spec. It would resist shrapnel, explosions, even plasma bolts from a handgun. Li Ming bypassed it altogether and stabbed the weapon through the back of the man's head. The steel effortlessly parted skin and crunched bone.

The White Tiger spasmed.

Li Ming pulled out the bloody blade. Stepped up. Aimed carefully at the first man he had knocked down with the locker. Thrust.

The ultra-sharp tip parted the high-strength aramids of his throat protector and sank deep into flesh. Li Ming stirred the weapon about, widening the wound channel. The White Tiger gurgled, grabbing the swordbreaker, trying to free himself. Li Ming stomped his face and yanked the weapon free. The last man—

Ghazan kicked him over and stabbed him, shoulder pocket, throat, armpit, everywhere that wasn't covered in hard armor.

Li Ming hopped over the bodies. Turned around, stomped the dying man one last time.

The light of the outside world blazed through the entrance. To his left and rear, men screamed and gurgled and died, their voices blending into an indistinguishable torrent of white noise that pounded Li Ming's brain. The only voice he could pick out was Cai Yan's, shrieking in rage.

Li Ming scanned. Men sprawled in chaotic piles at his feet, most moving, a few not. Through the black mist, Ghazan's aura blazed bright and hot and fierce, an all-consuming fire hungrily seeking fuel to burn.

Li Ming and Ghazan had broken through the White Tigers. They could roll up their flanks. Li Ming turned—

"DIE!" Ms. Rao screamed.

Outside the bunker, the remaining five White Tigers wrestled with Ms. Rao and the collectors. Stocks swinging, muzzles punching, they forced the civilians back and down. Behind them, Ouyang looked on, palms outstretched, the entirety of his being focused on maintaining the abyssal field.

Li Ming looked at Ghazan.

Ghazan pulled his bayonet from a dead man's throat.

In that glance, they exchanged ten thousand words.

"Go!" Ghazan urged. "I'll finish this lot!"

Li Ming sprinted out the bunker, swordbreaker held high. Ghazan whirled to the left, taking the remaining White Tigers from behind.

Ms. Rao broke free from the scrum and latched on to Ouyang's forearm.

And clawed his face.

The abyssal field vanished. The black qi dispersed as suddenly as it had come, dissipating in the bright sunlight, leaving no trace of itself behind.

"PROTECT MISS CAI!" Jiang Long shouted.

Infinity guns howled. Sun-bright plasma flashed in the dark bunker. Li heard or saw none of that. His world shrank down to the people in front of him, to the collectors, to Rao, to the White Tigers.

And Ouyang.

Ouyang whirled around, smashing his palm into Rao's forehead, forcing it back. He stepped in, blasting his right palm into her chin and his knee into her groin. Rao flew back with a pained grunt.

Too late. The abyssal field was down.

Li shot his left hand out, touching the essence of fire. A firebolt erupted from his palm, blasted through the air, bored through the exposed flank of the nearest White Tiger. The bolt caught him just below his pauldron, tunneled through his armpit, vaporizing his chest from the inside out.

Li punched his right fist. A pulse of pure force struck the next White Tiger in the head, knocking him down. A trio of collectors fell upon him, stabbing him with their work knives.

Li gulped down qi, forcing it into his left-hand crystal, and launched another firebolt. The third White Tiger saw it coming, turned to face Li, and caught it square on his chest plate. The bolt fizzled against the ceramic. Then Foreman Hu tackled him to the ground and stitched him up with his blade.

Another step. Another force punch. The fourth threat doubled over, covering his groin. A nearby collector forced himself back on his feet, grabbed his helmet, yanked up, slashed through his exposed throat.

The last White Tiger stepped back and lifted his infinity gun.

Li's shapers were dry. Too little energy, target too far away. That left...

He swung his swordbreaker.

The energy stored within its crystal flashed to metal qi. Electricity blasted through his palms. Thunder cracked. A qi-blade launched itself from the swordbreaker, a steel-gray crescent slashing and splitting and shaping the air itself, falling on the White Tiger.

The mercenary looked up.

The qi-blade cut into him, cut him open, cut him down. Down he went, blood gushing from an enormous wound bisecting his neck and upper chest.

And now there was only one left.

"OUYANG!" Li roared.

Raising his swordbreaker in both hands, rushing the martial immortal, he gulped down deep breaths, sending the qi screaming down his arms, down his hands, into the primordial crystal stored within the pommel, concentrating the entirety of his will into the weapon.

Ouyang extended his arms.

A huge force wave, invisible and irresistible, blasted from his palms. It blew Ms. Rao aside as if she were a paper doll. It slammed the collectors and their captors down to the ground. It screamed towards Li Ming, ripping up the dirt and air and everything in its path.

At the last moment, Li Ming generated a shield. An angular wedge of thick metal qi, it separated and split the force wave in two, redirecting it harmlessly into the forest. Bone-chilling wind howled past his ears, scourged his skin, buffeted his frame.

Ouyang fired.

He cracked off a string of shots, every one of them aimed at Li Ming's face. They splashed against his shield, blanking out his vision. Li Ming sprinted, an armored ram closing in for the kill. As his shield eroded, Li Ming sent fire qi to his legs, supercharging them, rocketing himself off the ground.

He was close, closer, even closer, so close he could see Ouyang's perfectly sculpted face, his hair done up in a neat topknot, his pistol spewing death with every trigger press.

Li Ming lunged.

Plasma flashed.

Li Ming slashed.

Ouyang flinched.

Metal smashed against metal.

Ouyang's pistol went flying into the air, spiraling into the forest.

Li Ming bit down a curse. He'd missed! He'd aimed for Ouyang's wrist! But the flashes and final jerk away had spoiled his aim. No matter. He stepped in again and—

A shockwave slammed into his chest, flinging him away. He soared through the air, bounced off the ground, dug a shallow furrow through the earth. He got up, shaking his head, just in time to feel qi rushing into Ouyang.

"HA!" Ouyang shouted.

An abyssal cloud blasted forth, smothering the world. Black mist wrapped around Li Ming, pulling him back, dragging him down, sapping his strength. Still Li Ming breathed, his weapon held low, still channeling what qi he could into his lungs, his muscles, his swordbreaker. The qi was slow, sluggish, dragged into the bottomless abyss—

Abyss.

Kan was the essence of water.

And earth conquered water.

Taking a deep breath, Li Ming sent qi surging into his swordbreaker's crystal, and willed the energy to become the embodiment of earth. Slow, heavy, solid energy oozed through the weapon, through the circuits, through the blade. The energy of earth, pushing aside the abyssal field, shaping watery qi around itself, standing fast against the relentless draining mist.

Ouyang's eyebrows narrowed.

"A magic swordbreaker. How did—"

Li Ming slashed.

Ouyang danced back, left hand flying to his straight sword. Li Ming flowed with the momentum, cycling it around through a tight circle, and slashed from hip to shoulder.

Ouyang drew.

Whirling, he met the swordbreaker with the flat of his blade, trying to shed its energy. The sheer concussive force of the swordbreaker rattled the jian in his hand. The straight sword leapt out of its sheath, unbalancing Ouyang for a moment. Li Ming took his swordbreaker in both hands and torqued around and swung down.

Ouyang shuffled out the way, the sharp tip hissing past his nose, and stomped his foot, regaining his balance.

Li Ming cursed. The swordbreaker was slow, too slow. If he'd been faster by a hair, he would have sundered Ouyang clean in half. He lifted the heavy blade and advanced.

Arcing his left hand high above his head, Ouyang leaned in and shot his blade straight out. Li Ming braked instantly, stopping just shy of the tip. Ouyang lunged. Li Ming jumped back.

Assumed the Sancai Shi, swordbreaker held by his waist.

Aimed the tip at Ouyang.

Waited.

Ouyang stared.

Li Ming stared back.

They waited some more.

Behind them, the sounds of war redoubled. Cai Yan screamed. Ghazan uttered a war cry. Someone gurgled in his death throes.

Li Ming eased his rear foot forward.

Ouyang remained still.

"You're an iron-ranked biaohang. How the devil did you get your hands on a weapon like this?" Ouyang said.

Li Ming adjusted his foot ever so slightly.

Ouyang dipped his sword to the left.

Li Ming shifted his swordbreaker.

Ouyang lifted the weapon to the right.

"Bold of you, to challenge me—"

Li Ming stepped in with a massive cut.

Ouyang retreated, sword flowing in a rising parry. An ordinary sword might have skipped off the flat of the razor-sharp jian. The swordbreaker just blew right through it, opening a hole in Ouyang's defenses. Li Ming cycled the enormously heavy weapon into him and thrust.

Ouyang nimbly hopped away, suddenly out of range, lifting his sword.

Li Ming slashed. Ouyang dodged. Li Ming thrust. Ouyang retreated. Now they stood in the dead ground between the airship and the fallen civilians. The strength bled from Li Ming's arms, and he settled into his guard. The weapon was a leaden weight, and he could not, *must not*, let it drop.

"I know what you're thinking," Ouyang said. "You're trying to force me away from the bunker and move the abyssal field away from it. Not a bad strategy, but the field extends to one *li* in all directions. You are not going to save your friends this way."

It was no idle boast. The mist hung over the world as far as Li Ming could see.

"Your friends aren't coming to help," Ouyang continued. "My men outnumber them. I don't know how you broke through, and frankly I don't care. Every moment you spend dallying here, my men are killing your friends."

As if to punctuate his statement, Jiang Long screamed in agony, his voice dissolving to liquid.

"I am immortal. I can maintain the abyssal field forever. Time is on *my* side."

Ouyang was right. Li Ming had to finish this fast, shut down the magic and take out the rest of the White Tigers.

But that was what Ouyang wanted. To goad Li Ming into rushing in with a clumsy attack, then a quick void and riposte. And that would be that.

Li Ming needed an edge.

His thoughts turned to the swordbreaker. A powerful tool, but only a tool. His primary weapon lay between his ears. If he used it poorly, it would be turned against him. Ouyang would surely exploit any openings Li Ming gave him.

Li Ming had only one course of action.

Give Ouyang what he wanted.

Li Ming thrust, questing for Ouyang's chest. Ouyang easily stepped aside, his sword flashing quick a tight arc. The weapon's mass conspired against Li, fighting him as he braked, reversed, snapped it back.

Too slow.

The point of Ouyang's sword sliced across the back of Li's right hand. It should have severed his tendons and rendered his fingers useless. His cut-resistant tactical glove held fast. Even so, the sword shocked his hand into temporary numbness.

And now Ouyang snapped his sword down to the horizontal, aligning it with Li Ming's exposed belly, and leapt.

Li Ming pulled the swordbreaker down into himself, its weight now aiding him, bringing it to bear against the incoming blade. The jian dashed itself against a raised ridge, throwing out sparks. Li Ming punched the swordbreaker out, lifting it through an uppercut-like motion, raising it above and over and past his head, deflecting the jian to the side. In that same motion, he spun, turning to Ouyang, and slashed.

Too slow.

Ouyang nimbly leapt out of the way. Waited for a split second, long enough for the swordbreaker to complete its arc. And thrust into Li Ming's exposed side.

Li Ming swiveled out of the way, smashing his swordbreaker into the sword. Steel clang against steel. The point sliced across his helmet, barely missing his ear. Li Ming let the swordbreaker fall, its weight carrying it through an arc, then stepped in and slashed upwards at Ouyang's retreating hand.

A ridge slammed into the hilt of the jian.

Ouyang's hand blasted away.

Yelling, Li Ming pounced and swung for Ouyang's head.

Ouyang stepped back.

The swordbreaker swung harmlessly through space.

Li brought his weapon into himself, back into the guard, aiming it at Ouyang, forestalling a counter. Ouyang assumed his own guard.

Stalemate.

No more games. No more talk. The men stared each other down. Ouyang's qi roared out of him like a waterfall, crashing into Li Ming, trying to drown him. Li Ming's own qi flared, but it was a candle in a downpour, flickering in the rain. Ouyang breathed smoothly and calmly. Li Ming panted, his entire body shaking, his arms trembling.

Li Ming's arms grew sore, his hands stiff, his muscles weary. This next exchange had to be the last. The others were counting on him.

Li Ming's weapon dipped.

Lowered.

Dropped.

Ouyang lunged in with a viper-quick thrust.

Li Ming stepped in to the right and torqued his swordbreaker to the left, the first half of the earth strike. The weapons clashed again. Ouyang's weapon dropped, covering his lowline, pre-empting a horizontal slash. Gripping his swordbreaker in both hands, roaring with a voice like thunder, Li Ming raised his weapon, leapt in, and swung.

Ouyang froze in place, shaken by the sudden rally. At the last moment he threw out his sword in a desperate block.

Keen edge rang on reinforced ridge.

Crumpled.

Shattered.

The jian snapped in twain, sending sparks flying in every direction.

Momentum drove the swordbreaker onward, accelerated by its augmented mass. The blade crashed into the immortal's collarbone, snapped it in half, and drove him down to the earth.

Ouyang gasped.

The abyssal field cut out.

And plasma fire raged anew.

Ouyang lay on the ground, gasping, twitching, trying to lift his now-useless sword arm, his face contorted in puzzlement and fear.

Li Ming stepped up to him, aiming the point at his eye.

"Surrender," Li Ming said.

"How... How did—"

"All warfare is based on deception."

The swordbreaker was slow, but it wasn't *that* slow. He was tired, but not *that* tired. Once he'd shown Ouyang what he'd wanted the immortal to see—what the immortal *wanted* to see—the final blow became inevitable.

Ouyang muttered a curse.

"How can a mortal defeat an immortal?" Ouyang asked.

"Happens all the time in the jianghu. Surrender now, and I won't—"

"WANJIAN WANSUI!"

Ouyang's qi blazed bright, surging into his reality shapers, his muscles, his lungs. His voice was thunder, his muscles quicksilver. Li Ming trembled under the weight of his voice. Ouyang rolled over, away from the swordbreaker.

Or tried.

The broken collarbone slowed him down. His right arm flopped, his qi faltered, his body lagged. He lurched, supported himself with his good arm, kicked up—

Li Ming drove the point of his swordbreaker through his skull.

Discharged the earth qi into the ground.

Blasted fire through the blade.

All at once, a huge surge of qi rushed from the body and dissipated into thin air.

Ouyang was done.

Li Ming pulled the weapon out of the remains. And scanned.

The shooting had stopped. Figures emerged from the darkness. The collectors got up, tending to their wounded. Ms. Rao lay on the ground, groaning, flopping about.

The airship's engines screamed.

Li spun around. The crew chief hung on to a grab rail for dear life with one hand, the other hovering over his sidearm. The pilots yelled at each other.

The door raised.

"STOP! STOP RIGHT THERE!"

The door shut.

The airship lifted off the ground.

Li Ming slashed.

A crescent of metal qi, hard and cutting, flashed from the swordbreaker. It crossed the distance in an instant, smashing into the port side thruster. The aircraft tilted sharply, trying to compensate.

Li Ming slashed again.

A second energy blade leapt forth and smashed the starboard thruster.

The Phoenix fell like the brick it was. It crashed straight down into the earth, throwing out a cloud of dirt, digging a shallow grave.

Running to the downed aircraft, Li Ming switched his swordbreaker to his other hand and drew his pistol.

The starboard door burst open. The crew chief stumbled out.

Li Ming aimed.

"HANDS UP! DO IT NOW!" he ordered.

The crew chief's hands flew into the air.

"We've got nothing to do with this! We didn't know!" he pleaded.

"Call out the rest of the crew!" Li Ming ordered. "Tell them to come with their hands up!"

"Guys! It's over! Raise your hands and come out!"

Nothing happened.

Li Ming swept his gaze left to right, searching for a trick, a sign, a way to cover all three men at once. If they abandoned the crew chief, broke to the port side—

The pilots staggered out the open door, their arms raised.

"On your knees, all of you!" Li Ming yelled.

"We're just the duty aircrew! Commander Ouyang didn't cut us in!" the pilot said.

"Shut up! Down on your knees!"

The men dropped to their knees, hands still raised.

"Don't kill us! We've got families! We're just doing our jobs! We didn't know he was planning to rip you off!" the crew chief blabbered.

"Then I'm sure you'll cooperate fully with the authorities," Li Ming said.

The men looked at each other and nodded vigorously.

"Yes, yes, we're not part of this plot!" the pilot said.

"Li Ming!" Cai Yan called.

"Over here! Do *not* approach from behind! Come to my left!"

Footsteps pounded behind him. Li Ming continued aiming at the aircrew with one hand, his weapon trembling. The cut had scored him good. With the adrenaline fading, pain blossomed across the back of his hand. His tendons froze. He didn't know if he could pull the trigger if he had to. But so long as the aircrew believed, it was enough.

Cai Yan stepped into his line of sight. And Ghazan.

"Is everyone okay?" Li Ming asked.

Cai Yan stopped. Sputtered. Looked away.

"We're the only ones left," Ghazan said.

His words were an icy fist to the gut. For a moment Li Ming couldn't speak. Then he sucked down a breath of air.

"Secure them," Li Ming said. "I'll cover."

Ghazan pulled flexicuffs from his bag—*why did he have such things on a hunting expedition?*—and cuffed the prisoners one by one. Cai Yan walked away, muttering to herself, wrapping her arms around her chest.

One by one, Ghazan tied the men's hands behind their backs. They didn't resist. Li Ming slowly put his weapons away and allowed himself to turn around.

The collectors had collected themselves. The wounded crawled off to the side, treating themselves if they could, helping others if they couldn't. The stronger among them checked the dead mercenaries and secured their weapons. Their foreman tended to Ms. Rao.

"Are you okay?" Li Ming asked.

Cai Yan shook her head, looking at the ground.

"They... protected... me," she whispered.

"It was their job."

"I... Why?"

Li Ming grabbed her shoulders.

"Cai Yan. Look at me."

She looked up. Tears streaked down her face. She'd shrunk into herself, her eyes wide open, her shoulders trembling.

"You're in charge now. That's why they protected you. Make their sacrifice worth it."

She let out a sob. Sucked down a breath. Leaned into him.

"Sorry. I... I'm not thinking straight now. I..."

He held her close, pressing her into his chest. The warmth of her enveloped him. She rested her hands on his spine, bracing herself against him, not quite settling into a full embrace.

"Breathe. Take your time."

They stayed that way for a moment.

Abruptly Cai Yan released herself from him. Raising her arms high, she closed her eyes and concentrated.

Warm, white light descended from the heavens. It washed over Li Ming, over the wounded, over the world. His pains vanished in an instant. His fatigue dissolved away. He wriggled his fingers, finding no trace of injury. He drew himself upright, renewed, refreshed, restored.

Ms. Rao moaned, rubbed her temples, and wobbled unsteadily to her feet.

"What... happened?" Ms. Rao whispered.

"I should ask you that," Li Ming said.

"Damned mercenaries betrayed us," Foreman Hu snarled.

The collectors were picking themselves up, wiping off their bloody blades, checking that the mercenaries were well and truly finished.

"What did they do?" Li Ming asked.

"We were processing the bodies when this mess started," Foreman Hu said. "They told us that Commander Ouyang wanted to speak to all of us. The five mercenaries over there escorted us here. They didn't tell us what they were doing, just to wait until Ouyang was done.

"Immediately after he shot your boss, the White Tigers aimed their weapons at us and told us to freeze. When you broke through their lines, you distracted them for a moment. Long enough for us to fight back."

"Thanks for helping us," Ms. Rao said.

"No problem," Cai Yan said.

"I took care of Ouyang," Li Ming said, gesturing at the body.

Ms. Rao snarled. "A dog's death is too good for him."

"You didn't know what he was up to?"

"None of us did. But I see you took prisoners."

"The aircrew says they don't know anything. Cai Yan, what about the attackers? Did you take any alive?"

She wiped her eyes. Inhaled deeply. Exhaled sharply. And only now did Li Ming see the blood splashed across her hands, her sleeves, her clothing, all of her. She stank of blood, of guts, of death, of war.

"No."

"*Gaisi*," Ms. Rao cursed. "What the devil did White Tiger want anyway?"

"Money drives men mad," Foreman Hu said darkly. "Between the beast carcasses and the artifacts, you could live like an emperor. Like a god."

"White Tiger is one of the Ten Corporations. They have more money than the heavens. Why would they do this?" Cai Yan said.

"We can worry about that later," Ghazan interjected. "We need to figure out what to do next."

All eyes turned on Cai Yan.

She deflated under their gaze. The strong, confident woman Li Ming had known was gone. Now there was only a picture of fractured femininity, a daughter who had lost her father and many of the men she had called brothers.

"We need to get out of here," Li Ming said.

"We go back to Lianghe and demand answers from White Tiger," Ghazan said.

Heat blossomed in Li's chest. An act like this cried out to the heavens for vengeance. When the wicked reared their heads, the righteous must cut them down. It was the way of the jianghu.

But...

"No," Li Ming said.

"Are you crazy? We must—"

"Think it through! Lianghe is crawling with cultivators. If we confront White Tiger there, we'll have to fight our way through the whole city. It's not a war we can win."

Ghazan spat a curse in Yueyu, dark and evil and venomous.

"They betrayed us! We cannot let them get away with it!" Ghazan said.

"We won't," Cai Yan said. "But we can't do that if we're dead."

"We must gather our strength before we take on the most powerful mercenary corporation in Xiazhou," Li Ming said.

"You won't be alone," Ms. Rao said. "The Jianghu Association will launch an investigation and sanction White Tiger. Even they cannot escape the wrath of the rivers and lakes."

"We'll gather the evidence, the bodies, the artifacts, everything that can be recovered. We return to Bao An, alert the authorities, and call in every biaohang who works for us," Li Ming said.

"And after that?" Ghazan demanded.

"We prepare for war," Cai Yan said.

Chapter Forty-Three

Brothers of the Blade

It was a long march to the cars. An even longer drive to Bao An.

As Ghazan stood watch over the prisoners, the task force organized the scene. The collectors recovered the bodies of the White Tigers and their gear. The women worked their phones. Li Ming retrieved the artifacts.

And the bodies of the biaohang.

There were so many. Lan Yi and Zhang Xinhua, who had held back the White Tigers with their bodies, buying everyone else time to regroup. Song Huizhong and Jiang Long, blasted at point-blank, in turn surrounded by more plasma-burned bodies. The Kang brothers, shot and stabbed and slashed side-by-side, keeping the remaining White Tigers away from Cai Yan. Cai Mengyang, the first martyr.

Blood ran like rivers and gathered in lakes across the floor of the bunker. Now released from this mortal coil, the men were united in death, their vital fluids mingling with one another to become a sea of red.

What a waste of life.

Gently, reverently, Li Ming and the collectors documented the scene and recovered the bodies. All of them. This was not women's work. They had suffered more than enough. One by one, they sucked the dead, their gear, and the artifacts into their interspatial bags.

An hour after the battle, all that remained was blood.

With the airship out of commission, they had to return to Dayong's rented vehicles. Everyone held together during the long trek. Li Ming took point, navigating through the hills and the forest. Ghazan managed the prisoners at the tail of the formation. The collectors armed themselves with confiscated infinity guns and pulled security, falling back on the tactics and techniques and procedures they had learned during their time as conscripts. Safely protected in the middle of the group, the women called up contacts and planned their next step.

The sun had set by the time they returned to the cars. Li Ming called a quick break for dinner and hygiene. Cai Yan had brought a portable camping toilet with her, and everyone took turns using it. Li Ming cut the prisoners loose and allowed them to feed themselves. The second they were done, the collectors tied them up with sturdy ropes.

Li Ming and Ghazan worked over the rented vehicles. They each had an onboard satellite navigation and tracking system. Perfect for cross-country expeditions, a liability when escaping and evading a mercenary company. With their multitools, they turned off and stripped out the vulnerable computers.

By the time Li Ming was done, a fresh wave of fatigue washed over him. His body was climbing down from the combat high, shifting into rest and digest mode. His qi was depleted, leaving him feeling like an empty shell. Aches and pains and tension came roaring back. His body screamed for rest. Even a bottle of beast broth did nothing for him.

But it was still a long way to Bao An.

The civilians volunteered to drive. It was the least they could do, they said, and the biaohang were close to collapse.

Li Ming was in no shape to protest. He simply climbed into the backseat of the second car, leaned back and closed his eyes.

Cai Yan sat next to him.

Slipped her fingers between his.

And rested her head against his shoulder.

They stayed that way until they reached Bao An.

Well after midnight, deep into the hour of the ox, the four-car convoy rolled into Bao An. For the last leg of the trip, Ghazan drove the lead vehicle to Luoyang District, to the Cai family home.

The streets were totally, completely, empty. Every window was darkened, every alley abandoned, every door locked. The streetlights illuminated a maze of desolated roads leading deeper into the heart of the sleeping city. In the nightlife districts, in the Cultivator Quarter, in the places where life never stopped, bright lights burned like distant beacons, staining the night and banishing the stars and moon. But here, in the historic district, there was only stillness and quiet.

Past the mouth of the hutong, Li made out two men. Cultivators. Their qi field dominated the narrow street, loose but alert, ready to condense into flame or frost at a moment's notice. Decked out in tactical gear, in full armor and infinity guns and reality shapers, they were ready to lay waste to the entire neighborhood.

And they wore Dayong patches.

Cai Yan called out to them. They snapped to attention, beckoning the party over. After a quick exchange of passwords and introductions, the guards let the party through the gates.

More biaohang stood in the inner garden, a four-man quick reaction force. Gathered around a table, they stood as Cai Yan strode through the entrance. Li Ming nodded at them as he passed.

Cai Yong waited by the waterfall. The moment she saw him, a sob escaped her lips.

"Yanyan!" he said. "Are you—"

She flew into her brother's arms. Cai Yong held her tight, rocking her gently, whispering into her ear. Cai Yan mumbled incoherently into his ear, tears staining his load carrier. By the gate, a man and a woman in formal robes stood in awkward silence, watching the scene.

The Cai elders.

Li Ming approached them and bowed.

"I am sorry for your loss."

They stiffened. Blood fled their faces. Grandmother Cai's eyes glistened. But they remained still, their faces stony, their dignity untouched.

"How did they die?" Grandfather Cai asked.

"They died protecting Cai Yan from mercenaries."

"A death worthy of the jianghu."

"They were all heroes. I did what I could but…"

"Xiao Yan told us you slew the enemy leader. You saved everyone. You have nothing to apologize for."

Li Ming nodded. Blinked. Drew in a breath.

"We recovered the remains of your son, and those of every Dayong biaohang who fell in battle."

"They were all our sons. Thank you."

The Cais bowed back.

Two men in dark suits strode through the inner gate. They donned sleek headsets, carried identical chunky scrolls, and wore shiny badges worn on lanyards around their necks. Li Ming instantly made them for who they were.

The shorter of the two held up his badge.

"I am Investigator Hong from the Criminal Investigation Bureau. This is my partner, Investigator Chen. On behalf of the Bureau, please accept our condolences."

"Thank you," Li Ming said.

"I understand this is a difficult time for everyone, and that you've just concluded a long drive. Ordinarily we'd arrange for interviews in the morning. However, we are given to understand you are in the possession of evidence and bodies."

"That's correct."

"We respectfully request that you hand them over to us. This will help us expedite the investigation."

"What do you need?"

"Everything."

Bodies. Guns. Gear. Even clothing. A team of crime scene technicians, stationed in the inner courtyard, collected and documented everything the team had recovered from the bunker. Li Ming had to hand over everything on his person before he was allowed to take a shower.

The rest of the night passed in a blur. The investigators took preliminary statements. The collectors collaborated with the technicians to account for the gear. Medics checked the wounded. Ms. Rao talked non-stop into her scroll, dropping so much jargon Li Ming couldn't follow. Representatives from the Jianghu Association took charge of the recovered relics. Police officers hauled the prisoners away and guarded key locations. Next to them, the biaohang stood watch, maintaining a war footing.

At dawn, the process was finally complete. The civilians took over the unoccupied guest rooms and living room. The Cais returned to the family estate, Ms. Rao still in tow. Li Ming flopped upon his bed. The second his head touched the pillow, he was out like a light.

Consciousness returned in the afternoon. He stared groggily at his clock for a few moments, until his brain kicked in and he realized it had been nearly half a day since their return. It was the first time he'd slept in so long for... He couldn't remember. Maybe his entire life.

He stood by the window and assumed the Sancai Shi.

And stood.

And breathed.

In the space of a day, his whole world had turned itself inside out. A hunting expedition became an exploration became a rip. How the devil had that happened? He had no idea. All he knew was that he had to ground himself, and zhan zhuang was his method.

Five minutes with the left side forward, five minutes with the right. Through it all, he breathed and stood and thought of nothing but the qi circulating through him. The fatigue mostly melted away, leaving a tingling in his arms and legs.

He was exhausted. Energy sensations ought to be much stronger than this.

The rest of the guest house was waking up. The collectors gathered in the living room, talking to each other, piecing together their stories. Ghazan sat at a table in the dining room, sipping at a bottle of beast broth.

Li's belly announced its existence. He ignored it.

He showered, shaved, slipped on a fresh suit. And made his way to the main hall.

Last night, before leaving, Investigators Chen and Hong had promised to return in the afternoon to take everyone's statements. They were here now, along with a platoon of their colleagues. In private rooms, in offices, in small nooks, the cops did their work, talking to everyone involved in the battle of the bunker, and at the periphery of the event.

Li Ming didn't have to talk to them now. But he wanted to get this over and done with as quickly as he could.

For the next half-hour, the investigators grilled him in the conference room. Li described the expedition from start to finish, from the moment he arrived in Lianghe to the convoy's return. It was like being in the military again, issuing a lengthy report. The investigators took copious notes and asked plenty of questions, but treated him as a witness, not a suspect.

At last, Investigator Chen wrapped up the interview.

"Thank you for your time. I'm sure you appreciate the sensitivity of the situation. Please refrain from sharing details of this investigation with anyone outside Dayong. Including and especially the media."

"What is the government going to do with White Tiger?" Li Ming asked.

"That remains to be decided."

"And what does that mean?"

"It means we'll have to conclude our investigation before taking action," Investigator Hong said.

"White Tiger ripped us off, killed my colleagues, and you say you have to 'conclude your investigation'?"

Investigator Chen held up his hands.

"All we're saying is that we need to respect due process. We must let the wheels of justice turn. Even in the jianghu, there are laws all men must obey."

"Does White Tiger answer to the law?"

"*Everyone* answers to the law."

"I hope so. I've got one last question."

"Go ahead."

"What does *wanjian wansui* mean?"

The investigators exchanged a glance.

"We'll have to get back to you on that," Investigator Chen said.

"I thought you said everyone answers to the law?"

"It's not like that," Investigator Hong said. "We need to clarify key details before we can answer that."

"Really."

"No need for cynicism here, Li Biaohang. We just want to make sure we have the facts before we can answer that."

"I'll hold you to that."

Questioning continued into the evening. Men and women in suits, armed with sleek devices and elegant bags, entered the main hall. Li Ming confined himself to his room, meditating and practicing gongfu, leaving only for dinner and for another shower.

The witnesses couldn't leave. Not until the interviews were over, until the Bureau decided if there were an ongoing threat to Dayong. The compound was the safest place in the city, and even White Tiger would hesitate to strike at Dayong here. Dinner was takeout from the eateries along the hutong, ordered over the phone and vetted by the cops.

Li Ming found Ghazan in the kitchen, working his way through a massive plate of steamed dumplings. Li Ming sat next to him and slurped up a carton of pork noodles.

For a while they ate in silence, two brothers of the blade collecting their thoughts and tending to their bodies. Halfway through his food, Li Ming finally spoke.

"Thanks for protecting Cai Yan."

"The others did the hard work. I only reached her at the end," Ghazan said.

"What happened after I left the bunker?"

"I flanked the enemy. Finished them with my bayonet. I got six of them."

Ghazan spoke calmly, matter-of-factly, as if he were describing the contents of his dumplings.

"Good work," Li Ming said.

"It was nothing. We escaped the worst of it."

"I heard the plasma fire when the abyssal field went down."

"I saw it. It was... terrible. Point blank gunfire. Mutual slayings. A few barely got shields up in time. The rest... you saw what happened."

"At least you weren't hurt."

"There is that. How did you defeat Ouyang?"

For the second time that day, he recounted his duel. But this time he was working through it with a fellow student of the martial arts. They broke it down step by step, dissected Li Ming's mistakes, figured out what he should do next time.

"I didn't know you had a magic swordbreaker," Ghazan said.

He kept his tone light, but his eyebrows furrowed and an accusatory tone stained his voice.

"Me neither. Father didn't tell me until after my first visit to the Three Worlds Emporium."

How long was that ago? A month? More? He couldn't recall. In his mind, everything that had come before the battle was an undifferentiated smear of sound and color, a vague recollection of a former life.

"You have a weapon fit for conquerors and bodyguards," Ghazan said.

"Now I just need to figure out how to use it."

Li Ming hadn't told him about the Li Family Magic Weapon Style. Some things had to be kept secret. Ghazan would understand.

At the hour of the pig, the final hour of the day, everyone gathered in the main hall. Investigators Chen and Hong waited for them at the far end, flanking a tall woman in an embroidered dress. Li Ming instantly knew she was an immortal. Her bearing, her flawless features, her old eyes and youthful grace, they betrayed her for what she was.

But she was no cultivator. Her qi score was a mere 104 points.

"Thank you for your cooperation," Investigator Chen said. "We've gathered your statements and have delivered the evidence to the labs for further testing. Our hearts are with you during this terrible time. Rest assured that the Criminal Investigation Bureau will do everything in its power to bring the perpetrators to justice."

"What about White Tiger?" Cai Yan asked.

The woman stepped up and bowed deeply.

"I am Wang Meilin, General Counsel of White Tiger. On behalf of my employer, please accept our most sincere apologies and condolences. We disavow the actions of Commander Ouyang Mingzhong. In complete violation of corporate policies and the law, he attempted to betray you and seize the Yue artifacts for himself. His deeds have blackened our names, and we shall strive to make things right."

"'Disavow'," Ghazan parroted with a sneer. "What if he had succeeded? Would you still be here?"

Now she stood ramrod-straight, her eyes burning.

"We would have deploedy our forces to hunt him down. Justice *will* be served."

"Lawyer Wang, a demi-platoon of White Tiger operatives went rogue and tried to make war on another biaoju," Cai Yong said. "You understand we cannot simply take your words at face value."

"I understand completely. I am authorized to reveal to you that the men who attacked your colleagues—your brothers and sister—were not White Tiger personnel."

"Who are they?" Li Ming demanded.

Lawyer Wang's mask of confidence crumbled. Or perhaps it was simply an act.

"Regrettably, we do not know. We have used many methods of attempting to verify their identity: retina scans, fingerprints, DNA tests. They were not on our payroll. The only person we can conclusively say who was part of White Tiger was Ouyang."

"What about the aircrew?"

"They were most cooperative," Investigator Hong said. "We are satisfied that they had nothing to do with this incident. They simply had the misfortune of being on duty when Ouyang executed his plot. He used his position to order them to ferry his men to the objective. That was the extent of their involvement."

"Does anyone else know who attacked us?" Cai Yan asked.

This time, Ms. Rao answered.

"They were martial cultivators from all over the province. Freelancers not affiliated with any registered organization. Half of them have criminal records and were expelled from the Jianghu Association."

"What do they have in common?"

"We're looking into it," Investigator Chen said.

"*Wanjian wansui*," Li Ming said. "Ouyang shouted that to signal the attack. Does that ring a bell?"

"That is the battle cry of the Wanjian Hui," Investigator Chen said.

"How do you write it?" Ghazan asked.

"'*Wan*' as in the number, '*jian*' as in the weapon, '*hui*' from the word 'society'."

Three characters floated into Li's head.

Ten Thousand Swords Society.

Ms. Rao paled. The collectors glanced at each other. A few of the older biaohang frowned and muttered to themselves.

"What is this Ten Thousand Swords Society?" Ghazan asked.

"Devil cultivators," Lawyer Wang spat.

"A secret society of criminal cultivators," Investigator Hong clarified. "While they originate from the Central Plains, their tentacles spread far and wide across Xiazhou. In the Zhongxia Republic, they've kept their activities low-key. But it seems the chance to loot a Yue bunker proved too tempting to pass up."

"What do they want?" Li Ming asked.

Cai Yong answered.

"Power."

Everyone turned to him.

"Power at any price. They believe that the weak are meat to the strong, and that only the strongest have the right to rule. They seek to overthrow the world order and rebuild society from the ground-up to reflect their ideology. They will stop at nothing to gain more power, more wealth, more influence. They walk the path of devils."

"Sounds like the Yue Dynasty," Investigator Hong remarked. "Only the most powerful cultivators were allowed to rule."

Ghazan glared at him but said nothing.

"They operate mainly in the underworld," Cai Yong continued. "In the Zhongxia Republic they are most active in Taiping and the coastal cities. The last time they were spotted in Bao An was twenty years ago, and Father crushed their cell after three years."

"Have they returned?" Cai Yan wondered. "Was this a revenge operation?"

"I wouldn't be surprised if it were," Cai Yong said. "Ouyang was an immortal, wasn't he? He had plenty of time to plot his revenge."

"We don't even know if the subjects belonged to the Wanjian Hui," Investigator Chen said. "Just because their leader used their battle cry doesn't mean they are part of the organization."

"But we have reason to suspect that the Wanjian Hui has infiltrated White Tiger," Li Ming said.

All eyes turned to Lawyer Wang.

"We will launch an internal investigation immediately. If we find any unlawful elements among our ranks, we will purge them immediately and hand them over to the police. On this we pledge our honor," she said.

"You'd better," Ghazan growled.

"That's not enough," Cai Yan said. "You allowed a devil cultivator to climb the ranks in your organization. You allowed him to create a gang of devil cultivators. You allowed him to command an expedition, requisition your company assets, and use them to kill my father and employees."

"We acknowledge that our internal processes failed to prevent this. We *will* fix them. We will make things right," Lawyer Wang promised.

"It's not enough. We are a small family-run company. We lost almost half our manpower in one day. A loss like this could destroy us!"

"We sympathize with your loss, but the Ten Thousand Swords Society was responsible for this."

"*You* were responsible for allowing Wanjian Hui members into your ranks. You armed them. The blood of my father and my biaohang are on *your* hands!"

Lawyer Wang glowered. Her nose lifted, her jaw set, her eyes grew bright. Now Li Ming sensed the true persona underneath, the corporate shark whose only objective was to protect White Tiger's reputation.

"What more do you want?" Lawyer Wang asked evenly.

"We demand reparations. Reparations for this act of perfidy by a high-ranking White Tiger member, for the murder of my father and fellow biaohang, for the damages your man caused us," Cao Yan said.

"He is not our man. Not anymore."

"You still bear responsibility. We will have satisfaction."

"We are a victim as much as you."

"Your negligence made this attack possible."

The women glared at each other. Cai Yan's qi erupted from her body, pounding into Lawyer Wang like a waterfall. The older woman stood where she was, meeting her gaze with eyes of flame, utterly unperturbed by the subtle assault.

Ms. Rao broke the deadlock.

"Ms. Cai is correct. Under the laws of the Zhongxia Republic, and the bylaws of the Jianghu Association, White Tiger bears responsibility for this attack."

"What do you mean?" Lawyer Wang demanded, now turning to Ms. Rao.

"While Ouyang might have acted as a member of the Ten Thousand Swords Society at the time of the assault, he used the powers and authority granted to him as a member of White Tiger to facilitate it. White Tiger may not have directly participated in the attack, but a case can be made that its internal failures led to the attack. Thus, White Tiger bears liability."

"Are you a lawyer?"

"No, but that's what the Jianghu Association's legal counsel told me. I'd be happy to get his words in writing for you. He also said that if White Tiger will not offer reparations, then Dayong has every right to take White Tiger to court."

Lawyer Wang frowned deeply.

"The Ten Thousand Swords Society is larger than this... trifling matter. Ms. Cai, have your lawyer contact me. I'm sure we can work out a suitable settlement."

"I'll do that," Cai Yan said.

The qi wave subsided. Everyone relaxed.

"What happens next?" Li Ming asked.

"You are now free to return to your lives," Investigator Chen said. "Ms. Rao, collectors, if you require transportation and police protection, please let us know. The Bureau will be glad to assist."

"For our part, we will pursue all available leads," Investigator Hong added. "We also trust that White Tiger will cooperate with our investigation."

"Of course," Lawyer Wang said.

"I have received special instructions from the headquarters of the Jianghu Association concerning this situation," Ms. Rao said.

"Let's hear it," Cai Yong said.

Ms. Rao pulled out her scroll and cleared her throat.

"Dayong has uncovered the find of the century. You have endured incredible hardships and retrieved many invaluable Yue artifacts. You will be compensated handsomely for your work. I will get an accurate figure from our assessors later, but you may expect a sum of no less than one hundred million yuan."

One. Hundred. Million. A number so astronomically huge Li Ming had no context to understand it.

"We do ask that you keep quiet about it," Ms. Rao added.

"It's hush money, isn't it?" Ghazan said.

Her voice grew cold and flat.

"There are countless people out there who seek Yue artifacts. Not all of them have your best interests at heart. The technology you have seen would rightly be classified as a state secret. I'm certain you do not wish for gangsters, devil cultivators and foreign spies to go hunting for you, or your prize."

"Thought so," Ghazan said, crossing his arms.

"Finally, Li, Ga San and Cai Biaohang will be promoted to the next rank, effective immediately."

The words hung in the air for a moment.

"Immediately?" Li Ming asked. "Why? *How?* I haven't even completed my six-month probation period!"

"You slew a number of novel nuhou, recovered multiple Yue relics, and defeated devil cultivators in battle, including one with a qi score over thirteen thousand points higher than yours. This is an achievement worthy of a gold ranker. I only regret that regulations forbid us from promoting you beyond bronze rank. For now."

Cai Yan beamed, but grief weighed down her eyes.

"Congratulations, Li Ming!" Cai Yan said.

"Thank you," Li Ming said, his heart numb.

He'd been looking forward to this moment. To becoming a bronze-ranked biaohang, a seasoned and trusted member of the jianghu. But... not like this. Not at such high cost.

"Is there a threat to us?" Cai Yong asked.

"Not that we know of. There are no indications that Dayong is being targeted specifically by the Ten Thousand Swords Society. For all we know, this could simply be an opportunistic hit. Ouyang might have planned to manipulate you into doing the difficult work of clearing out the ruins, then seize the artifacts and eliminate all witnesses."

With what little Li Ming knew, it was the only conclusion that made sense.

"Without prisoners to question, we can only speculate," Investigator Hong added. "However..."

His voice trailed off. He frowned, stroking his chin, as though trying to coax the words from his throat.

"'However'?" Cai Yong prompted.

Investigator Hong stayed where he was, his frown deepening. Li Ming just about sensed the gears in his brain seizing up, grinding to a halt, unable to put the finishing touches on a complex thought.

At last, Investigator Hong sighed, and spoke.

"You are all part of the jianghu. You are always in danger."

Chapter Forty-Four

Where All Suffering Ends

The traditional mourning period lasted for forty-nine days. It was the privilege of civilians. For warriors those who stood at the gates between civilization and barbarians, it was an extravagance no one could afford.

Li Ming missed most of it. The following day, the government, the Jianghu Association and White Tiger had requested his presence at the Yue bunker. Ghazan's, too. They wanted the two of them to walk through the site, recreate the final confrontation, account for the recovered artifacts—and guard the scene against trespassers.

Li Ming and Ghazan returned to the bunker ready for war, backed by a platoon of Special Military Police troopers. They had expected a battle with a horde of nuhou. They found only dried blood and silence. As the troopers moved off to clear the surrounding forest, the biaohang stood guard and tended to endless queries from countless officials.

Cai Yan, the bereaved, had the luxury of staying in Bao An—and the duty of organizing the funerals.

Half a day after their return to the bunker, the reclamation team arrived. Engineers, archaeologists, laborers, an official writer from the Jianghu Association, and embedded journalists from major news outlets. The bunker was the find of the year, of the decade, and the world clamored for more information.

Neither Li Ming nor Ghazan spoke to the journalists. They simply recited boilerplate statements composed by Dayong's lawyer and deferred them to the experts. Ordinarily, success in the jianghu required seizing glory whenever the chance reared its head, but the biaohang didn't want to let anyone know where they were. The Ten Thousand Swords Society least of all.

In his downtime, Li Ming consumed every bit of information he could find about the Wanjianhui. They were a secretive organization, leaving whispers and rumors in their wake. He found stories of duels, raids, massacres attributed to the secret society. Legends of ancient relics, powerful weapons, deadly beasts and spirits, all of them under the command of the society. Tales of the most powerful, dangerous, yet obscure martial immortals to walk the land, all of whom were pledged to the society.

Very, very, *very* few of these stories were verified facts.

The Jianghu Association offered what information they could, a ten-page dossier heavy on speculation and light on information. White Tiger claimed no knowledge of the Ten Thousand Swords Society. The government refused to disclose what they claimed was 'classified information'.

In the end, Li was no more knowledgeable about the Ten Thousand Swords than when he had left Bao An.

Save for one fact.

They still maintained a presence in the Central Plains.

The Central Plains tethered on the brink of anarchy. The perfect place for a secret society to do business. Though the Wanjianhui ran a handful of legitimate enterprises in the Central Plains, they kept an extremely low profile, disclosing little about their affairs. No doubt because they didn't want to give the local authorities a reason to investigate them in depth.

If Li Ming ever had cause to visit the Central Plains, he would have to take extra precautions.

Ghazan, too, spent his downtime reading. Usually he disappeared into a quiet corner, whipped out the scroll he had recovered, and engrossed himself in reading the ancient classics. Li Ming didn't blame him. He didn't think he had registered the relic with the Jianghu Association. It was technically a violation of the rules, but as Ghazan had said, it was just a consumer-grade device. Ghazan was simply reading about the history, traditions and culture of his ancestors.

Still, the few times Li Ming had caught him reading, Ghazan cleared the screen.

The following day, the specialists finally figured out how to safely recover the remaining Yue relics. Over the next four days, they dismantled the cosmic tap, pumped out the great vats, disassembled the computers, repaired the damaged stairwells, cleaned off the blood and feces and mold. By the time they were done, there was nothing left of the bunker but an empty shell.

That they could leave to lesser archaeologists and thrill-seekers. Everything of value was gone, claimed by the Zhongxia Republic and the Jianghu Association. Ms. Rao promised adequate compensation for Dayong's efforts. Li Ming would only believe it when he saw his paycheck.

Li Ming and Ghazan returned to Bao An on the final day of the wake, escorting the convoy to the branch headquarters of the Jianghu Association. In the waiting area, after receiving his paperwork, the receptionist handed Li Ming a large certificate.

"What's this?" Li Ming asked.

"You've been promoted to bronze rank. Congratulations!"

It was a strange thing. A sheet of cream-colored paper, framed in mahogany, bearing the signature of Chairman Huang, attesting that Li Ming was now a bronze-ranked member of the Jianghu Association.

"You're a full-fledged biaohang now," Ghazan said.

"That's right. We look forward to your continued service."

Li Ming had worked so hard and so long for this, but here and now, when he was finally seeing proof, did the weight of Ms. Rao's words finally rest on his shoulders. He'd known promotion was inevitable. He'd made it so. He'd just never expected it to feel so...

Hollow.

"Come on," Ghazan said. "The workday isn't over yet."

Cai Yan, dressed all in black, a hood of black sackcloth over her head, was waiting for them in the inner garden.

"You served with us during my father's and our brothers' final mission. Dayong and the Cai family would be honored if you served in the honor guard," she said.

Phrased like that, there was no way they could say no.

In downtown Bao An, Li Ming bought a suit of pure white and a pair of black leather shoes. Once he would have balked at such a purchase. Now, he simply noted that his bank account had more digits than the price of the clothing and paid for it immediately. It was a strange feeling—and yet, this purchase was for work, not for himself.

Back in Dayong, back in his room, he prepared himself for duty. He stripped down his weapons and thoroughly cleaned them. He wiped down his load carriage gear and their associated pouches. He polished his shoes to a mirror finish. He ironed his clothes. He took a long hot and cold shower, scrubbing off the last traces of the wilds. He shaved.

With great care, he dressed himself. Suit. Low-visibility battle belt. Shoes. Pistol. Infinity gun. Reality shaper.

Swordbreaker.

He saw Ghazan as he stepped out the room. He, too, was dressed all in white, with gleaming black shoes and Avenger with fixed bayonet.

The men nodded at each other. Checked their attire. And marched out.

Cai Yan let them into the family compound. It was the first time he was allowed into the inner sanctum. He only wished it were under more auspicious circumstances.

Like the Dayong compound, the Cai family residence was a siheyuan, built to a grander scale. The side halls were luxury villas, each as large as Dayong's main hall. The courtyard was mostly grass, with a concrete crossroad feeding to the entrances of every building. The northern road flowed up a short flight of steps. The main hall stood two stories tall, wearing steeply-arched roofs like a hat and skirt.

At the foot of the steps rested the remains of Cai Mengyang.

The coffin, resting on two high stools, was closed. There was nothing left of the face to view. Nonetheless, the head of the coffin pointed into the main house. Behind it stood a large altar, displaying a blown-up photo of the decedent's face. Atop the altar, incense sticks burned in large holders, surrounded by offerings of water and fruits. Wreaths of white irises surrounded the coffin. Yellow banners flanked the altar, emblazoned with lotuses and songbirds, displaying benedictions and praises for the deceased composed as rhyming couplets.

Armed biaohang stood guard at every corner, also dressed in white.

Li Ming and Ghazan took their posts, next to the gates. The job was simple: admit everyone on the guest list, keep out everyone who wasn't. Anybody could do it.

Li Ming dedicated his heart to it.

A steady stream of visitors flowed into the compound. High-ranking police, government and military officials. Businessmen and corporate representatives. The Jianghu Association branch head. Distant relatives.

The Cais greeted them all, accepting their condolences and well-wishes, and any gifts they had to offer. At the altar they placed flowers, fruits, candies. To Cai Yan, daughter of the deceased, and therefore the one who bore the funeral expenses, they gave white envelopes. It was *baijin*, white gold, a gift of money to help defray the costs of the funeral.

At sunset, Wang Meilin appeared.

Cai Yan wasn't happy to see her. But she was still on the guest list, and Li Ming allowed her through.

Lawyer Wang spoke to the Cais, bowing slightly. Cai Yan crossed her arms and nodded but refused to look her in the eye. They were too far away for Li Ming to hear clearly, but their body language was enough.

Workmen brought in a huge wreath, the largest wreath of all, adorned with calligraphic couplets written on white paper scrolls and the logo of White Tiger. More workmen arranged an elaborate offering of food on the altar, overwhelming the others. Lawyer Wang burned an enormous bundle of incense sticks, formally yet elegantly bowing three times to the deceased, and stuffed them into the overflowing incense holder.

Finally, she held out a white envelope.

Cai Yan stared at it for a moment. At her. Then, reluctantly, her face frozen, Cai Yan accepted.

After dark, a group of monks arrived. Hailing from the Temple of the Crescent Moon, they came equipped for the customs and traditions peculiar to those of the brotherhood of arms.

Most people would burn paper money, houses and other goods for the dead. Not the Cais. They held that the dead no longer needed material goods, and that burning paper did nothing more than create pollution. Rather, freed at last from this life of duty and danger, the deceased should be prepared for the world to come.

Thus, the monks prayed.

"Guanzizai Pusa xingshen boruo boluo miduo shi, zhaojian wuyun jiekong, du yiqie ku er..."

Every prayer and every scripture Li Ming knew, and more he didn't, the monks recited from memory. The Heart Classic. The Classic of Clarity and Tranquility. Praises to the Fo and Pusa. A final effort to purify the soul of base desires and guide him to the afterlife, to the Pure Land where all suffering ends and all beings could concentrate on gaining enlightenment.

The leader beat a wooden fish, keeping time. His assistant rang a bell at key intervals. Other monks clashed cymbals and banged a drum. Together, they chanted their litany at a mournful pace, dragging out every major syllable for the space of a long breath.

The prayers continued through the night, pausing only for the monks to drink water and rest their hands and throats in shifts. The Cais and the biaohang stood watch in shifts too. Civilians would indulge in an all-night marathon session of ma jiang and other games to guard the dead from evil spirits. The biaohang walked the length of the courtyard in silence, infinity guns shouldered, protecting the home from evil men. Retaliatory strikes against the family of the deceased were not unheard of in the jianghu. The code of the jianghu claimed that all debts and grudges ended in death, but there remained men who followed no code.

Li Ming alternated between standing guard and resting every hour. He dozed in his off-time to a chorus of prayers and awoke to the sound of cymbals and drums. The monks themselves seemed to be immune to the need for sleep, instead simply downing large quantities of water and meditating when they weren't on duty.

In the final ke before daybreak, the monks rose as one and sang the final prayer.

"Namo Amituofo!"

Five words. Five simple words. Yet Amituofo promised to take all beings who spoke them as few as ten times to the Pure Land.

Li Ming wondered if he would ever see it.

The sun peeked over the horizon. The monks withdrew to the main hall. The biaohang stayed.

Cai Yan and Cai Yong changed into black training uniforms.

They stood before their father. As one, they saluted him, palm over fist, hands over heart, and bowed. They turned to each other. Saluted again.

Unfolded into the Sancai Shi.

And flowed.

The five elements. The twelve animals. The linking forms. An Shen Pao. At the conclusion of the set, they switched seamlessly to yizhang. Now they demonstrated the eight palms and the two-man sets. Every technique, every form, every application, they performed the entire catalogue of An Family Gongfu, interpreted and passed down through the Cai clan.

They were showing their father everything they had learned, to assure him that Dayong was now in capable hands, that they in turn would pass down the teachings unto the next generation.

And yet, Cai Yan had changed.

Her movements, once fine and fluid, now carried a funereal air. Slow and stylized, they lacked the effortless grace he had felt when crossing hands with her. She was totally, completely, immersed in the movements, and yet the contents of her heart spilled out into her limbs and face.

Every technique had smoothness but no ease, circles but no spirals, lines but no curves, power but no center. He couldn't quite begin to describe it, only that it lacked an ineffable something that separated mere competence from true mastery.

Cold, gray qi wrapped around her like a shroud. Her movements, even hollowed out like this, were still beautiful. *She* was beautiful. And yet, he never wanted to see her like this again.

More workers came. Some cleared the altar and spruced up the coffin. Others set up large tents in the courtyard, and under those they placed tables and chairs, loudspeakers and audiovisual equipment. A catering company set up a cooking station in the corner, where they produced copious amounts of food.

Cai Mengyang enjoyed the first servings: fruits and vegetables, tea and wine, a chicken and a duck, a whole roast pig, rice, arrayed on special cups and platters on the altar. The monks came second. The caterers prepared special vegetarian dishes just for them. Last of all were the Cais and the biaohang. Li Ming ate little, just enough to fortify himself for the labors ahead.

At noon, the visitors came. Relatives. Friends of the family. Representatives from other biaoju in the province and the nation. They might have been business competitors, but before that they were all brothers of the rivers and lakes.

Lawyer Wang didn't show her face.

Under the tents, they ate and drank to the memory of the deceased. The Cais circulated the tables, thanking the guests for coming. Li Ming stayed where he was, on the border between the outside and the inside, watching for threats.

The meal wound down. The workers cleared the dishes. Cai Yan and Cai Yong knelt by the coffin, while their grandparents took the seats of honor. The guests settled.

The professional mourners arrived.

Dressed in white satin, the moirologists approached the altar, heralded by a ballad played on loudspeakers. They timed their approach perfectly, the strains fading out with the final step. As a choir of voices sang in soulful harmony, they gathered on the other side of the coffin, facing the Cais. The leader, a woman sporting twin pigtails, held up a microphone and stretched her palm to the heavens.

"Cai Mengyang! Head of the Dayong Biaoju! To us, he was the man who fearlessly defended this city from beasts and bandits. To his family, he was a good man, a filial son, a faithful husband, a dutiful father. He was a leader of warriors, a prince among immortals, a paragon of humanity. He is gone now! Gone to the next world! He has left this world with a heart filled with love, leaving us all behind!"

Wailing, moaning, she fell to her hands and knees, crawling around the coffin.

"You were a mountain, powerful and unshakable, a source of strength for your family and the nation! We never thought you would leave us so soon! Though the heavens gain an immortal, this world loses a hero!"

This was *kusang*. Crying for the dead. The audience joined in, sniffling and weeping, wiping their eyes and covering their ears. Li Ming, far at the back, felt her voice tugging at his heart.

He did not, could not, join in.

Where everyone else mourned, someone must still stand guard.

A man crawled up next to the leader. Together they sang a duet, a song of sorrow and farewells. The audience joined in, lending their voices to the song. The Cais bowed three times, touching their palms and foreheads to the floor.

One more song, and the Cais retreated.

The wailers' cries reached a crescendo. The monks emerged from the main hall. Swiftly they fastened paper seals on the coffin, protecting the body from evil spirits.

Everyone turned away from the sight. Everyone but Ghazan.

The monks returned to the hall. Suddenly the mood shifted. Pop music blared from the speakers. The mourners discreetly retreated. A woman in a sequined top and long skirt gyrated her way across the courtyard, lean arms and legs jittering and bouncing. She stopped before the coffin, turned to face the audience, smiled, and danced.

Li Ming's eyes popped. His jaw dropped. He had no idea what on earth he was looking at. A belly dance? At a *funeral*? Why? Was this how city people mourned the dead? He'd read about it before, but it hadn't been real to him until he saw it in person.

Even Ghazan stared in disbelief. The men exchanged puzzled glances. Ghazan tilted his head at the dancer, as if to ask what was going on. All Li Ming could do was shrug.

Strangely, amazingly, the audience began to smile and clap along to the beat. The dancer concluded her act with a flourish, sinking into a full split. She retreated to the sound of applause, and the mourners returned, this time outfitted in brightly-colored robes.

They sang. They danced. They belted out high-energy tunes and grooved to the beat. Lights flashed and strobed around them. The loudspeakers pumped up the volume. The Cais wiped away their tears and smiled.

The somber mood lifted. The audience clapped and cheered. The moirologists took their leave.

At the gate, Cai Yan discreetly passed their leader a bundle of banknotes. The mourners bowed to her. She bowed back.

Now came the pallbearers. Six male guests stepped up. The workmen assembled a scaffolding of wooden poles and sturdy rope. The men hoisted the coffin upon the frame, then gripped the poles and marched to the gate.

The monks reappeared, once again chanting and playing their instruments. Li Ming, Ghazan and the other biaohang escorted them past the gates, through the middle courtyard, and out the compound.

Life in the hutong paused. Everyone stopped as the funeral procession passed through the gates. Everyone turned away. A few bowed before they did. Some rubbed their eyes, symbolically washing off the yin qi from the dead.

Outside the hutong, the funeral convoy awaited. A massive portrait of Cai Mengyang was fastened to the roof of the hearse, adorned with paintings of lotuses and Pusa. White ribbons streamed down the hood and doors. The pallbearers loaded the coffin into the hearse. The Cais climbed in.

The monks boarded a pick-up truck behind the hearse and set up their instruments and loudspeakers. Relatives boarded the tail vehicle, a large minibus adorned with brightly-colored wreaths. As the convoy departed, the remaining guests dispersed.

The biaohang marched.

In the Zhongxia Republic, only three kinds of funerals were permitted the honor of an armed guard. State funerals, military and police funerals, and funerals for biaohang. The first two were for pomp and ceremony. The last was a necessity.

Weapon shouldered, Li Ming matched pace with the hearse. He scanned the streets, the windows, the roofs, everywhere that might hide a sniper, a bandit, a kill team. The true lead vehicle, a rented civilian car filled with biaohang in low-visibility gear, cleared the path ahead, while the actual chase vehicle covered the convoy's rear. Drones overflew the convoy, watching for wanted criminals and devil cultivators.

It was a long walk. Every step of the way, the monks recited scriptures, their voices blaring from loudspeakers. Civilian vehicles slowed and gave way. Police cars pulled over. Passers-by averted their gaze. A few clasped their hands in prayer.

Halfway down the route, in plazas and crosswalks, more funeral hearses appeared. Silent one-car processions, some bearing neither ribbons nor portraits. They bore the remains of the other Dayong biaohang who had fallen in battle.

The hearses linked up, snaking down the roads, forming a massive procession. The guards spread themselves down the line. Li Ming and Ghazan held their positions, letting the others take reference from them.

The convoy filed out the city and into the hills to the east. Here lay the resting grounds of the city's heroes. Soldiers, policemen and biaohang alike were buried here, in the most honored cemetery of Bao An.

The gravediggers were ready to receive them. They had prepared seven plots of land, not quite side by side, but clustered close together. A huge crowd of mourners—friends and relatives, not moirologists—waited. The biaohang fanned out, forming a protective circle around them.

The pallbearers brought out the coffins and surrendered them to the gravediggers. The swarthy men gently lowered the coffins into their graves. The monks chanted anew, calling upon Amituofo to liberate the departed from the wheel of suffering.

Cai Yan stood at the head of her father's grave, tall and clear-eyed. Surveyed the crowd. And spoke.

"Thank you for being here with us in the hour of our grief. My father, and all who fell under the Dayong banner, would be pleased to know they were well-loved in life.

"Though they were not born on the same day, the same month or the same year, they crossed over together on the same hour of the same day, the same month, and the same year. Though born to different mothers, through the shedding of blood they became brothers.

"This world is a world of suffering and bitterness. Even immortals may die. Yet they live on through us, we who will carry their memories into tomorrow..."

Li Ming tuned out the rest of her eulogy. He had to. He still had his duty.

The gravediggers laid sacred banners over the coffins. Blessed by the priests, written in special inks, covered in couplets, they would guide the souls on to the next life.

The monks rang bells and continued to chant. The workmen handed out incense sticks. Everyone lit them up, held them close, and faced the grave.

The monks bowed. Everyone bowed. One by one, they planted the incense sticks into the yielding earth. The family members of the bereaved threw the first handfuls of dirt into the graves, then retained a small fistful for their own family altars.

And then it was over. The monks departed. Then the guests. And the bereaved, last of all, thanking everyone for coming. Behind them, the gravediggers went about their work, finishing the task started by the families.

Li Ming finally relaxed, slinging his infinity gun and letting it hang from his neck. He stretched, careful to avoid disturbing everything else around him. He looked up to see Cai Yan sidle up.

"Thank you for your help," she said.

"All in a day's work."

A myriad of microexpressions flashed across her face, so subtle and fleeting he couldn't read them.

For a long moment, they stood there in silence, looking at each other. Ten thousand words floated through his mind, wrestling for the right to be spoken. A lifetime later, a coherent sentence emerged from the scrum.

"What do you plan to do next?"

She sighed. Crossed her arms. Looked away.

"There's so much to do. Insurance. Admin. Reports. You won't believe how much paperwork I have to file."

"What about jobs?"

"That's the biggest nightmare. With so many... so many biaohang gone, we've lost a significant chunk of our operational capability. We need to reorganize, to figure out which jobs we can take, how to replace our losses..."

Her voice faltered. A little part of his brain yearned to take her into his arms and hold her close. The rest of him remembered that she was still his employer—perhaps even his direct superior now. His mouth chose a compromise.

"How can I help?"

"You've done a lot already. I can't ask you to keep working. You should go home, take a break," Cai Yan replied.

"I can still work."

"You're not a machine. You'll burn out if this keeps up."

"I'm not burning out."

"Not yet. And… look, I don't think we have any jobs for you anyway. Until the rest of the family figures out how to continue running the business, all contracts are on hold. We're suspending operations for the time being.

"Go back home. Spend time with your family. Come back on Jia-Day. We should have something for you by then."

"You're asking me to go on leave?"

"Paid leave. Rest days. Whatever you want to call it. You've worked hard. You need time off."

"And you? Will you be okay?"

She smiled weakly.

"The Cai Family is made of steel. We will pull through."

"I'm not asking about the Cai Family. I'm asking about you."

The smile shattered. Her eyes grew bright with tears. She looked away and wiped them off.

"Father… Did he know that this expedition would be dangerous? Was that why he asked Cai Yong to stay home?"

"Our work is dangerous. Having a succession plan is wise."

"Yes, but… I insisted on joining the expedition. I told him that he needed a team shaper, and that I needed more field experience. He accepted, very reluctantly, and left Brother in charge of business in Bao An. What if…"

"Don't go there. Your father did what he thought was best. You identified the abyssal field early, which helped us in the fight. You brought the survivors back home. Dayong, and your family, endures."

"Could we have done better?"

"We did everything right. We just didn't know Ouyang would betray us. No one could have foreseen that. Don't beat yourself up over it. Just make sure something like that can't happen again."

She sniffled. Nodded. Breathed.

Again they looked at each other. Her irises dilated. Her lips parted slightly.

They stood there for a long while.

"Will you… Will you continue working with us?"

"My contract is still in force."

"*Shi… en… na ge…* Dayong took a major hit. Many men would jump ship."

"I'm not like those men. I gave my word, and I'll keep it."

"And after the contract? Then what?"

"Does Dayong still need me?"

"*I* do."

He stood there a moment longer, trying to process her words. Then, at last, he held out his arms.

She stepped in, wrapping her arms around him, burying her head into his chest. Hot tears stained his shirt. Her scent, sweet and light, yet sodden with sorrow, filled his nose. Li Ming pulled her close, as tightly as he dared.

"Thank you," she whispered.

She was the heir of one the most powerful families in Bao An. He was a dirt bun from Fuyang, with nothing to his name but the burdens of his ancestral history. To even dream of anything more than this was to be a toad lusting after a swan's flesh. The gulf between them was wider than the ocean.

But for now, this was enough.

Chapter Forty-Five

Heaven and Earth

Nightfall.

The city was winding down, contracting, preparing for bed. Dayong was closed, would remain closed for the rest of the week, though the lights of the Cai family residence continued to burn bright. With their employer disrupted, many of the resident biaohang had chosen to return home, wherever home was to them.

Not Ghazan.

He was a nomad, a descendant of nomads. His childhood home was a tent wandering across the steppes. In his former life the military had sent him all over the Yue Homelands. Today, home was wherever his registered address happened to be. He never stayed in one place for too long, his feet forever taking him to newer and stranger places all over Xiazhou.

He had nowhere else to go. Not in the Zhongxia Republic, not in the Homelands, not anywhere in the world. So he chose to stay where he was. For now.

He sat alone in his room, breathing deep. The Yue had developed many wondrous technologies, but the Celestial Empire had codified and transmitted the myriad methods of meditation and cultivation. He bore the Celestial Empire no ill will. The past was dead and buried—even if certain ill-mannered people insisted on resurrecting it.

Ordinarily he could spend hours in meditation. Today he spent only one ke in silence. Long enough to still the mind, steady the heart, gather his qi. His *boosted* qi.

Many people meditated for many reasons. Inner peace, calmness, spiritual pursuits. Martial cultivators used it as a tool to develop discipline and to grow their qi. He practiced it for war.

Warfare was a question of qi. How much qi you could gather, how much qi you could transmit, how long you could sustain it, what kind of qi you had at your disposal. From these questions came tactics, from tactics came strategy, from strategy came war.

His distant ancestors married their ways of war to the methods of cultivation, creating a new kind of warfare never seen before, a combined arms strategy that conquered Xiazhou. And he surely walked in his ancestors' footsteps.

Even now, cultivating at night, he honored them still. War was the province of Night. Death and deception, destruction and disruption, chaos and confusion, stealth and subtlety, these were the ways of war, and the properties of Night. The old tales sang of heroic feats in the light, but the older ones remembered deadly deeds done in the dark.

And for what he needed to do, he needed the powers of Night.

His phone alarm chimed. He turned it off. Turned off his phone, his headset, everything that could distract him. Then he retrieved his scroll. His *other* scroll.

He had carefully erased all mentions of the recovered artifact from his report. Li Ming had seen the device, but he had sneaked a peek at his report, and knew that he had only accounted for the artifacts he had recovered. Not Ghazan's.

The calculus was simple. If Ghazan had handed the scroll over to the Jianghu Association, he likely wouldn't see it again. A device that had remained powered for centuries, one that still retained its data storage, one that was perfectly functional, would be too tempting an artifact for the Zhongxia Republic. They might deign to offer him a high price for it, but they wouldn't give it back. Nor would Ghazan accept any offer, for its contents were priceless.

He unfurled the device and touched the wake button. Golden words flashed across the screen, requesting for his thumbprint. He pressed his thumb against a bright circle. If it were a fingerprint scanner, if the scroll were hard-locked, he'd be out of luck, and would have no choice but to sell his heritage to his conquerors.

Instead, the device read his genes in his fingerprint oils and unlocked.

It was primarily an entertainment device, and therefore one that needed no security beyond what was needed to keep a non-Yue from accessing it. Genetic scanner aside, its main point of departure from contemporary devices was that it was meant to be used in a vertical orientation, in keeping with the vertical Yue script. The scroll had many functions ubiquitous today. Music and video player. Gallery. Document viewer. Games.

Library.

Its previous owner had stuffed the library with thousands of titles, arranged in many shelves. Many of these titles were works of classical literature and philosophy, works he knew only second-hand, through references in everyday speech or studies of select quotations in school. Other titles were clearly works of fiction, stories of voyages to other realms and planets, adventures in foreign climes, romantic escapades.

And then there was that one title that had caught his eye.

He'd heard of that book. Among his people it was a lost tome, a myth, a legend. Every so often, someone would appear, claiming he had recovered a copy of it. But, always and always, serious investigation revealed that the book was only a collection of incomplete fragments, or else a complete forgery.

The proof was in the pudding. Or, in this case, cultivation.

And conquest.

That book was the cornerstone of the old Yue military. It was the manual they used to train their finest troops, they who had trampled kingdoms and emperors underfoot. Whenever the Yue Dynasty had a war to win, the Kheshig went, and always they returned in triumph.

And yet, over the centuries, their methods were lost. Once it was clear that the Yue Dynasty was no more, the survivors of the Kheshig chose to take their knowledge to the grave. Neither the Celestial Empire nor the Zhongxia Republic had recovered an intact copy of the manual, only scattered fragments. The government of the Yue Homelands offered a handsome bounty to anyone who could find one. But no one had.

Until now.

It was a martial manual. A military manual. A cultivation manual. A manual to rebuke Heaven and Earth. Scholars had many means of verifying the provenance of ancient artifacts. Ghazan had but one.

War.

Before the sudden betrayal, he had only read the first chapter. But it was enough. It was sparsely written but packed with detail. The anonymous author wrote precisely yet sparingly, using no excess words, yet concealed no secrets. Where words failed, he used diagrams to illustrate his points. There was so much information, it threatened to melt Ghazan's brain.

But it worked.

During the assault, Ghazan had applied the principles he'd remembered. Not the cultivation methods out of myth. Not the energy exercises promised in the table of contents. Not the promises of power. Only the first few fundamental principles.

And he won.

More than that, he triumphed. He'd blown through the enemy like a hurricane, feeding on their energies, fueling his inner fire with their own. Every strike sent a surge of power through him, every death recharged his own life.

This book was the real deal.

And if he mastered everything, he would be the master of the jianghu.

He touched the cover on the screen. It opened, going to the last page. He'd skimmed through it over the past few days, enough to check that every page was complete, every line uncorrupted, every visual clear. Now it was time to begin his studies in earnest.

He jumped back to the first page. The title, written in long lines of golden script against a field of black, stared back at him.

The Way of Conquering Heaven and Earth.

<<<<>>>

Chapter Forty-Six

Preview of LORD OF BEASTS

T hanks for reading Dawn of the Broken Sword! Turn the page to read a preview of Book 2 of Saga of the Swordbreaker: Lord of Beasts!

Chapter Forty-Seven

Bashe

Legend held that a bashe could grow so huge, it could swallow an elephant. Surely it was an exaggeration.

But not by much.

This close to the giant snake, Li Ming sensed its qi. A river of raw, vital force surging out the mouth of the dark cave that served as its den, emanating from an enormous living loop nestled deep within the bowels of the hill. It was easily the size of a house. And it was all coiled up, looping upon itself in multiple turns. Stretched out to its full length, it could easily cover half the length of a football field. At least.

Slowly, silently, Li Ming ascended the hill. He planted his feet on solid rock and unyielding earth, he leaned forward to counterbalance the bulk of his pack, he held his infinity gun close to his chest. Steering clear of vegetation and loose soil, his senses drinking in nothing and everything around him at once, he cut a serpentine path around countless trees and towards the mouth of the cave.

Below him, to his left, Ghazan followed. The tall, clean-limbed Yue was slightly slower, a little noisier, but he still made good time. Li Ming heard the soft rustle of vegetation, the scrape of steel soles against stone, once a soft curse when he lost his footing. He was a child of the steppes, not of the hills, but still he adapted quickly.

Bashe were diurnal. So the men made their approach at the third hour, the hour of the tiger, when the land was asleep and the moon hidden behind a sea of clouds. Li Ming navigated with his fusion goggles, seeing the world in infrared and thermal vision. His helmet visor projected a landscape of crisp black and white, low-fidelity daylight robbed of most color. Night-flying birds revealed themselves as swift-moving clouds of orange and yellow, their body heat betraying them.

Li Ming had grown up among hills and forest, farms and plateaus. This hill was steep and slippery, but he trusted in his experience and proprioception, intuitively stepping on solid ground and adjusting his weight for stealth and stability. He made good time, barely pausing, his subconscious mind driving his body to free his conscious mind for the task at hand.

The bashe had to die. There was no question about it. This close to civilization, just ten minutes from the closest town, it was a calamity in waiting. Already it had gobbled up dozens of sheep and goats in the past three days. Left unchecked, humans were next.

But ordinary humans couldn't fight a beast like that, so they turned to biaohang.

And in the armed escort business, Dayong Escort Agency was the gold standard.

The slope rounded off and flattened into a flat patch of earth, marking the entrance to the cave. Li Ming halted just below the crest, keeping low to the ground. The snake continued to snooze, ignorant of the biaohang's approach. Li Ming sneaked a peek behind him and saw Ghazan cover the final few paces.

Ghazan pressed himself against the earth, aiming his infinity gun at the cave opening. A bright silvery line betrayed his infrared laser. Li Ming shucked off his backpack, set it next to him, and reached for the smaller bag mounted on its back.

The Shanbang Belt Bag resembled a small clutch-sized bag, the kind of bag a man could wear over his lumbar in the wilds or a woman could sling over her shoulder on the street. On the outside, it appeared large enough to hold only essentials or to supplement a main pack. But on the inside, it was as large as a one-bedroom apartment.

It was no ordinary bag. It was an interspatial storage machine, with the form factor of a bag.

Li Ming worked the controls with both hands, calling up a holographic menu. Set to infrared mode, the floating window glowed in his visor but left the visible world in darkness.

Li Ming touched the first item on his inventory. The menu became a translucent three-dimensional image floating in mid-air. He aimed the backpack just so and pressed the eject button.

The image became a black hole. Within its depths, a tiny mote of white light rocketed to the surface and out into the real world. The mote swelled up, becoming a curved rectangular pouch. The hole closed instantly, and the pouch landed softly on the backpack.

Infinity gun slung over his back, Li Ming grabbed the pouch and crawled up to the cave. The beast's qi grew thicker, stronger, tasting of death and predation and violence. Li Ming's hackles rose. He breathed through the sensation, letting it pass, and opened the pouch to reveal a Type 99 antipersonnel mine.

It was such a small thing, a curved rectangular slab half the length of his forearm, but so much death was packed into it. Seven hundred steel balls packed in front of a layer of high explosive. Clack it off and any living thing within a hundred chi in front of it would cease to exist.

Screens large and small sang of the romance of the jianghu, the drama of the monster hunter, the splendid battles with the beasts and bandits of the world. In a role playing game, the intrepid biaohang would quest into the depths of the cave, battling lesser foes, until coming face to face with the serpent king on its throne. In the real world, the best hunts were ones that were boring, because everything went according to plan and the target never knew what hit it.

Li Ming ran his hands down the mine, finding the words 'This Side Towards Enemy' in raised characters on the front face, then deployed its twin bipods and oriented the device towards the cave. The mine had a tiny peep sight for aiming, but he didn't bother with it. It was impossible to align any kind of sight with fusion goggles. He just pointed it in the general direction of the opening.

Working by feel, he found the spool of firing wire snug in the pouch's larger outer pocket, took the blasting cap at the end of the wire, and connected it to the mine. He backed up, letting the wire play itself out, careful not to upset the mine, and returned to his pack. He took up his weapon and aimed it—and its laser—at the cave opening.

Now it was Ghazan's turn. He crawled up to the cave and emplaced his own mine, creating overlapping arcs of fire. Li Ming kept his attention trained on the laser dot and Ghazan in his peripheral vision. Ghazan added another step, daisy-chaining the mines together, allowing a single clacker to detonate both.

Ghazan slunk away, took up his weapon, and whispered into the team radio.

"Mines deployed."

The words flowed from his mouth like liquid chocolate, rounding off and muffling the tones that gave meaning and identity to each character.

"Roger. Return to fallback position," Cai Yan replied.

She was the leader of their little expedition, the daughter of the former owner of Dayong. After his murder, her twin brother had taken over the business, holding down the fort in their home city of Bao An. Which freed her—and a few select biaohang—to pursue contracts elsewhere.

The men retreated. The descent was slower, more agonizingly cautious, than the ascent. Li Ming allowed the wire to play out, keeping clear of anything that might snag on it and unbalance the mine. Ghazan cut across the trees, following Li Ming's footsteps.

Down they went, retracing their steps. Li Ming paused at the foot of the hill, long enough to check on Ghazan. He was still plodding along, still behind Li Ming. Li Ming turned back and climbed up another hill.

This hill was bare and gentle, the trees few and far between. He made good time, trekking across grassy earth at an angle away from the cave, allowing the wire to reach—

The spool played out completely.

And he was out in the open.

He cursed, but only in his mind. He'd been so focused on returning that he hadn't tracked how much wire he had left.

"I've run out of wire," Li Ming reported. "Moving to alternate position."

Li Ming reeled in the wire, going back down the hill. Ghazan stood in the dark, glaring silently at him, no doubt passing judgment. He'd picked a poor route. There was no cover, no concealment, not here on this hill. The closest was a tree at the foot of the hill.

The bashe's hill.

The men lay down by the tree, keeping most of its mass behind them and the cave. Li Ming wriggled about until he had a good line of sight to the cave. Ghazan adjusted too, pressing himself up against Li Ming. This close, the Yue's qi was a bonfire, spilling ethereal heat in every direction, threatening to smother Li Ming's. Somehow, over the months, the Yue's qi had grown by leaps and bounds, overtaking Li Ming's.

Li Ming didn't mind. He wasn't competing with Ghazan, not in this. Li Ming set his pouch down and opened the smaller outer pouch.

Here was the firing device. The device that would trigger hell in a small space.

He connected the clacker to the firing wire. And just like that, the mines were live.

Li Ming glanced at his heads up display. It was only slightly halfway past the hour. And there was no telling when the bashe would emerge from its cave.

Now came the hard part. The waiting.

Ghazan had hated this part of the plan. He was a man of action, a hunter and warrior, always eager to run down his prey and put it to the bayonet. It had taken a long time to talk him around and make him see the light.

He'd wanted to charge straight into the lair and kill the monster snake while it was still asleep. But in such close quarters, it was at the height of its strength, and it would be extremely difficult to escape if something went wrong. More to the point, Dayong would only be paid if it brought proof of the kill, and nobody wanted to drag out a humongous elephant-eating snake if they could avoid it. Better to let it come to them and do half their work.

The major downside of this plan was that it would yield a lesser harvest, and with it, lower pay. Li Ming didn't mind. Better to be paid modestly while keeping your life and limbs than to risk everything in chase of a higher payday. There would always be more beasts to hunt.

Fatigue crept into Li Ming's body. Every cell screamed at him to sleep. Li Ming massaged the Zhong Chong point on both hands, a spot just below the middle fingernail, on the side facing the thumb. A subtle bitter taste tingled across his tongue, waste energy flushing through his meridians, temporarily restoring his vitality.

The team was on fifty percent watch, one hour rotation. It was Ghazan's turn to rest. That left Li Ming staring into the darkness, left hand on the handguard of his infinity gun, right hand on the clacker.

The hour of the rabbit arrived with great reluctance. Ghazan signaled his wakefulness with a whisper.

"My turn on watch."

Li Ming handed over the clacker, then closed his eyes and breathed deep.

He drank in the qi of the earth and the air, circulating it throughout his body, replenishing the energy he had lost. He took care not to steal from Ghazan, not consciously at least, but this close to him it would be inevitable. The best Li Ming could do was to limit his body to taking only the excess qi his body expelled, the qi it couldn't use. Even so, it was like drinking from a waterfall.

Energy flowed through him like water, down his nose, lungs, dantian, curving to follow his perineum, up his spine and over his crown and back to his nose, joining the major meridians of his body in an unbroken circuit. Secondary circuits activated, sending waves of hot, heavy energy ebbing and flowing down his arms and legs, fingers and feet. It was healing, soothing, as if he were adrift on an ocean wave under the summer sun.

When he opened his eyes again, dawn broke. The goggles automatically cut off, allowing him to see the world in crystal clear color.

Ghazan stirred. Li Ming reached over to take the clacker.

"My turn," Li Ming whispered.

Ghazan nodded off. Li Ming watched. The snake slept.

Morning crawled past. The men took turns to have breakfast. Strips of mutton rougan for Ghazan, a compressed food bar for Li Ming. The beast continued to slumber. The men continued to watch.

The sun crept across the sky. The world brightened steadily. Sweat gathered in Li Ming's cracks and crevices. Itchiness followed. Li Ming remained still, recognizing the sensation and allowing it to leave, keeping his attention trained on the cave, on the snake. Bashe were cold-blooded, and it would awake only when it was warm enough.

At midday, the snake stirred.

Its energy shifted. It unwound itself, its head rising languidly to taste the air. Li Ming sensed it rather than felt it, a sinuous winding movement in its enormous qi field.

"Stand to. Target is waking up," Li Ming whispered.

"Roger," Wong Wan Lung said.

To the south, the sniper, the final member of the team, lay up among the trees and rolling hills. Wong Biaohang hailed from the Nanguang Federation, from the southern region of the continent. While he'd only recently joined Dayong, he had been in the business for years, longer than Ghazan and Li Ming combined. Li Ming didn't want to think too hard about Wong Biaohang sharing his observation point with Cai Yan. They were all professionals, but...

But that meant he had to focus, here and now.

The snake snapped to full alertness. Its body tensed and coiled. It froze for a moment, then slithered towards the cave mouth.

"The target is alert and exiting the cave," Li Ming reported.

"Think it sensed us?" Ghazan asked.

The bottom fell out of Li Ming's stomach. Of course it had. The enormous beast had a qi field to match its prodigious size, and the men were at the outer edges of the field. It could sense them as easily as Li Ming could sense it.

Li Ming's grip tightened around the clacker.

"Yes."

"Good."

Li Ming heard the smile—and the bloodlust—in the Yue's voice.

"Stand to, stand to," Cai Yan ordered.

Harsh sizzling reverberated within the cave, a primal sound from the dim and distant past, speaking directly to his genetic memory. It was the sound of scales slithering against stone, paired with the hissing of an animal the size of a truck. The sound shook Li Ming to the core, chilling his blood, stealing his breath. The bashe accelerated, its movements growing quicker and surer as its body warmed up. Li Ming glanced at his clacker, checking that, the wire was in, his fingers still safely pressed against its plastic body, and disengaged the safety latch.

The serpent appeared.

A gigantic head emerged from the mouth of the cave, scraping against its sides, revealing shining green scales and flat yellow eyes. Its black forked tongue flickered in and out, tasting the air. It danced back and forth in the air, revealing a pale white underbelly. It rose, higher and higher, rearing up to expose more of its length.

"Sights are hot," Wong Biaohang said.

"Fire," Cai ordered.

A sharp crack rang out, a crack unlike anything Li Ming had ever heard. It was as if the air was tearing itself apart, splitting under a mass of metal screaming forth at ludicrous velocities. Unlike the others, Wong Biaohang had armed himself with a coilgun, and it was the first time Li Ming had heard a kinetic weapon fired in anger.

Blood bloomed from the serpent's eye. Blood erupted from the other side of its skull. Blood showered the world.

And it dropped.

The ground quaked under its mass. Dust billowed. Stones showered down from the heavens. Qi spewed forth from the wound, dissipating in the air.

"Is it dead?" Wong Biaohang asked.

The rest of its qi field was intact.

"No," Ghazan said.

The bashe surged up again, curling up into a gigantic question mark in the blink of an eye. Its jaws opened wide, revealing fangs like sabers, hissing in pain and rage, training its surviving eye on Li Ming.

Li Ming squeezed the clacker.

The mines detonated with a ferocious double bang. Hundreds of high-velocity pellets shattered scales, sheared flesh, broke bones, chopping the beast clean in half. A red cloud burst forth, splattering the mouth of the cave, leaving behind a lingering mist. The beast slammed back down. More qi gushed out into the world. The bashe's upper half twitched and threshed about, snapping and biting at the air, at the dirt, at everything within range of its enormous fangs.

"Is it dead yet?" Wong Biaohang asked.

"Shoot it again," Li Ming urged.

Another thundercrack. Blood burst just behind its head. The monster hissed again, rearing up to its diminished height.

Blood dripped from a hundred tiny wounds. Blood gushed from the enormous stump. White bone, shattered and ragged, peeked out from the wounds. But the elephant-swallowing snake was still in the fight.

Rising to a knee, Li Ming brought up his infinity gun. As if sensing the motion, the snake dropped its head, falling out of his sight picture. Li Ming swung the gun down, and it swerved to the right, surging ever closer towards them.

A third thundercrack. The shot pierced through the beast's body and out the other side, and still the beast charged forward. A trio of plasma bolts followed, chewing away at its huge wound, barely slowing it down. Li Ming clicked to full auto and adjusted his aim and—

Ghazan.

Ghazan charged the beast, sunlight gleaming off his bayonet, bellowing a war cry in his native tongue. His dusky skin flashed white as a star. His platinum hair burned bright as the sun. Qi erupted from his body, spewing out his crown and hands, merging with the beast's own to become a volcano in full fury.

"Ghazan! What the devil are you doing?!"

The snake lunged.

Ghazan thrust.

A ray of blazing fire blasted through his bayonet, spearing the bashe clean through its jaws and out its brain. Everything it touched disintegrated. The killing light faded to reveal a gaping tunnel large enough for a child to crawl through.

The snake hurtled past Ghazan, missing him by a hair's breadth, struck the ground, rolled and flopped, and came to a rest by the tree.

And went completely still.

The bashe's qi was gone. So completely gone it was as if it had been ripped out of its body and scattered to the cosmos. The remaining energy from the bashe's lower half surrounded Ghazan like an aurora for a fleeting moment, and vanished into nothingness.

The Yue stood tall, the conqueror triumphant, spattered in blood, a maniacal grin stretching across his face.

A second chill ran down Li Ming's spine. He knew the Yue was a risk taker and a berserker. Point him at an enemy and he would close in and destroy it with fire and steel. But here, so close to him, it felt like he was standing before a beast that had taken rebirth in the form of a man.

Regardless of how he felt, though, he still had a job to do. Staying clear of its enormous jaws, Li Ming poked the snake's unwounded eye. It remained still.

"Target eliminated," Li Ming said.

"You sure love your bayonet, don't you?" Cai remarked.

"I told you we should have gone into its nest," Ghazan said. "I could have put it down with one blow."

"Ah, but can you process an entire bashe with one blow too?" Wong Biaohang asked.

It wasn't enough to kill the beast. Now they had to clean and gut it, to preserve what was valuable and discard the rest. And to do it before rot set in and spoiled everything.

Li Ming safed his weapon and drew his knife.

"Let's get to work."

Acknowledgments

I would like to thank the following people for their invaluable contributions to the manuscript:

Everyone who backed the series on IndieGoGo. Their faith in the story and the key concepts made this series possible.

The Story Forge and PulpRev, for invaluable feedback on the manuscript.

The Animal List, that eclectic group of foodies with a violence obsession, whose insights into violence and self-defense inform my works.

Denton Salle, who freely shared his knowledge of the Kenny Gong lineage of xingyiquan, fleshing out the combat and cultivation sequences in the series. Any errors and liberties I've taken with the internal martial arts are mine alone. A prolific author in his own right, you can check out his bibliography on Amazon.

And of course, you, dear reader, for purchasing and reading this book. If you've enjoyed this book, please leave a review on Amazon. This helps other readers like yourself find this book and helps me continue writing more books that you'll love.

Also By Kit Sun Cheah

Fiction:
Singularity Sunrise
Babylon
Dungeon Samurai
Nonfiction:
Pulp on Pulp: Tips and Tricks for Writing Pulp Fiction

About the Author

Kit Sun Cheah is Singapore's first Hugo and Dragon Award nominated writer. A blogger and martial artist, he is the Herald of the Pulp Revolution, combining the aesthetics and mindset of the pulp era with modern-day tastes and tradecraft. He has authored multiple series, most recently *Singularity Sunrise* and *Dungeon Samurai*.

Website: kitsuncheah.com
Twitter: @thebencheah
Facebook: benjamin.cheah.7
MeWe: bit.ly/2D1L2UK